Amitav Ghosh was born in Calcutta and spent his childhood in Bangladesh, Sri Lanka and northern India. He studied in Delhi, Oxford and Egypt and has taught in a number of Indian and American Universities. He is the author of three previous, highly acclaimed novels: *The Calcutta Chromosome*, *The Shadow Lines* and *The Glass Palace*. He is married and lives in New York

PRAISE FOR THE HUNGRY TIDE

He is a novelist in search of the distant frontiers that lie beyond your picture postcard realism, where ancient, telluric currents of ancestry continue to alter the script. As in *The Hungry Tide* ...What remain permanent, in terrifying beauty, are the river and the forest, and it is their overwhelming presence that provides *The Hungry Tide* a dark, elegiac elegance.

India Today

If there is a distinctive genre known as Indian Writing in English, then Amitav Ghosh is perhaps its most scholarly practitioner. Ghosh is a traveller in the physical as well as the metaphysical, a writer of formidable learning and intelligence. *The Hungry Tide* is a masterfully conceived and admirable book.

Indian Express

Ghosh's story-telling is at its best, tempting the reader on as if with an unsolved mystery, focussing dramatically on edgy exchanges between unusual individuals, blending tale into tale in a vast-seeming narrative close to the Bengali tradition of the river novel.

The Telegraph

The Hungry Tide, Ghosh's new novel... It is a fascinating, intense, tight book — perhaps the best Amitav Ghosh has written...He has created a constellation of immensely memorable characters, characters whose attraction, involvement – even hunger – for each other, set against the amplified canvas of nature at its most raw, makes for a very taut and pacy narrative... It has everything that makes for a masterful book. Read it.

Tehelka

This book is about confusion, misunderstandings, understandings and changes—all of which are played out in a world that's always changing, ever-silting, and in which the prey and the pursuer constantly switch positions.

The Hindustan Times

Ghosh is an anthropologist by training, and more than any of his contemporaries, part of his allotted task as a writer appears to be to dredge up lost stories in the way an archaeologist would, to analyse them in the way an anthropologist might, and to illuminate them in a way only a deeply sensitive writer can ... the trip of a lifetime.

Business Standard

Ghosh's scholarship is, as usual impeccable. His ability to collate huge amounts of data on a variety of subjects is astonishing as is his skill to make all this material a part of his story.

The Hindu

He is a writer who looks, listens and tells the story. If you want to see the Sunderbans painted in words, and read a bit of its history, myth, and the story of an American Indian in search of the rare river dolphins, an impromptu translator and a local guide, then grab a copy of *The Hungry Tide*. There are chances you may catapult into the tidal landscape of the Sunderbans.

The Pioneer

THE HUNGRY TIDE

AMITAV GHOSH

HarperCollins *Publishers* India
a joint venture with

New Delhi

First published in India in 2005 by
HarperCollins *Publishers* India
a joint venture with
The India Today Group
by arrangement with
HarperCollins *Publishers* Limited

First published in UK in 2004 by
HarperCollins *Publishers* Limited

HarperCollins *Publishers*
1A Hamilton House, Connaught Place, New Delhi 110 001, India
77-85 Fulham Palace Road, London W6 8JB, United Kingdom
Hazelton Lanes, 55 Avenue Road, Suite 2900, Toronto, Ontario M5R 3L2
and 1995 Markham Road, Scarborough, Ontario M1B 5M8, Canada
25 Ryde Road, Pymble, Sydney, NSW 2073, Australia
31 View Road, Glenfield, Auckland 10, New Zealand
10 East 53rd Street, New York NY 10022, USA

Printed and bound at
Thomson Press (India) Ltd.

For Lila

CONTENTS

PART ONE

The Ebb: *Bhata*

The Tide Country

Kanai spotted her the moment he stepped onto the crowded platform: he was deceived neither by her close-cropped black hair, nor by her clothes, which were those of a teenage boy – loose cotton pants and an oversized white shirt. Winding unerringly through the snack-vendors and tea-sellers who were hawking their wares on the station's platform, his eyes settled on her slim, shapely figure. Her face was long and narrow, with an elegance of line markedly at odds with the severity of her haircut. There was no *bindi* on her forehead and her arms were free of bangles and bracelets, but on one of her ears was a silver stud, glinting brightly against the sun-deepened darkness of her skin.

Kanai liked to think that he had the true connoisseur's ability to both praise and appraise women, and he was intrigued by the way she held herself, by the unaccustomed delineation of her stance. It occurred to him suddenly that perhaps, despite her silver nose-stud and the tint of her skin, she was not Indian, except by descent. And the moment the thought occurred to him, he was convinced of it: she was a foreigner; it was stamped in her posture, in the way she stood, balancing on her heels like a flyweight boxer, with her feet planted apart. Among a crowd of college girls on Kolkata's Park Street she might not have looked entirely out of place, but here, against the sooty backdrop of the commuter station at Dhakuria, the neatly composed androgyny of her appearance seemed out of place, almost exotic.

Why would a foreigner, a young woman, be standing in a south Kolkata commuter station, waiting for the train to Canning?

It was true of course that this line was the only rail connection to the Sundarbans. But so far as he knew it was never used by tourists – the few who travelled in that direction usually went by boat, hiring steamers or launches on Kolkata's riverfront. The train was mainly used by people who did *daily-passengeri*, coming in from outlying villages to work in the city.

He saw her turning to ask something of a bystander and was seized by an urge to listen in. Language was both his livelihood and his addiction and he was often preyed upon by a near-irresistible compulsion to eavesdrop on conversations in public places. Pushing his way through the crowd he arrived within earshot just in time to hear her finish a sentence that ended with the words 'train to Canning?' One of the onlookers began to explain, gesticulating with an upraised arm. But the explanation was in Bengali and it was lost on her. She stopped the man with a raised hand and said, in apology, that she knew no Bengali: *ami Bangla jani na.* He could tell from the awkwardness of her pronunciation that this was literally true: like strangers every-where, she had learnt just enough of the language to be able to provide due warning of her incomprehension.

Kanai was the one other 'outsider' on the platform and he quickly attracted his own share of attention. He was of medium height and at the age of forty-two his hair, which was still thick, had begun to show a few streaks of grey at the temples. In the tilt of his head, as in the width of his stance, there was a quiet certainty, an indication of a well-grounded belief in his ability to prevail, in most circumstances. Although his face was otherwise unlined, his eyes had fine wrinkles fanning out from their edges – but these grooves, by heightening the mobility of his face, emphasized more his youth than his age. Although he was once slight of build, his waist had thickened over the years but he still carried himself lightly, and with that alertness bred of the trav-eller's instinct for inhabiting the moment.

It so happened that Kanai was carrying a wheeled airline bag with a telescoping handle. To the vendors and travelling sales-men who plied their wares on the Canning line, this piece of luggage was just one of the many details of Kanai's appearance – along with his sunglasses, corduroy trousers and suede shoes –

4

that suggested middle-aged prosperity and metropolitan affluence. As a result he was besieged by hawkers, urchins and bands of youths who were raising funds for a varied assortment of causes: it was only when the green-and-yellow electric train finally pulled in that he was able to shake off this importuning entourage.

While climbing in, he noticed that the foreign girl was not without some experience in travel: she hefted her two huge backpacks herself, brushing aside the half-dozen porters who were hovering around her. There was a strength in her limbs that belied her diminutive size and wispy build; she swung the backpacks into the compartment with practised ease and pushed her way through a crowd of milling passengers. Briefly he wondered whether he ought to tell her that there was a special compartment for women. But she was swept inside and he lost sight of her.

Then the whistle blew and Kanai breasted the crowd himself. On stepping in he glimpsed a seat and quickly lowered himself into it. He had been planning to do some reading on this trip and in trying to get his papers out of his suitcase it struck him that the seat he had found was not altogether satisfactory. There was not enough light to read by and to his right there was a woman with a wailing baby: he knew it would be hard to concentrate if he were occupied in fending off a pair of tiny flying fists. It occurred to him, on reflection, that the seat on his left was preferable to his own, being right beside the window – the only problem was that it was occupied by a man immersed in a Bengali newspaper. Kanai took a moment to size up the newspaper reader and saw that he was an elderly and somewhat subdued-looking person, someone who might well be open to a bit of persuasion.

'*Aré moshai*, can I just say a word?' Kanai smiled as he bore down on his neighbour with the full force of his persuasiveness. 'If it isn't all that important to you, would you mind changing places with me? I have a lot of work to do and the light is better by the window.'

The newspaper reader goggled in astonishment and for a moment it seemed he might even protest or resist. But on taking in Kanai's clothes and all the other details of his appearance, he underwent a change of mind: this was clearly someone with a long reach, someone who might be on familiar terms with policemen, politicians and others of importance. Why court trouble? He gave in gracefully and made way for Kanai to sit beside the window.

Kanai was pleased to have achieved his end without a fuss. Nodding his thanks to the newspaper reader, he resolved to buy him a cup of tea when a *cha'ala* next appeared at the window. Then he reached into the outer flap of his suitcase and pulled out a few sheets of paper covered in closely written Bengali script. He smoothed the pages over his knees and began to read.

'In our legends it is said that the goddess Ganga's descent from the heavens would have split the earth had Lord Shiva not tamed her torrent by tying it into his ash-smeared locks. To hear this story is to see the river in a certain way: as a heavenly braid, for instance, an immense rope of water, unfurling through a wide and thirsty plain. That there is a further twist to the tale becomes apparent only in the final stages of the river's journey – and this part of the story always comes as a surprise, because it is never told and thus never imagined. It is this: there is a point at which the braid comes undone; where Lord Shiva's matted hair is washed apart into a vast, knotted tangle. Once past that point the river throws off its bindings and separates into hundreds, maybe thousands, of tangled strands.

'Until you behold it for yourself, it is almost impossible to believe that here, interposed between the sea and the plains of Bengal, lies an immense archipelago of islands. But that is what it is: an archipelago, stretching for almost three hundred kilometres, from the Hooghly River in West Bengal to the shores of the Meghna in Bangladesh.

'The islands are the trailing threads of India's fabric, the ragged fringe of her sari, the *ãchol* that follows her, half-wetted by the sea. They number in the thousands, these islands; some are immense and some no larger than sandbars; some have lasted through recorded history while others were washed into being just a year or two ago. These islands are the rivers' restitution, the offerings through which they return to the earth what they have taken from it, but in such a form as to assert their permanent dominion over their gift. The rivers' channels are spread across the land like a fine-mesh net, creating a terrain where the boundaries between land and water are always mutating, always unpredictable. Some of these channels are mighty waterways, so wide across that one shore is invisible from the other; others are no more than two or three kilometres long and only a few hundred metres across. Yet, each of these channels is a 'river' in its own right, each possessed of its own strangely evocative name. When these channels meet, it is often in clusters of four, five or even six: at these confluences, the water stretches to the far edges of the landscape and the forest dwindles into a distant rumour of land, echoing back from the horizon. In the language of the place, such a confluence is spoken of as a *mohona* – a strangely seductive word, wrapped in many layers of beguilement.

'There are no borders here to divide fresh water from salt, river from sea. The tides reach as far as three hundred kilometres inland and every day thousands of acres of forest disappear underwater only to re-emerge hours later. The currents are so powerful as to reshape the islands almost daily – some days the water tears away entire promontories and peninsulas; at other times it throws up new shelves and sandbanks where there were none before.

'When the tides create new land, overnight mangroves begin to gestate, and if the conditions are right they can spread so fast as to cover a new island within a few short years. A mangrove forest is a universe unto itself, utterly unlike other woodlands or jungles. There are no towering, vine-looped trees, no ferns, no wildflowers, no chattering monkeys or cockatoos. Mangrove leaves are tough and leathery, the branches gnarled and the foliage often impassably dense. Visibility is short and the air still and fetid. At no moment can human beings have any doubt of the terrain's utter hostility to their presence, of its cunning and resourcefulness, of its determination to destroy or expel them. Every year dozens of people perish in the embrace of that dense foliage, killed by tigers, snakes and crocodiles.

'There is no prettiness here to invite the stranger in: yet, to the world at large this archipelago is known as "the Sundarban", which means, "the beautiful forest". There are some who believe the word to be derived from the name of a common species of mangrove – the *sundari* tree, *Heriteria minor*. But the word's origin is no easier to account for than is its present prevalence, for in the record books of the Mughal emperors this region is named not in reference to a tree but to a tide – *bhati*. And to the inhabitants of the islands this land is known as *bhatir desh* – the tide country – except that *bhati* is not just the "tide" but one tide in particular, the ebb-tide, the *bhata*. This is a land half-submerged at high tide: it is only in *falling* that the water gives birth to the forest. To look upon this strange parturition, midwived by the moon, is to know why the name "tide country" is not just right but necessary. For as with Rilke's catkins hanging from the hazel and the spring rain upon the dark earth, when we behold the lowering tide

> *'we, who have always thought of joy*
> *as rising . . . feel the emotion*
> *that almost amazes us*
> *when a happy thing falls.'*

An Invitation

~~~~~~

The train was at a standstill, some twenty minutes outside Kolkata, when an unexpected stroke of luck presented Piya with an opportunity to avail herself of a seat beside a window. She had been sitting in the stuffiest part of the compartment, on the edge of a bench, with her backpacks arrayed around her: now, moving to the window, she saw that the train had stopped at a station called Champahati. A platform sloped down into a huddle of hutments before sinking into a pond filled with foaming grey sludge. She could tell, from the density of the crowds on the train, that this was how it would be all the way to Canning: strange to think that this was the threshold of the Sundarbans, this jungle of shacks and shanties, spanned by the tracks of a commuter train.

Looking over her shoulder, Piya spotted a tea-seller patrolling the platform. Reaching through the bars, she summoned him with a wave. She had never cared for the kind of *chai* on offer in Seattle, her hometown, but somehow, in the ten days she had spent in India she had developed an unexpected affinity for milky, overboiled tea served in earthenware cups. There were no spices in it for one thing, and this was more to her taste than the *chai* at home.

She paid for her tea and was trying to manoeuvre the cup through the bars of the window when the man in the seat opposite her own suddenly flipped over a page, jolting her hand. She turned her wrist quickly enough to make sure that most of the tea spilled out of the window, but she could not prevent a small trickle from shooting over his papers.

'Oh, I'm so sorry!' Piya was mortified: of everyone in the compartment, this was the last person she would have chosen to scald with her tea. She had noticed him while waiting on the platform in Kolkata and she had been struck by the self-satisfied tilt of his head and the unabashed way in which he stared at everyone around him, taking them in, sizing them up, sorting them all into their places. She had noticed the casual self-importance with which he had evicted the man who'd been sitting next to the window. She had been put in mind of some of her relatives in Kolkata: they too seemed to share the assumption that they had been granted some kind of entitlement (was it because of their class or their education?) that allowed them to expect that life's little obstacles and annoyances would always be swept away to suit their convenience.

'Here,' said Piya, producing a handful of tissues. 'Let me help you clean up.'

'There's nothing to be done,' he said testily. 'These pages are ruined anyway.'

She flinched as he crumpled up the papers he had been reading and tossed them out of the window. 'I hope they weren't important,' she said in a small voice.

'Nothing irreplaceable – just Xeroxes.'

For a moment she considered pointing out that it was he who had jogged her hand. But all she could bring herself to say was, 'I'm very sorry. I hope you'll excuse me.'

'Do I really have a choice?' he said in a tone more challenging than ironic. 'Does anyone have a choice when they're dealing with Americans these days?'

Piya had no wish to get into an argument so she let this pass. Instead she opened her eyes wide, feigning admiration, and said, 'But how did you guess?'

'About what?'

'About my being American? You're very observant.'

This seemed to mollify him. His shoulders relaxed as he leaned back in his seat. 'I didn't guess,' he said. 'I *knew*.'

'And how did you know?' she said. 'Was it my accent?'

'Yes,' he said with a nod. 'I'm very rarely wrong about accents. I'm a translator you see, and an interpreter as well, by profession.

I like to think that my ears are tuned to the nuances of spoken language.'

'Oh really?' She smiled so that her teeth shone brightly in the dark oval of her face. 'And how many languages do you know?'

'Six. Not including dialects.'

'Wow!' Her admiration was unfeigned now. 'I'm afraid English is my only language. And I wouldn't claim to be much good at it either.'

A frown of puzzlement appeared on his forehead. 'And you're on your way to Canning you said?'

'Yes.'

'But tell me this,' he said. 'If you don't know any Bengali or Hindi, how are you planning to find your way around over there?'

'I'll do what I usually do,' she said with a laugh. 'I'll try to wing it. Anyway, in my line of work there's not much talk needed.'

'And what is your line of work, if I may ask?'

'I'm a cetologist,' she said. 'That means—' She was beginning, almost apologetically, to expand on this when he sharply interrupted her.

'I know what it means,' he said sharply. 'You don't need to explain. It means you study marine mammals. Right?'

'Yes,' she said nodding. 'You're very well informed. Marine mammals are what I study – dolphins, whales, dugongs and so on. My work takes me out on the water for days sometimes, with no one to talk to – no one who speaks English, anyway.'

'So is it your work that takes you to Canning?'

'That's right. I'm hoping to wangle a permit to do a survey of the marine mammals of the Sundarbans.'

For once he was silenced, although only briefly. 'I'm amazed,' he said presently. 'I didn't even know there were any such.'

'Oh yes, there are,' she said. 'Or there used to be, anyway. Very large numbers of them.'

'Really? All we ever hear about is the tigers and the crocodiles.'

'I know,' she said, 'the cetacean population has kind of disappeared from view. No one knows whether it's because they're gone or because they haven't been studied. There hasn't ever been a proper survey.'

'And why's that?'

'Maybe because it's impossible to get permission?' she said. 'There was a team here last year. They prepared for months, sent in their papers and everything. But they didn't even make it out on the water. Their permits were withdrawn at the last minute.'

'And why do you think you'll fare any better?'

'It's easier to slip through the net if you're on your own,' she said. There was a brief pause and then, with a tight-lipped smile, she added, 'Besides, I have an uncle in Kolkata who's a big wheel in the government. He's spoken to someone in the Forestry Department's office in Canning. I'm keeping my fingers crossed.'

'I see.' He seemed to be impressed as much by her candour as her canniness. 'So you have relatives in Calcutta then?'

'Yes. In fact I was born there myself, although my parents left when I was just a year old.' She turned a sharp glance on him, raising an eyebrow. 'I see you still say "Calcutta". My father does that too.'

Kanai acknowledged the correction with a nod. 'You're right – I should be more careful, but the re-naming was so recent that I do get confused sometimes. I try to reserve "Calcutta" for the past and "Kolkata" for the present but occasionally I slip. Especially when I'm speaking English.' He smiled and put out a hand. 'I should introduce myself; I'm Kanai Dutt.'

'And I'm Piyali Roy – but everyone calls me Piya.'

She could tell he was surprised by the unmistakably Bengali sound of her name: evidently her ignorance of the language had given him the impression that her family's origins lay in some other part of India.

'You have a Bengali name,' he said, raising an eyebrow. 'And yet you know no Bangla?'

'It's not my fault really,' she said quickly, her voice growing defensive. 'I grew up in Seattle. I was so little when I left India that I never had a chance to learn.'

'By that token, having grown up in Calcutta, I should speak no English.'

'Except that I just happen to be terrible at languages . . .' She let the sentence trail away, unfinished, and then changed the subject quickly. 'And what brings *you* to Canning, Mr Dutt?'

12

'Kanai – call me Kanai.'

'Kan-ay.'

He was quick to correct her when she stumbled over the pronunciation: 'Say it to rhyme with Hawaii.'

'Kanaii?'

'Yes, that's right. And to answer your question – I'm on my way to visit an aunt of mine.'

'She lives in Canning?'

'No,' he said. 'She lives in a place called Lusibari. It's quite a long way from Canning.'

'Where exactly?' Piya unzipped a pocket in one of her backpacks and pulled out a map. 'Show me. On this.'

Kanai spread the map out and used a fingertip to trace a winding line through the tidal channels and waterways. 'Canning is the railhead for the Sundarbans,' he said, 'and Lusibari is the farthest of the inhabited islands. It's a long way upriver – you have to go past Annpur, Jamespur and Emilybari. And there it is: Lusibari.'

Piya knitted her eyebrows as she looked at the map. 'Strange names.'

'You'd be surprised how many places in the Sundarbans have names that come from English,' Kanai said. 'Lusibari just means "Lucy's House".'

'Lucy's House?' Piya looked up in surprise. 'As in the name "Lucy"?'

'Yes.' A gleam came into his eyes and he said, 'You should come and visit the place. I'll tell you the story of how it got its name.'

'Is that an invitation?' Piya said, smiling.

'Absolutely,' Kanai responded. 'Come. I'm inviting you. Your company will lighten the burden of my exile.'

Piya laughed. She had thought at first that Kanai was much too full of himself but now she was inclined to be slightly more generous in her assessment: she had caught sight of a glimmer of irony somewhere that made his self-centredness appear a little more interesting than she had first imagined.

'But how would I find you?' she said. 'Where would I look?'

'Just make your way to the hospital in Lusibari,' said Kanai, 'and ask for "Mashima". They'll take you to my aunt and she'll know where I am.'

'Mashima?' said Piya. 'But I have a "Mashima" too – doesn't it just mean "aunt"? There must be more than one aunt there: yours can't be the only one?'

'If you go to the hospital and ask for "Mashima",' said Kanai, 'everyone will know who you mean. My aunt founded it, you see, and she heads the organization that runs it – the Badabon Trust. She's a real personage on the island – everyone calls her "Mashima", even though her real name is Nilima Bose. They were quite a pair, she and her husband. People always called him "Saar" just as they call her "Mashima".'

'Saar? And what does that mean?'

Kanai laughed. 'It's just a Bangla way of saying "Sir". He was the headmaster of the local school, you see, so all his pupils called him "Sir". In time people forgot he had a real name – Nirmal Bose.'

'I notice you're speaking of him in the past tense.'

'Yes. He's been dead a long time.' No sooner had he spoken than Kanai pulled a face, as if to disclaim what he had just said. 'But to tell you the truth – right now it doesn't feel like he's been gone a long time.'

'How come?'

'Because he's risen from his ashes to summon me,' Kanai said with a smile. 'You see he'd left some papers for me at the time of his death. They'd been lost all these years, but now they've turned up again. That's why I'm on my way there: my aunt wanted me to come and look at them.'

Hearing a note of muted complaint in his voice, Piya said, 'It sounds as if you weren't too eager to go.'

'No, I wasn't, to be honest,' he said. 'I have a lot to attend to and this was a particularly busy time. It wasn't easy to take a week off.'

'Is this the first time you've come, then?' said Piya.

'No, it's not,' said Kanai. 'I was sent down here once, years ago.'

'Sent down? Why?'

'It's a story that involves the word "rusticate",' said Kanai with a smile. 'Are you familiar with it?'

14

'No. Can't say I am.'

'It was a punishment, dealt out to schoolboys who misbehaved,' said Kanai. 'They were sent off to suffer the company of rustics. As a boy I was of the opinion that I knew more about most things than my teachers did. There was an occasion once when I publicly humiliated a teacher who had the unfortunate habit of pronouncing the word "lion" as if it overlapped, in meaning as in rhyme, with the word "groin". I was about ten at the time. One thing led to another and my tutors persuaded my parents I had to be rusticated. I was sent off to stay with my aunt and uncle, in Lusibari.' He laughed at the memory. 'That was a long time ago, in 1970.'

The train had begun to slow down now and Kanai was interrupted by a sudden blast from the engine's horn. Glancing through the window he spotted a yellow signboard that said, 'Canning'.

'We're there,' he said. He seemed suddenly regretful that their conversation had come to an end. Tearing off a piece of paper, he wrote a few words on it and pressed it into her hands. 'Here – this'll help you remember where to find me.'

The train had ground to a halt now and people were surging towards the doors of the compartment. Rising to her feet, Piya slung her backpacks over her shoulder. 'Maybe we'll meet again.'

'I hope so.' He raised a hand to wave. 'Be careful with the maneaters.'

'Take care yourself. Goodbye.'

Canning

Kanai watched Piya's back with interest as she disappeared into the crowd on the platform. Although unmarried, he was, as he liked to say, rarely single: over the last many years, several women had drifted in and out of his life. More often than not, these relationships ended – or persisted – in a spirit of affectionate cordiality. The most recent however, which was with a well-known young Odissi dancer, had not ended well. Two weeks earlier she had stormed out of his house and forbidden him ever to call her again. He hadn't taken this seriously until he tried to call her cellphone only to find that she had given it to her driver. This had come as a considerable blow to his pride and in the aftermath he had tried to plunge himself into a brief affair of the kind that might serve to suture the wound suffered by his vanity: that was to say, he had sought, without success, a liaison where it would fall to him to decide both the beginning and the end. In coming to Lusibari, he had resigned himself to the idea of briefly interrupting this quest – but if life had taught him any lesson, it was that opportunities often appeared unexpectedly. Piya appeared to be a case in point. It was not often such a perfectly crafted situation presented itself: with his departure foreordained in nine days, his escape was assured. If Piya decided to avail herself of his invitation, then there was no reason not to savour whatever pleasures might be on offer.

Kanai waited till the crowd had thinned before stepping down to the platform. Then, with his suitcase resting between his feet, he paused to cast an unhurried glance around the station.

It was late November and the weather was crisp and cool, with a gentle breeze and honeyed sunlight. Yet the station had a look of bleak, downtrodden fatigue, like one of those grassless city parks, where the soil has been worn thin by the pressure of hurrying feet: the tracks glistened under slicks of shit, urine and refuse, and the platform looked as if it had been pounded into the earth by the sheer weight of the traffic that passed over it.

More than thirty years had passed since he first set foot in this station but he still remembered vividly the astonishment with which he had said to his uncle and aunt, 'But there are so many people here!'

Nirmal had smiled in surprise: 'What did you expect? A jungle?'

'Yes.'

'It's only in films, you know, that jungles are empty of people. Here there are places that are as crowded as any Kolkata bazaar. And on some of the rivers you'll find more boats than there are trucks on the Grand Trunk Road.'

Of all his faculties, Kanai most prided himself on his memory. When people praised him for his linguistic abilities, his response was usually to say that a good ear and a good memory were all it took to learn a language, and he was fortunate to possess both. It gave him a pleasurable feeling of satisfaction now to think that he could still recall the precise tone and timbre of Nirmal's voice, despite the decades that had passed since he had last heard it.

Kanai smiled to recall his last encounter with Nirmal, which dated back to the late 1970s when Kanai was a college student in Calcutta. He had been hurrying to get to a lecture, and while running past the displays of old books on the university's foot-paths he'd barrelled into someone who was browsing at one of the stalls. A book had gone flying into the air and landed in a puddle. Kanai was about to swear at the man he had bumped into, *Bokachoda!* Why didn't you get out of my way?, when he recognized his uncle's wide, wondering eyes blinking behind a pair of thick-rimmed eyeglasses.

'Kanai? Is that you?'

'*Aré tumi!*' In bending down to touch his uncle's feet, Kanai had also picked up the book he had dropped. His eyes had fallen

17

on the now-damaged spine, and he had noticed it was a translation of François Bernier's *Travels in the Mughal Empire*.

The bookseller in the meanwhile had begun to yell, 'You have to pay – it's expensive that book, and it's ruined now.' A glance at his uncle's stricken face told Kanai that he didn't have the money to buy that book. It so happened that Kanai had just been paid for an article he had sent to a newspaper. Reaching for his wallet, Kanai had paid the bookseller and thrust the book into Nirmal's hands, all in one flowing motion. Then, to forestall an awkward expression of gratitude on his uncle's part, he had mumbled, 'I'm late, have to run,' and had then fled, leaping over a puddle.

In the years since he had always imagined that when he next ran into Nirmal it would be in a similar fashion – he would be in a bookshop fondling some volume he could not afford and he, Kanai, would reach discreetly into his own pocket to buy him the book. But it hadn't happened that way: two years after that accidental encounter, Nirmal had died in Lusibari, after a long illness. Nilima had told Kanai then that his uncle had remembered him on his deathbed: he had said something about some writings that he wanted to send to him. But Nirmal had been incoherent for many months and Nilima had not known what to make of this declaration. After his death, she had looked everywhere, just in case there was something to it. Nothing had turned up, so she had assumed Nirmal's mind had been wandering, as it often did.

Then suddenly one morning, two months before, Nilima had called Kanai at his flat in New Delhi's Chittaranjan Park; she was in Gosaba, a town near Lusibari, calling from a telephone booth. Kanai was sitting at his dining table, waiting for his cook to bring him his breakfast, when the telephone rang.

'Kanai-ré?'

They were exchanging the usual greetings and polite inquiries when he detected a note of constraint in her voice. He said, 'Is something the matter? Are you calling for some special reason?'

'Actually, yes,' she said, a little awkwardly.

'What is it? Tell me.'

'I was thinking it would be good if you could come to Lusibari soon, Kanai,' she said. 'Do you think you could?'

Kanai was taken aback. It so happened that Nilima was child-less and he, Kanai, was her closest relative, yet he could not remember any occasion when she had made such a demand. She had always been very much her own person and it was out of character for her to ask favours. 'Why do you want me to come to Lusibari?' Kanai said, in surprise.

The phone went quiet for a moment and then she said, 'Do you remember, Kanai, I told you years ago that Nirmal had left some writings for you?'

'Yes,' said Kanai. 'Of course I remember. But they were never found, were they?'

'That's the thing,' said Nilima. 'I think I've found them: a packet addressed to you has turned up.'

'Where?' said Kanai.

'In Nirmal's study. It's on the roof of the place where I live, on top of the Trust's Guest House. All these years, after he died, it's been locked just as it was. But now it's going to be torn down, because we need to build another floor. I was clearing it out the other day and that was when I found it.'

'And what was inside?'

'It must be all the essays and poems he wrote over the years. But the truth is, I don't know. I didn't open it because I knew he'd have wanted you to look at them first. He never trusted my literary judgement – and it's true I'm not much good at that kind of thing. That's why I was hoping you could come. Perhaps you could even arrange to have them published. You know some publishers, don't you?'

'Yes, I do,' he said, flustered. 'But going to Lusibari? It's so far after all – from New Delhi it'll take two days to get there. I mean, of course, I'd like to but—'

'I'd be very grateful if you could, Kanai.'

This was said in the quiet but firm tone of voice Nilima used when she was determined to get her way. Kanai knew now that she was in earnest and would not be put off easily. In their family, Nilima was legendary for her persistence – her doggedness and tenacity had built the Badabon Trust into what it was, an organization widely cited as a model for NGOs working in rural India.

19

Kanai made one last attempt to give her the slip. 'Couldn't you just send this packet by post?'

'I wouldn't trust a thing like this to the post,' she said, in a shocked voice. 'Who knows what might happen to it?'

'It's just that this is a very busy time,' said Kanai. 'I have so much to do.'

'But Kanai,' she said, 'with you it's always a busy time.'

'That's true enough.' Kanai was the founder and chief executive of a small but thriving business. He ran a bureau of translators and interpreters that specialized in serving the expatriate communities of New Delhi: foreign diplomats, aid workers, charitable organizations, multinational companies and the like. Being the only such organization in the city, the services of Kanai's agency were hugely in demand. This meant its employees were all overworked – none more so than Kanai himself.

'So will you come, then?' she said. 'Every year you say you'll visit but you never come. And I'm not getting any younger.'

He caught the pleading note in her voice and decided to check his impulse to fob her off. He had always been fond of Nilima and his affection had deepened after the death of his own mother, whom she closely resembled, in appearance if not temperament. His admiration for her was genuine too: in founding his own business he had come afresh upon an appreciation of what it took to build up and maintain an organization like hers – especially considering that, unlike his own agency, the Trust was not run for profit. He remembered, from his first visit, the dire poverty of the tide country and he thought it both inexplicable and remarkable that she had chosen to dedicate her life to working for the betterment of the people who lived there. Not that her work had gone unrecognized – the year before the president had actually decorated her with one of the country's highest honours. But still, it amazed him that someone from a background like hers had actually lasted in Lusibari as long as she had – he knew from his mother's accounts that they belonged to a family that was notable for its attachment to the creature comforts. And in Lusibari, as he knew from experience, there was little to be had by way of comforts and amenities.

Kanai had always extolled Nilima to his friends as someone

20

who had made great sacrifices in the public interest, as a figure who was a throwback to an earlier era when people of means and education were less narrow, less selfish than now. All this made it somehow impossible to turn down Nilima's simple request.

'If you want me to come,' he said, reluctantly, 'then there's nothing more to it. I'll try to come for maybe ten days. Do you want me to leave immediately?'

'No, no,' Nilima said quickly. 'You don't have to come right away.'

'That makes it a lot easier for me,' said Kanai, in relief. His stormy but absorbing involvement with the Odissi dancer was then still heading in an interesting direction. To interrupt the natural trajectory of that relationship would have been a considerable sacrifice and he was glad he was not going to be put to that test. 'I'll be there in a month or two. I'll let you know as soon as I've made the arrangements.'

'I'll be waiting.'

And now there she was, Nilima, sitting on a bench in the shaded section of the platform, sipping tea while a couple of dozen people milled around her, some vying for attention and some being held at bay by her entourage. Kanai made his way quietly to the outer edge of the circle and stood listening. A few among the crowd were supplicants who wanted jobs and some were would-be politicians hoping to enlist her support. But for the most part, the people there were just well-wishers who wanted nothing more than to look at Nilima and to be warmed by her gaze.

At the age of seventy-six, Nilima Bose was almost circular in shape and her face had the dimpled roundness of a waxing moon. Her voice was soft and it had the splintered quality of a note sounded on a length of cracked bamboo. She was small in height and her wispy hair, which she wore in a knot at the back of her head, was still more dark than grey. It was her practice to dress in saris woven and crafted in the workshops of the Badabon Trust, garments almost always of cotton, with spidery borders executed in batik. It was in one such, a plain white widow's sari, thinly bordered in black, that she had come to the station to receive Kanai.

21

Nilima's customary manner was one of abstracted indulgence. Yet when the occasion demanded she was also capable of commanding prompt and unquestioning obedience – few would willingly cross her, for it was well known that Mashima, like many another figure of maternal nurture, could be just as inventive in visiting retribution as she was in dispensing her benedictions. Now, on catching sight of Kanai, it took her no more than a snap of her fingers to silence the people around her. The crowd parted almost instantly to let Kanai through.

'Kanai!' Nilima cried. 'Where were you?' She ran a hand over his head as he bent down to touch her feet. 'I was beginning to think you'd missed the train.'

'I'm here now.' She looked much more frail than Kanai remembered and he slipped an arm around her to help her to her feet. While members of her entourage took charge of his luggage, Kanai took hold of her elbow and led her towards the station's exit.

'You shouldn't have taken the trouble to come to the station,' said Kanai. 'I could have found my way to Lusibari.' This was a polite lie for Kanai would have been at a loss to know how to proceed to Lusibari on his own. What was more, he would have been extremely annoyed if he had been left to fend for himself in Canning.

But Nilima took his words at face value. 'I wanted to come,' she said. 'It's nice to get away from Lusibari sometimes. But tell me, how was your ride on the train? I hope you weren't bored.'

'No,' said Kanai. 'I wasn't. Actually I met an interesting young woman. An American.'

'Oh?' said Nilima. 'What was she doing here?'

'She's doing research on dolphins and such like,' Kanai said. 'I asked her to visit us in Lusibari.'

'Good. I hope she comes.'

'Yes,' said Kanai. 'I hope so too.'

Suddenly Nilima came to a halt and snatched at Kanai's elbow. 'I sent you some pages that Nirmal had written,' she said anxiously. 'Did you get them?'

'Yes,' he said, nodding. 'In fact, I was reading them on the train. Were they from the packet he left for me?'

'No, no,' said Nilima. 'That was just something he wrote long ago. There was a time, you know, when he was so depressed I thought he needed something to keep him going. I asked him to write a little thing about the Sundarbans. I was hoping to be able to use it in one of our brochures, but it wasn't really appropriate. Still, I thought it might interest you.'

'O,' said Kanai. 'I somehow assumed it was a part of whatever he'd left for me.'

'No,' said Nilima. 'I don't know what's in the packet: it's sealed and I haven't opened it. I know Nirmal wanted you to see it first. He told me that, just before his death.'

Kanai frowned. 'Weren't you curious, though?'

Nilima shook her head. 'When you get to my age, Kanai,' she said, 'you'll see it's not easy to deal with reminders of loved ones who've moved on and left you behind. That's why I wanted you to come.'

They stepped out of the station into a dusty street where *paan*-shops and snack-stands jostled for space with rows of tiny shops.

'Kanai, I'm very glad you're here at last,' said Nilima. 'But there's one thing I don't understand.'

'What?'

'Why did you insist on coming through Canning? It would have been so much easier if you had come through Basonti. No one comes this way nowadays.'

'Really? Why not?'

'Because of the river,' she said. 'It's changed.'

'How?'

She glanced up at him. 'Wait. You'll see soon enough.'

'On the banks of every great river you'll find a monument to excess.'

Kanai remembered the list of examples Nirmal had provided to prove this: the opera house of Manaus, the temple of Karnak, the ten thousand pagodas of Pagan. In the years since he had visited many of those places, and it made him laugh to think his uncle had insisted that Canning too had a place on that list: 'The mighty Matla's monument is Port Canning.'

The bazaars of Canning were much as he remembered, a jumble of narrow lanes, cramped shops and mildewed houses. There were a great many stalls selling patent medicines for neuralgia and dyspepsia – concoctions with names like 'Hajmozyne' and 'Dardocytin'. The only buildings of any note were the cinema halls; immense in their ungainly solidity, they sat upon the town like sandbags, as though to prevent it from being washed away.

The bazaars ended in a causeway that led away from the town towards the Matla River. Although the causeway was a long one, it fell well short of the river: on reaching its end Kanai saw what Nilima had meant when she said the river had changed. He remembered the Matla as a vast waterway, one of the most formidable rivers he had ever seen. But it was low tide now and the river in the distance was no wider than a narrow ditch, flowing along the centre of a kilometre-wide bed. The freshly laid silt that bordered the water glistened in the sun like dunes of melted chocolate. From time to time, bubbles of air rose from the depths and burst through to the top, leaving rings upon the burnished surface. The sounds seemed almost to form articulate patterns, as if to suggest they were giving voice to the depths of the earth itself.

'Look over there,' said Nilima, pointing downstream to a boat that had come sputtering down the remains of the river. Although the vessel could not have been more than nine metres in length, it was carrying at least a hundred passengers and possibly more: it was so heavily loaded that the water was within fifteen centimetres of its gunwales. It came to a halt and the crew proceeded to extrude a long gangplank that led directly into the mudbank.

Kanai froze in disbelief. What would happen now? How would the boat's passengers make their way across that vast expanse of billowing mud?

On the boat, preparations for the crossing were already in train. The women had hitched up their saris and the men were rolling up their *lungis* and trousers. On stepping off the plank, there was a long-drawn-out moment when each passenger sank slowly into the mud, like a spoon disappearing into a bowl of very thick *daal*; only when they were in up to their hips did their descent end and their forward movement begin. With their legs

24

hidden from sight, all that was visible of their struggles was the twisting of their upper bodies.

Nilima frowned as she watched the men and women who were floundering through the mud. 'Even to look at that hurts my knees,' said Nilima. 'I could do it once, but I can't any more – it's too much for my legs. That's the problem you see: there isn't as much water in the river nowadays and at low tide it gets very shallow. We brought the Trust's launch to take you to Lusibari, but it'll be at least two hours before it can make its way here to pick us up.' She directed an accusatory glance at Kanai. 'It really would have been so much easier if you had come through Basonti.'

'I didn't know,' said Kanai ruefully. 'I wish you'd told me. The only reason I wanted to come through Canning was that this was the route we took when you brought me to Lusibari in 1970.'

As he looked around, taking in the sights, Kanai had a vivid recollection of Nirmal's silhouette, outlined against the sky. Nirmal had put him in mind of a long-legged waterbird – maybe a heron or a stork. The impression was heightened by his clothes and umbrella: his loose white drapes had flapped in the wind like a mantle of feathers, while the shape of his *chhata* was not unlike that of a long, pointed bill.

'I still remember him, standing here, while we were waiting for a boat.'

'Nirmal?'

'Yes. He was dressed in his usual white *dhuti-panjabi* and he had his umbrella in his hands.'

Suddenly Nilima seized his elbow. 'Stop, Kanai. Don't talk about it. I can't bear it.'

Kanai cut himself short. 'Is it still upsetting for you? After all these years?'

Nilima shivered. 'It's just this place – this is where he was found, you know. Right here on the embankment in Canning. He only lived another couple of months after that. He must have been out in the rain, because he caught pneumonia.'

'I didn't know about that,' Kanai said. 'What brought him to Canning?'

25

'I still don't know for sure,' Nilima said. 'His behaviour had become very erratic, as it tended to when he was under stress. He had retired as headmaster some months before and was never the same again. He would disappear without leaving any word. It was around the time of the Morichjhāpi incident so I was beside myself with worry.'

'Oh?' said Kanai. 'What was that? I don't recall it exactly.'

'Some refugees had occupied one of the islands in the forest,' Nilima said. 'There was a confrontation with the authorities that resulted in a lot of violence. The government wanted to force the refugees to return to their resettlement camp in central India. They were being put into trucks and buses and taken away. In the meanwhile the whole district was filled with rumours. I was terrified of what might happen to Nirmal if he was found wandering around on his own: for all I knew he'd just been forced on to a bus and sent off.'

'Is that what happened?'

'That's my suspicion,' said Nilima. 'But someone must have recognized him and let him off somewhere. He managed to make his way back to Canning – and this was where he was found, right here on this embankment.'

'Didn't you ask him where he'd been?' Kanai said.

'Of course I did, Kanai,' Nilima said. 'But by that time he was incapable of answering rationally; it was impossible to get any sense out of him. His only moment of clarity after that was when he mentioned this packet of writings he'd left for you. At the time I thought his mind was wandering again – but it turns out it wasn't.'

Kanai put an arm around her shoulders. 'It must have been very hard for you.'

Nilima raised a hand to wipe her eyes. 'I still remember coming here to get him,' Nilima said. 'He was standing here shouting, "The Matla will rise! The Matla will rise!" His clothes were all soiled and there was mud on his face. I'll never get that image out of my head.'

A long-buried memory stirred in Kanai's mind. '"The Matla will rise." Is that what he was saying? He must have been thinking of that story he used to tell.'

'What story?' Nilima said sharply.

'Don't you remember? About the viceroy who built this port and Mr Piddington, the man who invented the word "cyclone", and how he predicted that the Matla would rise to drown Canning?'

'Stop!' Nilima clapped her hands over her ears. 'Please don't talk about it, Kanai. I can't bear to remember all that. That's why I wanted you to deal with this packet of his. I just don't have the strength to revisit all of that.'

'Of course,' said Kanai, remorsefully. 'I know it's hard for you. I won't mention it.'

Then too Kanai remembered, there had been a long wait on the embankment. Not because of the tides or the mud, but because of a simple lack of boats heading in the right direction. He had sat with Nilima in a tea-stall while Nirmal was sent to stand atop the embankment to watch for boats.

Nirmal, Kanai remembered, had not been very effective at keeping watch. On his most recent visit to a bookshop, in Calcutta, he had bought a copy of a Bangla translation of Rainer Maria Rilke's *Duino Elegies* – the translator, Buddhadeb Basu, was a poet he had once known. All the while he was meant to be watching for a boat, Nirmal's attention had kept returning to his recent acquisition. For fear of Nilima he hadn't dared to open the book. Instead, he had held it aslant across his chest, and stolen glances whenever he could.

Fortunately for them, they had not had to depend on Nirmal to find a boat. Someone had come to their rescue of his own accord. '*Aré* Mashima! You here?' Before they could look around, a young man had come running up the embankment to touch Nilima's feet.

'Is it Horen?' Nilima had said, squinting closely at his face. 'Horen Naskor? Is it you?'

'Yes, Mashima; it's me.' He was squat of build and heavily muscled, his face broad and flat, with eyes permanently narrowed against the sun. He was dressed in a threadbare *lungi* and a mud-stained vest.

'And what are you doing in Canning, Horen?' Nilima said.

'*Jongol korté geslam*, I went to "do jungle" yesterday, Mashima,'

27

Horen replied, 'and Bon Bibi granted me enough honey to fill two bottles. I came here to sell them.'

At this point Kanai had whispered into Nilima's ear, 'Who is Bon Bibi?'

'The goddess of the forest,' Nilima had whispered back. 'In these parts, people believe she rules over all the animals of the jungle.'

'*O?*' Kanai had been astonished to think that a grown-up, a big strong man at that, could entertain such an idea. He had been unable to suppress the snort of laughter that rose to his lips.

'Kanai!' Nilima had been quick to scold. 'Don't act like you know everything. You're not in Calcutta now.'

Kanai's laugh had caught Horen's attention too, and he had stooped to bring their faces level. 'And who is this, Mashima?'

'My nephew – my sister's son,' Nilima had explained. 'He got into trouble in school so his parents sent him here – to teach him a lesson.'

'You should send him over to me, Mashima,' Horen had said with a smile. 'I have three children of my own, and my oldest is not much smaller than him. I know what has to be done to teach a boy a lesson.'

'Do you hear that, Kanai?' Mashima had said. 'That's what I'll do if there's any nonsense from you – I'll send you to live with Horen.'

This prospect had instantly sobered Kanai, removing the smile from his face. He had been greatly relieved when Horen had turned away from him to reach for Nilima's luggage.

'So, Mashima, are you waiting for a boat?'

'Yes, Horen. We've been sitting here a long time.'

'No more sitting, Mashima!' Horen had said, hefting one of her bags on to his shoulders. 'My own boat is here – I'll take all of you home.'

Nilima had made a few unconvincing protests. 'But it's out of your way, Horen, isn't it?'

'Not far,' Horen had said. 'And you've done so much for Kusum. Why can't I do this? You just wait here – I'll bring the boat around.'

With that he had gone hurrying away, along the embankment.

28

After he was out of earshot, Kanai had said to Nilima, 'Who is that man? And what was he talking about? Who is Kusum?'

Horen was a fisherman, Nilima had explained, and he lived on an island called Satjelia, not far from Lusibari. He was younger than he looked, probably not yet twenty, but like many other tide country boys, he had been married off early – at the age of fourteen in his case. This was why he was already a father of three while still in his teens.

As for Kusum, she was a girl from his village, a fifteen-year-old, whom he had put into the care of the Women's Union in Lusibari. Her father had died while foraging for firewood and her mother, without other means of support, had been forced to look for a job in the city. 'It wasn't safe for her on her own,' Nilima had said. 'All kinds of people tried to take advantage of her. Someone was even trying to sell her off. If Horen hadn't rescued her who knows what might have happened?'

This had piqued Kanai's interest. 'Why?' he had said. 'What might have happened?'

Nilima's eyes had grown sad as they tended to do when she was reminded of those of the world's ills she was powerless to remedy. 'She might have been forced to lose her self-respect and honour; it happens often enough to poor girls who're caught in that kind of situation.'

'Oh?' For all his precocity Kanai was unable to unravel the precise implications of Nilima's euphemisms – yet he had understood enough of their meaning for his breath to quicken.

'And where is this girl now?' he had said.

'In Lusibari,' Nilima had replied. 'You'll meet her. Our Women's Union is still looking after her.'

The conversation had ended, Kanai remembered, with his sprinting up the embankment to stand beside Nirmal. Kanai had scanned the river with eager eyes, looking for Horen's boat. Till then the prospect of going to Lusibari had inspired nothing other than bored resentment, but the prospect of meeting this Kusum was something to look forward to.

The Launch

Deep in the interior of Canning's bazaar Piya had come to a halt at the gates of the Forest Department's offices. Because of the circumstances of her work she had, over the years, developed a reluctant familiarity with the officialdom of forests and fisheries. She had been expecting a grimy bureaucratic honeycomb and was taken aback to find herself looking at a small brightly painted bungalow. But still, before stepping up to the entrance she steeled herself for what promised to be a very long day.

But as it turned out, her experience was not quite as grim as she had anticipated. It did indeed take a full hour of waiting before she could even make her way past the first doorkeeper, but once she was inside her progress was unexpectedly swift. Thanks to her uncle's influence, she was led almost immediately into the presence of a harried but obliging senior ranger. After a polite exchange she was handed over to a subordinate, who led her down a number of corridors, through cubicles of diminishing size. In between were long intervals of drinking tea, waiting, and staring at walls blotched with red *paan*-stains. But, apace or not, the paperwork did proceed and within a mere four hours of her entry into the building she was in possession of all the necessary documents.

It was only then, just as she was about to march out of the office, giddy with joy at her triumph, that she learnt that the procedures weren't quite over yet – the last remaining requirement for her survey was that she be accompanied by a forest guard. Her face fell in dismay for she knew from previous experience that official escorts were always a hindrance and sometimes needed more attention than the survey itself; she would have far preferred to travel on her own, with only a boatman or pilot for company. But it was quickly made clear that this was not an option. In fact, a guard had already been assigned to her, a man who knew the route and would help with the hiring of a boat and all the other arrangements. She dropped the matter without further demur. It was good enough that she had got her papers so quickly – better not try her luck too far.

The guard, dressed in a starched khaki uniform, proved to be a small ferret-faced man. He greeted her with a deferential smile and his appearance provided no cause for misgiving – not until he produced a leather bandolier and a rifle. The sight of the weapons induced her to make her way back down the corridors to ask if the gun was really necessary. The answer was yes, it was; regulations required it because her route would take her through the tiger reserve. There was always the possibility of an attack.

There was nothing more to be said. Shouldering her backpacks, she followed the guard out of the bungalow.

They had not gone far before the guard's demeanour began to change. Where he had been almost obsequious before, he now became quite officious, herding her ahead without any explanation of where they were going or why. In a short while she found herself at a teashop on the embankment, meeting with a man of vaguely thuggish appearance. The man's name, so far as she could tell, was Mej-da: he was squat of build and there were many shiny chains and amulets hanging beneath his large, fleshy face. Neither he nor the guard spoke English but it was explained to her through intermediaries that Mej-da owned a launch that was available for hire: he was a seasoned guide who knew the area better than anyone else.

She asked to see the launch and was told that that would not be possible – it was anchored some distance away and they would have to take a boat to get to it. On inquiring about the price she was quoted a clearly excessive figure. She knew now that this was a set-up and she was being cheated. She made a desultory effort to find other boat-owners, but the sight of Mej-da and the guard scared them off. No one would approach her.

31

At this point she knew she was faced with a choice. She could either go back to lodge a complaint at the Forestry Department's office or she could agree to the proposed arrangement and get started on her survey. After having spent most of the day in that office, she could not bear to think of returning. She gave in and agreed to hire Mej-da's launch.

On the way to the launch, remorse set in. Perhaps she was judging these men too harshly? Perhaps they really did possess great funds of local knowledge? In any event, there was no harm in seeing if they could be of help. In one of her backpacks she had a display card she had chosen especially for this survey. It pictured the two species of river dolphin known to inhabit these waters – the Gangetic dolphin and the Irrawaddy dolphin. The drawings were copied from a monograph that dated back to 1878. They were not the best or most lifelike pictures she had ever come across (she knew of innumerable more accurate or more realistic photographs and diagrams) but for some reason she'd always had good luck with these drawings: they seemed to make the animals more recognizable than other, more realistic representations.

In the past, on other rivers, display cards like these had sometimes been of great help in gathering information. When communication was possible, she would show them to fishermen and boatmen and ask questions about sightings, abundance, behaviour, seasonal distribution and so on. When there was no one to translate she would hold up the cards and wait for a response. This often worked; they would recognize the animal and point her to places where they were commonly seen. But as a rule only the most observant and experienced fishermen were able to make the connection between the pictures and the animals they represented. Relatively few had ever seen the whole, living creature and their view of it was generally restricted to a momentary glimpse of a blowhole or a dorsal fin. This being so, it was not unusual for the cards to elicit unexpected reactions – but never before had this illustration provoked a response as strange as the one she got from Mej-da. First he turned the card around and looked at the picture upside down. Then, pointing to the illustration of the Gangetic dolphin he asked if it were a bird. She understood him because he used the English word: 'Bird? Bird?'

Piya was so startled that she looked at the picture again, with fresh eyes, wondering what he might be thinking of. The mystery was resolved when he stabbed a finger at the animal's long snout with its twin rows of needle-like teeth. Like an illusionist drawing, the picture seemed to change shape as she looked at it; she had the feeling that she was looking at it through his eyes. She understood how the mistake might be possible, given the animal's plump, dovelike body and its spoon-shaped bill, not unlike a heron's. And of course the Gangetic dolphin had no dorsal fin to speak of. But then the ludicrousness of the notion had hit her – the Gangetic dolphin a bird? She took the card back and put it away quickly, turning her face aside to hide her smile.

The smile lingered for the rest of the ride, vanishing only when her eyes alighted on Mej-da's launch – it was a decrepit diesel steamer that had been adapted for the tourist trade, with rows of plastic chairs lined up behind the wheelhouse, under a soot-blackened awning. She would have liked a skiff or a light fibreglass shell, outfitted with an outboard motor. Experience had taught her that this was the kind of boat of greatest use in river surveys. She began to regret the impulse that had led her to agree to this arrangement, but now it was too late to turn back.

As she walked up the gangplank, the stench of diesel fuel struck her like a slap in the face. There were some half-dozen or so young helpers tinkering with the engine. When they started it up, the volume was deafening, even up on deck. Then, to her surprise, Mej-da ordered all the helpers to leave the launch. Evidently the crew was to consist of no one other than himself and the guard. Why just these two and no one else? There was something about this that was not quite right. She watched in concern as the boys filed off the launch and her misgivings only deepened when Mej-da proceeded to enact a curious little pantomime, as if to welcome her on to his vessel. It so happened that he was dressed exactly as she was, in blue pants and a white shirt. She hadn't remarked on this herself, but the coincidence had evidently seized his interest. He made a series of gestures, pointing to himself and at her, providing a wordless inventory of the points of similarity in their appearance – their clothes, their skin colour, the dark tint of their eyes and the cut of their short, curly hair. But the performance ended with a gesture both puzzling and peculiarly obscene. Bursting into laughter, he gesticulated in the direction of his tongue and his crotch. She looked away quickly, frowning, puzzled as to the meaning of this bizarre coda. It was not till later that she realized that this pairing of the organs of language and sex was intended as a commentary on the twin mysteries of their difference.

The laughter that followed on this performance sharpened her doubts about this pair. It was not that she was unused to the company of watchers and minders. The year before, while surveying on the Irrawaddy she had been forced – 'advised' was the government's euphemism – to take on three extra men. They were identically dressed, the three men, in knit golf shirts and chequered sarongs, and they had all sported steel-rimmed aviator sunglasses. She had heard later that they were from military intelligence, government spies, but she had never felt any unease around them, nor any sense of personal threat. Besides, she had always felt herself to be protected by the sheer matter-of-factness of what she did: the long hours of standing in unsteady boats, under blazing skies, scanning the water's surface with her binoculars, taking breaks only to fill in half-hourly data sheets. She had not realized then that on the Irrawaddy, as on the Mekong and the Mahakam, she had also been protected by her unmistakable foreignness. It was written all over her face, her black, close-cropped hair, the sun-darkened tint of her skin. It was ironic that here – in a place where she felt even more a stranger than elsewhere – her appearance had robbed her of that protection. Would these men have adopted the same attitude if she had been say, a white European, or Japanese? She doubted it. Nor for that matter would they have dared to behave similarly with her Kolkata cousins, who wielded the insignia of their upper-middle-class upbringing like laser-guided weaponry. They would have known exactly how to deploy those armaments against men like these and they would have called it 'putting them in their place'. But as for herself she had no more idea of what her own place was in the great scheme of things than she did of theirs – and it was exactly this, she knew, that had occasioned their behaviour.

Lusibari

The tide was running low when the Trust's launch brought Kanai and Nilima to Lusibari and this seemed to augment the height of the tall embankment that ringed the island: from the water nothing could be seen of what lay on the far side. But on climbing the earthworks Kanai found himself looking down on Lusibari village and suddenly it was as if his memory had rolled out a map so that the whole island lay spread out before his eyes.

Lusibari was about two kilometres long from end to end, and was shaped somewhat like a conch shell. It was the most southerly of the inhabited islands of the tide country – in the fifty kilometres of mangrove that separated it from the open sea, there was no other settlement to be found. Although there were many other islands nearby, Lusibari was cut off from these by four encircling rivers. Of these rivers two were of medium size, while the third was so modest as almost to melt into the mud at low tide. But the pointed end of the island – the narrowest spiral of the conch – jutted into a river that was one of the mightiest in the tide country, the Raimangal.

Seen from Lusibari at high tide, the Raimangal did not look like a river at all: it looked more like a limb of the sea, a bay perhaps, or a very wide estuary. Five other channels flowed into the river here, forming an immense mohona. At low tide, the mouths of the other rivers were clearly visible in the distance – gigantic portals piercing the ring of green galleries that encircled the mohona. But Kanai knew that once the tide turned everything would disappear: the rising waters of the mohona would swallow up the jungle as well as the rivers and their openings.

If it were not for the tips of a few *kewra* trees you would think you were gazing at a body of water that reached beyond the horizon. Depending on the level of the tide, he remembered, the view was either exhilarating or terrifying. At low tide, when the embankment was riding high on the water, Lusibari looked like some gigantic earthen ark, floating serenely above its surroundings. Only at high tide was it evident that the interior of the island lay well below the level of the water. At such times the unsinkable ship of a few hours before took on the appearance of a flimsy saucer that could tip over at any moment and go circling down into the depths.

From the narrow end of the island a mudbank extended a long way into the water. This spit was like a terrestrial windsock, changing direction with the prevailing currents. But just as a windsock can generally be counted on to remain attached to its mast, the mudbank too was doggedly tenacious in keeping a hold upon the island. It formed a natural pier and that was where ferries and boats usually unloaded their passengers. There were no docks or jetties on Lusibari, for the currents and tides that flowed around it were too powerful to permit the construction of permanent structures.

The island's main village – also known as Lusibari – was situated close to the base of the mudspit, in the lee of the embankment. A newcomer, looking down at Lusibari from the crest of the *bādh*, would see a village that seemed at first glance no different from thousands of others in Bengal: a tightly packed settlement of palm-thatched huts and bamboo-walled stalls and shacks. But a closer examination would reveal a different and far from commonplace design.

At the centre of the village was a *maidan*, an open space not quite geometrical enough to be termed a square. At one end of this ragged-edged maidan was a marketplace, a jumble of stalls that lay unused through most of the week, coming alive only on Saturdays, which was the weekly market day. At the other end of the maidan, dominating the village, stood a school. This was the building that was chiefly responsible for endowing the village with an element of visual surprise. Although not large, it loomed like a cathedral over the shacks, huts and shanties that surrounded it. Outlined in brick, over the keystone of the main entrance were the school's name and the date of its completion: 'Sir Daniel Hamilton High School 1938'. The façade consisted of a long shaded veranda, equipped with fluted columns, neoclassical pediments, vaguely Saracenic arches and other such elements of the school-house architecture of its time. The rooms were large and airy, with tall shuttered windows.

Not far from the school lay a compound cut off from public view by a screen of trees. The house that occupied the centre of this compound was much smaller and less visible than the school. Yet its appearance was, if anything, even more arresting. Built entirely of wood, it stood on a two-metre-tall trestle of stilts, as if to suggest it belonged more in the Himalayas than in the tide country. The roof was a steeply pitched wooden pyramid, sitting upon a grid of symmetrical lines: stilts and columns, windows and balustrades. Rows of French windows were set into the walls and their floor-to-ceiling shutters opened into a shaded veranda that ran all the way around the house. In front there was a lily-covered pond, skirted by a pathway of mossy bricks.

In 1970, Kanai recalled, this compound had seemed lonely and secluded. Although it was situated in the centre of the settle-ment there were few other dwellings nearby. It was as though some lingering attitude of deference or respect had prompted the islanders to keep their distance from that wooden house. But that had changed now. It was clear at a glance that the area around the compound was among the most heavily trafficked in the whole island. Clusters of huts, houses, stalls, sweetshops and the like had grown up around the compound. The lanes that snaked around its perimeter echoed to the sound of *filmi* music and the air was heavy with the smell of freshly fried *jilipis*.

Kanai glanced over his shoulder and saw that Nilima was busy discussing Trust business with a couple of office-holders of the Women's Union. Slipping away, he pushed open the compound's gate and went hurrying up the mossy pathway that led up to the house. To his surprise, none of the noise and bustle of the village seemed to filter into the compound and for a moment he felt as though he were stepping through a warp in time. The house seemed at once very old and very new. The wood,

38

discoloured by the sun and rain, had acquired a silvery patina, like certain kinds of bark; it reflected the light in such a way as to appear almost translucent, like a skin of mirrored metal. It seemed now to be almost blue in colour, reflecting the tint of the sky.

On reaching the stilts, Kanai stopped to peer at the dappled underside of the house – the geometric pattern of shadows was exactly as he remembered. He went up the steps and was starting towards the front door when he heard his uncle's voice, echoing back from the past.

'You can't go in that way,' Nirmal was saying. 'Don't you remember? The key to the front door was lost years ago. We'll have to go all the way around.'

Retracing the steps of that earlier visit, Kanai went down the veranda, around the corner of the balcony and along the next wing until he came to a small door at the rear of the house. The door opened at a touch and, on stepping in, the first object to meet his eyes was an old-fashioned porcelain toilet with a wooden seat. Next to it was an enormous cast-iron bathtub with clawed feet and a curling rim. The head of a shower curled over it, like a flower drooping on a wilted stem.

The fittings seemed somewhat more rusty since he had first seen them, but they were otherwise unchanged. Kanai remembered how eagerly, as a boy, he'd taken them in. Since coming to Lusibari he'd had to bathe in a pond, just as Nirmal and Nilima did – he'd longed to step under that shower.

'This is a *shahebi choubachcha*, a white man's tank,' Nirmal had said, pointing to the bathtub. '*Shahebs* use them to bathe in.'

Kanai remembered that he had been struck by the aptness of the description while also being offended at being spoken to as if he were a yokel who'd never seen such things. 'I know what that is,' he had said. 'It's a bathtub.'

A door led out from the bathroom, into the interior of the house. Pushing it open, Kanai found himself in a cavernous, wood-panelled room. Clouds of dust hung, as if frozen, in the angled shafts of light admitted by the louvred shutters. A huge iron bedstead stood marooned in the middle of the floor, like the remains of a drowned atoll. On the walls there were fading portraits in heavy frames; the pictures were of *memsahibs* in long dresses and men in knee-length breeches.

Kanai came to a stop in front of a portrait of a young woman in a lacy dress, sitting on a grassy moor dotted with yellow wild-flowers. In the background were steep slopes covered with purple gorse and mountains flecked with snow. A grimy copper plate beneath the picture said, 'Lucy McKay Hamilton, Isle of Arran.'

'Who was she?' Kanai could hear his voice echoing back from the past. 'Who was this Lucy Hamilton?'

'She's the woman from whom this island takes its name.'

'Did she live here? In this house?'

'No. She was on her way here, from the far end of Europe, when her ship capsized. She never got to see the house but because it had been built for her, people used to call it *Lusi'r-bari*. Then this was shortened to Lusibari and that was how the island took this name. But even though this house was the original Lusibari, people stopped calling it that. Now everyone speaks of it as the "Hamilton House".'

'Why?'

'Because it was built by Sir Daniel MacKinnon Hamilton, Lucy's uncle. Haven't you seen his name on the school?'

'And who was he?'

'You really want to know?'

'Yes.'

'All right, then. Listen.' The knob-knuckled finger rose to point to the heavens. 'Now that you've asked you'll have to listen. And pay attention, for all of this is true.'

The Fall

The day was drawing to an end when a distant fishing boat drew
a scratch across Piya's line of vision, interrupting the rhythm
of her vigil. At first it was no more than a pinpoint on the
lens of her binoculars, a stationary speck, anchored on the far
side of a confluence of many rivers. After a while, when the dot
had grown a little, Piya saw that it represented a small canoe-
like craft with a hooped covering at the rear. There seemed to
be only one fisherman on board. He was going through the
motions of casting a net, standing upright to make his throw and
stooping to pull his catch in.

Piya had now spent three hours in her 'on effort' position, in
the bow of the launch. With her binoculars fitted to her eyes,
she had scanned the water, waiting for a flash of black or grey
to break through the dun surface. But so far her vigil had gone
unrewarded: she had had no sightings all afternoon, not one.
There had been one hopeful moment but it had ended with a
glimpse of a gliding stingray, shooting into the air, with its tail
trailing behind it like the string of a kite. Soon afterwards there
was another false alarm. Mej-da had come running up in great
excitement, pointing and gesticulating, giving her the impression
that he had seen a dolphin. But it turned out that his attention
had been caught by a group of crocodiles that were sunning
themselves on a mudbank. Mej-da's motives for bringing them
to her notice were made evident when he rubbed his fingers
together to let her know that he deserved a tip. This had annoyed
her and she had brushed him off with a peremptory gesture.

She had spotted the crocodiles long before him of course – she had seen them when they were a couple of kilometres away. There were four of them, and they were huge: from tip to tail, the largest of them was probably about the same length as the launch. She had wondered what it would be like to encounter one of these monsters up close and the thought had prompted an involuntary shudder.

But this was all. She had seen nothing else of note. Even though she hadn't known what to expect she had not foreseen as complete a blank as this. That these waters had once contained large numbers of dolphins was known beyond a doubt. Several nineteenth-century zoologists had testified to it. The 'discoverer' of the Gangetic dolphin, William Roxburgh, had said explicitly that the freshwater dolphins of the Ganges delighted in the 'labyrinth of rivers, and creeks to the South and South-East of Calcutta'. This was exactly where she was and yet, after hours of careful surveillance she had still to spot her first dolphin. Nor had she seen many fishermen: Piya had been hoping that the trip would yield a few encounters with knowledgeable boat people but such opportunities had been scarce today. She had seen many overcrowded ferries and steamers but very few fishing boats – so few as to suggest that the area was off-limits for fishing. The canoe-like craft in the distance was the first boat she had seen in a long time and it was clear the launch would pass within a couple of hundred metres of it. She began to wonder if it was worth a detour.

Reaching for her belt, Piya unhooked her rangefinder. The instrument had the look of a pair of truncated binoculars, with two eyepieces at one end but only a single Cyclopean lens at the other. She focused this lens on the fishing boat and pressed a button to get a reading of the distance between them. A moment later, to the accompaniment of an exclamatory beep, the instrument posted the answer: 1.1 kilometres.

Piya could not see the fisherman clearly but it seemed to her that he had the grizzled look of an experienced hand: around his chin and mouth was a dusting of white that suggested stubble or a beard. There was some kind of turban wrapped around his head but his body was bare except for a single twist of cloth, wound between his legs and around his waist. His frame was skeletal, almost wasted, in the way of a man who'd grown old on the water, slowly yielding his flesh to the wind and the sun. She had come across many such fishermen on other rivers and they had often been sources of good tips and useful information. She decided it would be well worth her while to take a few minutes to show him her flashcards.

Twice before she had asked for detours, but Mej-da, who was steering, had grown increasingly hostile after the incident with the crocodiles; he had ignored her on both occasions. But this time she was determined to have her way.

Mej-da and the guard were in the boat's glass-fronted wheel-house, sitting shoulder to shoulder. Stepping away from the bow, she turned to face the two men. Mej-da was at the wheel and he dropped his eyes on her approach – the furtiveness of his manner indicated all too plainly that he had been talking about her.

Pulling out a flashcard, she went to the wheelhouse and positioned herself directly in front of Mej-da. 'Stop!' she said, pressing an open palm on the glass. Mej-da's eyes followed her finger to the boat, now clearly visible ahead. 'Head over there,' she said. 'Toward that boat. I want to see if he recognizes this.' She held up the card, in explanation.

The wheelhouse door swung open and the guard stepped out, hitching up his khaki trousers. He made his way across the deck and leaned on the gunwale, shading his eyes. A frown appeared on his face as he squinted at the boat. Spitting into the water, he muttered something to the pilot. There was a quick exchange of words and then Mej-da nodded and spun the wheel. The bow of the launch began to turn in the direction of the boat.

'Good,' said Piya but the guard ignored her; his attention was now wholly focused on the boat. The intensity of his expression puzzled her; there was a predatory look in his eye that made it hard to believe he was doing this solely out of deference to her wishes.

In the distance the fisherman was standing up to make another cast: the boat had stayed where it was, growing a little larger each time it crossed her line of vision. It was now less than a kilometre away and she kept her binoculars trained on it as the launch turned. The fisherman had so far appeared to be unaware of their presence, but when it became apparent that the launch was changing course he checked himself in the act of casting his net and turned to look in their direction. Suddenly his eyes flared in alarm. She could see them through her glasses, outlined against the darkness of his skin. He turned to one side and his lips seemed to move as though he were speaking to someone. Shifting focus, Piya saw that the fisherman was not alone in the boat, as she had thought: there was a child with him – a nephew or grandson? The boy was sitting crouched in the prow. She guessed it was he who had alerted the fisherman to the launch's approach. He was pointing in their direction and cowering, as though in terror.

Within moments it became clear that both man and boy had taken fright. The man pulled out a pair of oars and began to row, furiously, while the boy scurried across the length of the boat and hid under the hooped covering at its rear. The boat had been positioned some fifty metres from the mouth of a narrow creek – a distance that could be covered with a few dozen oarstrokes. It was towards this opening that they were heading. The forests that lined the creek's banks had been half-submerged by the tide and the boat was small enough to give the launch the slip by heading directly into the mangroves. The water was still at a height where it would carry them deep into the forest in perfect concealment. They would be well hidden and would be able to make an escape.

There was something about the situation that puzzled Piya. On the Irrawaddy and the Mekong too fishermen had sometimes taken fright at the prospect of being interrogated by strangers, especially when there was a whiff of an official connection. Yet she had never known a fishing boat actually to attempt an escape.

Piya looked to her right. The guard was standing in the bow of the launch now and his rifle was slung over his shoulder. He had fetched it while her attention was fixed on the boat. Suddenly the fisherman's response made sense. Turning on the guard, she stabbed a finger at his gun. 'What's that for?' she said. 'Why do you need that?' The guard ignored her and she raised her voice: 'Put that gun away. It's not necessary.' He waved her away with a brusque gesture and turned to shout something to Mej-da. At once, the pitch of the engine rose and the launch lurched forward, closing in on the boat.

She understood now that the situation, although of her own making, was wholly outside her control and even her comprehension. The one explanation she could think of was that the fisherman had been working in an off-limits area, which might account for this pursuit. Whatever the reasons, it was clearly up to her to put a stop to this chase – her work would be in jeopardy if word got out that she was interfering with local people.

Turning to the wheelhouse, she signalled urgently to Mej-da, 'Stop! We're not going any further; this is it.' She was about to walk over to him when the guard began to bellow at the boat. The rifle was at his shoulder now, upraised, and he was evidently threatening to open fire.

She was appalled. 'What the hell do you think you're doing?' She rushed at him and lunged at his arm, trying to push away the barrel of the gun. He saw her coming and thrust out his elbow. It caught her in the collarbone and sent her reeling back. The display card went flying from her grip as she steadied herself, clutching her shoulder.

The fisherman had stopped rowing now and Mej-da cut the engine as the launch pulled up to the boat. Shouting an order the guard threw over a rope and the fisherman tethered it to his boat. The child, Piya noticed, was watching everything from his hiding place, under the darkness of the boat's hooped covering.

The guard barked a question that elicited a muttered response from the fisherman. The answer was clearly much to the guard's liking for he turned to Mej-da and smiled, as if in satisfaction. The two men had a quick exchange of words and then the guard turned to Piya and spat out the word 'poacher' in a tone of accusation.

'What?' said Piya. Even if she had been disposed to believe him, this charge would not have been credible. She shook her head dismissively. 'He was just fishing – that's all he was doing.'

'Poacher,' the guard said again, pointing his rifle at the fisherman. 'Poacher.'

It was all clear to her now: just as she had thought, the

fisherman had been casting his net in an off-limits area. He had chosen that spot so he would be able to get away if an official boat came along. He had assumed the launch to be just another tourist boat and hadn't realized until too late that there was an armed forest guard on board. Now he was going to have to pay either a bribe or a fine.

The fisherman was standing wearily upright in the boat, leaning on his oar. The sight of him startled Piya, for it was evident at close quarters that he was not at all the elderly greybeard she had taken him to be – he was of about her own age, in his late twenties. His frame was not wasted but very lean and his long, stringy limbs were almost fleshless in their muscularity. Nor was it because of a beard that his chin sported a dusting of white: the flakes were crystals of salt, left behind by a long day's deposits of brackish water. His face was narrow and angular and its gauntness seemed to emphasize the size of his eyes. The cloth tied around his middle was no more than a faded rag and it gave his skeletal frame a look of utter destitution. Yet there was a defiance in his stance at odds with the seeming defencelessness of his unclothed chest and his protruding bones. He was watching the guard with wary eyes, as though he were trying to reckon exactly how much money he was going to lose. At least a week's earnings, Piya guessed, if not a whole month's.

As if to remind her of her part in the situation, the guard stooped to pick her display card off the deck. He seemed to be in no hurry, now that he had caught up with his prey. Handing her the card he made a gesture in the direction of the boat, urging her to show it to the fisherman.

Piya could scarcely believe that he was asking her to carry on as if nothing had happened. She drew her hands back, shaking her head. He thrust the card at her again and this time his rifle seemed to move with his arm, as if to prod her in the direction of the fisherman. She shrugged. 'All right.' Undoing her equipment belt, she stowed it in her backpack along with her binoculars. Then she picked up the display card and stepped up to the gunwale. The boat was directly below, tethered close to the launch, and the fisherman's face was now on a level with her knee.

On catching sight of her, the fisherman started. His attention

46

had been focused on the guard and he hadn't realized there was a woman on the launch. Her presence seemed to make him suddenly self-conscious. He reached for the cloth tied around his head and yanked it down. It sprang apart and fell open around him, unrolling over his body like a curtain. When he had fastened it at the waist, she saw that the twist of cloth that she had taken to be a turban was, in fact, a rolled-up sarong. There was a consideration in this gesture, an acknowledgement of her presence, that touched her: it seemed like the first normal human contact she had had since stepping on the launch. Despite the strangeness of the circumstances, she was suddenly eager to see his response to the pictures.

She lowered herself to one knee and when their heads were level she held out the card. She tried to give him a smile of reassurance but he would not meet her eye. He glanced from the card to her face and raised a hand to point upriver. The gesture was so quick and matter of fact that for a moment she thought he had misunderstood. Then she looked into his eyes and he nodded, as if to say, yes, that's where I saw them. But which ones? She thrust the card at him again, expecting that he would point to the picture of the Gangetic dolphin, the more common of the two species. To her astonishment, his finger dropped to the illustration of the Irrawaddy dolphin, *Orcaella brevirostris*. He said something in Bengali and held up six fingers.

'Six?' she said. She was suddenly very excited. 'You're sure?'

She was interrupted by a child's cry. Looking up, she saw that the guard had taken advantage of her conversation with the fisherman to board the boat. Now he was rifling through the possessions that lay bundled under the boat's hooped covering. The child was cowering against the side of the boat, clutching his hands to his chest. With a sudden lunge, the guard caught hold of the child and pried his hands open: evidently the boy had been trying to conceal a thin wad of banknotes. The guard tore the money from his grip and slipped it into his own pocket. Then he gave the boy a parting slap and climbed back into the launch.

Piya, looking on from above, suddenly recalled her own wad of money, stashed in the money-belt she was wearing around her waist. She undid the zip surreptitiously, slipped her hand in and pulled out a handful of notes. Rolling them tight in her palm, she waited until the launch had started up again. When the guard had turned his back, she leaned over the side and stretched her arm towards the fisherman. 'Here! Here!' She kept her voice low and it was drowned by the hammering of the engine. Now a wedge of water had opened up between the boat and the launch but she felt sure she would be able to throw the money over if only she could climb a little higher. There was a plastic chair nearby and she pushed it to the side of the deck. Then she climbed up, balancing her weight against the gunwale. 'Here!' She threw over the money, and accompanied it with a loud hissing sound. This time she succeeded in catching the fisherman's attention and he jumped to his feet in surprise. But the guard had heard her too and he came barrelling across the deck. One of his feet crashed into the chair, throwing her forward, tipping her weight over the gunwale. Suddenly she was falling and the muddy brown water was rushing up to meet her face.

S'Daniel

'One of the many ways,' said Nirmal, 'in which the tide country resembles a desert is that it can trick the eye with mirages. This is what it did to Sir Daniel Hamilton. When this Scotsman looked upon the crab-covered shores of the tide country, he saw not mud, but something that shone brighter than gold. "Look how much this mud is worth," he said. "A single acre of Bengal's mud yields fifteen maunds of rice. What does a square mile of gold yield? Nothing."'

Nirmal raised a hand to point to one of the portraits on the wall. 'Look,' he said. 'That's him, Daniel Hamilton, on the day when he became a knight. After that his name was forever S'Daniel.'

The picture was of a man in stockings and knee breeches, wearing buckled shoes and a jacket with brass buttons. On his upper lip was a bushy white moustache and at his waist hung something that looked like the hilt of a sword. His eyes looked directly into the viewer's, at once stern and kindly, austere and somewhat eccentric. There was something about his gaze that discomfited Kanai. As if by instinct, he slipped behind his uncle to elude those penetrating eyes.

'S'Daniel's schooling,' Nirmal said, 'was in Scotland, which was a harsh and rocky place, cold and unforgiving. In school his teachers taught him that life's most important lesson is "labour conquers everything", even rocks and stones if need be – even mud. As with many of his countrymen, a time came when Daniel Hamilton had to leave his native land to seek his fortune, and what better place to do that than India? He came to Calcutta and joined MacKinnon & McKenzie, a company with which he had a family connection. This company sold tickets for the P&O shipping line, which was then one of the largest in the world. Young Daniel worked hard and sold many, many tickets: first class, second class, third class, steerage. For every ship that sailed from Calcutta there were hundreds of tickets to be sold and only one ticket agent. Soon S'Daniel was the head of the company and master of an immense fortune, one of the richest men in India. He was, in other words, what we call a *monopolikapitalist*. Another man might have taken his money and left – or spent it all on palaces and luxury. But not S'Daniel.'

'Why not?'

'I'm getting to it. Wait. Look at the picture on the wall and close your eyes. Think of that man, S'Daniel, standing on the prow of a P&O liner as it sails away from Calcutta and makes its way towards the Bay of Bengal. The other *shahebs* and *mems* are laughing and drinking, shouting and dancing, but not S'Daniel. Standing on deck, his eyes drink in these vast rivers, these mudflats, these mangrove-covered islands and it occurs to him to ask, "Why does no one live here? Why are these islands empty of people? Why is this valuable soil allowed to lie fallow?" A crewman sees him peering into the forest and points out the ruins of an old temple and a mosque. See, he says, people lived here once, but they were driven away by tempests and tides, tigers and crocodiles. *"Tai naki?"* says S'Daniel. Is that so? "But if people lived here once, why shouldn't they again?" This is after all no remote and lonely frontier – this is India's doormat, the threshold of a teeming subcontinent. Everyone who has ever taken the eastern route into the Gangetic heartland has had to pass through it – the Arakanese, the Khmer, the Javanese, the Dutch, the Malays, the Chinese, the Portuguese, the English. It is common knowledge that almost every island in the tide country has been inhabited at some time or another. But to look at them you would never know: the speciality of mangroves is that they do not merely recolonize land; they erase time. Every generation creates its own population of ghosts.

'On his return to Calcutta S'Daniel sought out knowledgeable people. He learnt that of all the hazards of the Sundarbans none is more dangerous than the Forest Department, which treats the area as its own kingdom. But S'Daniel cared nothing for the Forest Department. In 1903 he bought ten thousand acres of the tide country from the British *sarkar*.'

'Ten thousand acres! How much land is that?'

'Many islands' worth, Kanai. Many islands. The British *sarkar* was happy to let him have them. Gosaba, Rangabelia, Satjelia – these were all his. And to these he later added this island you're standing on: Lusibari. S'Daniel wanted his newly bought lands to be called Andrewpur, after St Andrew of Scotland – a poor man, who, having neither silver nor gold, found the money to create it. But that name never took; people grew used to speaking of these islands as Hamilton-abad. And as the population grew, villages sprouted and S'Daniel gave them names. One village became "Shobnomoskar", "welcome to all", and another became "Rajat Jubilee", to mark the Silver Jubilee of some king or the other. And to some he gave the names of his relatives – that's why we have here a Jamespur, an Annpur and an Emilybari. Lusibari was another such.'

'And who lived in those places?'

'No one – in the beginning. Remember, at that time there was nothing but forest here. There were no people, no embankments, no fields. Just *kādā ār bādā*, mud and mangrove. At high tide most of the land vanished under water. And everywhere you looked there were predators – tigers, crocodiles, sharks, leopards.'

'So why did people come, then?'

'For the land, Kanai. What else? This was at a time when people were so desperate for land that they were willing to sell themselves in exchange for a *bigha* or two. And this land here was in their own country, not far from Calcutta: they didn't need to take a boat to Burma or Malaya or Fiji or Trinidad. And what was more, it was free.'

'So they came?'

'By the thousand. Everyone who was willing to work was welcome, S'Daniel said, but on one condition. They could not bring all their petty little divisions and differences. Here there would be no Brahmins or Untouchables, no Bengalis and no Oriyas. Everyone would have to live and work together. When the news of this spread, people came pouring in, from northern Orissa, from eastern Bengal, from the Santhal Parganas. They came in boats and dinghies and whatever else they could lay their hands on. When the waters fell the settlers hacked at the forest with their daas, and when the tides rose they waited out the flood on stilt-mounted platforms. At night they slept in hammocks that were hung so as to keep them safe from the high tide.

'Think of what it was like: think of the tigers, crocodiles and snakes that lived in the creeks and *nalas* that covered the islands. This was a feast for them. They killed hundreds of people. So many were killed that S'Daniel began to give out rewards to anyone who killed a tiger or crocodile.'

'But what did they kill them with?'

'With their hands. With knives. With bamboo spears. Whatever they could find at hand. Do you remember Horen, the boatman, who brought us here from Canning?'

'Yes.' Kanai nodded.

'His uncle Bolai killed a tiger once, while he was out fishing. S'Daniel gave him two *bighas* of land, right here in Lusibari. For years afterwards, Bolai was the hero of the island.'

'But what was the purpose of all this?' said Kanai. 'Was it money?'

'No,' said Nirmal. 'Money S'Daniel already had. What he wanted was to build a new society, a new kind of country. It would be a country run by co-operatives, he said. Here people wouldn't exploit each other and everyone would have a share in the land. S'Daniel spoke with Mahatma Gandhi, Rabindranath Thakur and many other *bujuwa* nationalists. The bourgeoisie all agreed with S'Daniel that this place could be a model for all of India; it could be a new kind of country.'

'But how could this be a country?' said Kanai in disbelief. 'There's nothing here – no electricity, no roads, nothing.'

Nirmal smiled. 'All that was to come,' he said. 'Look.' He pointed to a discoloured wire that ran along the wall. 'See. S'Daniel had made arrangements for electricity. In the beginning there was a huge generator, right next to the school. But after his death it broke down and no one ever replaced it.'

Kneeling beside a table, Nirmal pointed to another set of wires. 'Look: there were even telephone lines here. Long before phones had come to Kolkata, S'Daniel had put in phones in Gosaba. Everything was provided for; nothing was left to chance. There was a Central Bank of Gosaba and there was even a Gosaba currency.'

Nirmal reached into one of the bookshelves that lined the wall and took out a torn and dusty piece of paper. 'Look, here is one of his banknotes. See what it says: "The Note is based on the living man, not on the dead coin. It costs practically nothing, and yields a dividend of One Hundred Per Cent in land reclaimed, tanks excavated, houses built, &c. and in a more healthy and abundant LIFE."'

Nirmal held the paper out to Kanai. 'See!' he said. 'The words could have been written by Marx himself: it is just the Labour Theory of Value. But look at the signature. What does it say? Sir Daniel MacKinnon Hamilton.'

Kanai turned the piece of paper over in his hands. 'But what was it all *for*? If it wasn't to make money, then why did he go to all the trouble? I don't understand.'

'It was a dream, Kanai,' said Nirmal. 'What he wanted was no different from what dreamers have always wanted. He wanted to build a place where no one would exploit anyone and people would live together without petty social distinctions and differences. He dreamed of a place where men and women could be farmers in the morning, poets in the afternoon and carpenters in the evening.'

Kanai burst into laughter. 'And look what he ended up with,' he said. 'These rat-eaten islands.'

That a child could be so self-assuredly cynical came as a shock to Nirmal. After opening and shutting his mouth several times, he said weakly, 'Don't laugh, Kanai – it was just that the tide country wasn't ready yet. Some day, who knows? It may yet come to be.'

Snell's Window

In the clear waters of the open sea the light of the sun wells downwards from the surface in an inverted cone that ends in the beholder's eye. The base of this cone is a transparent disk that hangs above the observer's head like a floating halo. It is through this prism, known as Snell's window, that the oceanic dolphin perceives the world beyond the water; in submersion, this circular portal follows it everywhere, creating a single clear opening in the unbroken expanse of shimmering silver that forms the water's surface as seen from below.

Rivers like the Ganga and the Brahmaputra shroud this window with a curtain of silt: in their occluded waters light loses its directionality within a few centimetres of the surface. Beneath this lies a flowing stream of suspended matter in which visibility does not extend beyond an arm's length. With no lighted portal to point the way, top and bottom and up and down become very quickly confused. As if to address this the Gangetic dolphin habitually swims on its side, parallel to the surface, with one of its lateral fins trailing the bottom, as though to anchor itself in its darkened world by keeping a hold upon its floor.

In the open sea Piya would have had no difficulty dealing with a fall such as that she had just sustained. She was a competent swimmer and would have been able to hold her own against the current. It was the disorientation caused by the peculiar conditions of light in the silted water that made her panic. With her breath running out, she felt herself to be enveloped inside a cocoon of eerily glowing murk and could not tell whether she was looking up or down. In her head there was a smell, or rather, a metallic savour she knew to be, not blood, but inhaled mud. It had entered her mouth, her nose, her throat, her eyes – it had become a shroud closing in on her, folding her in its cloudy wrappings. She threw her hands at it, scratching, lunging and pummelling, but its edges seemed always to recede, like the slippery walls of a placental sac. Then she felt something brush against her back and at that moment there was no touch that would not have made her respond as if to the probing of a reptilian snout. Her body began to twitch convulsively, and she tried to look over her shoulder, but could see nothing except that impenetrable sepia glow. Although her limbs were growing rigid and her strength was ebbing, she tried to defend herself by hitting out and flailing her arms in the water. But then something came shooting through the water and struck her in the face: she felt herself being propelled through the water and was unable to resist. Suddenly her head broke free and there was a lightness on her skin that she knew to be the touch of air. But still she could not breathe: her nose and her mouth were swamped with mud and water.

Thrashing her arms, she tried to lift herself from the water, only to be struck on the face again, by another powerful blow. Then, to her amazement, a pair of arms appeared around her chest. A hand caught hold of her neck, jerking back her head and another set of teeth were suddenly clamped against her own. There was a sucking sensation in her mouth and something seemed to shoot out of her gullet. A moment later she felt a whiff of air in her throat and began to gasp for more. A clasped arm was holding her upright in the water and on her left shoulder was a sharp, prickling sensation. Even as she was struggling to swallow mouthfuls of air, it filtered through to her consciousness that it was the fisherman who was holding her and that his stubble was abrading her skin. The stinging seemed to clear her mind and she forced herself to loosen her panicked muscles, calming her body to the point where he could begin to swim.

The current had carried them a long way from the boat and she knew that he would not be able to tow her unless she lay still. Rolling over in the water she arched her back, to stay afloat, and hooked her arm through his, making herself almost weightless. Even then the push of the current was like a gravitational force, and she could feel him straining for each inch, as though he were dragging her up a steep slope.

At last, when her hands were on the gunwale, he corkscrewed his body under her, pushing her out of the water and into the boat. She landed on her belly and instantly a jet of swallowed water rose to choke her gorge. Suddenly it was as if she were drowning all over again. With water streaming from her mouth and her nose, she clutched at her throat, clawing at the base of her neck with her fingers as though she were trying to loosen a garrotte. Then again, his hands fastened on her shoulders, flipping her over. Throwing a leg across her hips, he weighed her down with his body and fastened his mouth on hers, sucking the water from her throat and pumping air into her lungs.

When her windpipe was clear again, he broke away. She heard him spitting into the water and knew he was cleaning the taste of her vomit from his mouth.

As the rhythm of her breathing returned, she caught the sound of voices and opened her eyes. It was the forest guard and his friend, the pilot: they were leering at her from the launch, lounging against the rails and exchanging whispers as they watched her fighting for her breath. When the guard saw she had opened her eyes, he began to point to his watch and to the sun, which was now slipping below the horizon in a blaze of crimson. At first she could make no sense of these gesticulations but when he started to make beckoning motions, she understood: darkness was fast approaching and he wanted her to hurry up and get back on to the launch so they could proceed to wherever it was they were going.

The abruptness of this summons made Piya's hackles rise. The man had evidently assumed she had no choice but to follow his orders, that she would put up with whatever demands he chose to make. From the start she had sensed a threat from the guard and his friend: she knew that to return to the launch in these circumstances would be an acknowledgement of helplessness. If she placed herself in their power now, she would be marked as an acquiescent victim. She could not board that launch again – and yet, what else could she do?

Suddenly a word flashed through her mind, taking her by surprise. She sat up and tried to enunciate it before it could escape. The fisherman was squatting in the bow, bare-bodied except for his loincloth. He had torn off his *lungi* before plunging into the water, and the little boy was using it now to mop the water from his head. When Piya sat up, the boy whispered something and the fisherman turned to look at her. Quickly, before the word could slip away, she said, 'Lusibari?' He frowned as if to say that he hadn't heard her right, so she said the word again, 'Lusibari?' and added, 'Mashima?' At this, he gave her a nod that seemed to indicate he knew those names.

Piya's eyes widened: could it really be that he knew this woman? To confirm, she said again, 'Mashima?' He nodded once more and gave her a smile, as if to say, yes, he knew exactly who she was referring to. But she still could not tell whether he had understood the full import of what she was asking of him. So, just to be sure, she made a sign, pointing first to herself and then at the horizon, to tell him she wanted him to take her there, in his boat. He nodded again, and added, as if in confirmation, 'Lusibari.'

'Yes.' Shutting her eyes in relief, she unclenched her stomach and let her breath flow out.

Standing on the launch, the guard snapped his fingers at Piya as if to wake her from a long sleep. She pulled herself to her feet, leaning against the boat's bamboo awning for support, and signalled to him to pass over her backpacks. He handed over the first without demur, and it was only when she asked for the second that he understood she was not coming back to the launch. His smirk changed into a scowl, and he began to shout, not at her, but at the fisherman, whose response was nothing more than a quiet shrug and a murmur. This seemed to make the guard angrier still, and he began to threaten the fisherman with gestures of his fist.

Piya tried to intervene with a shout of her own. 'It's not his fault. Why're you yelling at him?' Now, unexpectedly, the pilot added his voice to hers. He too began to remonstrate with the guard, pointing to the horizon to remind him of the fast-approaching sunset. This jolted the guard's attention back to Piya. He held up her second backpack and rubbed his finger and thumb together, to indicate that it would not be given over without a payment.

Her money, she remembered, was enclosed inside her water-proofed money-belt. She reached for the zip and was relieved to find the belt intact, its contents undamaged. She counted out the equivalent of a day's hire for the boat and a day's wages for the guard. Then, as she was handing the money over, just to ensure herself of a quick riddance, she added a few extra notes. Without another word, the guard grabbed the money and tossed over her backpack.

She could scarcely believe she had succeeded in ridding herself of them. She had expected more scenes and more yelling, fresh demands for money. On cue, as if to show her that she had not got off lightly, the guard held up her Walkman – he had managed to extricate it from her belongings before handing them over. Then, to celebrate his theft, he began to make lurid gestures, pumping his pelvis and milking his finger with his fist.

Piya was as oblivious to these obscenities as to the loss of her music: she would be grateful just to see the guard and his friend depart. She shut her eyes and waited till the sound of the launch had faded away.

The Trust

Despite its small size the island of Lusibari supported a population of several thousand. Some of its people were descended from the first settlers, who had arrived in the 1920s. Others had come in successive waves, some after the partition of the subcontinent in 1947 and some after the Bangladesh war of 1971. Many had come even more recently, when other nearby islands were forcibly depopulated in order to make room for wildlife conservation projects. As a result, the pressure of population in Lusibari was such that no patch of land was allowed to lie fallow. The green fields that quilted the island were dotted with clusters of mud huts and crossed by many well-trodden pathways. The broadest of these paths were even paved with bricks and shaded with rows of casuarina trees. But these elements of an ordinary rural existence did not entirely conceal the fact that life in Lusibari was lived at the sufferance of a single feature of its topography. This was its *bãdh*, the tall embankment that encircled its perimeter, holding back the twice-daily flood.

The compound of the Badabon Trust was at the rounded end of the conch-shaped island, a kilometre's distance from Lusibari village. Nilima lived there in a small building that doubled also as a guest house for the Trust's visitors.

It took a while for Kanai and Nilima to make their way to this end of the island. They had disembarked on the mudspit, near Lusibari village, and by the time they departed for the Trust's compound, it was near sunset. The vehicle that had been arranged for their transport was new to Kanai – there had been none on the island at the time of his last visit. It was a cycle-van, a bicycle-trolley with a square platform mounted behind the driver's saddle. The platform served to carry luggage and livestock as well as passengers, who sat on it either with their legs folded or with their feet dangling over the edge. Since the platforms were flat, with no handholds, the passengers had to cling on as best they could. When the vehicles hit bumps or potholes, they locked arms to hold each other in place.

'Are you sure we'll all fit on that?' said Kanai dubiously, eyeing the vehicle.

'Yes, of course,' said Nilima. 'Just get on and we'll hold you down.'

They set off with Kanai's suitcase lodged among baskets of vegetables and squawking clutches of fowl. The van turned on to a path paved with uncemented brick, many of which had come loose, leaving gaps in the track's surface. When the wheels hit these holes, the platform flew up as if to catapult its passengers from the vehicle. Kanai would have gone rocketing off if the others hadn't kept him in place by holding on to his shirt.

'I hope you'll be comfortable in our Guest House,' said Nilima anxiously. 'Our set-up is very simple, so don't expect any luxuries. A room's been prepared for you and your dinner should be waiting, in a tiffin carrier. I've told one of our trainee nurses to make arrangements for your food. If you need anything, just let her know. Her name is Moyna – she should be there now, waiting for us.'

At the mention of the name the van's driver suddenly corkscrewed around in his seat. 'Mashima, are you talking about Moyna Mandol?'

'Yes.'

'But you won't find her at the guest house, Mashima,' the driver said. 'Haven't you heard yet?'

'What?'

'Moyna's husband, that fellow Fokir, has gone missing again. And he's taken the boy too – their son. Moyna's running all over the place, asking after them.'

'No! Is that true?'

'Yes.' A couple of other passengers confirmed this with vigorous nods.

60

Mashima clicked her tongue. 'Poor Moyna. That fellow gives her so much trouble.'

Kanai had been listening to this exchange and, on seeing the look of consternation on Mashima's face, said, 'Will this upset all the arrangements?'

'No,' said Mashima. 'We'll manage one way or the other. I'm just worried about Moyna. That husband of hers is going to drive her mad one day.'

'Who is he? Her husband I mean?'

'You won't know him—' Breaking off in mid-sentence Nilima clutched at Kanai's arm. 'Wait! Actually you do know him – not him, I mean, but his mother.'

'His mother?'

'Yes. Do you remember a girl called Kusum?'

'Of course,' said Kanai. 'Of course I remember her. She was the only friend I had in this place.'

Nilima gave a slow nod. 'Yes,' said Nilima. 'I remember now: you two used to play together. Anyway, this man we're talking about – Fokir? He's Kusum's son. He's married to Moyna.'

'Is he the one who's missing?'

'Yes, that's him.'

'And what about Kusum? What became of her?'

Nilima let out a deep sigh. 'She ran off, Kanai; it must have been some months after you visited us. For years we didn't have any news of her, but then she showed up again. It was very unfortunate.'

'Why? What happened?'

Nilima closed her eyes as if to shut out the memory. 'She was killed.'

'How?'

'I'll tell you later,' said Nilima in an undertone. 'Not now.'

'And her son?' Kanai persisted. 'How old was he when Kusum died?'

'He was just a child,' Nilima said. 'Maybe five years old or so. He was brought up by Horen, who was a relative.'

A large building suddenly came into view, capturing Kanai's attention. 'What's that, over there?'

'That's the hospital,' said Nilima. 'Is this the first time you're seeing it?'

61

'Yes,' said Kanai. 'I haven't been to Lusibari since it was built.'

The lights that flanked the hospital's entrance each seemed to be enclosed within a moving, buzzing halo of its own. When the cycle-van rolled past, Kanai saw that this effect was created by clouds of insects. Also clustered beneath the bulbs were groups of schoolchildren, with books open on their laps.

'Aren't those electric lights?' Kanai said in surprise.

'Yes, they are.'

'But I thought Lusibari hadn't got electricity yet?'

'We have electricity within this compound,' said Nilima. 'But just for a few hours each day, from sunset till about nine.'

One of the Trust's benefactors, Nilima explained, had donated a generator, and the machine was turned on for a few hours each evening so that the hospital's staff could have a period of heightened activity in which to prepare for the stillness of the night. As for the children, they too were drawn to the hospital by its lights. It was easier to study there than at home and cheaper too, since it saved oil and candles.

'And that's where we're going,' said Nilima pointing ahead, to a two-storey house separated from the hospital by a pond and a stand of coconut trees. Small and brightly painted, the house had the cheerful look of a whitewashed elementary school. The guest rooms were upstairs, Nilima explained, while the flat on the ground floor was the home in which she and her late husband had lived since the mid-1970s. Nirmal's study, where all his papers were stored, was on the roof.

After Nilima had dismounted from the cycle-van, she handed Kanai a key: 'This opens the door to your uncle's study. You should go upstairs and have a look – you'll find the packet on his desk. I wanted to take you there myself but I'm too tired.'

'I'll manage on my own,' said Kanai. 'Don't worry about me. I'll see you in the morning.'

Kanai was heading for the stairs with his suitcase, when Nilima called out, as an afterthought, 'The generator will be switched off at nine, so be prepared. Don't be caught off guard when the lights go off.'

Fokir

Only after the launch had disappeared from view was Piya able to breathe freely again. But now, as her muscles loosened, the delayed shock she had been half-expecting set in as well. Her limbs began to quiver and suddenly her chin was knocking a drumbeat on her kneecaps; in a moment she was shivering hard enough to shake the boat, sending ripples across the water.

There was a touch on her shoulder and she turned sideways to see the child, standing beside her. He put his arm around her and clung to her back, hugging her, trying to warm her body with his own. She closed her eyes and did not open them again until the chattering of her teeth had stopped.

Now it was the fisherman who was in front of her, squatting on his haunches and looking into her face with an inquiring frown. Slowly, as her shivering passed, his face relaxed into a smile. With a finger on his chest, pointing at himself, he said, 'Fokir.' She understood that this was his name and responded with her own: 'Piya.' With a nod of acknowledgement, he turned to the boy and said, 'Tutul.' Then his forefinger moved, from himself to the boy and back again, and she knew he was telling her the boy was his son.

'Tutul.'

Looking closely at the child she saw he was even younger than she had thought, perhaps no more than five years old. He was wearing a threadbare sweater, against the November chill. Below this hung a pair of huge, discoloured shorts that looked as though they had once belonged to a school uniform. He had something in his hands, and when he held it up she saw it was

63

her laminated placard. She had no idea where he had found it but was pleased to see it again. He brought it to her, holding it in front of him like a tray, and gave her fingers a squeeze, as though to assure her of his protection.

The gesture had the paradoxical effect of making her suddenly aware of her own vulnerability. This was not a feeling she was accustomed to – she was used to being on her own in out-of-the-way places, with only strangers for company. But her experience with the guard had bruised her confidence and she felt as though she were recovering from an assault. This made her all the more grateful for the child's presence: she knew that if it weren't for him it would have been much harder for her to put her trust in a complete stranger as she had done. It was true, then, that in a way the boy was her protector. The recognition of this made her do something that did not come easily. She was not given to displays of affection but now, in a brief gesture of gratitude, she opened her arms and gave the boy a hug.

As she was releasing the child, she noticed he was looking intently at her hands – her wallet was still wedged between her fingers. With a guilty start, she remembered that she had made no mention of money to the fisherman. Opening the wallet she took out a wad of Indian currency and separated a thin sheaf of notes from the rest. She was counting out the money when she became aware of their attention and looked up. They appeared to be transfixed and their eyes were following her fingers as though she were performing some intricate feat of jugglery. There was a wonderment in their faces that told her that their absorption was not a function of greed; it was just that they had never before been in the proximity of so large a sum of money and so many crisp currency notes. Yet, despite the closeness of this scrutiny, Fokir seemed not to have understood that it was for him that she was counting the money: when she offered the notes to him, he recoiled guiltily, as though she'd offered him some kind of contraband.

The sum she had counted out was small, no more than she might elsewhere have paid for a few sandwiches and a couple of coffees. Her research grant was too tight to allow her to be lavish, but this small token, at least, she felt she did owe him, and if he had had a shirt she would have tucked the money right into his pocket. As it happened, apart from his wet loincloth he was wearing nothing but a small cylindrical medallion tied to his arm with a string, just above the bicep. Unable to think of any other expedient, she twisted the notes into a roll and thrust them under the medallion. His skin, she noticed, was bristling with goosebumps and she could not tell whether this was a reaction to her touch or to the chilly evening wind.

A loud exclamation followed as Fokir retrieved the money. When the notes were in his hands, he examined them as if in disbelief, holding them at a distance from his face. Presently, with a gesture in the direction of the recently departed launch, he peeled a single note from the bundle and held it aloft. She understood that he was telling her that he would accept that one note as compensation for the money that had been taken from him. He handed this to the boy, who darted off to hide it somewhere in the thatch of the boat's hood.

The other notes he gave back to her, and when she attempted to protest, he pointed towards the horizon and repeated the word she herself had uttered earlier: 'Lusibari.' She recognized he was deferring the matter of payment until they arrived at Lusibari, and there she was content to let the matter rest.

The Letter

The Guest House occupied the whole of the second floor and was accessed by a narrow staircase. There were four rooms, all identically furnished with two narrow beds, a desk and a chair. They opened into a space that was part corridor, part dining room, part kitchen. At the far end of the corridor lay the building's one claim to luxury, a bathroom with a shower, a toilet and running water. Kanai had been dreading the thought of bathing in a pond and heaved a sigh of relief on catching sight of these unexpected amenities.

On the dining table stood a stainless-steel tiffin carrier and Kanai guessed it contained his dinner. Evidently, despite her cares, Moyna had not neglected to provide his evening meal. Exploring further, he deposited his suitcase in the room that appeared to have been readied for him and headed for the stairs.

On making his way up to the roof Kanai was rewarded with a fine view of a tide country sunset: with the rivers running low, the surrounding islands were riding high on the reddening water. With his first circumambulation of the roof, Kanai found he could count no fewer than six islands and eight 'rivers' in the immediate vicinity of Lusibari. He saw also that Lusibari was the most southerly of the inhabited islands; on the islands beyond were no fields or houses, nothing other than dense forests of mangrove.

On one side of the roof was a long, tin-roofed room with a locked door. This, Kanai realized, was Nirmal's study. He tried the lock and found that it opened to the key Nilima had given him. Pushing the door open, he stepped in to find himself facing a wall stacked with books and papers. There was only one window and on opening it Kanai saw it looked westwards, in the direction of the Raimangal's mohona. The desk beneath this window was laid out as if for Nirmal's use, with an inkwell, a stack of fountain pens and an old-fashioned, crescent-shaped blotter. Under the blotter was a large sealed packet that had Kanai's name written on it. The packet was wrapped in layers of plastic that had been pasted together with some kind of crude industrial glue. On top was a piece of paper that looked as if it had been torn from a notebook, and written upon it, in his uncle's hand, were Kanai's name and his address of twenty years before. Kanai squeezed the packet between his fingers but could not make out exactly what lay inside. Nor could he see how he was to open it; the layers of plastic seemed almost to be fused together. Looking around him, he saw half a razor blade lying on the window sill. He picked up the sharp-edged sliver of metal and applied it to the plastic sheets, pinching it carefully between his fingertips. After cutting through a few layers, he saw, lying inside, like an egg in a nest, a small cardboard-covered notebook, a *khata*, of the kind generally used by school-children. This surprised him for he had been expecting loose sheets – poems, essays – anything but a single notebook. He flipped it open and saw that it was covered in Bengali lettering, in Nirmal's hand. The writing was cramped, as if in order to save space, and the penmanship was so unruly as to suggest that the lines had been written in great haste. In places there was much crossing out and filling in, and the words often spilled into the thin margin. Despite the many layers of plastic, the paper was covered with damp spots. In some places, the ink too had begun to fade.

Kanai had to raise the notebook to within a couple of inches of his eyes before he could decipher the first few letters. There was a date in the top left-hand corner, written in English: May 15, 1979, 5.30 a.m. Immediately below this was Kanai's name. Although there were none of the customary salutations of a letter, it was clear these pages had been addressed directly to him, Kanai, in the form of some kind of extended letter.

This was confirmed when Kanai read the first few lines: 'I am writing these words in a place that you will probably never have heard of: an island on the southern edge of the tide country, a place called Morichjhāpi . . .'

Kanai looked up from the page and turned the name over in his mind: Morichjhāpi. As if by habit, he found himself translating the word: 'Pepper-island'.

He lowered his eyes once more to the notebook:

The hours are slow in passing as they always are when you are waiting in fear for you know not what: I am reminded of the moments before the coming of a cyclone, when you have barricaded yourself into your dwelling and have nothing else to do but wait. The moments will not pass; the air hangs still and heavy; it is as though time itself has been slowed by the friction of fear.

*In other circumstances perhaps I would have tried to read. But I have nothing with me here except this notebook, one ballpoint pen, one pencil, and my copies of Rilke's **Duino Elegies**, in Bangla and English translation. Nor, in the hours preceding this, would it have been possible to read, for it is daybreak and I am in a thatch-roofed hut with no candles available. From a chink in the bamboo wall, I can see the Gāral, one of the rivers that flows past this island. The sun has shown itself in the east and, as if to meet it, the tide too is quickly rising. The nearby islands are sliding gradually beneath the water and soon, like icebergs in a polar sea, they will be mostly hidden; only the tops of their tallest trees will remain in sight. Already their mudbanks and the webbed roots that hold them together have become ghostly discolorations, shimmering under the surface, like shoals of wave-stirred seaweed. In the distance a flock of herons can be seen heading across the water in preparation for the coming inundation: driven from a drowning island they have taken wing in search of a more secure perch. It is, in other words, a dawn that is beautiful in the way only a tide country dawn can be.*

This hut is not mine; I am a guest. It belongs to someone you once knew: Kusum. She has lived in it with her son for almost a year.

As I look on the scene before me I cannot help wondering what it has meant to them – to Fokir, to Kusum – to wake to this sight, through the better part of a year? Has it provided any recompense for everything they have had to live through? Who could presume to know the answer? At this moment, lying in wait, I can think only of the Poet's words:

'beauty is nothing
but the start of terror we can hardly bear,
and we adore it because of the serene scorn
it could kill us with . . .'

All night long, I have been asking myself, what is it I am afraid of?
Now, with the rising of the sun, I have understood what it is: I am afraid
because I know that after the storm passes, the events that have preceded
its coming will be forgotten. No one knows better than I how skilful the
tide country is in silting over its past.

There is nothing I can do to stop what lies ahead. But I was once a
writer; perhaps I can make sure at least that what happened here leaves
some trace, some hold upon the memory of the world. The thought of
this, along with the fear that preceded it, has made it possible for me to
do what I have not been able to for the last thirty years – to put my pen
to paper again.

I do not know how much time I have; maybe not much more than
the course of this day. In this time, I will try to write what I can in the
hope that somehow these words will find their way to you. You will be
asking, why you? All I need say, for the time being, is that this is not
my story. It concerns, rather, the only friend you made when you were
here in Lusibari: Kusum. If not for my sake, then for hers, read on.

The Boat

Fokir's five-metre-long boat was just about broad enough in the middle to allow two people to squat side by side. Once Piya had taken stock of her immediate surroundings she realized the boat was the nautical equivalent of a shanty, put together out of bits of bamboo thatch, splintered wood and torn sheets of polythene. The planks of the outer shell were unplaned and had been caulked with what appeared to be tar. The deck was fashioned out of plywood strips that had been torn from discarded tea-crates: some still bore remnants of their old markings. These improvised deck-slats were not nailed in: they rested on a ledge and could be moved at will. There were storage spaces in the bilges below and, in the hold at the fore end of the boat, crabs could be seen crawling about in a jumble of mangrove branches and decaying sea-grass. This was where the day's catch was stored – the vegetation provided moisture for the crabs and kept them from tearing each other apart.

The hooped awning at the rear of the boat was made of thatch and bent spokes of bamboo. This hood was just about large enough to shelter a couple of people from the rain and the sun. As water-proofing, a sheet of speckled grey plastic had been tucked between the hoops and the thatch. Piya recognized the markings on this sheet: they were from a mailbag, of a kind that she herself had often used in posting surface mail from the US. At the stern end of the boat, between the shelter and the curved sternpost, was a small, flat platform, covered with a plank of wood pocked with burn marks.

The deck beneath the shelter concealed yet another hold, and when Fokir moved the slats, Piya saw that this was the boat's equivalent of a storage cupboard. It was separated from the fore-hold by an internal bulwark, and was crudely but effectively waterproofed with a sheet of blue tarpaulin. It held a small, neatly packed cargo of dry clothes, cooking utensils, food and drinking water. Reaching into this space now, Fokir pulled out a length of folded fabric. When he shook it out Piya saw it was a cheap, printed sari.

The manoeuvres that followed caused Piya some initial puzzle-ment. After sending Tutul to the bow, Fokir reached for her back-packs and stowed them under the shelter. Then he slipped out himself and motioned to her to go in. Once she had squirmed inside he draped the sari over the mouth of the shelter, hiding her from view.

It took her a while to understand that he had created an enclosure to give her the privacy to change her wet clothes. In absorbing this, she was at first a little embarrassed to think that it was he rather than she herself, who had been the first to pay heed to the matter of her modesty. But the very thought of this – even the word itself, 'modesty', with its evocation of flutter-ing veils and old comic strips – made her want to smile: after years of sharing showers in co-ed dorms and living with men in cramped seaboard quarters, the idea seemed quaint but also, somehow, touching. It was not just that he had thought to create a space for her; it was as if he had chosen to include her in some simple, practised family ritual, found a way to let her know that despite the inescapable muteness of their exchanges, she was a person to him and not, as it were, a representative of a species, a faceless, tongueless foreigner. But where had this recognition come from? He had probably never met anyone like her before, any more than she had ever met anyone like him.

After she had finished changing, she reached out to touch the sari. Running the cloth between her fingers, she could tell that it had gone through many rigorous washings. She remembered the feel of the cloth. This was exactly the texture of the saris her mother had worn at home, in Seattle – soft, crumpled, worn thin. They had been a great grievance for her once, those faded greying saris: it was impossible to bring friends to a home where

71

the mother was dressed in something that looked like an old bedsheet.

Whom did the sari belong to? His wife? The boy's mother? Were the two the same? Although she would have liked to know, it caused her no great regret that she lacked the means of finding out. In a way it was a relief to be spared the responsibilities that came with a knowledge of the details of another life.

Crawling out of the boat's shelter, Piya saw that Fokir had already drawn in the anchor and was lowering his oars. He too had changed, she noticed, and had even taken the time to comb his hair. It lay flat on his head, parted down the middle. With the salt gone from his face, he looked unexpectedly youthful, almost impish. He was dressed in a faded, buff-coloured T-shirt and a fresh lungi. The old one – the one he had been wearing when she first spotted him with her binoculars – had been laid out to dry on the boat's hood.

In the meanwhile the sun had begun to set, and a comet of colour had come shooting over the horizon and plunged, flaming, into the heart of the mohona. With darkness approaching quickly, Piya knew they would soon have to find a place to wait out the night. Only in the light of day could a boat of this size hope to find its way through this watery labyrinth. She guessed that Fokir had probably already decided on an anchorage for the night and was trying to get them there as quickly as possible.

When the boat started to move, Piya stood up, with a beltful of equipment hanging at her waist, and began to scan the water ahead. Her binoculars' gaze seemed to fall on the landscape like a shower of rain, mellowing its edges, diminishing her sense of disorientation and unpreparedness. The boat's rolling did nothing to interrupt the metronomic precision of her movements; her binoculars held to their course, turning from right to left and back again, as steady as the beam of a lighthouse. Over years of practice, her musculature had become attuned to the water and she had learned to keep her balance almost without effort, flexing her knees instinctively to counteract the rolling.

This was what Piya loved best about her work: being out on the water, alert and on watch, with the wind in her face and her equipment at her fingertips. Buckled to her waist was a rock-climber's belt, which she had adapted so that the hooks served to attach a clipboard as well as a few instruments. The first and most important of these was the hand-held monitor that kept track of her location, through the Global Positioning System. When she was 'on effort', actively searching for dolphins, this instrument recorded her movements down to every metre and every second. With its help, she could, if necessary, find her way across the open ocean, back to the very spot where, at a certain moment on a certain day, she had caught a momentary glimpse of a dolphin's flukes before they disappeared under the waves.

Along with the GPS monitor was a rangefinder and a depth-sounder, so named because it could provide an exact reading of the depth when its sensor was dipped beneath the surface. Although these instruments were all essential to her work, none was as valuable as the binoculars strapped around her neck. Piya had had to reach deep into her pocket to pay for them but the money had not been ill spent. The glasses' outer casing had been bleached by the sun and dulled by the gnawing of sand and salt, yet the waterproofed armouring had done its job in protecting the instrument's essential functions. After six years of constant use the lens still delivered an image of undiminished sharpness. The left eye-piece had a built-in compass that displayed its readings through an aperture. This allowed Piya to calibrate her movements so that the sweep of her gaze covered an almost exact semicircle, a precise one hundred and eighty degrees.

Piya had acquired her binoculars long before she had any real need of them, when she was barely a year into her graduate programme at the Scripps Institution of Oceanography in California. Early though it was then, she had had no doubts about the purchase; by that time she was already sure of her mind and knew exactly what she was going to be doing in the years ahead. She had wanted to be absolutely sure about getting the best and had gone through dozens of catalogues before sending her cheque to the mail-order company.

When the package arrived she was surprised by its weight. At the time she was living in a room that looked down on one of the busier walkways in the university. She had stood by the window and turned the glasses on the throngs of students below, focusing on their faces and even their books and newspapers, marvelling at the clarity of the resolution and the brilliance of the image. She had tried turning the instrument from side to side and was surprised by the effort it took: it came as a discovery that you could not do a hundred-and-eighty-degree turn just by swivelling your head – the movement had to torque through the whole of your body, beginning at the ankles and extending through the hips and shoulders, reaching almost as far as your temples. Within a few minutes she had grown tired and her arms had begun to ache. Was it possible she'd ever be able to heft an instrument of this weight through the length of a twelve-hour day? It didn't seem possible. How did they do it, the others?

She was used to being dwarfed by her contemporaries. Through her childhood and adolescence she had always been among the smallest in her age group. But she had never in her life felt as tiny as she did that day in La Jolla when she walked into her first cetology lecture – 'a minnow among the whale-watchers' one of her professors had said. The others were natural athletes, raw-boned and finely muscled. The women especially, seemed all to have come of age on the warm, surf-spangled beaches of southern California or Hawaii or New Zealand; they had grown up diving, snorkelling, kayaking, canoeing, playing volleyball in the sand. Under their golden tans the fine hair on their forearms shone like powdered silica. Piya had never cared for sport of any kind and this had added to her sense of apartness. She had become a kind of departmental mascot – 'the little East Indian girl'.

It was not until her first survey cruise, off the coast of Costa Rica, that her doubts about her strength were put at rest. For the first few days they had seen nothing and she had laboured under the weight of the binoculars – to the point where her co-workers had taken pity on her, giving her extra turns on the 'Big Eye', the deck-mounted binoculars. On the fourth day, they had caught up with what they had thought was a small herd of maybe twenty spinners. But the number had kept growing, from twenty to a hundred to maybe as many as seven thousand – there were so many that the numbers were beyond accurate estimation; they filled the sea from horizon to horizon so that even the white caps of the waves seemed to be outnumbered by the glint of pointed beaks and shining dorsal fins. That was when she learned how it happened – how at a certain moment, the binoculars' weight ceased to matter; it was not just that your arms developed huge ropy muscles (which they did) – it was also that the glasses fetched you the water with such vividness and particularity that you could not think of anything else.

Nirmal and Nilima

Nirmal and Nilima Bose first came to Lusibari in search of a safe haven. This was in 1950 and they had been married less than a year.

Nirmal was originally from Dhaka but had come to Calcutta as a student. The events of Partition had cut him off from his family and he had elected to stay on in Calcutta where he had made a name for himself as a leftist intellectual and a writer of promise. He was teaching English literature at Ashutosh College when his path crossed Nilima's: she happened to be a student in one of his classes.

Nilima's circumstances were utterly unlike Nirmal's. She was from a family well known for its tradition of public service. Her grandfather was one of the founding members of the Congress Party and her father (Kanai's grandfather) was an eminent barrister at the Calcutta High Court. As an adolescent Nilima had developed severe asthma and when it came time to send her to college her family had decided to spare her the rigours of a long daily commute. They had enrolled her in Ashutosh College, which was just a short drive from their home in Ballygunge Place. The family car, a Packard, made the trip twice a day, dropping her in the morning and picking her up in the afternoon.

One day she sent the driver away, on a pretext, and followed her English teacher on to a bus: it was as if the light of idealism in his eye was a flame and she a moth. Many other girls in her class had been mesmerized by Nirmal's fiery lectures and impassioned recitations; although many of them claimed to be in love with him, none of them had Nilima's resolve and resourcefulness. That day on the bus, she managed to find a seat next to Nirmal and within the space of a few months was able to announce to her outraged family that she knew exactly whom she wanted to marry. Her family's opposition served only to strengthen her resolve and in 1949 the young couple were married in a civil ceremony. The wedding was presided over by one of Nirmal's comrades and was solemnized by readings of Blake, Mayakovsky and Jibanananda Das.

They had not been married a month when the police came knocking at the door of their tiny flat in Mudiali. It so happened that the year before Nirmal had participated in a conference convened by the Socialist International, in Calcutta. (In telling this story Nirmal would pause here, to note parenthetically that this conference was one of the pivotal events of the postwar world: within a decade or two, Western intelligence agencies and their clients were to trace every major Asian uprising – the Vietnamese insurrection, the Malayan insurgency, the Red Flag rebellion in Burma and much else – to the policy of 'armed struggle' adopted in Calcutta in 1948. There was no reason, he would add, why anyone should know or remember this: yet in the tide country, where life was lived on the margins of greater events, it was useful also to be reminded that no place was so remote as to escape the flood of history.)

Nirmal had played only a small part in the conference, serving merely as a guide and general dogsbody for the Burmese delegation. But now, with a Communist insurgency raging in Burma, the authorities were keen to know whether he had picked up anything of interest from his Burmese contacts.

Although his detainment lasted only a day or two, the experience had a profoundly unsettling effect on Nirmal, following as it did on his rejection by Nilima's family and his separation from his own. He could not bring himself to go to the college and there were days when he would not even get out of bed. Recognizing that something had snapped, Nilima threw herself upon her family's mercies and went to see her mother. Although her marriage was never quite forgiven, Nilima's family rallied to her side and promised to help in whatever way they could. At her father's bidding, a couple of doctors came to see Nirmal and their advice was that he would do well to spend some time outside the city. This view was endorsed by Nirmal's comrades who had come to recognize that he was of too frail a temperament to be of much use to their cause. For her part Nilima welcomed the idea of putting distance between herself and the city – as much for her own asthma as for Nirmal's sake. The problem was, where were they to go? It so happened that Nilima's father handled some of the affairs of the Hamilton Estate and he learnt that the estate's managers were looking for a teacher to run the Lusibari school.

Sir Daniel Hamilton had died in 1939 and the estate had since passed into the possession of his nephew, James Hamilton. The new owner lived on the isle of Arran in Scotland and had never been to India before coming into his inheritance. After Sir Daniel's death he had paid a brief visit to Gosaba but for every practical purpose, the estate was now entirely in the hands of its management: if Nilima's father were to put in a word, Nirmal would almost certainly get the job.

Nirmal was initially horrified at the thought of being associated with an enterprise founded by a leading capitalist, but after much pleading from Nilima he eventually agreed to go to Gosaba for an exploratory visit. They travelled down to the estate together and their stay happened to coincide with the annual celebration of the founder's birthday. They discovered, to their astonishment, that this occasion was observed with many of the ceremonial trappings of a *puja*. Statues of Sir Daniel, of which there were many scattered through the estate, were garlanded, smeared with vermilion and accorded many other marks of reverence. It was clear that in the eyes of the local people the visionary Scotsman was, if not quite a deity, then certainly a venerated ancestral spirit. In listening to the settlers' remembrances of the estate's idealistic founder, Nirmal and Nilima were forced to revise their initial scepticism. It shamed them to think that this man – a foreigner, a Burra Sahib, a rich capitalist – had taken it upon himself to address the issue of rural poverty when they themselves, despite all their radical talk, had scarcely any knowledge of life outside the city.

It took them just a couple of days to make their minds up:

without so much as setting foot in Lusibari they decided that they would spend a couple of years on the island. They went back to Calcutta, packed their few belongings and left immediately after the monsoons.

For their first few months on the island they were in a state akin to shock. Nothing was familiar; everything was new. What little they knew of rural life was derived from the villages of the plains: the realities of the tide country were of a strangeness beyond reckoning. How was it possible that these islands were a mere ninety-seven kilometres from home and yet so little was known about them? How was it possible that people spoke so much about the immemorial traditions of village India and yet no one knew about this other world, where it was impossible to tell who was who, and what their castes and religions and beliefs were? And where was the shared wealth of the Republic of Co-operative Credit? What had become of its currency and banks? Where was the gold that was to have been distilled from the tide country's mud?

The destitution of the tide country was such as to remind them of the terrible famine that had devastated Bengal in 1942 – except that in Lusibari hunger and catastrophe were a way of life. They learnt that after decades of settlement, the land had still not been wholly leached of its salt. The soil bore poor crops and could not be farmed all year round. Most families subsisted on a single daily meal. Despite all the labour that had been invested in the embankments, there were still periodic breaches because of floods and storms: each such inundation rendered the land infertile for several years at a time. The settlers were mainly of farming stock who had been drawn to Lusibari by the promise of free farmland. Hunger drove them to hunting and fishing and the results were often disastrous. Many died of drowning, and many more were picked off by crocodiles and estuarine sharks. Nor did the mangroves offer much of immediate value to human beings – yet thousands risked death in order to collect meagre quantities of honey, wax, firewood and the sour fruit of the *kewra* tree. No day seemed to pass without news of someone being killed by a tiger, a snake or a crocodile.

As for the school, it had little to offer other than its roof and walls. The estate was almost bankrupt. Although funds were said to have been earmarked for clinics, education and public works, very little evidence was ever seen of these. The rumour was that this money went to the estate's managers, and the overseers' henchmen savagely beat settlers who protested or attempted to resist. The methods were those of a penal colony and the atmosphere that of a prison camp.

They had not expected a utopia but nor had they expected such destitution. Faced with this situation they saw what it really meant to ask a question such as 'What is to be done?'

Nirmal, overwhelmed, read and reread Lenin's pamphlet without being able to find any definite answers. Nilima, ever practical, began to talk to the women who gathered at the wells and the ponds.

Within a few weeks of her arrival in Lusibari, Nilima noticed that a startlingly large proportion of the island's women were dressed as widows. These women were easily identified because of their borderless white saris and their lack of adornment: no bangles or vermilion. At the wells and by the *ghats* there often seemed to be no one who was not a widow. Making inquiries, she learnt that in the tide country girls were brought up on the assumption that if they married, they would be widowed in their twenties – their thirties if they were lucky. This assumption was woven, like a skein of dark wool, into the fabric of their lives: when the menfolk went fishing it was the custom for their wives to change into the garments of widowhood. They would put away their marital reds and dress in white saris; they would take off their bangles and wash the vermilion from their heads. It was as though they were trying to hold misfortune at bay by living through it over and over again. Or was it merely a way of preparing themselves for that which they knew to be inevitable?

There was an enormity in these acts that appalled Nilima. She knew that for her mother, her sisters, her friends, the deliberate shedding of these symbols of marriage would have been unthinkable, equivalent to wishing death upon their husbands. Even she, who believed herself to be a revolutionary, could no more have broken her marital bangles than she could have driven a stake through her husband's heart. But for these women the imagining of early widowhood was not a wasted effort: the hazards of life in the tide country were so great; so many people perished in their youth, men especially, that almost without exception the fate they had prepared themselves for did indeed befall them. It was true that here, on the margins of the Hindu world, widows were not condemned to lifelong bereavement: they were free to remarry if they could. But in a place where men of marriageable age were few, this meant little. Here, Nilima learnt, even more than on the mainland, widowhood often meant a lifetime of dependence and years of abuse and exploitation.

What to make of these women and their plight? Searching for a collective noun for them, Nilima was tempted to settle on *sreni*, class. But Nirmal would not hear of it. Workers were a class, he said, but to speak of workers' widows as a class was to introduce a false and unsustainable division.

But if they were not a class, what were they?

It was thus, when reality ran afoul of her vocabulary, that Nilima had her epiphany. It did not matter what they were; what mattered was that they should not remain what they were. She knew a widow who lived near the school, a young woman of twenty-five. One day she asked her if she would be willing to go to Gosaba, to buy soap, matches and provisions. The rates charged by Lusibari's professional shopkeepers were exorbitant; even after the fares for the ferry there would be a considerable saving. Half of this, the woman could keep for herself. This tiny seedling of an idea was to lead to the foundation of the island's Mohila Sangothon – the Women's Union – and ultimately to the Badabon Trust.

Within a few years of Nirmal and Nilima's arrival in Lusibari, *zamindaris* were abolished and large landholdings were broken up by law. What remained of the Hamilton Estate was soon crippled by lawsuits. The union Nilima had founded, on the other hand, continued to grow, drawing in more and more members and offering an ever-increasing number of services – medical, paralegal, agricultural. At a certain point the movement grew so large that it had to be reorganized, and that was when the Badabon Development Trust was formed.

81

Nirmal was by no means wholly supportive of Nilima's efforts – for him they bore the ineradicable stigma of 'social service', *shomaj sheba* – but it was he who gave the Trust its name, which came from the Bengali word for 'mangrove'.

Badabon was a word Nirmal loved. He liked to point out that like the English 'bedouin', *badabon* derived from the Arabic *badiya*, which means 'desert'. 'But "Bedouin" is merely an anglicizing of Arabic,' he said to Nilima, 'while our Bangla word joins Arabic to Sanskrit – "bada" to "bon", or "forest". It is as though the word itself were an island, born of the meeting of two great rivers of language – just as the tide country is begotten of the Ganga's union with the Brahmaputra. What better name could there be for your "Trust"?' And so was the Trust's name decided upon.

One of the Badabon Trust's first acts was to acquire a tract of land in the interior of the island. There, in the late 1970s, its hospital, workshops, offices and Guest House were to be built. But in 1970, the year of Kanai's first visit, these developments were still a decade in the offing. At that time, the meetings of the Women's Union were still held in the courtyard of Nirmal's 'bungalow'. It was there that Kanai met Kusum.

At Anchor

In the failing light the boat approached a bend that led into a wide channel. The far shore, several kilometres away, had already been obscured, but in midstream something lay anchored that seemed to suggest a floating stockade. Fetching her binoculars, Piya saw that this object was actually a cluster of six fishing boats, similar in size and design to the one she was in. The boats were roped tightly together, side by side, and they were tethered against the current by a battery of ropes. Although they were more than a kilometre away, her binoculars provided a clear view of the crewmen as they went about their business. Some were sitting alone, smoking bidis; others were drinking tea or playing cards; a few were washing clothes and utensils, drawing water from the river in steel buckets. A boat in the centre of the cluster was sending up puffs of smoke and she guessed that this was where the communal dinner was being cooked. The sight was both familiar and puzzling. She was reminded of riverside hamlets on the Mekong and the Irrawaddy: there too, at the approach of nightfall, time had seemed both to accelerate and stand still, with lazy spirals of smoke rising into the twilight while bathers came hurrying down the banks to wash off the day's dust. But the difference here was that this village had taken leave of the shore and tethered itself in midstream. Why?

Catching sight of the boats, Tutul gave a shout and launched into an animated conversation with his father. She could tell that they had recognized the boats in the little flotilla. Perhaps they belonged to friends or relatives? She had spent enough time on rivers to know that the people who lived on their shores were rarely strangers to each other. It was almost a certainty that Fokir and his son knew the people in that floating hamlet and that they would be welcomed there. It was easy to imagine how, for them, this might well be the best possible conclusion to the day – an opportunity to mull over the day's events and to show off the stranger who had landed in their midst. Maybe this had been the plan all along – to anchor here, with their friends?

As the boat rounded the bend, she became convinced of this and found herself thinking of the hours that lay ahead. She had long experience of such encounters, having been on many river surveys where the days ended in unforeseen meetings of this kind. She knew exactly what would follow, the surprise that would be occasioned by her presence, the questions, the explanations, the words of welcome she didn't understand but would have to respond to with enforced good humour. The prospect dismayed her, not because of any concern for her own safety – she knew she had nothing to fear from these fishermen – but because, for the moment, all she wanted was to be in this boat, in this small island of silence, afloat on the muteness of the river. It was all she could do to keep herself from appealing to Fokir to keep on going, to hug the shore and keep their boat well hidden.

Of course, none of this could have been said, not even if she had had the words, and it was precisely because nothing was said, that she was taken by surprise when she saw the boat's bow turning in exactly the direction she had hoped for. Soon it was clear that Fokir was steering them away from the floating hamlet, slipping by along the shadows of the shore. She did not betray her relief by any outward alteration of her stance and nor did her practised hands fail to keep her binoculars fixed to her eyes – but inside, it was as though there were a child leaping up to celebrate an unexpected treat, a rare surprise.

Shortly after the last flicker of daylight had faded Fokir pulled the boat over and dropped anchor in a channel that the ebb-tide had turned into a sheltered creek. It was clear that they could not have gone much farther that night, and yet there was something about his manner that told Piya that he was disappointed – that he had decided on another spot in which to anchor and was annoyed with himself for not having reached it.

But now that they were at anchor, with the surprises of the day behind them, a sense of unhurried lassitude descended on the boat. Fokir put a match to an oil-blackened lamp and lit a *biri* from the flame. After he had smoked it down to a stub, he went aft, and showed Piya, by indication and gesture, how the squared platform at the stern end of the boat could be screened off, for use as a lavatory and bathroom. By way of example, he drew a bucket of water and proceeded to bathe Tutul, using the brackish water of the river to soap him, and dipping sparsely into a fresh-water canister to wash off the suds.

With the setting of the sun, the night had turned chilly and the boy's teeth chattered as he stood dripping on deck. Producing a chequered cloth, Fokir rubbed him down before bundling him into his clothes. This towel was made of reddish cotton and was one of several similar pieces Piya had seen around the boat; they had stirred a faint sense of recognition but she could not recall where from.

Once Tutul was done with dressing, it was his turn to bathe his father. After Fokir had stripped down to his breechcloth, Tutul upended streams of cold water over his head, to the accompaniment of much laughter and many loud yells. Piya could see the bones of Fokir's chest, pushing against his skin, like the ribs of a tin that had been stripped of its label. The water made patterns around him, sluicing off the contours of his body as though it were tumbling down the tiers of a fountain.

When both father and son were finished it was Piya's turn. A bucket load of water was pulled up and the shelter was screened off with the sari. In the confinement of the boat it was no easy matter to change places; it was impossible for all three of them to be on their feet at the same time so they had to lie prone and squirm through the hooped hood, in a jumble of elbows, hips and bellies, with Fokir holding down his *lungi* to prevent it from riding up. As they were wriggling past each other Piya caught his eye and they both laughed.

Piya emerged at the far end to find the river glowing like quicksilver. All but the brightest of the stars had been obscured by the moon and apart from their one lamp, no other light was to be seen, either on land or on the water. Nor was there any sound, other than the lapping of the water, for the shore was so distant that even the insects of the forest were inaudible. Except at sea, she had never known the human trace to be so faint, so close to undetectable. Yet on looking around her tiny bathroom, she discovered, by the yellow light of the lamp, that amenities far beyond her expectation had been provided. There was a half-canister of fresh water and next to it a bucket filled with the brackish water of the river; there was a cake of soap on a ledge, and beside it, a tiny but astonishing object – a plastic sachet of shampoo. She had seen strings of these dangling in the tea-shops in Canning and yet, when she picked it up to examine it, its presence seemed oddly intrusive. She would have liked to throw it away, except that she knew that here, in the island that was this boat, the sachet was a treasure of a kind (bought at the expense of how many crabs?) and that it had been put there in her honour. To throw it away would be to abuse this offering; so even though she had never felt less inclined to use shampoo, she put a little bit of it in her hair and washed it into the water, hoping they would see, from the bubbles flowing past the bow, that she had accepted the gift and put it to use.

Only when it was too late and she was shivering against the chill, squatting on the wet boards and hugging her knees, did she remember that she had no towel nor anything else with which to dry herself. But a further search revealed that even this had been provided for: one of those rectangles of chequered cloth had been left draped on the bamboo awning for her use. It was already dry, which suggested it had been there for some time. When she touched it, to pick it up, she had an intuition that this was what Fokir had been wearing when he had dived in after her. These lengths of cloth served many purposes, she knew, and when she put it to her nose she had the impression that she could smell, along with the tartness of the sun and the metallic muddiness of the river, also the salty scent of his sweat.

Now, suddenly she recalled where it was that she had seen a towel like this before: it was tied to the doorknob of her father's wardrobe, in the eleventh-floor apartment of her childhood. Through the years of her adolescence, the fabric had grown old and tattered and she would have thrown it away but for her father's protests. He was, in general, the least sentimental of men, especially where it concerned 'home'. Where others sought to preserve their memories of the 'old country', he had always tried to expunge them. His feet were in the present, he had liked to say, by which he meant they were planted firmly on the rungs of his company's career ladder. But when she had asked whether she could throw away that rotting bit of old cloth, he had responded almost with shock. It had been with him for many years, he said, it was almost a part of his body, like his hair or his nail clippings; his luck was woven into it; he could not think of parting with it, of throwing away this—. What was it he had called it? She had known the word once, but time had erased it from her memory.

Kusum

From the far side of the Guest House roof Kanai could see all the way across the island to the Hamilton High School and even beyond, to the spot where Nirmal's house had once stood. It was gone now but the image of it that flickered in his memory was no less real to him than the newly constructed student hostel that had taken its place. Although the house had always been referred to as a 'bungalow' its size, design and proportions were those of a cabin. Its walls and floors were made of wood and nowhere was a brick or a single smudge of cement to be seen. The structure, held up by a set of stumpy little stilts, stood a foot or so off the ground. As a result, the floors were uneven and their tilt tended to vary with the seasons, dipping during the rains when the ground turned soggy and firming up in the dry winter months.

The 'bungalow' had only two proper rooms, of which one was a bedroom while the other was a kind of study, used by both Nirmal and Nilima. A cot was rigged up in the study, for Kanai, and like the big bed, it was enclosed in a permanent canopy of heavy netting. Mosquitoes were the least of the creatures this net was intended to exclude; its absence, at any time, night or day, would have been an invitation for snakes and scorpions to make their way between the sheets. In a hut by the pond a woman was even said to have found a large dead fish in her bed. This was a *koimachh* or tree perch, a species known to be able to manipulate its spiny fins in such a way as to drag itself overground for short distances. It had found its way into the bed only to suffocate on the mattress.

To preclude night-time collapses of the mosquito netting, the bindings were checked and retied every evening. The tide country being what it was, there were twists even to this commonplace household chore. Once, soon after she first came to Lusibari, Nilima had made the mistake of trying to put up the net in near-darkness. The only light was from a candle, placed on a window sill at the other end of the room. Being short, as well as very short-sighted, she could not see exactly what her fingers were doing as they knotted the net to the bed's bamboo poles: even on tiptoe the strings were far above her head. Suddenly one of the strings had come alive; to the accompaniment of a sharp hiss, it had snapped a whiplike tail across the palm of her hand. She had snatched her arm back, just in time to see a long thin shape dropping from the pole. She had caught a glimpse of it before it wriggled under the door. It was an extremely venomous arboreal snake that inhabited the upper branches of some of the more slender mangroves: in the poles of the mosquito net it had evidently found a perch much to its liking.

At night, lying on his cot, Kanai would imagine that the roof had come alive; the thatch would rustle and shake and there would be frantic little outbursts of squeals and hisses. From time to time there would be loud plops as creatures of various kinds fell to the floor; usually they would go shooting off again and slip away under the door, but every once in a while Kanai would wake up in the morning and find a dead snake or a clutch of birds' eggs lying on the ground, providing a feast for any army of beetles and ants. At times these creatures would fall right into the bed's netting, weighing it down in the middle and shaking the posts. When this happened you had to take your pillow, shut your eyes and give the net a whack from below. Usually the creature, whatever it was, would go shooting off into the air and that was the last you'd see of it. But sometimes it would just go straight up and land right back in the net and then you'd have to start all over again.

At the back of the bungalow was an open courtyard where the meetings of the Lusibari Women's Union were held. At the time of Kanai's banishment to Lusibari, in 1970, the Union was a small, improvised affair. Several times a week the Union's members would gather in the courtyard to work on 'income-generating projects' – knitting, sewing, dyeing yarn and so on. But the members also used these occasions to talk and give vent to their anger and grief.

These outbursts were strangely disquieting and in the beginning Kanai went to great lengths to stay away from the bungalow when the Union was in session there. But that too was not without its pitfalls, for he had no friends in Lusibari and nowhere particular to go to. When he encountered children of his age they seemed either simple-minded, silent or inexplicably hostile. Knowing that his suspension from school would be over in a few weeks, he felt no particular compulsion to unbend towards these rustics. After twice being attacked with stones, thrown by unseen hands, Kanai decided that he might be better off inside the bungalow than outside. And soon enough, from the safety of the study, he was eavesdropping avidly on the exchanges in the courtyard.

It was at one of those meetings that Kanai first saw Kusum. She had a chipped front tooth and her hair was cut short, making her something of an oddity among the girls of the island. Her head had been shaved the year before, after an attack of typhoid. She had only narrowly survived and was still treated as something of an invalid. It was for this reason that she was allowed to while away her time at the Union's meetings; it was possibly for this reason also that she was still, in her mid-teens, dressed in the frilly 'frock' of a child instead of a woman's sari – or perhaps it was simply in order to wring a few more months' wear out of a set of still-usable clothes.

One day, during a meeting in the courtyard, a woman began to recount a story in exceptionally vivid detail. Her husband being away on a boat, her father-in-law had come home drunk one night and forced his way into the room where she was sleeping with her children. In front of her children, he had held the sharpened edge of a *dá* to her throat and tried to pull off her sari. When she tried to fight him off, he had gashed her arm with the machete, almost severing the thumb of her left hand. She had flung a kerosene lamp at him and his lungi had caught fire giving him severe burns. For this she had been turned out of her marital home, although her fault was only that she had tried to protect herself and her children.

90

Here, as if to corroborate her story, her voice rose and she cried out, 'And this is where he cut me, here and here.'

At this point Kanai, unable to restrain his curiosity, thrust his head through the doorway to steal a glance. The woman who had told the story was hidden from his view, and since everyone in the courtyard was looking in her direction no one noticed Kanai – no one, that is, but Kusum, who had averted her eyes from the storyteller. Kanai and Kusum held each other's gaze, and for the duration of that moment it was as though they were staring across the most primeval divide in creation, each assessing the dangers that lay on the other side; it seemed scarcely imaginable that here, in the gap that separated them, lay the potential for these extremes of emotion, this violence. But the mystery of it was that the result of this assessment was nothing so simple as fear or revulsion – what he saw in her eyes was rather an awakened curiosity he knew to be a reflection of his own.

So far as Kanai could remember, it was Kusum who spoke to him first, not on that day, but some other morning. He was sitting on the floor, wearing nothing but a pair of khaki shorts. He had his back against a wall and there was a book standing on his belly with its spine propped up against his knees. He looked up from the page to see her peering through the doorway, a strangely self-possessed figure, despite her close-cropped hair and tattered red frock. Scowling at him, she said, in a tone of querulous accusation, 'What are you doing here?'

'Reading.'

'I saw – you were listening.'

'So?' He shrugged.

'I'll tell.'

'So go and tell.' Despite the show of bravado he was rattled by the threat. As if to keep her from carrying it out, he moved up to make room for her to sit. She sank down and sat beside him with her back to the wall, and her knees drawn up to her chin. Although he didn't dare look at her too closely, he became aware that their bodies were grazing each other at the shoulder, the elbows, the hips and the knees. Presently he saw that there was a mole on the swell of her left breast: it was very small, but he could not tear his eyes from it.

'Show me your book,' she said.

Kanai was reading an English mystery story and he dismissed her request with a shrug. 'Why do you want to look at this book? It won't make any sense to you.'

'Why not?'

'Do you know English?' Kanai demanded.

'No.'

'Then? Why are you asking?'

She watched him for a moment, unabashed, and then sticking her fist under his nose, unfurled her fingers. 'Do you know what this is?'

Kanai saw that she had a grasshopper in her hand and his lip curled in contempt. 'Those are everywhere. Who's not seen one of those?'

'Look.' Lifting up her hand, Kusum put the insect in her mouth and closed her lips.

This caught Kanai's attention and he finally deigned to lower his book. 'Did you swallow it?'

Suddenly her lips sprang apart and the grasshopper jumped straight into Kanai's face. He let out a shout and fell over backwards, while she watched, laughing.

'It's just an insect,' she said. 'Don't be afraid.'

Words

After Piya had dressed and changed, she crawled back to the front of the boat with the chequered towel in her hands. She tried to ask Fokir the name of the fabric, but her gestures of inquiry elicited only a raised eyebrow and a puzzled frown. This was only to be expected, for he had so far shown little interest in pointing to things and telling her their Bengali names. She had been somewhat intrigued by this for, in her experience, people almost automatically went through a ritual of naming when they were with a stranger of another language. Fokir was an exception in that he had made no such attempts – so it was scarcely surprising that he should be puzzled by her interest in the word for this towel.

But she persisted, making signs and gestures until finally he understood. '*Gamchha*,' he said laconically, and of course, that was it; she had known it all along: *Gamchha, gamchha.*

How do you lose a word? Does it vanish into your memory, like an old toy in a cupboard, and lie hidden in the cobwebs and dust, waiting to be cleaned out or rediscovered?

There was a time once when the Bengali language was an angry flood trying to break down her door. She would crawl into a wardrobe and lock herself in, stuffing her ears to shut out those sounds. But the doors were no defence against her parents' voices: it was in that language that they fought, and the sounds of their quarrels would always find ways of trickling in, under the door and through the cracks, the level rising until she thought she would drown in the flood. Their voices had a way of finding her, no matter how well she hid. The accumulated resentments of their life were always phrased in that language, so that for her, its sound had come to represent the music of unhappiness. As she lay curled in the cupboard, she would dream of washing her head of those sounds; she wanted words with the heft of stainless steel, sounds that had been boiled clean, like a surgeon's instruments, tools with nothing attached except meanings that could be looked up in a dictionary – empty of pain and memory and inwardness.

In the bedroom of Piya's early childhood there was one window that afforded a glimpse of Puget Sound. The apartment was small – two bedrooms, a living room and a kitchen – and the sliver of a view afforded by the one westward-facing window in the master bedroom was its one noteworthy attraction.

There was never any question that she, two-year-old Piya, would be allotted that room. Piya was the altarpiece around which their lives were arranged; the apartment was a temple to her and her room was its shrine. Her parents took the other bedroom, so small that they had to get into bed by climbing over the foot of the bedstead. This enclosed space became the echo chamber for the airing of their mutual grievances. They would while away hours, bickering over trivia, only occasionally generating enough energy to launch into full-throated quarrels.

Piya had the larger room to herself for some five years before her mother abruptly ousted her from it. She could no longer bear the circumstances of her confinement with Piya's father and wanted nothing more than to shut out the entire family.

Shortly afterwards she would be diagnosed with cervical cancer. But in between was a period when she would allow Piya to sit beside her on her bed. Piya was the only person allowed into her presence, permitted to touch and see her. Everyone else was excluded – her father most of all. Her mother's voice would greet her as soon as she let herself into the flat, on coming home from school: 'Come Piya, come and sit.' It was strange that she could not remember the sound of those words (were they in English or Bengali?) but she could perfectly recall the meaning, the intent, the voice. She would go in and find her mother curled up in bed, dressed in an old sari: she would have spent the whole morning in the bathroom, trying to cleanse herself of some

94

imaginary defilement, and her skin would be dimpled from its long immersion.

It was only then, sitting beside her, looking towards Puget Sound, that she learnt that her mother had spent a part of her girlhood staring at a view of a river – the Brahmaputra, which had bordered on the Assam tea estate where her father had been manager. Resting her eyes on the Sound, she would tell stories of another, happier life, of playing in sunlit gardens, of cruises on the river.

Later, when Piya was in graduate school, people had sometimes asked if her interest in river dolphins had anything to do with her family history. The suggestion never failed to annoy her, not just because she resented the implication that her interests had been determined by her parentage, but also because it bore no relation to the truth. And this was that neither her father nor her mother had ever thought to tell her about any aspect of her Indian 'heritage' that would have held her interest – all they ever spoke of was history, family, duty, language.

They had said much about Calcutta, for instance, yet had never thought to mention that the first known specimen of *Orcaella brevirostris* was found there, that strange cousin of the majestic killer whales of Puget Sound.

Soon it became clear that Fokir was making preparations for a meal. From the bilges below deck, he pulled out a couple of large and lively crabs. These he imprisoned in a soot-blackened pot, before reaching into the hold again for a knife and a few utensils – including a large cylindrical object that appeared to be an earthenware vessel. But there was a hole in the side of this vessel, and when he began to stuff bits of firewood into it, she realized it was a portable stove, made of clay. He took the stove to the stern, and when it was well out of the way of the shelter's inflammable roof, he lit a match and blew the firewood into flame. Then he washed some rice, drained it into a battered tin utensil, poured in some water and put it on the stove. While the rice was coming to the boil, he dismembered the crabs, cracking their claws with his knife. When the rice was done, he took the pot off the fire and replaced it with yet another blackened aluminium pot. Next he opened a battered tin container and took out some half-dozen twists of paper, which he unrolled and laid out in a semicircle around the stove. There were spices inside and their colours – red, yellow, bronze – were bright in the light of the hissing flame. After he had splashed some oil into the pot, his hands began to fly over the slips of paper, peppering the spitting oil with pinches of turmeric and chilli, coriander and cumin.

The smells were harsh on Piya's nose. It was a long time now since she had eaten food of this kind: while in the field she rarely ate anything not from a can, a jar or a packet. Three years before, when working on Malampaya Sound, in the Philippines, she had been incautious in her eating and had suffered to the point where she had had to be medevacked by helicopter to Manila. On every survey since, she had equipped herself with a cache of mineral water and portable food – principally high-protein nutrition bars. On occasion, she also carried a jar or two of Ovaltine, or some other kind of powder for making malted milk. When there was milk to be had, fresh or condensed, she treated herself to a glass of Ovaltine; otherwise, she managed to get by on very little, a couple of protein bars a day was all she needed. This procedure had the added advantage of limiting the use of unfamiliar, and sometimes unspeakable, toilets.

Now, as she sat watching Fokir at the stove, she knew he would offer her some of his food and she knew also she would refuse. And yet, even as she recoiled from the smell, she could not tear her eyes from his flying fingers: it was as though she were a child again, standing on tiptoe to look at a clutch of stainless-steel containers, lying arrayed on the counter, beside a stove; it was her mother's hands she was watching, as they flew between those colours and the flames. They were almost lost to her, those images of the past, and nowhere had she less expected to see them than on this boat.

There was a time when those were the smells of home; she would sniff them on her mother, on the way back from school; they would fill the lift on its journey up to their floor. When she stepped inside they had greeted her, like domesticated animals, creatures with lives of their own, sustaining themselves on the close, hot air of the apartment. She had imagined the kitchen as a cage from which they never ventured out, which was why it came doubly as a shock when she discovered, from pointed jokes and chance playground comments, that they followed her everywhere, like unseen pets. Her response was to fight back, with a quietly ferocious tenacity, against them and against her mother, shutting them away with closed doors, sealing them into the kitchen.

But here, the ghosts of these creatures seemed to be quieted by their surroundings. The spell of Fokir's fingers was broken only when a breeze carried the acrid odour of burning chillies directly into her face. And then suddenly the phantoms came alive again, clawing at her throat and her eyes, attacking her as though she were an enemy who had crossed over undetected. She retreated to the bow and when he followed her there, with a plateful of rice and cooked crab, she fended him off with her protein bars and her bottled water, smiling and bobbing her head in apology, to show she meant no offence.

He accepted her refusal with a readiness that surprised her; she had expected protests, exclamations, a show of being wounded or hurt. But there was none of that; instead, he gave her a nod and a long, cool look of appraisal, as though he were mentally going through a list of reasons why she might decline to accept food from his hands. It alarmed her that he might imagine that it was for some mysterious reason of caste or religion that she had refused to eat his food, so she placed a hand on her belly and acted out a little charade of her intestinal sufferings. This seemed to serve the purpose, for he laughed, throwing his head back, and gave the plate to Tutul, who devoured it greedily.

After the meal, the utensils and the stove were put back in the hold and an armload of mats and blankets was taken out. Tutul, already drowsy, unrolled one of the mats under the shelter and fell asleep quickly, with a blanket pulled over his head. Unfurling a second mat, next to the boy's, Fokir made a sign to Piya, indicating that this was to be her place for the night. But she had a mat of her own, a thin sheet of blue foam tied to the frame of one of her backpacks. Undoing the bungee cord that held it in place, she unrolled the mat so that its head was pointing to the bow, almost touching the boat's rounded prow.

He started in alarm on realizing that this was where she was planning to spend the night. Shaking his head, he raised a finger of warning to point to the forested shores in the distance. The gesture was intentionally vague and only by inference did she understand that his warning concerned an animal, a predator. And now at last, she had an inkling of why the boat had been anchored in this odd position: was it perhaps to put it beyond the reach of tigers? She had never had much interest in terrestrial carnivores, but she could not imagine that even the hungriest of them would choose to stage an attack so far from shore. And if it did, what difference would it make whether you were in the stern or the bow? Presumably the whole boat would tip over under a tiger's weight.

There was a cumulative absurdity about these propositions that made her smile. To include him in the joke, she made her hands into claws, as if to mime a tiger. But before she could complete the gesture, he clamped his hands on her wrists, vehemently shaking his head, as if to forbid her from making any reference to the subject. She decided it was best to shrug the matter off and, smoothing her mat, she lay down. This seemed the most economical way of letting him know that she was not going to spend the night huddled in the shelter for fear of an aquatic feline. To her great relief, he accepted this without protest. Removing the sari from the thatched hood, he folded it into a pillow and handed it to her, along with one of his grimy, grey blankets.

Then, retreating to the centre of the boat, he draped a blanket over his shoulders and lit a *biri*. In a while, just as she was drifting off to sleep, she heard a snatch of a tune and realized he was humming. She raised herself on her elbow and said, 'Sing.' He gave her a puzzled glance and she responded by making an upwards gesture with an open palm. 'Louder. Sing louder.'

At this he tilted his head back and sang a few notes. The melody surprised her, for it bore no resemblance to any Indian music she had ever heard before – not the Hindi film music her father liked nor the Bengali songs her mother had sometimes sung. His voice sounded almost hoarse and it seemed to crack and sob as it roamed the notes. There was a suggestion of grief in it that unsettled and disturbed her.

She had thought that she had seen a muscular quality of innocence in him, a likable kind of *naïveté*, but now, listening to this song, she began to ask herself whether it was she who was naive. She would have liked to know what he was singing about and what the lyrics meant – but she knew too that a river of words would not be able to tell her exactly what made the song sound as it did right then, in that place.

The Glory of Bon Bibi

~~~~~~~

Kusum was from the nearby island of Satjelia. Her father had died while foraging for firewood in a place that was off-limits to villagers. He had not been in possession of a permit at the time, so Kusum's mother had received no compensation. With no means of livelihood she was reduced to a state of such destitution that she considered herself fortunate when a man from their village, a landowner by the name of Dilip Choudhury, had offered to find her a job in the city.

Knowing that he had found employment for other women, Kusum's mother could see no reason why she should not accept Dilip's offer. Leaving Kusum with relatives, she had gone off with him to take the train into Calcutta. Returning alone, Dilip had told Kusum that her mother was doing housework for a good family and would send for her shortly. That time came soon enough: a month or so later, Dilip came to see Kusum and told her that her mother had sent word, asking him to bring Kusum to Calcutta.

It was at this stage that Horen had got to know of Dilip's plan. Horen had worked with Kusum's father, and he also happened to be distantly related to her through his wife. He had sought her out and warned her that Dilip was linked to a gang that trafficked in women. What kind of job could this procurer have found for Kusum's mother? She was probably trapped in a brothel somewhere in Sonargachhi. As for Kusum, she was of much greater value to him than her mother had been – young girls like her were known to fetch large sums of money. If Dilip had his way, she would end up either in Calcutta's red light district

100

or, worse still, in some brothel in Bombay. Instead, Horen had brought Kusum to Lusibari and put her in the custody of the Women's Union. Pending some more permanent arrangement, all the Union's members, in turn, were looking after her.

During the months she had spent in Lusibari, Kusum had come to know the island well and she became Kanai's guide and mentor: she told him about its people and their children and about everything happening around it – cockfights and *pujas*, births and deaths. Kanai in turn, would tell her about his school, his friends and the ways of the city. Although these stories seemed pale to him, in comparison with hers, she would listen with rapt attention, breaking in from time to time to ask questions.

'Do you think I can come to the city with you?' she asked once. 'I'd like to see where you live.'

This silenced Kanai. It amazed him that Kusum should even ask such a question. Did she have no idea at all of how things worked? He tried to think of taking her home to Calcutta and cringed to imagine the tone of voice in which his mother would speak to her and the questions the neighbours would ask. 'Is that your new *jhi*? But don't you already have that other maid servant coming to do the washing and sweeping? Why do you need this one?'

'You wouldn't like Calcutta,' Kanai said at length. 'You wouldn't feel at home.'

It was from Kusum that Kanai learnt that a troupe of travelling actors was soon to come to Lusibari to stage performances of *The Glory of Bon Bibi*. He had heard mention of this story a couple of times on the island but was unsure about its particulars. When he asked Kusum about it, she gasped as if in shock: 'You mean you don't know the story of Bon Bibi?'

'No.'

'Then whom do you call on when you're afraid?'

Unable to untangle the implications of this, Kanai changed the subject. But the question nagged at his mind, and, later in the day, he asked Nirmal about the story of Bon Bibi.

Nirmal waved him airily away. 'It's just a tale they tell around here. Don't bother yourself with it. It's just false consciousness; that's all it is.'

'But tell me about it.'

'Horen is the one you should ask,' said Nirmal. 'If you did he would tell you that Bon Bibi rules over the jungle, that the tigers, crocodiles and other animals do her bidding. Haven't you noticed the little shrines outside the houses here? The statues are of Bon Bibi. You would think that in a place like this people would pay close attention to the true wonders of the reality around them. But no, they prefer the imaginary miracles of gods and saints.'

'But tell me the story,' said Kanai. 'Who is it about? What happens?'

'It's all the usual stuff,' Nirmal threw up his hands in impatience. 'Gods, saints, animals, demons. It's too long for me to tell, better you find out for yourself. Go to the performance.'

The stage for *The Glory of Bon Bibi* was erected on the open expanse of Lusibari's maidan, between the compound of the Hamilton House and the school. Its design was so simple that it took less than a day to set up. The floor, a few planks of wood, was laid on a trestle and enclosed within an open scaffolding of bamboo poles. During performances, sheets of painted cloth were suspended from the poles at the rear. These served as backdrops for the audience and as screens for the actors, so that they could eat, smoke and change costumes out of public view. Several large, hissing gas lamps served to illuminate the spectacle and music was provided by a battery-operated cassette recorder and loudspeakers.

As a rule, night came early to Lusibari. Candles and lamps were expensive and used as sparingly as possible. People ate their evening meal in the glow of twilight and by the time darkness fell, the island had usually fallen silent except for the few animal sounds that carried across the water. For this reason, a nighttime diversion was a major occasion, the anticipation of which provided at least as much pleasure as the event itself. Great numbers of people, Kanai and Kusum among them, stayed up, night after night, to attend the performances.

For Kanai the greatest surprise came right at the start of the show. This was because the story of the tiger-goddess did not begin either in the heavens or on the banks of the Ganges, like the mythological tales with which he was familiar. Instead, the opening scene was set in a city in Arabia and the backdrop was painted with mosques and minarets.

The setting was Medina, one of the holiest places in Islam; here lived a man called Ibrahim, a childless but pious Muslim who led the austere life of a Sufi *faqir*. Through the intervention of the archangel Gabriel, Ibrahim became the father of blessed twins, Bon Bibi and Shah Jongoli. When the twins came of age, the archangel brought them word that they had been chosen for a divine mission: they were to travel from Arabia to 'the country of eighteen tides' – *athhero bhatir desh* – in order to make it fit for human habitation. Thus charged, Bon Bibi and Shah Jongoli set off for the mangrove forests of Bengal dressed in the simple robes of Sufi mendicants.

The jungles of 'the country of eighteen tides' were then the realm of Dokkhin Rai, a powerful demon king, who held sway over every being that lived in the forest – every animal as well as every ghoul, ghost and malevolent spirit. Towards mankind he harboured a hatred coupled with insatiable desires – for the pleasures afforded by human flesh he had a craving that knew no limit.

One day Dokkhin Rai heard strange new voices in the jungle calling out the *azán*, the Muslim call to prayer; this was his notice that Bon Bibi and Shah Jongoli had come into his realm. Rousing his hordes the incensed demon set upon the trespassers, only to be put to rout in a pitched battle. But Bon Bibi was merciful in victory and she decided that one half of the tide country would remain a wilderness; this part of the forest she left to Dokkhin Rai and his demon hordes. The rest she claimed for herself, and under her rule this once-forested domain was soon made safe for human settlement. Thus order was brought to the land of eighteen tides, with its two halves, the wild and the sown, being held in careful balance. All was well until human greed intruded to upset this order.

On the edges of the tide country lived a man called Dhona who had put together a fleet of seven ships in the hope of making a fortune in the jungle. Dhona's fleet was about to set sail when it was discovered that the crew was exactly one man short of a full complement. The only person at hand was a young lad called Dukhey, 'sorrowful', a name nothing if not apt, for this boy had long been cursed with misfortune: he had lost his father as a child and now lived in great poverty with his old and ailing mother. It was with the greatest reluctance that the old woman allowed her son to go, and at the time of leave-taking, she gave him a last word of advice – were he ever to find himself in trouble, he was to call on Bon Bibi; she was the saviour of the weak and a mother of mercy to the poor; she was sure to come to his aid.

The expedition set off and wound its way down the rivers of the tide country until at last it came to an island by the name of Kedokhali Char. It so happened that this island fell within Dokkhin Rai's territory and unknown to the sailors, the demon king had already prepared a surprise for them. When they went into the forest strange things began to happen: they were given tantalizing glimpses of plump hives hanging from branches, but when they approached, the hives seemed to disappear only to reappear again at a distance. They could not avail themselves of even one and Dhona was reduced to despair. But that night, Dokkhin Rai revealed himself to Dhona in a dream and proposed a pact in which they would each provide for the satisfaction of the other's desires. The demon wanted the boy that Dhona had brought on his boat; it was an age since he had been able to sate his appetite for human beings and he was now riven with a longing for the taste of Dukhey's flesh. In exchange he would give Dhona wealth beyond imagining, as much as could be carried on the boats.

Overcome by greed, Dhona agreed to the bargain and at once the creatures of the forest, the demons and ghosts, even the bees themselves, began to load Dhona's boats with a great cargo of honey and wax. Soon the vessels were full and could carry no more and then it was time for Dhona to keep his part of the bargain. Summoning Dukhey, he told him to go ashore to fetch some firewood.

The boy had no recourse but to obey and on his return found his worst misgivings confirmed: the ships were gone. And then, standing alone on the bank, trapped between river and forest, the boy's eye was caught by a shimmer of black and gold – he was being stalked by a tiger, hidden in the greenery on the far shore. The animal was none other than Dokkhin Rai in disguise, and the demon shook the earth with a roar as he started his charge. At the sight of that immense body and those vast jowls, flapping in the wind like sails, mortal terror seized Dukhey's soul. Even as he was losing consciousness, he recalled his mother's parting words, and called out: 'O mother of mercy, Bon Bibi, save me, come to my side.'

Bon Bibi was far away, but she crossed the waters in an instant. She revived the boy, taking him into her lap, while her brother Shah Jangoli dealt a terrible chastisement to the demon. Then, transporting Dukhey to her home, she nursed him back to health. When it was time for him to return, she sent him back to his mother with a great treasure trove of honey and wax. Thus did Bon Bibi show the world the law of the forest, which was that the rich and the greedy would be punished while the poor and righteous were rewarded.

Kanai had expected to be bored by this rustic entertainment: in Calcutta he was accustomed to going to theatres like the Academy of Fine Arts and cinemas like the Globe. But much to his surprise, he was utterly absorbed and even after the show had ended was unable to erase some of the scenes from his mind. The terror he had felt when the demon charged Dukhey was real and immediate, even though there was nothing convincing about the tiger and it could be plainly seen that the animal was only a man, dressed in a painted sheet and a mask. No less real were the tears of joy and gratitude that flowed from his eyes when Bon Bibi appeared at Dukhey's side. Nor was he the only one: everyone in the audience wept, although the actress's arrival was anything but instantaneous. On the contrary, the audience had actually had to hurry her along a little, because even as Dukhey lay unconscious with the tiger poised to devour him, she had stopped to lean over the side of the stage in order to clear her mouth of a great wad of *paan*. But the flow of the story was such that none of this seemed to matter and even before the performance had ended Kanai knew he wanted to see it again.

The last performance of *The Glory of Bon Bibi* was something of a special event and many people came in from other islands. The crowd was much rowdier than on other days and Kanai kept to the maidan's fringes, watching from a distance. By this time he knew the first part of the show well enough to be bored by it. At a certain point he dozed off, and found, on waking, that he was sitting next to Kusum. 'What's happening?' he whispered. 'Where have they got to?' There was no answer; she was so rapt in the performance that she seemed to be oblivious to his presence. Her absorption prompted him to glance at the stage and he saw that he had slept longer than he had thought. The action was well advanced now: Dhona and his fleet had arrived at Kedokhali Char and would soon make his pact with the devil.

'Kusum?' whispered Kanai, and when she turned briefly to look at him he saw, in the reflected glow of the gas lamps, that she was biting her lip and her face was streaked with tears. Having seen for himself the emotions the story could evoke, he was not particularly surprised to see she was crying. But then, when she suddenly leaned over to bury her face in her knees, he knew there was more at issue here than could be accounted for by the performance alone. On an impulse, thinking to console her, he slid his hand along the ground, hoping to find her fingers. But her hand was not where he had expected it to be and instead he found his fist entangled in the folds of her frock. His fingers grew frantic as he tried to extricate them and instead of finding their way out they encountered a soft and unexpectedly warm part of her body. The shock sparked by this contact passed through both of them like a bolt of electricity.

Suppressing a cry, she jumped to her feet and went stumbling into the darkness. He would have run after her right then, but some furtive instinct of prudence prompted him to think of how this might look to watching eyes. He waited a minute or two and then pretended to head in the other direction. Circling back in the shadows, he caught up with her as she was nearing the compound of the Hamilton House: 'Kusum – wait! Stop!'

There was just enough light from the now-distant gas lamps for him to see that she was stumbling ahead, turning from time to time to wipe her dripping nose on her shoulder. 'Kusum,' he cried, keeping his voice low. 'Stop.' He had caught up with her now and he gave her elbow a tug. 'It was a mistake.'

She came to a halt and he steeled himself for a flood of reproach. But she said nothing and when he looked into her eyes he knew that his link with her perturbation was only incidental and that her grief sprang from a much deeper source than could be plumbed by a boy's mistaken touch.

They were now very close to the gate that led into the compound of the Hamilton House. On an impulse Kanai vaulted over the gate and gestured to Kusum: 'Come on. Come.' After a moment's hesitation, she followed and he took her hand and went racing up the mossy flagstones that flanked the pond. They came to the steps that led up to the house and Kanai led Kusum up to the shaded veranda. They seated themselves on the floor, with their backs to the old wooden walls. From this position they had a clear view of the maidan, and they could even see Dukhey lying prone on the stage, beseeching Bon Bibi to save him.

It was Kusum who spoke first. 'I called her too,' she said. 'But she never came.'

'Who?'

'Bon Bibi. The day my father died. I saw it all, it happened in front of me, and I called her again and again . . .'

It was an ordinary day, no different from any other, and it happened under the full light of a blazing noonday sun. There was money in the house and food as well, because her father had come back, just the day before, from a long and successful fishing trip: the one untoward thing he had had to report was that he had lost his *gamchha*. He had wanted to eat well, so her mother had made rice, *dāl* and vegetables, but just when it came time to cook some fish, the firewood had run out. On being told of this, he had flown into a rage: it was many days since he had had a good meal and he was not going to be deprived of one now. He stormed out of the house, saying he would be back soon with more firewood.

Their hut was in the lee of the embankment, on the shore of a narrow creek; it took just ten or fifteen minutes of rowing to get to the forest on the far bank. Although this was a 'reserve' area it was common for people of their village to forage for fire-wood there. Kusum followed him out of the house and stood on the embankment as he rowed across the river. This took longer than usual because there was a strong wind blowing in from the far shore. He was pushing the boat up the bank when she saw it – not the whole animal but just enough of its flashing black and gold coat to know it was there.

'Do you mean,' Kanai interrupted, 'that you saw a—?' But even before he could say the word *bāgh*, tiger, she had slammed a hand over his mouth: 'No you can't use the word – to say it is to call it.'

The animal was in the trees that lined the shore, and from the direction of its advance she knew it had watched the boat as it came across the river. At her first scream her mother and many others from the hamlet came running up to the embankment. But her father, for whom the shout of warning had been intended, didn't hear her for the wind was blowing in the wrong direction.

Within moments dozens of people had joined her on the embankment and they all saw what she had seen: the animal was stalking her father. The men of the village raced to get their boats into the water, while the women shouted and banged on pots and pans, making as much noise as they could. But it made no difference, for the wind was against them – the sound did not carry to the man on the far bank. The animal too was upwind of its prey and they could see its coat flashing as it closed in; because of the distinctiveness of its own odour, it was skilled in dealing with the wind and it knew that the people on the other bank were powerless against these gusts. So great was its confidence that in the last stretch it actually broke cover and went racing along the shore, in full view of the far shore; intent on its prey, it no longer cared about concealment. This was in itself an astonishing sight, almost without precedent, for the great cats of the tide country were like ghosts, never revealing their presence except through marks, sounds and smells. They were so rarely seen that to behold one, it was said, was to be as good as dead – and indeed the sight caused several of the women on the embankment to lose consciousness.

But as for Kusum, she sank to her knees and began to whisper, 'Help, O Mother of Mercy, O Bon Bibi, save my father.' She had shut her eyes so she didn't see the end but she heard everything. Because of the wind's direction, the sounds that accompanied the kill carried across the water with exceptional clarity: Kusum heard the roar that froze her father; she heard his cry for help – *bachao!* – she heard the sound of his bones cracking as the animal swiped a paw across his neck; she heard the rustle of the mangrove as the animal dragged the corpse into the forest.

And all through this she never once stopped reciting Bon Bibi's name.

It was Horen who picked her off the dust. 'Bon Bibi's heard you,' he told her. 'Sometimes this is the means she chooses to call those who are closest to her: men like your father, *bauleys*, they're always the first to go.'

Kusum's body had crumpled as she was telling this story, leaving her slumped against Kanai's shoulder and he could feel her hair on his skin. Her story had caused an upwelling of emotion in him that constricted his throat; he wanted to fold her in his arms, to ward off her grief; he wanted to wipe away her tears, he wanted his body to become a buffer between her and the world. This was the most intense physical sensation he had ever experienced, this need to protect, to defend, to make a bodily expression of his sympathy. He brushed her eyes with his lips and the softness and warmth was such that he could not stop: he put an arm around her and pulled her towards him, pressing his head against hers.

Suddenly they heard the sound of running feet, flying up the teak stairs of the Hamilton bungalow. 'Kusum! Kusum!' It was Horen's voice, calling to her in a hoarse whisper.

Kusum stood up. 'Yes, I'm here.'

Horen appeared in front of them, panting. 'Kusum,' he said, 'we have to go. I saw Dilip – he's here with some men, looking for you. You're not safe here. You have to get away.'

Horen squatted beside Kanai and stuck a finger in his face. 'And as for you, little *babu* – if you tell anyone where she's gone or with whom, you won't be safe either. Do you understand?' Without waiting for any response from Kanai, he took hold of Kusum's hand and led her off, at a run.

This was Kanai's last glimpse of Kusum. The next day Nirmal announced to him that his exile was over and he was to be taken back to Kolkata.

Stirrings

Although the moon was only three-quarters full, it cast such a bright sheen upon the river's surface that the water seemed to be glowing from within. Although the night was cool, there was no wind and not a sound was to be heard from the shores. Turning over in drowsy discomfort, Piya adjusted the sari that was her pillow and found her head resting against the boat's wooden prow. Her sleep was suddenly interrupted by the sound of a great bustle: a restless, scraping, scratching noise was echoing through the timber, percolating up from the boat's bowels. It took a few minutes for Piya to work out that this was merely the sound of the boat's live cargo of crabs, scurrying about in the hold. She could hear the rattle of their shells, the clattering of their claws and the rustling of leaves and branches: it was as though she were a giant listening to the stirrings of a subterranean city.

The boat rocked as if under the shifting of someone's weight and she glanced down to see that Fokir was sitting up in the centre of the craft, with a blanket draped tent-like around his shoulders. She had thought him to be asleep, under the shelter, but there was a boulder-like immobility about him that suggested he had been sitting there for some time. He seemed to feel the touch of her gaze, for he turned to look in her direction, and when he saw she was awake gave her a smile that was both apologetic and self-mocking, as if he were making fun of himself. It warmed her to think of him sitting there, keeping watch as she and Tutul slept. She remembered the moment when his hand had touched her in the water and how violently she had tried to fight it off until she understood it was not a predator that had touched her but a human being, someone she could trust, someone who would not hurt her. In remembering this, she was amazed to think that no more than a few hours had passed since she had tumbled out of that launch and into the water. The memory caused a tremor to shake her body, and when she shut her eyes it was as if the water had closed around her again and she was back in those swift, eerily glowing depths where the sunlight had no orientation and it was impossible to know which way was up and which down.

She felt the boat move under her and realized she was shivering. She was trying to calm herself, taking one deep breath after another, when suddenly she felt a firm, cool touch on her shoulder – and this too was strangely reminiscent of her fall, for she knew it was Fokir. Opening her eyes, she saw he was looking worriedly into her face and she tried to force a smile – but it turned into a grimace for her body would not stop its convulsive shaking. She could feel his anxiety deepening now, so she placed her hand on his and he took hold of it and stretched himself out beside her. His salty, sun-soaked smell was in her nostrils now, and through the blanket that separated them she could feel the sharpness of his ribs. His body seemed to warm her coverings, dissipating the clammy sensation that had seized her limbs. When her shivering stopped she sat up abruptly, in embarrassment. He sprang back at the same time and she knew he was just as discomfited as she was and she wished she could think of a way to let him know it was all right – nothing had been misunderstood, no wrong had been done. But all she could do was clear her throat noisily and say thank you. Then, mercifully, as if to rescue them from the awkwardness of the moment, Tutul cried out in his sleep. Immediately Fokir slid away to comfort his son.

Piya lowered her head again to the bunched-up sari she was using as a pillow, and it seemed to her now that in the folds of the fabric she could smell the presence of the garment's owner: it was almost as if this other woman had suddenly materialized in the boat. Piya was glad to think she could have said to her exactly what she had said to Fokir: that no wrong had been done and nothing at all had happened.

And what could have happened anyway? Although she knew little else about Fokir, she did know he had a child and was married. And as for herself, no thought was farther from her mind than the idea of a personal entanglement. She was out on assignment, working in the field – it was the exclusion of intimate involvements that made a place into a field and the line between the two was marked by a taboo she could not cross, except at the risk of betraying her vocation.

The boat was already moving when Piya woke next morning. She opened her eyes to find that a dense fog had resulted from the collision between the cold night air and the water's warmth. She could not see much beyond her own feet and her blankets were wet with dew. It was only because of a faint glow in the eastern sky that she knew that the sun had already risen. It astonished her that Fokir could steer in such bad light: clearly, he knew this stretch of water well enough to feel his way along the river's edge.

There was no pressing reason to get up, so she allowed herself to fall back into a doze. In a while the boat came to a stop, waking her again. She looked up to find that the fog was still thick around the boat and nothing could be seen of the surrounding terrain. There was a sound astern as of an anchor dropping and she wondered idly why Fokir had chosen to stop here. She decided it must have something to do with the visibility – perhaps they had reached a stretch of open water where it would be impossible to steer in the fog?

She was about to drop off again when she heard something that suddenly made her sit upright. Cupping her hands around her ears, she listened hard, and there it was again, a rippling in the water followed by a muffled snort, as of a man blowing his nose into a thick wad of Kleenex.

'Shit!' She sprang into a kneeling position, and listened carefully, tuning her ears to the fog. A few minutes of close attention was all it took to know that there were several dolphins in the vicinity of the boat. The sounds were scattered in direction and seemed to change location frequently: some were faint and far away while others were close at hand. She had spent great lengths of time listening to these muffled grunts and she knew exactly what they were: only the Irrawaddy dolphin, *Orcaella brevirostris*, produced this particular kind of sound. Evidently a group of travelling Orcaella had decided to make a brief halt in the vicinity of the boat. It was typical of her luck that this had happened at a time when she could not see beyond her arm: from her experience of such encounters, she knew that the dolphins would become restless in a matter of minutes. They would probably be gone even before she could unpack her equipment.

'Fokir!' She said his name in an urgent whisper, to make sure he had heard the sounds. The boat rocked and she knew from its motion that he was working his way forward. But he still took her by surprise when he emerged from the fog: his head seemed to be floating on a cloud, with tendrils of mist swirling around his neck.

'Listen!' she cried, holding a hand to her ear, pointing in the direction of the exhalations. He nodded, but without showing any surprise; it was as though there were nothing unexpected about this encounter and he had known all along that they would be there. Could it be that this was the spot he had been aiming for the night before – with the idea of showing her the dolphins?

This baffled her still more: how could he have known that they would run into a group of Orcaella, right then and right in that place? It was possible of course, that dolphins frequented that route and were often seen in this stretch of water – but even then, how could he have known that they would be there on that day, at that time? Groups of migrating Orcaella were anything but predictable in their movements. She decided to shrug off these questions for the time being. The job at hand was to record all the data that could be conjured out of this fog.

Despite the urgency of the moment, Piya's movements were unhurried and methodical as she went about the business of unpacking her equipment. Just as she was fixing a sheaf of data sheets into her clipboard, a dolphin surfaced a metre away: it was so close she could feel the spray from its breath. She caught sight of a dorsal fin and a bluntly rounded snout. There was no further room for doubt now: these were definitely Orcaella. Although she had been almost sure from the start, it was still

113

good to have visual confirmation. The animal had surfaced so close to the boat that she had only to extend her arm to get a reading on the GPS monitor. She recorded the figures with a sense of triumph: even if the dolphins took flight this very minute, this little scrap of data would have made the encounter credible and worthwhile.

By this time the fog had thinned and with the tide at its lowest ebb, the shore was revealed to be no more than a few hundred metres away. Piya saw that Fokir had stopped the boat at a point where the shore curved, like the inside of an arm, creating a long patch of unperturbed water in the crook of the river's elbow. It was evident also that the boat was anchored in the only remaining stretch of deep water. This consisted of a boomerang-shaped area about a kilometre in length. It was in this stretch that the dolphins were circling, as if within the limits of an invisible pool.

Soon the dawn fog was as distant a memory as the chill of the night. With the mudbanks and the forests holding back the wind, no breeze could find its way down to the water. In the stillness, the river seemed to give birth to a second sun, so that there was almost as much heat radiating from the water's surface as from the cloudless sky above. As the temperature peaked, subterranean currents of life rose seething to the surface of the nearby mudbanks, with legions of crabs scuttling to salvage the rich haul of leaves and other debris left behind by the retreating tide.

By midday Piya had enough data to make an informed guess about the size of the group. There were seven individuals, she estimated, but this included a pair that appeared to be swimming in tandem, usually surfacing together. One of these was smaller in size than the other animals, and she knew this to be a calf, probably a newborn, yet too young to swim independently of its mother. Time and again she observed it coming to the surface in a 'corkscrew' pattern, with its little head protruding out of the water – an indication that it had still to learn to breathe smoothly. Her heart leapt every time she caught sight of that little head: it was exhilarating to know that the population was still reproducing. Rarely, if ever, did the animals venture away from the bend in the river: they seemed instead to be content to circle within that small stretch of deep water. Nor was it the boat's presence that kept them there: whatever interest they had had in it had long since been exhausted.

Why were they lingering there? What had brought them here and what were they waiting for? It was all very confusing and yet Piya knew intuitively that something very interesting was going on here – something that might be very important to the understanding of the Irrawaddy dolphin and its patterns of behaviour. She just had to puzzle out what it was.

Morichjhãpi

Sunlight, streaming in through an uncurtained window, woke Kanai shortly after dawn. A little later, having washed and changed, he went downstairs and tapped on Nilima's door.

The voice that answered was uncharacteristically tremulous: '*Ke?*'

'It's me – Kanai.'

'Come in. The door's open.'

Kanai entered to find a bleary-eyed Nilima sitting propped up in bed, with a bank of pillows behind her and a large quilt piled over her legs. There was a cup of tea on the bedside table, and next to it, a saucer filled with Marie biscuits. No clothes or personal effects were anywhere to be seen while books and files lay stacked everywhere – under the bed, on the floor and even in the swell of the mosquito net. The room was sparsely utilitarian in appearance, with very few furnishings other than file cabinets and bookcases. But for the presence of a large four-poster bed, it would have been easy to mistake it for an extension of the Trust's offices.

'You're not looking well,' said Kanai. 'Has a doctor been sent for?'

Nilima blew her nose into a handkerchief. 'It's just a cold,' she said. 'Why do I need a doctor to tell me that?'

'You shouldn't have come to Canning yesterday,' said Kanai. 'It was too much for you. You should take better care of your health.'

Nilima brushed this off with a flick of her hand. 'Enough about me,' she said. 'Sit down over here and tell me how you've been faring. Did you sleep well last night?'

'Well enough.'

'And the packet?' she cried eagerly. 'Did you find it?'

'Yes. It was exactly where you said it would be.'

'So then, *bal to ré*, tell me,' said Nilima, 'were they poems or stories?'

Kanai could tell, from the expectant tone of her voice, that she had already begun to believe that her husband's literary reputation would be posthumously restored by the contents of the packet she had found. It pained him to disappoint her and he tried to let her down as gently as he could. 'Actually, it's not what I'd expected,' he said. 'I thought I'd find poems, essays, stories. But what I found instead was some kind of journal or diary. It was written in an exercise book – just a common *khata*, like schoolchildren use.'

'Oh?' Nilima's eyes dimmed and she breathed a sigh of dejection. 'And when was it written? Does it say?'

'Yes,' said Kanai. 'It was written in 1979.'

'1979?' Nilima was quiet for a moment as she thought this over. 'But that was the year of his death. He died in July. Are you sure it was written in that year?'

'Yes,' said Kanai. 'Why should that surprise you?'

'I'll tell you why,' she said. 'Because that was the one year of his life when he did no writing at all. He had retired as headmaster of the Lusibari school the year before and it was a very difficult time for him. The school had been his whole life for almost three decades – ever since we came to Lusibari. His behaviour became very erratic at this time. As you know he had a history of mental instability, so it was very worrying for me. He used to disappear for days and afterwards he wouldn't be able to recall where he had been. He was all in an uproar that year. He was in no state to do any writing.'

'Maybe he had a brief period of lucidity,' Kanai said. 'I have the impression the entire notebook was written over one or two days.'

'And do you know the dates?' said Nilima, watching him closely.

'Yes,' said Kanai. 'He started writing it on the morning of 15 May 1979. In a place called Morichjhãpi.'

117

'Morichjhãpi!' There was a sudden intake of breath as Nilima said the word.

'Yes,' said Kanai. 'Tell me exactly what happened there.'

Morichjhãpi, said Nilima, was a tide country island, a couple of hours from Lusibari by boat. It fell within a part of the Sundarbans reserved for tiger conservation but unlike many such islands it was relatively easily accessible from the mainland. In 1978 it happened that a great number of people suddenly appeared in Morichjhãpi. In this place where there had been no inhabitants before there were now thousands, almost overnight. Within a matter of weeks they had cleared the mangroves, built bãdhs and put up huts. It happened so quickly that in the beginning no one even knew who these people were. But in time it came to be learnt that they were refugees, originally from Bangladesh. Some had come to India after Partition, while others had trickled over later. In Bangladesh they had been among the poorest of rural people, oppressed and exploited both by Muslim communalists and by Hindus of the upper castes.

'Most of them were Dalits, as we say now,' said Nilima. 'Harijans, as we used to say then.'

But it was not from Bangladesh that these refugees were fleeing when they came to Morichjhãpi; it was from a government resettlement camp in central India. In the years after Partition the authorities had removed the refugees to a place called Dandakaranya, deep in the forests of Madhya Pradesh, hundreds of kilometres from Bengal.

'They called it "resettlement",' said Nilima, 'but people say it was more like a concentration camp, or a prison. They were surrounded by security forces and forbidden to leave. Those who tried to get away were hunted down.'

The soil was rocky and the environment was nothing like they had ever known. They could not speak the languages of that area and the local people treated them as intruders, attacking them with bows, arrows and other weapons. For many years they put up with these conditions. Then in 1978 some of them organized themselves and broke out of the camp. By train and on foot they moved eastwards in the hope of settling in the Sundarbans. Morichjhãpi was the place they decided on.

Earlier that year a Left Front ministry had taken power in West Bengal and the refugees may have assumed that they would not face much opposition from the state government. But this was a miscalculation: the authorities had declared that Morichjhãpi was a protected forest reserve and they had proved unbending in their determination to evict the settlers. Over a period of about a year there had been a series of confrontations between the settlers and government forces.

'And the final clash,' Nilima said, 'if I recall correctly was in mid-May of that year, 1979.'

'So do you think Nirmal was there at the time?' Kanai stopped to consider another possibility. 'Or was it perhaps just a fantasy?'

'I don't know, Kanai,' Nilima said, looking down at her hands. 'I really don't know. He became a stranger to me that year. He wouldn't talk to me. He would hide things. It was as if I had become his enemy.'

Kanai could see that Nilima was close to tears and his heart went out to her. 'It must have been very hard for you.'

'It was,' she said. 'I could see that he had developed some kind of obsession with Morichjhãpi and I was very uneasy about it. I knew there was going to be trouble and I just wanted to keep him from harm.'

Kanai scratched his head. 'I still don't understand. Why did this cause have so much appeal for him?'

Nilima's answer was slow in coming. 'You have to remember, Kanai,' she said at length, 'that as a young man Nirmal was in love with the idea of revolution. Men like that, even when they turn their backs on their party and their comrades, can never let go of the idea: it's the secret god that rules their hearts. It is what makes them come alive; they revel in the danger, the exquisite pain. It is to them what childbirth is to a woman, or war to a mercenary.'

'But these settlers weren't revolutionaries, were they?'

'No,' said Nilima. 'Not at all. Their aims were quite straight-forward. They just wanted a little land to settle on. But for that they were willing to pit themselves against the government. They were prepared to resist until the end. That was enough. This was the closest Nirmal would ever come to a revolutionary moment.

He desperately wanted to be a part of it. Perhaps it was his way of delaying the recognition of his age.'

Kanai was hard put to reconcile the gentle, *dhoti*-clad man of his memories with this image of a revolutionary. 'Did you try to reason with him?'

'Yes, of course,' Nilima said. 'But he would say, "You've joined the rulers; you've begun to think like them. That's what comes of doing the sort of 'social work' you've been doing all these years. You've lost sight of the important things." She shut her eyes as she recalled the contempt with which her own husband had dismissed her life's work. She turned her head to brush away the tears dripping from her eyes. 'We were like two ghosts living in the same house. At the end he seemed to want only to hurt me. Just think about it, Kanai – why else would he have insisted on leaving this notebook to you and not to me?'

'I don't know what to say.' Kanai had assumed that Nirmal had wanted him to have the notebook because he, Kanai, represented a slender connection to the ears of an unheeding world. He had not for a moment considered the possibility that Nirmal had intended to wound Nilima. The idea shocked him. He had always known Nirmal to be eccentric but he had never thought him to be capable of malice or cruelty, especially to his own wife. Like everyone who knew them he had always assumed that Nilima and Nirmal were content in their marriage, that theirs was a happy, if unlikely, pairing. He realized now that it was only because Nirmal never left Lusibari that they had been able to sustain this illusion.

Thinking of what Nilima had been through all these years, an unfamiliar lump arose in Kanai's throat. 'Look,' he said, rising to his feet. 'I'll give you that notebook right now. You can keep it or throw it away – do whatever you like. I don't want to have anything more to do with it.'

'No, Kanai!' cried Nilima. 'Sit down.' Reaching for his hand, she pulled him back into his chair. 'Kanai, listen to me: I always did my best to do my duty by Nirmal. It's very important to me that his last wishes are not dishonoured. I don't know why he wanted you to have the book; I don't know what's in it – but that's how it must be.'

Kanai went to sit beside her on the bed. He had been uneasy so far, about broaching the subject of Kusum, but he could see no way around it. 'Tell me,' he said gently. 'Do you think Kusum might have had something to do with it?'

She flinched at the sound of the name. 'There were rumours, Kanai. Yes, I won't deny it.'

'But how did Kusum end up at Morichjhāpi?'

'I don't know exactly how it happened. But somehow she did.'

'And did you ever see her while she was there?' Kanai said.

Nilima nodded. 'Yes. Just once. She came to see me, in this very room.'

She was working at her desk, said Nilima, one morning in 1978, when a nurse came to tell her she had a visitor, someone who claimed to know her. Nilima asked what her name was, but the nurse didn't know. 'All right,' said Nilima. 'Bring her here.' A few minutes later the door opened to admit a young woman and a child, a boy of four or five. The woman looked to be in her early twenties but she was dressed in a white sari and there were no bangles on her wrists and no vermilion in her hair: elsewhere, Nilima would have known immediately she was a widow, but in Lusibari she could not be sure.

There was something familiar about the woman – not so much her face as the look in her eye – but Nilima could not remember her name. When the visitor bowed to touch her feet, she said, 'Tell me now, who are you?'

'Mashima,' came the answer, 'my name is Kusum. Don't you remember me?'

'Kusum!' Almost at once Nilima began to scold her. 'Why didn't you send news, Kusum? Where have you been? Didn't you know we were looking for you?'

Kusum's answer was to laugh. 'Mashima, there was too much to tell. More than I could put into a letter.'

When she stood up Nilima saw that Kusum had grown into a sturdy, bright-eyed young woman. 'And who is this boy, Kusum?'

'That's my son,' she answered. 'His name is Fokir – Fokirchand Mandol.'

'And his father?'

121

'His father died, Mashima. I'm all he has now.'

Nilima was glad to see that premature widowhood had not robbed Kusum of her ready laugh. 'Tell me, Kusum. What brings you here?'

It was then that Kusum revealed that she was living in Morichjhãpi: she had come to Lusibari in the hope of persuading Nilima to send medical help for the settlers.

Nilima was immediately on her guard. She told her that she would have liked to help, but it was impossible. The government had made it known that they would stop at nothing to evict the settlers: anyone suspected of helping them was sure to get into trouble. Nilima had the hospital and the Union to think of: she could not afford to alienate the government. She had to consider the greater good.

After half an hour Kusum left and Nilima never saw her again.

'So what happened after that?' Kanai said. 'Where did she go?'

'She didn't go anywhere, Kanai. She was killed.'

'Killed?' said Kanai. 'How? What happened?'

'She died in the massacre, Kanai,' Nilima said. 'The massacre at Morichjhãpi.'

She covered her face with her hands. 'I'm tired now; I think I'd better rest for a while.'

An Epiphany

In the afternoon, as the waters began to rise, Piya noticed that she was seeing less and less of the dolphins. This was confirmed by a glance at her data sheets: it seemed the animals had begun to disperse with the turning of the tide.

Through the early hours of the day the pace of Piya's work had been dictated by the belief that this was a school of migrating dolphins that might depart at any minute. But now she began to wonder: these animals hadn't given her the impression of being headed anywhere in particular. On the contrary, she had got the feeling that they had gathered here to wait out the ebb-tide until the water rose again. But that made no sense either, she told herself; it just didn't fit with what she knew about these animals.

Orcaella were of two kinds: one tribe liked the salt waters of the coast while the other preferred rivers and fresh water. The difference between these two communities was not anatomical – it had only to do with their choice of habitat. Of the two populations, the coastal was by far the more numerous. The waters of southern Asia and northern Australia were reliably believed to contain several thousand of them. Fresh-water Orcaella on the other hand were a rare and dwindling breed. Only a few hundred now remained in Asia's rivers. Coastal Orcaella were not known to linger for hours in one place and were more likely to range freely along the shore. Their fresh-water cousins on the other hand, were more territorial and not nearly so gregarious. In times of heavy rainfall, when the rivers rose, they would range far afield, chasing their prey into minor tributaries and even into flooded rice fields. But in dry periods, when the rivers began to drop, they would make their way back to certain spots. These were usually deep-water 'pools', created by quirks of geology in the riverbed, or by the water's patterns of flow. In Cambodia Piya had tracked populations of Orcaella in several pools along the Mekong, from Phnom Penh to the Laos border. She had found the same individuals, returning to the same pools year after year. But when the seasons changed these dolphins travelled hundreds of kilometres downriver; in one unfortunate instance an animal had swum all the way down from the Laos border only to drown in a gill-net near Phnom Penh.

Piya had come to the Sundarbans believing that any Orcaella she found there would be of the coastal variety: this seemed only logical considering how salty the waters were in this region. But what she had seen today made her wonder if she hadn't made a mistake. If these were coastal Orcaella what were they doing congregating in a pool? That was out of character for them – only their river-dwelling kin did that. But on the other hand these could not be river dolphins either. The water was too salty. And anyway, riverine Orcaella didn't leave their pools in the middle of the day; they spent a whole season in them. So what kind of animal was this and what did this odd behaviour mean?

As she was mulling over these questions a thought came into Piya's mind. Was it possible that these Sundarbans Orcaella did twice each day what their Mekong cousins did once every year? Had they found a novel way of adapting their behaviour to this tidal ecology? Could it be that they had compressed the annual seasonal rhythms of their Mekong relatives so as to fit them into the daily cycle of tides?

Piya knew that if she could establish any of this she would have a hypothesis of stunning elegance and economy – a thing of beauty, such as was rarely to be found in the messy domain of mammalian behaviour. What was more, the idea might well have profound implications for the conservation of this endangered species: protective measures would be very much more effective if they could be focused on particular pools and specific movement corridors. But the hypothesis begged as many questions as it answered.

What for instance were the physiological mechanisms that attuned the animals to the flow of the tides? Obviously, it could not be their circadian rhythms since the timing of the tides changed from day to day. What happened in the monsoon, when the flow of fresh water increased and the balance of salinity changed? Was the daily cycle of migration inscribed upon the palimpsest of a longer seasonal rhythm?

Piya remembered a study which had shown that there were more species of fish in the Sundarbans than could be found in the whole continent of Europe. This proliferation of aquatic life was thought to be the result of the unusually varied composition of the water itself. The waters of river and sea did not intermingle evenly in this part of the delta; rather, they interpenetrated each other, creating hundreds of different ecological niches, with streams of fresh water running along the floors of some channels, creating variations of salinity and turbidity. These microenvironments were like balloons suspended in the water, and they had their own patterns of flow. They changed position constantly, sometimes floating into midstream and then wafting back towards the shore, at times being carried well out to sea and at others, retreating deep inland. Each balloon was a floating biodome, filled with endemic fauna and flora, and as they made their way through the waters, strings of predators followed trailing in their wake. This proliferation of environments was responsible for creating and sustaining a dazzling variety of aquatic life forms – from gargantuan crocodiles to microscopic fish.

Now, as she sat in the boat, thinking about these connections and interrelations, Piya had to close her eyes, so dazzling was the universe of possibilities that opened suddenly in her mind. There was so much to do, so many queries to answer, so many leads to follow: she would have to acquire a working knowledge of a whole range of subjects – hydraulics, sedimentation geology, water-chemistry, climatology; she would have to do seasonal censuses of the Orcaella population; she would have to map the dolphins' movement corridors, she would have to scrounge for grants, apply for permits and permissions; there was no horizon to the work that lay ahead. She had been sent to the Sundarbans for a fortnight, to do a small survey, on a shoestring budget –

125

but to follow through on the questions now buzzing in her mind would take not a week or two, but years, even decades. She had perhaps fifteen to twenty years of active field research ahead of her; she could tell, from the outlines of the project taking shape in her mind, that it would consume all those years and more: it was the work of a lifetime.

Piya had often envied those field biologists who had found monumental subjects to work on – Jane Goodall in the mountains of Kenya, Helene Marsh in the swamps of Queensland. Being unambitious by nature, she had never imagined that something similar might come her own way one day. And yet, here it was – and she had stumbled on it by chance, exactly when things seemed to be going wrong. She recalled the mythologies of discovery that had attracted her to the sciences as a child, and how the most miraculous seemed always to be those that had the most quotidian origins – Archimedes and his bathtub, Newton and his apple. Not that her work would be in any way comparable or similar – but now at least she could see what it was about, how it happened that an idea floated unexpectedly into your mind and you knew in an instant that this was an errand that would detain you for the rest of your life.

She had never had high aspirations for herself as a scientist. Although she liked cetaceans and felt an affinity for them, she knew it was not just for the animals that she did what she did. As with many of her peers, she had been drawn to field biology as much for the life it offered as for its intellectual content – because it allowed her to be on her own, to have no fixed address, to be far from the familiar, while still being a part of a loyal but loose-knit community. This would not change any of that; for the most part it would be the usual grind of writing applications, trying to find funding and so on. Whatever came of it in the end, it was a certainty that it was not going to create an upheaval in science. But at the same time, who would have thought that it would be so intensely satisfying to have your future resolved, to know what you were going to be doing next year and the year after that and so on and so on, until who knew when? And yes, it was true that whatever came of it would not revolutionize the sciences, or even a minor branch of them, but it was also true that if she were able to go through with it – even a part of it – it would be as fine a piece of descriptive science as any. It would be enough; as an alibi for a life, it would do; she would not need to apologize for how she had spent her time on this earth.

Moyna

It was well past noon when Kanai went down to knock again on Nilima's door. He was glad to find her dressed and on her feet.

'*Aré*, Kanai,' she said, smiling. 'There you are. Come in.'

On her face there was no sign of the anguish Kanai had seen that morning, and he guessed that the change in her spirits was due to her being at her desk. It was in this way, he realized, that she had coped with Nirmal's death and the years of loneliness that had followed – by immersing herself in her work.

'Moyna should be here any minute now,' Nilima said. 'I've asked her to show you around the hospital.'

'What exactly does Moyna do here?' said Kanai.

'She's one of our trainees,' replied Nilima. 'She joined the Trust years ago, when we started our "barefoot nurse" programme. It's an outreach project, for providing medical assistance to people in out-of-the-way villages. We give the nurses some basic training in hygiene, nutrition, first aid, midwifery, and other things that might be useful – how to cope with drowning, for instance, since that's a situation they often have to face. Then they go back to their villages and hold training classes of their own.'

'But I take it Moyna has risen in the ranks?'

'Yes,' said Nilima. 'She's not a barefoot nurse any more. She's training to be a fully fledged nurse in the hospital. She applied a couple of years ago and since her record was very good we were happy to take her in. The strange thing was that even though she had worked for us for a long time, we had no idea who she was – in the sense that we didn't know she was married to

Kusum's son. And even when I found out, it was almost by accident.'

'What happened?'

'I was in the market, one day,' Nilima said, 'and I saw her with a young man and a child. Now you have to remember I hadn't seen Fokir since he was a boy of five, so of course I didn't recognize him. I said to her, "Moyna, is this *chhélé-chhokra* your husband, then?" and she replied, "Yes, Mashima; this is him." "So what's his name then?" I asked, and she said, "Fokir Mondol." It's a common enough name, but I knew at once. I said, "*Éki ré?* Who are you? Are you our Kusum's Fokir? And he said yes.'

'So at least that part of it turned out well,' said Kanai. 'He was here, safe in Lusibari.'

'I wish it were that simple,' said Nilima. 'But the truth is, it hasn't gone well at all.'

'Oh? Why not?'

Moyna was both ambitious and bright, Nilima said. Through her own efforts, with no encouragement from her family, she had managed to give herself an education. There was no school in her village, so she had walked every day to another village kilometres away. She had done well in her school-leaving exams and had wanted to go on to college, in Canning or some other nearby town. She had made all her preparations and had even got her Scheduled Caste certificate. But her family had balked at the prospect of her departure and to thwart her plans had insisted she get married. The man chosen to be her husband was Fokir – by all accounts, a perfectly fine young fellow except that he could neither read nor write and made his living by catching crabs.

'But the remarkable thing is that Moyna hasn't abandoned her dreams,' said Nilima. 'She's so determined to qualify as a nurse that she made Fokir move to Lusibari while she was in training.'

'And is Fokir happy about that?'

'I don't think so,' Nilima said. 'I hear they've been having trouble – that might be why he disappears sometimes. I don't know the details; the girls don't tell me everything. But I do know that Moyna's been having a difficult time. This morning, for instance, she looked completely distraught.'

129

'So she came by, did she?'

'Yes,' said Nilima. 'In fact, she should be here again any minute. I sent her to the hospital to get me some medicine.'

'But Fokir isn't back yet?'

'No,' said Nilima, 'and Moyna's sick with worry. I've asked her to show you around the hospital because I thought it would take her mind off this thing a little for a bit.'

There was a tapping sound on the front door, and Nilima responded by calling out, 'Moyna? Is that you?'

'Yes, Mashima.'

'*Esho.* Come.'

Kanai turned around to see a young woman standing at the entrance, with her sari drawn over her head. A stream of sunlight, flooding in from the open doorway, had cast her face into shadow so that all he could see of her was the three glinting points of her earrings and her nose stud: in the dark oval of her face they seemed to shine like stars in a constellation.

'Moyna, this is Kanai-babu,' said Nilima. 'He's my nephew.'

'*Nomoshkar,*' she said, stepping in.

'Nomoshkar.' The light had caught her face now and seeing her close up Kanai saw that the *kajol* had spilled over the rims of her eyes. Her complexion was dark and silky and her raven-black hair shone with oil. Her face was marked by a sharply outlined brow and a prominent jaw; he could tell at a glance that she was not one to be shy of pitting her will against the world. Yet from the redness of her eyes, it was clear she had been crying.

'Listen, Kanai,' said Mashima, switching suddenly to English so as not to be understood by Moyna. 'Be careful with this girl – she's clearly very upset.'

'Of course,' said Kanai.

'Righty-oh, then,' said Nilima. 'I suppose you had better be going.'

'Righty-oh!' It was not often that Kanai heard his aunt speak English and he was struck by her distinctive and unexpected diction. Her Bengali, after years of living in the tide country, had almost converged with the local dialect, having been stripped of the inflections of her urban upbringing. But her English, possibly because she spoke it so rarely, had survived like a fern suspended in amber, untouched by time and unspoiled by the rigours of regular usage, a perfect specimen of a tongue learnt in the schools of the Raj. It was like listening to a lost language, the dialect of a vanished colonial upper middle class, spoken with the crisp enunciation once taught in elocution classes and debating societies.

As they were starting down the path to the hospital, Kanai said to Moyna, 'Did Mashima tell you I knew your mother-in-law?'

'No!' cried Moyna, throwing him a look of surprise. 'Mashima didn't mention it. Did you really know her?'

'Yes,' said Kanai. 'I did. It was a long time ago of course. She must have been about fifteen. And I was younger.'

'What was she like?'

'What I remember is her *tej*,' Kanai said. 'Even at that age she was very spirited.'

Moyna nodded. 'I've heard people say she was like a storm, a *jhor*.'

'Yes,' said Kanai. 'That's a good way of putting it. Of course, you never knew her yourself, did you?'

'No,' said Moyna. 'I was just a baby when she died. But I've heard many stories about her.'

'Does your husband talk about her?'

Moyna's face had brightened in speaking of Kusum, but now, at the mention of Fokir, it fell again. 'No,' she said. 'He never speaks of her. I don't think he remembers much of her either. After all, he was very little when she died—' She shrugged, cutting herself short and Kanai thought it better to let the subject drop.

They were nearing the hospital now and seeing the building close up gave Kanai a renewed appreciation of the sheer scale of Nilima's achievement. It was not that the building was overly large or particularly striking in its design; a mere two storeys high, it was built in the shape of a squat shoebox. Its outer walls were painted grey, while the windows and the railings of its long corridors were outlined in white. There was a garden in front, planted largely with marigolds. Yet, plain as it was, in this tide country setting, where mud and mildew encrusted everything, the building's crisp lines and fresh paint were enough to give it the exclamatory salience of a skyscraper. Kanai could tell that the mere sight of it gave heart to the people it served.

This was clearly the effect it had on Moyna for there was a noticeable improvement in her demeanour as she led Kanai to the hospital. With every step her carriage seemed to become a little straighter and her movements more assured: it was as though the mere proximity of the building had caused a brisk professional to emerge from the chrysalis of a careworn wife and mother.

Leading Kanai through the hospital's entrance, Moyna ushered him to a door. Then, speaking in a voice hushed with pride, she announced, 'And this is the Maternity Ward.'

Hospitals were not, as a rule, of much interest to Kanai, but this was an exception: he could not help being impressed by the impeccable maintenance of the wards. Every part of the hospital seemed to be spotlessly clean and even though it had only forty beds, it was, for its size, well equipped. The equipment had come from donors, Moyna explained, some Indian and others foreign. There was a diagnostic laboratory, an X-ray room and even a dialysis machine. On the top floor lived two resident doctors, one of whom had been in Lusibari ten years. The other was a new arrival who had just completed his residency requirements at the prestigious medical college of Vellore. They were both, Moyna said, prominent and much-beloved figures on the islands. Every patient who came to the hospital made it a point to leave an offering at their door – a coconut, or a few *kewra* fruit or a fish wrapped in leaves, or even sometimes, a live chicken or two.

Such was the hospital's reputation, Moyna said, that people now came there from great distances. Many who could have travelled more conveniently to Canning, or even Kolkata, chose to come to Lusibari instead: the hospital was known to provide, at a nominal cost, a standard of care that could not be had elsewhere even at exorbitant rates. This traffic, in turn, had led to the growth of a small service industry around the hospital's perimeters. Over the years, a number of tea-shops, guest houses and stands for cycle-vans had taken root and flourished. Directly or indirectly the hospital now provided employment to the majority of Lusibari's inhabitants.

On the upper storey Moyna pointed out Nirmal's single contribution to the hospital: a large ward specially equipped to withstand cyclones. The windows had thick wooden shutters and the doors were reinforced with steel. Although he rarely interfered in anything to do with the Trust, when the hospital was under construction Nirmal had taken the trouble to find out if any anti-cyclone measures had been provided for. He was horrified to learn that they hadn't: did nobody know about the tide country's history of catastrophic cyclones? Did they think that Lusibari was the one place where history would not repeat itself? It was at his insistence that this ward was built.

From a veranda on the second floor, Moyna pointed to the stalls and hutments that ringed the perimeter of the compound. 'Look over there, Kanai-babu,' she said. 'Look at the shops and stalls that have come up around the hospital. See how many there are?'

Kanai was touched, moved even, by Moyna's evident pride in the institution. 'Have you ever brought Fokir here?' he said.

She answered this with a small shake of her head. 'No.'

'Why not?'

She pulled a face. 'He doesn't like to come – he feels out of place.'

'In the hospital, you mean? Or in Lusibari?'

'Both,' she said. 'He doesn't like it here.'

'And why is that?'

'Things are different here than they were in the village.'

'In what way?' Kanai asked.

She shrugged. 'Over there he was always with Tutul – our son,' she said. 'Because of my work with the Trust I was out of the house a lot, so Tutul was with him on the river all day. But after we came here I had to put a stop to that.'

'Really? Why?'

'Because Tutul has to go to school, doesn't he?' she said sharply. 'I don't want him growing up catching crabs. Where's the future in that?'

'But that's what Fokir does.'

133

'Yes, but for how long?' she said. 'Mashima says that in fifteen years the fish will all be gone. What with the new nets and all. And after that what?'

'What new nets?'

'These new nylon nets, which they use to catch *chingrir meen* – the spawn of tiger prawns. The nets are so fine that they catch the eggs of all the other fish as well. Mashima wanted to get the nets banned, but it was impossible.'

'Why?'

'Why else?' she said. 'Because there's a lot of money in prawns and the traders had paid off the politicians. What do they care – or the politicians for that matter? It's people like us who're going to suffer and it's up to us to think ahead. That's why I have to make sure Tutul gets an education. Otherwise, what's his future going to be?'

'I'm sure Fokir would understand if you explained,' Kanai said.

'Do you think I haven't tried?' she said, her voice rising. 'I've tried so many times. But what does he understand? He's illiterate – it's impossible to explain these things to him.'

It occurred to Kanai as she was speaking that for someone in her circumstances, Moyna possessed a very sure grasp of the world and how she could get on in it. It was astonishing to think of how much had changed in the tide country since his last visit, not just in material matters but even in people's hopes and desires. Nothing was better proof of this than the very existence of this hospital and the opportunities it provided and aspirations it nurtured. This made it seem all the more unfortunate that someone with Moyna's talents should be held back by a husband who could not keep step.

'Look.'

They had come to an operating theatre now and Moyna broke off abruptly to look through the circular window that pierced the door. She lingered there so long that Kanai began to wonder whether there was an operation under way inside. But when at last she moved aside to let him look, he saw that the room was empty, except for its equipment.

'What were you looking at?' he said.

'I just like to look at all the new equipment,' she said with a

134

laugh. 'Who knows? Maybe if I finish this course, one day I'll be working in there myself.'

'Of course you will.'

She pursed her lips. 'God knows.'

Kanai could tell, from the sound of Moyna's voice, that her dream of becoming a nurse was no ordinary yearning: it was the product of a desire as richly and completely imagined as a novel or a poem. It recalled for him what it meant to be driven to better yourself, to lay claim to a wider world. It was as though, in listening to Moyna, he were looking back on that earlier incarnation of himself.

In the circular pane of the theatre's window, he saw Moyna's face appear beside his own. She tapped on the glass and pointed into the dark interior of the operating room. 'That was where my Tutul was born,' she said. 'Mashima arranged for my admission. I was the first girl from my family to give birth in a hospital. There were three nurses to tend to me and they passed the baby to each other before they handed him to me. All I could think of was how fortunate they were and how much I wanted to be one of them.'

Her ambition was so plainly written on her face that Kanai was assailed by the kind of tenderness we sometimes feel when we come across childhood pictures of ourselves – photographs that reveal all-too-unguardedly the desires people spend lifetimes in learning to dissimulate.

'Don't worry, Moyna,' said Kanai. 'You'll be there soon.' It was only after he had spoken that he realized he had addressed her as *tumi* – using a familiar form, without asking the customary permission. There was an intimacy in this that he had not intended but he made no apology, for it seemed best to let it pass unremarked.

Crafts

Around midday, with the level of the water edging ever higher, it was clear that the dolphins had begun to disperse. Piya's last set of sightings was of the newborn and its mother and they put on a display the like of which she had rarely seen. First there was a series of surfacings in which they exposed almost the entire length of their bodies: the calf was seen to be about a metre in length while the older animal was almost half as large again. Next she was afforded a couple of beautiful sightings in which they shot water from their mouths, creating fountains in the air. 'Spitting behaviour' of this kind was a characteristic of the species – she believed the dolphins used it as a strategy to confuse their prey. The sightings were so good that she put away her data sheets and picked up her camera. Minutes later she was rewarded with a rare view of a young Orcaella tossing a fish into the air and catching it in its mouth. The propensity to play with prey was a family trait – Orcaella shared it with its relative, the killer whale – but Piya had witnessed it only some six times in all her years of tracking Orcaella and this was the only occasion on which she had got a clear shot of it.

Shortly afterwards the pair vanished. Now it remained only to be seen if they would come back when the water ebbed again, in the evening.

While Piya was in the bow, watching the water, Fokir and Tutul were sitting in the stern, patiently tending a set of fishing lines. The lines had worried Piya at first, for dolphins had been known to get themselves tangled in certain kinds of fishing gear. But a close look had shown that Fokir's tackle was too flimsy to

136

pose a threat to animals of that size and she had let the matter pass, deciding that it was all right to ignore such lightweight lines. The fish, evidently, had come to the same conclusion for neither father nor son had a single strike all morning. But this didn't seem to worry them – they seemed content where they were, at least for the time being.

But when would Fokir and Tutul demand to leave? The night before, she had hoped they would set off at first light. But the dolphins had changed everything: she saw now that it was imperative that she stay till the next day. This was the only way she could discover whether there was any truth to her intuition that these dolphins had adapted their behaviour to suit the ebb and flow of the water – by staying here through a whole cycle of tides. It was possible of course that this was just a fantasy and, in any event, it would take years to find the supportive data. For now all she needed was a few more shreds of evidence, a few indications to suggest that she was thinking along the right lines. If only she could remain here till the next sunrise – that would be enough.

As the hours passed, Piya's anxieties shifted focus, moving away from the dolphins and settling on Fokir and the boy. How much longer before they grew impatient and demanded to leave? What would she have to do to persuade them to stay on? She had noticed that their clay stove had not been lit all morning – they had eaten nothing but some dry *chapatis*. This was not a good sign; it could mean they were running low on supplies. In other circumstances she might have offered Fokir a bonus, as compensation for whatever inconvenience he might have to suffer. But this was not an option here: the child could not be expected to defer his hunger in order to earn money for his father.

Her own supply of water was running low, but she knew she could make it last if she was careful. It was the two of them she was worried about, and her anxiety prompted her to do something unprecedented: digging into her carefully hoarded stock of nutrition bars she offered them some. Fokir declined, but Tutul accepted one and ate it with evident relish. This reassured her a little: if need be, she would sacrifice a few more bars – it would be well worth it if she could only persuade them to stay on. But her anxieties would not be quieted: even as she was filling in her data sheets, she kept casting glances in their direction. Their every movement made her start: was this it? Had they decided to leave now?

Unaccountably, nothing happened. Neither of them seemed to have any interest in getting the boat under way. After a meagre midday meal of chapatis and honey, they both fell asleep in the shade of the shelter.

Piya was now in a state of such anxiety and expectation that she knew she would not be able to sit still and wait for the hours to pass. Instead, she decided to spend the rest of the afternoon mapping the riverbed to see whether or not there was an under-water 'pool' where the Orcaella had gathered. She had some experience of this kind of mapping and knew it to be a simple, if painstaking task: it would require her to take depth-soundings that could be linked together to create contour lines. Thanks to the Global Positioning System it was easy to ensure the exact placement of each sounding, so that the readings were taken along regular, geometrical quadrants.

But how was this to be explained to Fokir?

She made her way to the shelter and found Fokir and the boy fast asleep. They were lying on their sides, with Tutul's small form nested inside the larger curve of his father's body. The boy, she noticed, had a slight pudginess that contrasted sharply with his father's near-skeletal leanness: Fokir was all muscle and bone, a male anatomy reduced to its essentials. Was the boy better fed than his father? There was a story here that she wished she understood: who looked after the boy? Did someone have to deprive himself to make sure Tutul was properly fed?

Their chests were moving in unison as they slept and the rhythm of their breathing reminded her of the pair of dolphins she had been watching earlier. It calmed her to see them sleeping so peacefully – the contrast with her own state of mind could not have been more marked. She hesitated in extending her arm to wake Fokir: would he be annoyed at being woken from his siesta? Was this when he would demand to leave for home? She noticed a bead of sweat travelling down his temple, towards the corner of his eye and without thinking, she put out a finger to flick it away.

He awoke instantly and sat up, rubbing the spot where her fingertip had touched his skin. She backed away, in embarrassment. 'I'm sorry,' she said. 'I didn't mean—' He shrugged indifferently, and dug his fists into his eyes as though he were trying to rub away the remnants of his sleep.

'Look.' She thrust her positioning monitor in front of him and pointed to the screen. 'Over here.' To her surprise, his attention was caught immediately. He paid careful attention as she tried to show him the meaning of the dots and the lines.

The hardest part was to explain the correspondence between their own position and their place on the screen. She tried pointing, in various combinations, to the screen, to herself and to him and the boy. But the purpose was not served: she saw he had grown flustered and realized that her gestures had given him the impression that she wanted him to move closer to her. The misunderstanding disconcerted her and she fetched a sheet of paper, deciding on a change in strategy. Surely it would be easier if she were to reduce the problem to two dimensions, by drawing a simple diagram, with stick figures, like those familiar to every child? The trouble was, she had never been much good at drawing, and now, halfway into the sketch she was brought up short by an unanticipated misgiving. In the past, she had always used a triangular skirt to distinguish her stick women from her men – but this didn't quite make sense in a situation where the man was in a lungi and the woman in pants. She crumpled up the sheet and would have tossed it away if Fokir hadn't taken it from her hands, to save for kindling.

With her next drawing she started with the outlines of the landscape, sketching in the curve of the shore before indicating their own position. Just as she had thought, the reduction to two dimensions made all the difference: once she had shown him how the diagram corresponded with the lines on the monitor's screen, the rest was easy. It took only a few strokes of her pencil to convey that she needed him to row the boat in parallel lines over a quadrant shaped roughly like a triangle, with its apex almost touching the far shore.

She had expected some reluctance, and possibly even resistance. But there was none. On the contrary, he seemed quite pleased and went so far as to rouse Tutul with a cheerful shout. It was the prospect of traversing the water in straight lines that seemed to enthuse him most – and she discovered why when he pulled a roll of line out of the hold. Evidently he wanted to use this opportunity to do some fishing.

But the line puzzled her; in all the time she had spent on Asian rivers she had never seen its like. It was made of thick, strong nylon, and all along its length, at intervals of a metre or so, were weights – small fragments of broken tile. Stranger still, there were no hooks – instead, spaced between the weights, were bits of fish-bone and dried cartilage, tied to the line with cord. It was difficult to see how the tackle worked: the expectation seemed to be that a fish would just attach itself to the line and permit itself to be reeled in. But no fish would do that surely? Then what could he be fishing for? She was at a loss for an answer. It was clear in any event, that the line presented no threat to the dolphins and she could see no reason to object to his laying it so long as the boat kept to the right course.

She went back to her position in the bow and readied herself to proceed with her mapping. With her monitor in hand she directed Fokir to the position from which they were to start. Then, just as Tutul was dropping the first weight in the water, she dipped the echo-sounder and pressed the button.

The initial run was about a kilometre long, and by the time they reached the end the whole line had been paid out. It was after they had turned to retrace their course, that Piya discovered what the line was for: it was pulled in with a live crab hanging on to every ninth or tenth morsel of bait. The creatures had snapped their claws on the cartilage and would not let go. Fokir and Tutul had only to peel them off with a net and drop them into a pot filled with leaves. The sight made Piya laugh: so this was where the word 'crabby' came from, a creature so stubborn that it would rather be captured than let go?

It took only a few more runs to confirm Piya's guess that the dolphins had congregated in a declivity. Her soundings showed that the riverbed dipped by a good five to eight metres there, more than enough to provide for the dolphins' comfort when the water was running low.

But it was not just for dolphins that the pool was a hospitable habitat: crabs too seemed to flourish there and Fokir's catch grew steadily with each successive run. At the start, she had thought they might end up disrupting each other's work – that her soundings would get in the way of his fishing or the other way around. But, to her surprise, no such difficulties arose: the stops required for the laying of the line seemed to be ideally timed for the taking of soundings. What was more, the line acted like a guide-rail, keeping the boat to a straight and unvarying tack, and at the end of each run it led them right back to the precise point from which they had started. In other circumstances, Piya would have had to use the Global Positioning System to be sure of this, but here the line served the same purpose. She needed her monitor only to make sure that each run began at a point five metres farther along the quadrant. This was just as much to Fokir's advantage as it was to hers since it ensured that his line never fell twice in the same place.

It was surprising enough that their jobs had not proved to be utterly incompatible – especially considering that one of the tasks required the input of geostationary satellites while the other depended on bits of shark-bone and broken tile. But that it had proved possible for two such different people to pursue their own ends simultaneously – people who could not exchange a word with each other and had no idea of what was going on in one another's heads – was far more than surprising: it seemed almost miraculous. And nor was she the only one to remark on this: once, when her glance happened accidentally to cross Fokir's, she saw something in his expression that told her that he too was amazed by the seamless intertwining of their pleasures and their purposes.

When the crab pot was full, Fokir covered its mouth with an aluminium plate and passed it to her so she could release the catch into the hold. Looking in, she saw that there were some fifteen crabs inside the pot, eyeing her balefully, snapping their claws. When she tipped the pot over they tumbled out in a chain and disappeared into the hold with an angry outburst of clicking and clattering. The unlikely eloquence of the sound drew a laugh from Piya. Her birthday was in July and she had often wondered why the ancients had included a crab in the Zodiac when there were so many other more interesting animals to choose from. But now, as she watched the creatures scuttling about in the hold she found herself wishing that she knew more about crabs. She recalled a class in which the teacher had demonstrated how some kinds of crab actually laundered the mud they lived in, scrubbing it grain by grain. Their feet and their sides were lined with hairs that formed microscopic brushes and spoons. They used these to scrape off the diatoms and other edible matter attached to each grain of sand. They were a sanitation department and a janitorial team rolled into one: they kept the mangroves alive by removing their leaves and litter; without them the trees would choke on their own debris. Didn't they represent some fantastically large proportion of the system's biomass? Didn't they outweigh even the trees and the leaves? Hadn't someone said that intertidal forests should be named after crabs rather than mangroves since it was they – certainly not the crocodile or the tiger or the dolphin – who were the keystone species of the entire ecosystem?

She had thought of these concepts – keystone species, biomass – as ideas that applied to things other than herself. To nature, in short – for who was it who had said that the definition of 'nature' was that it included everything not formed by human intention? But it was not her own intention that had brought her here today; it was the crabs – because they were Fokir's livelihood and without them he would not have known to lead her to this pool where the Orcaella came. Maybe the ancients had got it right after all – perhaps it was the crab that ruled the tide of her destiny.

Travels

Returning to the Guest House, Kanai found that Moyna had left him his lunch in a tiffin carrier. The meal was simple: plain rice, *musuri'r dāl*, a quick-cooked *chorchori* of potatoes, fish-bones and a kind of green leaf he could not identify. Finally, there was a watery *jhol* of a tiny but toothsome fish called *murola*. Even cold, the food was delicious. Kanai's cook was from Lucknow and his table at home, in New Delhi, tended to be set with elaborately Mughlai dishes. It was a long time since he had eaten simple Bengali food and the tastes seemed to explode in his head. At the end of the meal he was giddily replete.

After he had put away the utensils, Kanai made his way up the stairs, to Nirmal's study. Shutting the door behind him, he pulled a chair up to the desk and flipped open the notebook.

You, Kanai, were among the last to see Kusum in Lusibari, in 1970. That year, on the eve of the performance of the Bon Bibi Johuranama, she vanished as if into the eye of a storm. No one knew where she went; no trace of her remained. That was the last we heard of Kusum and, to be truthful, we paid little mind to her fate. Sadly, it is all too common in these parts for young people and children to disappear into the city: there are so many such that one loses track of them.

The years went by and the time of my retirement approached. I would be lying if I did not admit that the prospect filled my heart with trepidation. I had been headmaster for close to thirty years: the school, my pupils, my teaching – these things had become my life. Without the pattern and order of a classroom routine, what would become of me? I remembered my days of disorder when the world looked so irredeemably confused that to lie abed seemed the best possible course. Would this condition beset me again? You can imagine my despondency.

The true tragedy of a routinely spent life is that its wastefulness does not become apparent till it is too late. For years I had been telling Nilima that I'd been writing up in my study. She was glad for me; she took no pleasure in the fact that she enjoyed so much esteem in the world and I so little. She wanted me to be known for what she believed me to be – a writer, a poet. But the truth was that I had not written a single word in all my time in Lusibari; not just that, I had even abandoned my other great pleasure – reading. Regret and remorse attacked me on all these counts as the day of my superannuation neared. One day I went to Kolkata and scoured my favourite stalls and bookshops – only to realize that I could no longer afford to buy books. I returned to Lusibari with only one new volume in my possession – the copy of Bernier's Travels that you were so kind as to buy for me.

As my final day in school drew nigh it became increasingly apparent that the other masters were keenly awaiting my departure – not, I think, out of a spirit of malice, but merely from an eagerness to see what the future might hold. Someone who has stayed in the same job for thirty years becomes like mildew on the wall – everybody longs to see it wither in the bright light of a new day.

As word of my impending retirement spread, I began to receive invitations to visit schools on other islands. In the past perhaps I would have declined, but I now recalled the Poet's dictum – 'To stay is to be nowhere' – and I was happy to accept. One such invitation was from an old acquaintance who lived in Kumirmari, which is a good distance from here: to get to it requires several changes of ferry. I decided to go.

The morning came and it so happened that Nilima was away, making one of her trips on behalf of the Trust. Left to my own devices, I spent too much time packing the jhola I had planned to take with me; I put in one book and then another – the journey was not a short one after all, and I would need plenty to read. In the process I misjudged many things – the timing of the ferries, how long it would take to get to the jetty and so on. Suffice it to say that I missed the first connection, which meant that I would miss all the rest.

I was sitting in despair on the bādh when suddenly I spotted a familiar figure, going by in a boat. I had not seen Horen for many years

144

but I recognized at once his squat build and narrowed eyes: there was a teenage boy with him and I knew this must be his oldest son.

I hurried down the embankment and accosted them: 'Horen! Horen! Wait!'

When I drew level with them, he said, in amazement, 'Saar? You here? I was bringing my son to see you – he wants to enrol in your school.'

I put a hand on the boy's shoulder: 'I'll make sure he gets in – but in return there's something you must do for me.'

'Yes, Saar. What is it?'

'Horen, I have to go to Kumirmari. Can you take me?'

'Why, Saar, yes; for you anything. Get in.' He gave his son a pat on the shoulder and told him to find his own way home. Then without a backward glance, we set off in the direction of Kumirmari.

Once we were on the water, it struck me that it was a long time since I had sat in a nouko like Horen's. In recent years, when I felt the need to travel outside Lusibari – and this happened seldom enough – I generally took ferries and bhotbhotis. Sitting in the boat, the familiar scenery began to take on a different aspect: it was as if I were seeing it in a new way. Under the shade of my umbrella, I opened one of the books I had brought with me – my copy of Bernier's 'Travels' – and, as if by magic, the pages fell open to his account of his travels in the tide country.

Presently, Horen said, 'Saar, what is that you're reading? Are there any stories in it? Why not tell me too, since we have such a long way to go.'

'All right, then,' I said. 'Listen.'

This book was by a Christian priest, I told him, a Frenchman who'd come to India in the year 1665. At that time Chaitanya Mahaprabhu's memory was still fresh in our villages and the Emperor Jahangir was sitting on the Mughal throne. The priest's name was François Bernier and he was of the Jesuit 'shomproday'. He had with him two Portuguese pilots as well as a considerable company of servants. On their first day among the mangroves, they found themselves beset with hunger. Although they had food, they were nervous about going ashore to cook it. They had heard many stories of the ferocity of the local tigers and they wanted to take every possible precaution. Late in the day a suitable sandbank was found and two chickens and a fish were prepared. After consuming

145

this meal, the Jesuit and his party set off again and rowed until dark. When night approached, they took their boat into a 'snug creek' and anchored it at a distance from the shore where they judged themselves to be safe from predators. But they took the additional precaution of maintaining a watch through the night and this proved lucky for the priest. When his turn came he was privileged to witness a truly amazing spectacle: a rainbow made by the moon.

'Oh!' cried Horen. 'I know where this happened: they must have been at Gerafitola.'

'Rubbish, Horen,' I said. 'How could you know such a thing? This happened over three hundred years ago.'

'But I've seen it too,' Horen protested, 'and it's exactly as you describe – a creek, just off a big river. That's the only place where you can see the moon's rainbow – it happens when there's a full moon and a fog. But never mind all that, Saar – go on with the story.'

'On the third day Bernier and his party discovered that they were lost. They wandered through creeks and rivers and became more and more distracted, thinking that they were trapped forever in this labyrinth of waterways. And then again an amazing thing happened. They saw some people in the distance, working on a sandbank, so they headed in that direction. These would be local fishermen, they assumed, who would show them the way. But on getting there they discovered that these men were Portuguese. They were making salt.'

'Ah!' said Horen with a long drawn-out sigh. 'I know that place. It's on the way to Kedokhali. There's a place there where people still some-times go to make salt. My chhotokaka spent the night there once, and all night long he heard strange voices uttering strange words: it must have been those same ghosts they saw. But never mind all that, Saar – just go on.'

'The fourth day found the priest and his party still in the tide country, and in the evening they withdrew once again into the shelter of a creek. Then there followed "a most extraordinary night". First, the wind died down so that not a leaf stirred in the forest. Next the air around the boat began to heat up and it soon became so hot that the priest and his party could scarcely breathe. Then, all of a sudden, the mangroves around the boat seemed to burst into flame as the greenery was invaded by great swarms of glow-worms. These insects hovered in such a way as to give the impression that fires were dancing in the mangroves' roots and branches. This caused panic among the sailors who, the Jesuit says, "did not doubt that they were so many devils".'

'But Saar,' said Horen, with a puzzled look in my direction. 'Why should they doubt it? What else could they be?'

'I don't know, Horen. I'm just telling you what the priest says.'

'Go on Saar. Go on.'

'The night that followed was still worse – "altogether dreadful and perilous" says the priest. Suddenly, with no warning, a violent storm arose and pursued the priest and his party into a creek. They took their boat close to shore and, using all their ropes, tied the boat to a tree. But the storm raged with such ferocity that their cables could not long withstand the wind. Suddenly the ropes snapped and it seemed certain the boat would be blown out of its shelter, into a storm-tossed mohona where the waves were sure to rip apart the joins of the timber. All the while "the rain fell as if poured into the boat from buckets" and the "lightning and thunder were so vivid and loud, and so near our heads, that we despaired of surviving this horrible night".

'At this juncture, in a "sudden and spontaneous movement" the priest and his two Portuguese pilots took hold of a tree and entwined their arms into the mangroves' twisted stilts. Their arms became living roots like those of the tree that had given them shelter. In this way they clung on "for the space of two hours, while the tempest raged with unabated force".'

'Ei re!' cried Horen. 'They must have crossed the line.'

'What line, Horen?'

'Didn't you say they were lost, Saar?'

'Yes, I did.'

'That's what happened, then. They crossed the line by mistake and ended up on one of Dokkhin Rai's islands. Whenever you have a storm like that – one that appears so suddenly, out of nowhere – you know it's the doing of Dokkhin Rai and his demons.'

I grew impatient and I said, 'Horen! A storm is an atmospheric disturbance: it has neither intention nor motive.'

I had spoken so sharply that he would not disagree with me, although he could not bring himself to agree either. 'As to that, Saar,' he said, 'let us leave each other to our beliefs and see what the future holds.'

Here was a man, I thought, whom the Poet would have recognized: 'filled with muscle and simplicity'.

I have gone on at too great a length – hours have passed, the ink in my ballpoint is running down. This is what happens when you have not written for years: every moment takes on a startling clarity; small things become the world in microcosm.

Kusum and Horen have left me here with Fokir. They have gone to find out if the rumours are true; if Morichjhāpi is soon to be attacked, and if so when the assault will come.

To think of all the years when I had nothing but time and yet wrote not one word. And now like some misplaced, misgendered Scheherazade, I am trying to stave the night off with a flying, fleeting pen . . .

Garjontola

The final run brought Fokir's boat into shallow water, within a few metres of the shore. Piya's guess had been amply confirmed by this time: her soundings showed that there was a kilometre-long depression in the sheltered crook of the river's elbow. The declivity formed a gentle, kidney-shaped basin, with a rounded bottom and sides: although the drop exceeded eight metres in some places, on average it was only some five metres deeper than the rest of the riverbed. The 'pool', in short, was similar in most particulars, to those frequented by the Orcaella of the Mekong during the dry season.

With the water running high, the band of mud on the shore had thinned to the width of a few paces and the mangroves' trunks were at last on eye-level, neither above nor below the boat. The water was so shallow here that there was no point in taking soundings; for the first time in hours, Piya went 'off effort', dropping her binoculars and resting her eyes on the greenery of the shore. Presently, her gaze was drawn to what looked like a fragment of brick, lying in the mud. She looked more closely and her glasses confirmed her impression: this was indeed a bit of broken brick, and nor was it the only one – the shore was littered with them. Examining the tangled greenery, she discovered that some of the mangroves were growing out of mud walls while others had chunks of brick entwined in their roots.

She called out to Fokir, 'Look – there.' He threw a glance at the shore, over his shoulder and nodded. 'Garjontola,' he said, with a gesture in the direction of the shore. She guessed that this was the name of whatever settlement had once stood there.

'Garjontola?' He nodded in confirmation. She was glad to know the name and noted it quickly: the dolphins' tidal pool, she decided, would be named after this abandoned village – 'the Garjontola pool'.

All of a sudden Tutul jumped to his feet, rocking the boat. Looking up from her notebook, she saw that he was pointing into the middle distance, to a tree that was taller than the others and looked more like a birch than a mangrove: it was slender-limbed, with light-coloured bark, and foliage that seemed almost silvery against the dense, heavy green of the surrounding mangroves.

At the end of the run, Fokir surprised her by turning the boat's bow in the direction of the shore. This was the closest she had been to the forest and she felt as though she were facing it for the first time: before, it had been either half-submerged, or a distant silhouette, looking down on the water from the heights of the shore. Looking into it now, she was struck by the way the greenery worked to confound the eye. It was not just that it was a barrier, like a screen or a wall: it seemed to trick the human gaze, in the manner of a cleverly drawn optical illusion. There was such a profusion of shapes, forms, hues and textures, that even things that were in plain view seemed to disappear, vanish-ing into the tangle of lines like the hidden objects in children's puzzles.

Fokir pulled the oars in, after a last, powerful stroke and the boat's bow nudged into the mud. Then he rose to his feet and, as if by magic, his *lungi* became a loincloth, transformed by a single flick of his wrist. Swinging his legs over the side, he dropped into the water and gave the boat a push that sent it ploughing deep into the bank. Piya, sitting in the bow, found herself lodged halfway up the bank, with a tangled barrier of mangrove blocking off the slope ahead.

After lifting Tutul off the boat, Fokir made a beckoning motion with his arm and she understood that he was asking her to follow him off the boat. But where was he going? She sketched a gesture of interrogation and he responded by pointing in the direction of the island's interior, past the first barrier of mangrove.

'In there?'

Now he was beckoning again, motioning to her to hurry. She hesitated for a moment, held back by her aversion to mud, insects and dense vegetation, all of which were present aplenty on the shore. In any other circumstances she would not even have considered heading into forest cover of that kind, but with Fokir it was different. Somehow she knew she would be safe.

'OK. I'm coming.' Rolling her pants up to her knees, she swung her bare feet over the gunwale. The mud parted under her weight, sucking her feet in with a wet slurping sound. She was taken completely by surprise for the mud hadn't seemed deep at all when Fokir was running up the bank. The slight forward momentum of her body, as she came off the boat, was enough to unbalance her: the grip of the mud pulled her ankles backwards, away from her centre of gravity. Suddenly she was tipping over, falling face-forwards, extending her arm to keep herself from slamming into the mud. But at just the right moment, Fokir appeared directly in front of her, with his body positioned to block her fall. She landed heavily on his shoulder and once again she found herself soaking in the salty smell of his skin. In blocking her fall, she had thrown her arms around his torso as though he were a pillar or a tree trunk and one of her hands had caught hold of his shoulder-blade, digging into the recess between muscle and bone. Her other hand had slid down his bare skin, coming to rest in the small of his back, and, for an instant, she was paralysed with embarrassment. Then, she became aware of Tutul's voice, somewhere nearby – he was laughing at her discomfiture, in childish delight – and she began to pull away from Fokir, withdrawing her fingers gingerly. When he put a steadying hand under her elbow, she saw he was laughing too, but not in a way that seemed unkind – he seemed to be amused more by her surprise at the depth of the mud than by her fall.

After she was on her feet again he enacted a little pantomime to show her how to negotiate the bank: lifting up a foot, he curled the toe like a crab's claw and dug it into the mud. She tried it herself, and it worked for a couple of steps, but then her foot slipped again. Fortunately, he was still beside her and she held on to his arm until they had left the mud behind and pushed their way into the tangle of greenery that lined the shore.

She saw now he had a machete with him. He went ahead of her, swinging the blade and clearing a path through the dense foliage. Suddenly, the green barrier came to an end and they broke through to a grassy clearing dotted with stunted palm trees.

Tutul ran ahead to the far side of the clearing and stopped in front of what seemed to be a small shack built on stilts. On approaching closer she saw it was not a shack at all, but a leaf-thatched altar or shrine: it reminded her distantly of her mother's *puja*-table, except that the images inside didn't represent any of the Hindu gods she was familiar with. There was a large-eyed female figure in a sari and beside it a slightly smaller figure of a man. Crouching between them was a tiger, recognizable because of its painted stripes.

Piya stood by and watched as Fokir and Tutul performed a little ceremony. First they fetched some leaves and flowers and placed them in front of the images. Then, standing before the shrine, Fokir began to recite some kind of chant, with his head bowed and his hands joined in an attitude of prayer. After she had listened for a few minutes, Piya recognized a refrain that occurred over and over again – it contained a word that sounded like 'Allah'. She had not thought to speculate about Fokir's religion, but it occurred to her now that he might be Muslim. But no sooner had she thought this, than it struck her that a Muslim was hardly likely to pray to an image like this one. What Fokir was performing looked very much like her mother's Hindu *pujas* – and yet the words seemed to suggest otherwise.

But what did it matter either way? She was glad just to be there, as a witness to this strange little ritual.

A few minutes later they headed back and, on breaking free of the mangrove, Piya saw that the sun had dipped in the sky and the level of the water had begun to fall. She tiptoed carefully across the mud and was about to climb into the boat when Fokir waved to catch her attention. He was twenty metres away, kneeling, with his hand pointing downward, to the ground. Piya went over to look and saw that he was pointing to a depression in the mud filled with scurrying crabs. She raised her eyebrows, and he held up a hand, as if to tell her that that was what it was – the mark of a hand. She frowned in incomprehension:

what hand could have touched that mud other than his? Then it struck her that maybe he meant, not 'hand' but 'foot' or 'paw'. 'Tiger?' she was about to say but he raised a finger to prevent her: she understood now that this was indeed some kind of superstition – to say that word or even to make a gestural reference to it was taboo.

She looked at it again and could see nothing to suggest that it was what he had said. The placement of the mark contributed to her scepticism: the animal would have had to be in full view and she would have seen it from the water. And would Fokir himself be quite so unconcerned if there really was a tiger nearby? It just didn't add up.

Then she heard the sound of an exhalation, and all thought of the tiger was banished from her mind. Picking up her binoculars she spotted two humps breaking the river's surface: it was the adult orcaella, swimming in tandem with the calf. With the water ebbing, the dolphins had returned: their movements seemed to follow exactly the pattern she had inferred.

A Disturbance

Kanai was still in his uncle's study, reading, when the light above the desk flickered and went out. He lit a candle and sat still as the throbbing of the generator faded and a cloud of stillness crept slowly over the island. Listening to its advance, it occurred to him to wonder why, in English, silence is commonly said to 'fall' or 'descend' as though it were a curtain or a knife. There was nothing precipitous about the hush that followed the shutting off of the generator: the quiet was more like a fog or a mist, creeping in slowly, from a distance, wrapping itself around certain sounds while revealing others: the sawing of a cicada, a snatch of music from a distant radio, the cackle of an owl. Each of these made themselves heard briefly, only to vanish again into the creeping fog. It was in just this way that yet another sound, unfamiliar to Kanai, revealed itself, very briefly, and then died away again. The echo had carried across the water from such a distance that it would have been inaudible if the generator had been on; yet it bespoke a nakedness of assertion, a power and menace, that had no relationship to its volume. Small as it was, every other sound seemed to wither for an instant, only to be followed by a loud and furious outbreak of disquiet – marked most prominently by a frenzy of barking, from all over the island.

Shutting the door behind him, he stepped out on to the roof and discovered that the landscape, in its epic mutability, had undergone yet another transformation: the moonlight had turned it into a silvery negative of its daytime image. Now it was the darkened islands that looked like lakes of liquid, while the water lay spread across the earth like a vast slick of solid metal.

'Kanai-babu?'

He turned to see a woman standing silhouetted in the doorway, with her sari drawn over her head.

'Moyna?'

'Yes.'

'Did you hear?' No sooner had he said the words than he heard the sound again: it was the same indistinct echo, not unlike the bellowing of a faraway train, and again it was followed by an outburst of barks as though all the island's dogs had been waiting to hear it repeated.

'Is it a—?' Kanai began, and then, seeing her flinch, cut himself short. 'I shouldn't say the word, should I?'

'No,' she said. 'It's not to be spoken aloud.'

'Where do you think it's coming from?'

'It could be from anywhere,' she said. 'I was just sitting in my room, waiting, but then I heard it and I couldn't sit still any more.'

'So Fokir isn't back yet?'

'No.'

Kanai understood now that the animal's roar had a direct connection with her anxiety. 'You shouldn't worry,' he said, trying to reassure her. 'I'm sure Fokir will take all the right precautions. He knows what to do.'

'Him?' Anger seethed in her voice as she said this. 'If you knew him you wouldn't say that. Whatever other people do, he does just the opposite. The other fishermen – my father, my brothers, everyone – when they're out there at night, they tie their boats together, in mid-stream so they won't be defenceless if they're attacked. But Fokir won't do that; he'll be off on his own somewhere without another human being in sight.'

'Why?'

'That's just how he is, Kanai-babu,' she said. 'He can't help himself. He's like a child.'

The moonlight caught the three points of gold on her face and once again Kanai was reminded of stars, lined up in a constellation. Even though her āchol was drawn carefully over her head, there was a restlessness in the tilt of her face that was at odds with the demure draping of her sari.

'Moyna, tell me,' said Kanai, in a half-jocular, teasing tone, 'was Fokir a stranger to you before you married him? Didn't you know what he was like?'

'Yes,' said Moyna, 'I did know him, Kanai-babu. After his mother died, he was brought up by Horen Naskor. Our village was not far from theirs.'

'You're a bright girl, Moyna,' Kanai said. 'If you knew what he was like, why did you marry him?'

She smiled, as if to herself. 'You wouldn't understand,' she said.

He was nettled by the certainty in her voice. '*I* wouldn't understand?' he said sharply. 'I know five languages; I've travelled all over the world. Why wouldn't I understand?'

She let her *āchol* drop from her head and gave him a sweet smile. 'It doesn't matter how many languages you know,' she said. 'You're not a woman and you don't know him. You won't understand.'

Leaving him standing, she whirled around and left.

Listening

~~~~~

The dolphins' quiet, regular breathing had lulled Piya into a doze from which she was woken by a sound that seemed to come booming out of a dream. By the time she opened her eyes and sat up, the forest was quiet again and the echoes had already faded. The river was lapping gently at the boat's hull and the stars above had become faint pinpricks of light, their glow dimmed by the brightness of the moon.

Then the boat began to rock and she knew that Fokir was awake too. Raising her head she saw that he had seated himself in the centre of the boat, with his blanket draped shawl-like around his shoulders. Now she roused herself and made her way like a crab along the boat, seating herself beside him. 'What was it?' she mimed the question with raised eyebrows and a turn of her hand. He gave her a smile but made no direct answer, only raising a hand to point vaguely across the water. Then, resting his chin on his knees, he fixed his eyes on the island they had visited earlier, visible now as a faint silver filigree across the water.

For a while they sat listening companionably to the Orcaella as they circled around the boat. Then she heard him humming a tune, deep in his throat, so she laughed and said, 'Sing. Louder. Sing.' She had to exhort him a few more times and then he did sing out loud, but keeping his voice very low. The melody was very different from that of the day before, alternately lively and pensive, but it mirrored her mood and she felt a sense of perfect contentment as she sat there listening to his voice, against the percussive counterpoint of the dolphins' breathing. What greater

happiness could there be than this: to be on the water with someone you trusted, at this magical hour, listening to the serene
sound of these animals?

They sat a while in silence and presently she sensed that
despite the direction of his gaze, he was not really watching the
far shore. Was he perhaps half-asleep, she wondered, as people
sometimes are even when they seem to be awake? Or was he
just lost in thought, with his mind racing to retrieve some almost-
forgotten shard of recollection from his past?

What did he see when he looked back? She pictured a hut
like those she had seen on the fringes of Canning, with mud
walls and straw thatch and shutters of plaited bamboo. His father
was a fisherman like him, with long stringy limbs and a face
imprinted by the sun and wind, and his mother was a sturdy
but tired woman, worn to the bone by the daily labour of carrying baskets full of fish and crabs to the market. There were many
children, many playmates for little Fokir, and although they were
poor their lives did not lack for warmth or companionship: it
was a family like those she had heard her father talk about – in
which want and deprivation made people pull together all the
more tightly.

Had he seen his wife's face before the wedding? Her own parents,
she remembered, had actually been allowed to meet and talk to
each other, although there had been many relatives present – but
of course they were city people, middle class and educated. A
meeting between the unwed would not, surely, be allowed in the
village Fokir lived in? The couple would have first set eyes on
each other when they were seated at the sacred fire and even
then the girl would not have looked up: she would have kept her
eyes downcast until it was night and they were lying beside each
other in the mud-walled room of their hut. Only then would she
allow herself to look at this boy who was her man and thank her
fate for giving her a husband who was young, with fine clean
limbs and wide, deep eyes, someone who could almost have been
the dark god of her prayers and dreams.

She decided to get up and go back to the bed she had made
for herself in the bow of the boat. She flipped over and lay on
her stomach, turning her attention back to the dolphins. They

were still in the pool, even though the tide was now in full flood: evidently this meant they preferred not to hunt by night. It remained to be seen whether they would leave the pool when the tide rose again the next day.

She imagined the animals circling drowsily, listening to echoes pinging through the water, painting pictures in three dimensions – images that only they could decode. The thought of experiencing your surroundings in that way never failed to fascinate her: the idea that to 'see' was also to 'speak' to others of your kind, where simply to exist was to communicate.

And in contrast, there was the immeasurable distance that separated her from Fokir. What was he thinking about as he stared at the moonlit river? The forest, the crabs? Whatever it was, she would never know: not just because they had no language in common but because that was how it was with human beings, who came equipped, as a species, with the means of shutting each other out. The two of them, Fokir and herself, they could have been boulders or trees for all they knew of each other: and wasn't it better in a way, more honest, that they could not speak? For if you compared it to the ways in which dolphins' echoes mirrored the world, speech was only a bag of tricks that fooled you into believing that you could see through the eyes of another being.

Blown Ashore

And so to Kumirmari: that day, I heard for the first time of the events unfolding at Morichjhāpi. The islands were close by, and in the school I was visiting there were many teachers who had witnessed the progress of the exodus: they had seen tens of thousands of settlers making their way to the island, in boats, dinghies and bhotbhotis. Many of their own people had gone off to join the movement, drawn by the prospect of free land. But even as they marvelled at the refugees' boldness, there were those who predicted trouble: the island belonged to the Forest Department and the government would not allow the squatters to remain.

I thought no more of it; it was no business of mine.

At midday there was a meal and shortly afterwards Horen and I set off to return to Lusibari. We were on the river, heading home, when the wind suddenly started up. Within moments it was on us – it attacked with that peculiar, wilful malevolence that causes people to think of these storms as something other than wholly natural. The river had been calm minutes before, but now we found ourselves picked up and shaken by huge waves. Before, Horen had been sweating to make the boat move – now we were being swept along against our will.

'Are we going to be finished off this time?' I said.

'No, Saar,' he said quickly. 'I've lived through much worse than this.'

'When?'

'In 1970, Saar, during the Agunmukha cyclone. If you had seen that, this would not seem like a storm at all. But that's too long a story to tell to you now: what's important for us at this minute is to go ashore.' He pointed to his right.

'Morichjhãpi, Saar. We can take shelter there until the storm subsides.'

There was nothing more to be said. With the wind behind us we were driven quickly to the shore. I helped Horen push his boat up the bank and after he had secured it, he said, 'Saar, we have to take shelter, under a roof.'

'But where can we go, Horen?'

'Over there, Saar. I see a dwelling.'

Without another question I set off after him, running through the pounding rain. With water streaming down my glasses, it was all I could do to keep my eyes on Horen's back.

Soon we were at the door of a small shack – of the usual kind, made with bamboo and palm-leaf thatch. At the door, Horen shouted, 'Eijé – ké achhish? Who's there?'

The door sprang suddenly open and I stepped in. I was standing there, blinking, wiping the rain from my glasses, when I heard someone say, 'Saar? Is that you?'

I looked down and saw a young woman kneeling in front of me, touching my feet. That I could not identify her was no more a surprise than that she should know me: if you have been in one place long enough, as a schoolteacher, then this happens with almost everyone you meet. Your pupils grow up and your memory fails to grow with them. Their new faces do not match the old.

'Saar,' she said, 'it's Kusum.'

Of all the people I might have expected to meet in that place, she was surely the last. 'Impossible.'

Now that my glasses were dry I noticed there was a small child hiding behind her. 'And who is that?' I said.

'That's my son, Fokir.'

I reached out to pat his head but he darted away.

'He's very shy,' said Kusum with a laugh.

I noticed now that Horen had not entered the dwelling and I realized that this was probably as a show of respect to me. I was both pleased and annoyed. Who, after all, is so egalitarian as not to value the respect of another human being? Yet, it seemed strange that he did not know of my aversion to servility.

I put my head around the door and saw him standing outside, waiting patiently in the pouring rain. 'What's the matter with you, Horen?' I said. 'Come inside. This is no time to be standing on ceremony.'

So Horen came in and there ensued a silence of the kind that often descends when people meet after a long time. 'You?' said Kusum at last, and Horen answered with one of his customary mumbles. Then she pushed the boy forward and said, 'Here is Fokir, my son.' Horen ran his hand through the boy's hair and said, 'Besh! Good.'

'And what about your family?' she said. 'Your children must be quite grown now?'

'My youngest is five,' said Horen, 'and the oldest is fourteen.'

She smiled, as if to tease him: 'Almost of an age to be married, then?'

'No,' said Horen, with sudden vehemence. 'I would not do to him what was done to me.'

I recount this only as an example of the way in which, even in extraordinary circumstances, people will often speak of the most inconsequential things.

'Look at you,' I said. 'It's Kusum who's been away for all these years – and here we are talking about Horen and his children.'

There was a mat on the floor and I sat down. I asked where she had been and how she had ended in Morichjhãpi?

'What can I tell you, Saar?' she said. 'It would take too long to tell.'

The wind was howling outside and the rain was still pouring down. 'There's nothing else to do now, anyway,' I said. 'So I'm ready to hear whatever you have to say.'

She laughed. 'All right, Saar. How can I say no to you? I'll tell you how it happened.'

I remember that her voice changed as she was recounting her story; it assumed new rhythms and distinctive cadences. Is it merely a trick of memory? It doesn't matter: her words have come flooding back to me in a torrent. My pen will have to race to keep up: she is the muse and I am just a scribe.

'Where was my mother? I only knew what I'd heard – from Lusibari I went as if to the dark: she had been taken, they said, to a town called Dhanbad. I asked a few questions and found out where to go; switching from this train to that, I made my way there.

'At the station it struck me: what would I do now? It was a mining town, the air was filled with smoke; the people were strangers, I'd never known their like; their words were like iron, they rang when they spoke;

when their gaze turned on you, their eyes smouldered like coal. I was on my own, a girl dressed in a torn frock; I'd had no fear till then – now my courage ran dry.

'But I was fortunate, although I didn't know, a blessed power was watching: she showed me where to go. There was a man at the station, selling ghugni, I spoke to him and found he was from the tide country! His house was in Basonti, his name was Rajen; his people were poor and he had left home as a boy. He had been lamed in Kolkata by a speeding bus; started selling food, in stations and on trains. Chance had brought him to Dhanbad, there he'd found a shack; it was in a bosti, right beside the railtrack. When he heard why I was there, he said he would help – but in the meanwhile, what would I do with myself? "Come with me," he said. "You will be fine in my shack. Like you I'm on my own. There'll be room for us both." I followed him there, along the gravelled railtrack. I was fearful when I entered: would I be safe? All night I lay awake and listened to the trains.

'Many days passed and he gave me no cause for shame; he was a good, kind man: how many such are there? It's true that some said, "Look who's with Rajen the lame" – I let them say what they wanted. What did I care?

'It was Rajen who brought me word of my mother; she was working in a place where truck-drivers came, to sleep on charpais and buy women for the night. I went there with Rajen and in secret we met: I fell upon Ma, but couldn't bring myself to speak. For so long I'd been waiting, but now my heart broke: her body was wasted, her face thin and drawn. "Don't look, Kusum," she said. "Don't touch me with your eyes; think of me as I was, before your father died. I blame that Dilip; he's more demon than man. He said he'd find me work, and look where he brought me: to eat leaves at home, would have been a better fate. He sold me, that danob, to others of his kind. This is no place for you, Kusum. You must go back. But stay a few days; come and see me once more."

'We went home that night, and came back a week later. Then Rajen said something that stopped our very breath: "Let Kusum marry me; let her be my wife. She'll be with me forever; I'll give her my life." At last I saw Ma smile: what better news could there be? "Fortunate Kusum, you've been blessed by Bon Bibi." "You'll come too," said Rajen. "Ma, we'll steal you away. This is no place for you; you'll die if you stay."*

We went back together, to Rajen's little shack; in Ma's presence we were married, Rajen and I. Who could have known then that this would be Ma's bidai? To see me was her release; three months later she died. That was her fate – nothing could be done; if she had lived but two years, she would have seen Fokir, our son.

'Many months passed and we spoke of coming back here: that place was not home; there was nothing for us there. Walking on iron, we longed for the touch of mud; encircled by rails, we dreamed of the Raimangal in flood. We dreamed of storm-tossed islands, straining at their anchors and of the rivers that bound them in golden fetters We thought of high tide, and the mohonas mounting, of islands submerged, like underwater clouds. By night we remembered, we talked and we dreamed – by day coal and metal were the stuff of our lives.

'Four years went by and then that life came to an end: a train began to move, with Rajen still unpaid. As the engine picked up speed, he ran to keep up, then his bad leg crumpled and he made a misstep: he was pulled from the platform, thrown before the wheels. What can I say? He was taken before his time. He kept his word to me: he gave me his whole life. Never had I thought he would leave me like that, but at least I had Fokir, my son, was his gift. Once again I thought of making my way back home; but now, with a child, I hadn't the courage on my own. Whom would I go to there? Who would I ask for help? What if I couldn't make do and it came to the worst? What if I had to fall begging, at Dilip's feet?

'Maybe Bon Bibi was keeping watch over me, for one night I heard tell of a great march to the east. They passed us next day – like ghosts, covered in dust, strung out in a line, shuffling beside the railtracks. They had children on their shoulders, bundles on their backs. Where were they heading? From what city had they come? They were not from those parts; they were strangers to us. I saw someone stumble, a woman as old as Ma. I took her back home with the help of some others. I gave them food and water; I saw they needed rest. "Stay, sit, raho behtho," I said. "Get back your strength." Did you notice the words? See: I'd spoken in Hindi, but it was in Bangla they spoke back to me. I was amazed: the very same words, the same tongue! "Who are you?" I said. "Tell me: where are you headed?" "Listen, sister, we'll tell you; this is the story.

'"Once we lived in Bangladesh, in Khulna jila: we're tide country

164

people, from the Sundarbans' edge. When the war broke out, our village
was burned to ash; we crossed the border, there was nowhere else to go.
We were met by the police and taken away; in buses they drove us, to
a settlement camp. We'd never seen such a place, such a dry emptiness;
the earth was so red it seemed to be stained with blood. For those who
lived there, that dust was as good as gold, they loved it just as we love
our tide country mud. But no matter how we tried, we couldn't settle
there: rivers ran in our heads, the tides were in our blood. Our fathers
had once answered Hamilton's call: they had wrested the estate from
the sway of the tides. What they'd done for another, couldn't we do for
ourselves? There are many such islands in the bhatir desh. We sent some
people ahead, and they found the right place; it's a large empty island
called Morichjhãpi. For months we prepared, we sold everything we
owned. But the police fell on us the moment we moved: they swarmed
on the trains, they put blocks on the road – but we still would not go
back; we began to walk."

'*I listened to them talk and hope blossomed in my heart; these were*
my people, how could I stand apart? We shared the same tongue, we
were joined in our bones; the dreams they had dreamt were no differ-
ent from my own. They too had hankered for our tide country mud; they
too had longed to watch the tide rise to full flood. If we stayed on in
Dhanbad, what would our future be? A lifetime of toil, in a city of rust?
I gathered our things, put clothes on Fokir's back; with Rajen in our
hearts, we stepped away from the shack.

'*And there you have it, Saar. I have told you the story. That's how*
Fokir and I came to Morichjhãpi.'

And so we fell silent, each of us alone with our thoughts, Kusum
and Fokir, Horen and I. In my mind's eye I saw them walking, these
thousands of people, who wanted nothing more than to plunge their
hands once again in our soft, yielding tide country mud. I saw them
coming, young and old, quick and halt, with their lives bundled on
their heads, and knew it was of them the Poet had spoken when he
said:

'*Each slow turn of the world carries such disinherited*
ones to whom neither the past nor the future belong.'

A Hunt

～⁓

In the morning Fokir still showed no great eagerness to be gone, and Piya, for her part, saw no reason to hurry him: she was glad to be able to spend more time with the dolphins.

The animals remained in the pool till midmorning, when the waters began to rise. Then again, over a period of about half an hour, they vanished. It happened exactly as it had the day before, except for the difference in the timing of the tide.

What remained to be seen now was where they went when they left the pool: it was quite possible that Fokir might know the answer to this. Through a combination of gestures she managed to convey to him that she wanted to follow the dolphins – would it be possible to track them in the boat? He nodded eagerly and quickly pulled in the anchor.

They left the pool while the tide was still coming in and the current added a little to their pace. Leaving Garjontola behind, they entered a mohona. Keeping watch in the bow, Piya saw that, with the tide in flood, the surrounding islands were sliding gradually beneath the water.

Looking ahead with her binoculars, she suddenly spotted a pair of fins, far out in front. By the time they had crossed the mohona, the fins were nowhere in sight. But Fokir seemed sure of the way, for he turned unhesitatingly into a wide channel, and then veered off into another that was narrower. Shortly afterwards he downed his oars and pointed to the shore. Veering around with her binoculars, Piya spotted three crocodiles – she had missed them because her attention had been focused on the water. She guessed that Fokir had seen them before, in this very stretch of water. They were lying exposed to view but their mud-caked bodies blended so well into the surroundings that it was hard to judge their size. One had its jaws open and it seemed to Piya that the gap was wide enough to take the measure of a human being – certainly one of her own size.

The channel was a relatively narrow one and if the tide had been low they would have passed very close to the crocodiles, but with the water running high, the reptiles were well up on the shore. They gave no indication of having noticed the boat's passage, but a while later when Piya turned her binoculars on them again, she saw that there were only two animals left on the bank. The third had slithered into the water and the trough it had carved in the mudbank had begun to fill up again. Within minutes the depression vanished and the bank was restored to its lacquered smoothness.

Then Tutul uttered a wordless shout and pointed ahead. Piya swung her binoculars around just in time to catch a glimpse of a dolphin's flukes. They disappeared almost at once and she was annoyed with herself for being distracted by the crocodiles. But a minute later the flukes appeared again, rising vertically out of the water, as if the animal were standing on its head. Then another pair of flukes appeared beside the first, similarly upended and Piya recognized the mother-and-calf couple she had observed before, in the 'pool'. The flood tide had created dozens of tiny creeks that reached deep into the interior of the surrounding banks and islands. It was in one of these that the dolphins were foraging, a gully clearly too shallow even for Fokir's boat.

Piya knew exactly what the dolphins were doing: they had herded a school of fish into shallow water and the hunted crea-tures had buried themselves in the mud, in a futile effort to evade their pursuers. Now, much like rabbits uprooting a harvest of carrots, the dolphins were picking the fish from the riverbed.

Piya had witnessed a variation on this very scene once, on the Irrawaddy River. In the course of a survey, she had made time to visit two fishermen who lived in a small village north of Mandalay. The visit had come about at the urging of a fellow cetologist who'd told her that these men would show her some-thing she would be hard put to believe.

167

The two fishermen proved to be a middle-aged man and his teenage son. At eleven in the morning they took Piya and her interpreter out on the river in their fishing boat. The boat was about the same size as Fokir's, but it had no hood. The heat was so fierce that even the water seemed to be in a stupor, showing few discernible signs of movement. Piya was relieved to find they had not far to go. When they were some twenty metres from shore the older man produced a wooden stick and began to drum on the boat's gunwale. A few minutes later a sharply raked dorsal fin broke the water's surface, soon to be followed by several others. Then the younger man picked up a fishing net and began to rattle the metal weights that were attached to its fringe. The sound prompted a pair of dolphins to break off from the pod. While the others hung back, this pair made a close approach to the boat. When they were a few metres from the bow, they began to swim in circles, almost as if they were chasing each other's tails. Through the interpreter, the fishermen explained that the dolphins were herding a school of fish towards the boat.

For a while, the fishermen observed in silence, and then the younger man rose to his feet. Giving voice to a strange, gobbling call he swirled the net around his head and made a cast. The net landed right in the centre of the perimeter the dolphins had been patrolling. Now, as the net sank, the water's surface began to froth. Small silver fish leapt in the air, while the two patrolling dolphins swam faster and faster in tightening circles. The other dolphins in the pod joined in and began to make darting charges, thrashing the surface with their flukes in order to drive the fast-scattering fish back towards the net.

The fishermen pulled the net in, and a wriggling, writhing mass of silver spilt out and lay scattered around the deck: it was as though a *piñata* had burst, releasing a great mass of tinsel. The dolphins in the meanwhile, were celebrating a catch of their own. In sinking to the bottom, the net had pushed a great number of fish into the soft floor of the river; the dolphins were now free to feast on this underwater harvest. They fell to it with gusto, upending themselves in the water, creating a small thicket of wriggling flukes.

Piya was awestruck. Did there exist any more remarkable instance of symbiosis between human beings and a population of wild animals? She could not think of one. There was truly no limit, it seemed, to the cetacean gift for springing surprises.

Dreams

With the storm raging outside, there was no question of trying to get back to Lusibari that night.

'Saar,' Horen said at last, with a sigh, 'I think we'll have to sleep here, on Kusum's floor, tonight.'

'It's for you to judge, Horen,' I said. 'I'll do what you say.'

Later, Kusum boiled some rice and cooked a few small fish, a handful of little tangra-machh that Fokir had caught. After we had eaten, Kusum laid out mats for Horen and me at one end of the room, while she went with Fokir to sleep in the far corner. Late at night, when the storm had died down, I heard the door open and knew that Horen had gone to see to the safety of his boat. I fell into a fitful, feverish sleep, stirring and tossing.

'Saar.' I heard Kusum's voice, although I couldn't see her face in the dark. 'Are you all right?'

'Yes,' I said. 'I'm fine. Why do you ask?'

'Because you cried out in your sleep.'

I felt her hand, stroking my forehead and tears came to my eyes. 'Just an old man's night-time fears,' I said at last. 'But I'm fine now. Go back to your son. Go back to sleep.'

I rose in the morning to find, as so often after a storm, that there was not a cloud in the sky. The island and river were bathed in brilliant sunshine. I stepped away from Kusum's dwelling and saw others beside it, a little distance away. I walked a little farther and saw still more dwellings, scattered over cleared fields. These were huts, shacks and shanties built with the usual materials of the tide country – mud, thatch and bamboo – yet a pattern was evident here: these dwellings had not been laid out at random.

What had I expected? A mere jumble, perhaps, untidy heaps of people, piled high upon each other? That is after all, what the word 'rifugi' has come to mean. But what I saw was quite different from the picture in my mind's eye. Paths had been laid, the bādh *– that guarantor of island life – had been augmented; little plots of land had been enclosed with fences; fishing nets had been hung up to dry. There were men and women sitting outside their huts, repairing their nets and stringing their crab lines with bits of bait and bone.*

Such industry! Such diligence! Yet it was only a few weeks since they had come.

Taking in these sights, I felt the onrush of a strange, heady excitement: suddenly it dawned on me that I was watching the birth of something new, something hitherto unseen. This, I thought, is what Daniel Hamilton must have felt when he stood upon the deck of his launch and watched the mangroves being shorn from the islands. But between what was happening at Morichjhāpi and what Hamilton had done there was one vital aspect of difference: this was not one man's vision. This dream had been dreamt by the very people who were trying to make it real.

I could walk no more. I stood transfixed on the still-wet pathway, leaning on my umbrella while the wind snatched at my crumpled dhoti. *I felt something changing within me: how astonishing it was that I, an ageing, bookish schoolmaster, should live to see this, an experiment, imagined not by those with learning and power, but by those without!*

I felt all of existence swelling in my veins. Letting my umbrella drop, I flung back my head to open myself to the wind and the sun. It was as though in the course of one night I had cast away the emptiness I had so long held in my arms.

In great excitement, I went back to Kusum's door.

'What's the matter, Saar?' she said in alarm. 'Why are your clothes muddy, your face red? Where have you left your umbrella?'

'Never mind all that,' I said, impatiently. 'Tell me: who is in charge? Is there a committee? Are there leaders?'

'Yes, of course. Why?'

'I want to meet with them.'

'Why, Saar?'

'Because I want to have some part in what is happening here. I want to be of help.'

171

'Saar, if that's what you want, who am I to say no?'

The island, she said, had been divided into wards. People in charge of each of these wards took decisions and helped organize every essential activity.

'Take me to the head of your ward,' I said, and she led me to a door a short distance away.

The leader of the ward was a sharp, energetic man, no dreamer, and not someone to put up with trespasses on his time: in his demeanour I glimpsed the euphoric reticence of someone who knows that success is within reach. Clearly, he was busy, but when he heard I was a headmaster – although soon to be retired – he took the time to show me around. We walked along the newly cleared paths and he pointed out all that had been done in the weeks since they had first arrived. I was amazed, not just by what they had built but the care they had invested in creating organizations, institutions. They had set up their own government and taken a census – there were some thirty thousand people on the island already and there was space for many more. The island had been divided into five zones and each family of settlers had been given five acres of land. Yet, they had also recognized, shrewdly enough, that their enterprise could not succeed if they didn't have the support of their neighbours on the surrounding islands. With this in mind they had reserved one quarter of the island for people from other parts of the tide country. Hundreds of families had come flocking in.

At the end of the brief tour, I clasped my guide's hand: 'Destiny is on your side, comrade.'

He smiled and said, 'But still, we cannot succeed without help.'

It was clear at once that he was thinking of all the ways in which I might be of use to him. This impressed me. It was a good sign, I thought, that he was applying his mind in this practical way.

'I want to be of help,' I said. 'Tell me what I can do.'

'That depends,' he said. 'What's most important to us at this time is to mobilize public opinion, to bring pressure on the government, to get them to leave us alone. They're putting it out that we're destroying this place; they want people to think we're gangsters who've occupied this place by force. We need to let people know what we're doing and why we're here. We have to tell the world about all we've done and all we've achieved. Can you help us with this? Do you have contacts with the press in Kolkata?'

I didn't begrudge him his attitude; it seemed to me he was right to take this approach. 'There was a time once', I said regretfully, 'when I knew people in the press. But no more.'

'Then do you know anyone with power? Policemen? Forest Rangers? Politicians?'

'No,' I said. 'No one.'

'Then what can you do for us?' he said, growing peevish. 'Of what use could you be?'

What use indeed, was I? There are people in this world who are truly useful, who lead useful lives: Nilima for instance. But a schoolteacher such as me?

'There's only one thing I know to do,' I said. 'And that is to teach.'

'Teach?' I could see he was struggling to suppress a smile. 'What could you teach here?'

'I could teach your children about this place that you've come to: the tide country. I have time – I am soon to retire.'

He lost interest in me. 'Our children here have no time to waste,' he said. 'Most of them have to help their families find food to eat.' Then, after a little more thought, he added, 'however, if you can find pupils who're willing, then why should I prevent you? It's up to you: teach all you want.'

I went back to Kusum triumphantly and told her what had transpired. In evident alarm, she said, 'But whom will you teach, Saar?'

'Why?' I said. 'There's your son, Fokir. There must be others like him. Mustn't there?' A look of reluctance had come into her face, so I added, almost pleading: 'It wouldn't be every day. Maybe just for a little while, each week. I'll come over from Lusibari.'

'But, Saar,' she said, 'Fokir can't write nor read, and that's true of many of these children. What will you teach them?'

I hadn't given this matter any thought, but the answer came to me at once, I said, 'Kusum, I'll teach them to dream.'

Pursued

While the dolphin and its calf were foraging in the creek, Fokir was fighting hard to hold his boat steady in the adjoining channel. The water was flowing fast here and he was turning the boat around in circles so that Piya could keep the dolphins in view. Even though there was no wind, the water's surface was so densely marked with ripples and eddies that it seemed almost to be simmering as it flowed.

Having filled in six data sheets, Piya decided to measure the water's depth. She was in the bow, as usual, while Fokir was in the mid-section, turning rapidly from left to right as he dipped his oars alternately on either side of the boat. He happened to look up just as Piya was lowering her depth-sounder into the water. His eyes flared and he uttered a shout that made her freeze, with her wrist still submerged in the water. Pulling his oars into the boat, Fokir threw himself at Piya, diving across the length of the boat, snatching wildly at her wrist. Piya fell over backwards, and her arm snapped out of the water, cata-pulting the depth-sounder over the boat.

Suddenly the water boiled over and a pair of massive jaws came shooting out of the river, breaking the surface exactly where Piya's wrist had been a moment before. From the corner of one eye, Piya saw two sets of interlocking teeth making a snatching, twisting movement as they lunged at her still-extended arm: they passed so close that the hard tip of the snout grazed her elbow and the spray from the nostrils wetted her forearm. A second later the boat shook under the impact of a massive underwater blow: the shock was powerful enough to send the bilge water shooting up, out of the innards of the craft: there was a creaking sound and the boat tipped to such an angle that it seemed almost inevitable it would roll over. Piya's clipboard, which was lying at her feet, slipped into the water, and many of the plywood slats that covered the deck tumbled out, like falling dominoes.

Tutul who'd been sitting in the shade of the hood, curled himself into a ball and rolled forward to correct his balance. The boat righted itself, with a thump that threw up a curtain of water. A moment later there was another massive blow to its underside, somewhere near the stern. With the boat rolling wildly, Fokir rose to a kneeling position and took hold of one of his oars. Raising it above his head he turned it so that its head became a blade and brought it crashing down into the water. The oar hammered into the head of the crocodile just as it was surfacing to make another lunge and the force of the impact snapped shut the gaping jaws. The oar splintered and the blade broke from the handle and went cartwheeling across the water. The water bubbled again as the reptile sank out of sight: for a moment after its submersion a ghostly outline of its shape remained imprinted on the surface and Piya saw that it was almost as large as the boat.

In the meanwhile, Fokir had dropped to his haunches and seized a pair of oars. The current had already carried the boat several hundred metres from the creek where the dolphins had been foraging. Now, Fokir began to heave at the oars, turning the boat from one creek into another, labouring to lengthen the distance.

After some twenty minutes of furious rowing they came to an inlet that curved deep into the interior of a thickly forested island. Fokir kept the boat moving until they came to a spot where the boat was well sheltered from the currents of the main channel. Here, after dropping anchor, he tore off his drenched T-shirt and reached for a gamchha to wipe away the sweat that was pouring down his chest.

After he had caught his breath, he glanced at Piya and said, 'Lusibari?'

Piya was only too glad to assent. 'Yes,' she said. 'Let's head for Lusibari: it's time.'

PART TWO

The Flood: *Jowar*

Beginning Again

I had thought that on the way to Lusibari my face would lose the flush it had acquired in Morichjhãpi: the brisk air of the river would cool my skin and the rocking of Horen's boat would slow the pace of my heart. But no, exactly the opposite happened; with every turn a new vista seemed to open in front of me. I could not keep still. I put away my umbrella and stood up, opening my arms as if to embrace the wind. My dhoti *became a sail and I a mast, tugging the boat towards the horizon.*

'Saar!' cried Horen. 'Sit down; the boat will roll over – you'll fall.'

'Horen, you are the best of boatmen. You'll find a way of keeping us afloat.'

'But Saar,' said Horen. 'What's the matter with you today? You don't seem like your old self.'

'You are right, Horen: I am not my old self any more. And it's you who's responsible.'

'And how's that, Saar?'

'Wasn't it you who took me to Morichjhãpi?'

'No, Saar. It was the storm.'

Forever modest, our Horen. 'All right, then. It was the storm.' I laughed. 'It was the storm that showed me that a man can be transformed even in retirement; that he can begin again.'

'Begin what, Saar?'

'Begin a new life, Horen, a new life. The next time we come to Morichjhãpi my students will be waiting. I'll teach as I have never taught before.'

'And what will you teach them, Saar? What will the lesson be?'

'Why, I'll tell them about—'

179

And what indeed was I to tell them about? Expert boatman that he was, Horen had found a way of spilling the wind from my sails.

I sat down: this was a matter that needed careful thought.

I would start, I decided, with magical tales of the kind to which these children were accustomed. 'Tell me, children,' I would begin. 'What do our old myths have in common with geology?'

This would catch their interest. Their eyes would narrow, they would puzzle over my question for a minute or two before giving up.

'Tell us, Saar.'

'Goddesses, children,' I would announce in triumph. 'Don't you see: goddesses are what they have in common.'

They would look at each and whisper, 'Is he teasing? Is this a joke?' Presently a small, hesitant voice would speak up: 'But, Saar, what do you mean?'

'Think about it,' I would say, 'and you'll see: it's not just the goddesses – there's a lot more in common between myth and geology. Look at the size of their heroes, how immense they are – heavenly deities on the one hand, and on the other, the titanic stirrings of the earth itself – both equally otherworldly, equally remote from us. Then there is the way in which the plots go round and around in both kinds of story, so that every episode is both a beginning and an end and every outcome leads to others. And then, of course, there is the scale of time – yugas and epochs, Kaliyuga and the Quaternary. And yet – mind this! – in both, these vast durations are telescoped in such a way as to permit the telling of a story.'

'How, Saar, how? Tell us one of these stories.'

And so I would begin.

Maybe I would start with the story of Vishnu, in his incarnation as a divine dwarf, measuring out the universe in three giant strides: I would tell them about the god's misstep and how an errant toenail on one of his feet created a tiny scratch on the fabric of creation. It was this pore, I'd tell them, that became the source of the immortal and eternal Ganga that flows through the heavens, washing away the sins of the universe – this was the stream that would become the greatest of all the earth's rivers.

'The Ganga? Greatest of all rivers?' They would rise up, provoked beyond endurance by my mischievous phrasings. 'But, Saar, many rivers are longer than our Ganga: the Nile, the Amazon, the Mississippi, the Yangtze.'

And then I would produce my secret treasure, a present sent to me by a former student – a map of the sea-floor, made by geologists. In the reversed

180

relief of this map they would see with their own eyes that the Ganga does not come to an end after it flows into the Bay of Bengal. It joins with the Brahmaputra in scouring a long, clearly marked channel along the floor of the bay. The map would reveal to them what is otherwise hidden underwater: and this is that the course of this underwater river exceeds by far the length of the river's overland channel.

'Look comrades, look,' I would say. 'This map shows that in geology, as in myth, there is a visible Ganga and a hidden Ganga: one flows on land and one beneath the water. Put them together and you have what is by far the greatest of the earth's rivers.'

And, to follow this, I decided, I'd tell them the story of the Greek goddess who was the Ganga's mother. I would take them back to the deep, deep time of geology and I would show them that where the Ganga now runs there was once a coastline – a shore that marked the southern extremity of the Asian landmass. India was far, far away then, in another hemisphere. It was attached to Australia and Antarctica. I would show them the sea and tell them about its name, Tethys, in Greek mythology the wife of Oceanus. There were no Himalayas then and no holy rivers, no Jamuna, no Ganga, no Saraswati, no Brahmaputra. And since there were no rivers, there was also no delta, no flood plain, no silting, no mangroves – no Bengal, in other words. The green coastline of Tamilnadu and Andhra Pradesh was then a frozen waste with ice running to depths of sixty metres. Where the southern shore of the Ganges now lies was a length of frozen beach that dipped gently into the waters of the now-vanished Tethys Sea.

I would show them how it happened that India broke away suddenly, a hundred and forty million years ago, and began its journey from Antarctica to the north. They would see how their subcontinent had moved, at a speed no other landmass had ever attained before; they would see how its weight forced the rise of the Himalayas; they would see the Ganga emerging, as a brook on a rising hill. In front of their eyes they would see how, as India travelled, the Tethys shrank, how she grew thinner and thinner as the channel closed. They would watch as she withered – the two landmasses finally colliding at the expense of the mother ocean: they would see her dying but they would shed no tears, for they would see also the birth of the two rivers in which her memory would be preserved, her twin children – the Indus and the Ganga.

'And do you know how you can tell that the Sindhu and the Ganga were once conjoined?'

'How, Saar?'

'Because of the 'shushuk' – the river dolphin. This creature of the sea was the legacy left to the twins by their mother, Tethys. The rivers nurtured it and made it their own. Nowhere else in the world is the shushuk to be found, but in the twin rivers, the Ganga and the Sindhu.'

And if their interest wandered, I would tell them, in the end, a love story, about a king called Shantanu and how, on the banks of the great river, he spotted a woman of dazzling beauty. This was, of course, none other than the Ganga herself, but the king had no knowledge of this. On the banks of rivers even the most temperate men lose their heads. King Shantanu fell in love, wholly, madly; he promised the river goddess that he would grant her whatever she wanted, if she chose even to drown her own children he would not stand in her way.

A single besotted moment beside a river, and thus was launched a parva of the Mahabharata.

Why should a schoolmaster deny that which even the old mythmakers acknowledge? Love flows deep in rivers.

'Children, this is the lesson; hear it in the words of the Poet:

"To sing about someone you love is one thing; but, oh, the blood's hidden guilty river-god is something else".'

Landfall

At the start, with the currents flowing in the wrong direction and Fokir labouring alone at the oars, the going was painfully slow. Piya was not surprised when after an hour of rowing she checked the boat's position on the GPS and found that they had travelled only three kilometres. It struck her then, belatedly, that Fokir might have yet another pair of oars. On signalling the question, she was glad to discover he did: they were stored underfoot, in the boat's bilges.

The oars were no less crudely crafted than the boat itself – they consisted of two oblong pieces of wood nailed awkwardly to a couple of shorn mangrove branches. There were no oarlocks on the gunwales and the handles had to be engaged in little protrusions of wood. When Piya dipped the oars in the water the current twisted them around and nearly tore them from her grip. It took her a while to grow used to the feel of them but with two of them rowing the pace quickened.

As the hours wore on, Piya found it increasingly difficult to keep going: a crop of blisters appeared on her hands and the creases of her face and neck seemed to be marbled with veins of salt. Towards sunset she pulled in her oars and yielded finally to the temptation to ask how much longer it would be before they arrived at their destination. 'Lusibari?'

Fokir had been rowing almost without a break since morning but she was still unable to see any signs of tiredness in him. Now, pausing briefly to glance over his shoulder, he pointed to a tongue of land just visible in the distance: its deforested shore-line marked it out from the other islands in the vicinity. It was heartening to have the place finally within sight, but Piya knew it would be a while yet before they made landfall, and she was right.

By the time they had moored the boat and collected their things, the sun had set and darkness was closing in. Fokir picked up one of her backpacks while she took the other and they set off in single file, with Tutul in the lead. Piya's attention was focused on keeping the two of them in sight and she took nothing in of the surroundings until Fokir came suddenly to a halt and pointed ahead. 'Mashima,' he said, and she saw he was gesturing towards a flight of steps that led up to a closed door.

Was this it? She was wondering what to do next when he lifted the backpack off his shoulders and handed it to her. Then both he and the boy withdrew a little – Fokir with his catch of crabs rolled in a length of netting, and Tutul with a bundle of clothes balanced on his head. Fokir motioned to her again to step up to the door and Piya sensed now, from the incline of their bodies that they were poised to turn away, leaving her where she was. Suddenly she was in the grip of a kind of panic. 'Wait!' she cried. 'Where are you going?'

She had envisaged many possibilities but not this – not that they would just walk away with nothing said, not even a goodbye. Nor had it occurred to her that the prospect of their departure would result in such an icy feeling of abandonment.

'Wait. Just a minute.'

Just then a generator was switched on, somewhere in the distance, and a flood of light came pouring out of a nearby window. Piya's eyes had grown unaccustomed to electricity and she was momentarily blinded by the bright, flat light. Blinking, she dug her fists into her face, and when she opened her eyes again they were gone, both of them, Fokir and the boy.

She remembered that she hadn't given Fokir any money for bringing her here. How was she ever to find him again? She didn't know where he lived – she didn't even know his full name. Cupping her hands around her mouth, she shouted into the darkness, 'Fokir!'

'*Ké?*' The answer was spoken in a woman's voice, and it came

184

not from ahead of her, but from behind. Then the door swung open and Piya found herself facing a small, elderly woman with wispy hair and gold-rimmed eyeglasses. '*Ké?*'

Collecting herself quickly, Piya went up the steps. 'Please excuse me. I don't know if I've come to the right place. I'm looking for Mashima.' She said this in a rush, not knowing whether she would be understood or not.

There was an awkward moment during which Piya felt herself to be subjected to a shrewd and searching scrutiny: the gold-rimmed glasses rose and fell as they took in her salt-streaked face and muddy cotton pants. Then, greatly to her relief, she heard a voice say, in soft, fluting English, 'You are indeed in the right place. But tell me – who are you? Do I know you?'

'No,' said Piya. 'You don't know me. My name is Piyali Roy. I met your nephew on the train.'

'Kanai?'

'Yes. Kanai. He invited me to visit.'

'Well, do come in. Kanai will be down any minute.' She stepped aside to let Piya through. 'How did you find your way here? Surely you didn't come alone?'

'No,' said Piya. 'I'd never have been able to find you on my own.'

'Then who brought you? I didn't see anyone outside.'

'They left just as you opened the door—' Before Piya could say any more, the door swung open and Kanai stepped in. He stood in the doorway squinting in surprise. 'Piya? Is that you?'

'Yes. It is.'

'So you made it after all?'

'That's right.'

'Good!' He gave her a broad smile. He hadn't expected to see her quite so soon and was flattered as well as pleased: it seemed like a good augury. 'Looks like you had an eventful trip.' He looked her up and down, taking in her mud-splattered clothes. 'How did you get here?'

'In a rowboat.'

'A rowboat?'

'Yes,' said Piya. 'You see, I had an accident soon after I met you.'

185

In a few short sentences, Piya told them about the events that had led to her fall from the launch. 'And then the fisherman jumped in after me – I don't know what would have happened if he hadn't. I'd swallowed a lot of water but he managed to get me back into the boat. But after that I decided it wasn't safe to get back in the launch with that guard. So I took a chance and asked the fisherman if he knew Mashima. It turned out he did so I said I'd pay him if he brought me to Lusibari. We would have been here sooner, except that we had some unexpected encounters.'

'With what?'

'First we met up with some dolphins,' said Piya. 'Then this morning we had a brush with a crocodile.'

'Upon my word!' said Nilima. 'No injuries I hope.'

'No,' said Piya. 'But there could have been. He fought it off with an oar – it was incredible.'

'My goodness!' said Nilima. 'And who was this man? Did he tell you his name?'

'Sure,' said Piya. 'His name's Fokir.'

'Fokir?' cried Nilima. 'Do you mean Fokir Mondol by any chance?'

'He didn't tell me his surname.'

'Was there a little boy with him?' said Nilima.

'Yes, there was,' said Piya. 'Tutul.'

'That's him.' Nilima directed a glance in Kanai's direction. 'So that's where he was.'

'Were people looking for them?'

'Yes,' said Kanai. 'Fokir's wife, Moyna, works at the hospital here and she's been half out of her mind with worry.'

'Oh?' said Piya guiltily. 'It's probably my fault. I kept them out there longer than they'd have stayed.'

'Well,' said Nilima pursing her lips. 'As long as they're back now – no harm done.'

'I hope not,' said Piya. 'I'd hate to think I'd gotten him into some kind of trouble. He saved my life, you know. And it wasn't just that – he also led me straight to a pod of dolphins.'

'Is that so?' said Kanai, in surprise. 'But how did he even know you were looking for dolphins?'

'I showed him a picture, a flashcard,' Piya said. 'And that was all it took. He led me straight to the dolphins. In a way, that fall was the luckiest thing that could have happened to me – I'd never have found the dolphins on my own. I really need to see him again. I've got to pay him, for one thing.'

'Don't worry about that,' said Nilima. 'They live nearby – in the Trust's quarters. Kanai will take you there tomorrow morning.'

Piya turned on him eagerly. 'It'd be great if you could.'

'Yes,' said Kanai. 'Of course I will. But that can wait. For the time being, we've got to get you settled so you can rest and change up.'

Piya had given no thought to what would happen next and now, with the euphoria of her arrival beginning to fade, she was suddenly aware of a weighty backlog of fatigue. 'Settled?' she said, looking around herself vaguely. 'Where?'

'Here,' said Kanai. 'Or rather, upstairs.'

She was discomfited to think he had assumed she would stay with him. 'Are there any hotels around here?'

'I'm afraid not,' said Nilima. 'But there's a guest house upstairs, with three empty rooms. You're very welcome to stay there. There's no one in it but Kanai. And if he bothers you, just come down and let me know.'

Piya smiled. 'I'll be fine – I know how to look after myself.' But she was glad the invitation had come from Mashima: some- how, it made it easier to accept. 'Thank you,' she said. 'I'd really appreciate a good night's rest. Are you sure I won't be in your way if I stay a couple of days?'

'Stay as long as you like,' said Nilima. 'Kanai will show you around.'

'Come on,' said Kanai, reaching for one of her backpacks. 'It's this way.' Kanai led her upstairs and, after pointing out the kitchen and bathroom, unlatched a door and switched on a neon light. The bedroom was no different from the one he had occupied himself: there were two narrow beds in it, each equipped with its own mosquito net. The replastered cement walls were blotched with damp spots and cracks, left behind by the last monsoon. On the far side was a barred window that looked out over the rice-fields that adjoined the Trust's compound.

'Will this do?' said Kanai, depositing her backpack on one of the beds.

Piya stepped in and looked around. Although bare in appearance, the room was comfortable enough: the sheets looked clean and there was even a towel lying neatly folded at the foot of the bed. By the window stood a desk and a straight-backed chair. The door, she was glad to note, had a sturdy latch that could be attached from the inside.

'This is more than I expected,' Piya said. 'Thanks so much.'

Kanai shook his head. 'You don't have to thank me,' he said. 'It'll be nice to have you here. I was getting a bit lonely on my own.'

She didn't know what to make of this, so she gave him a neutral smile.

'Anyway, I'll leave you to settle in,' said Kanai. 'I'll be upstairs in my uncle's study. Knock if you need anything.'

A Feast

Any excuse to return to Morichjhāpi would have sufficed, but none could have been better than that which Horen presented me. I had, in the meanwhile, arranged for his son's admission, so it happened that I often ran into him in the school's vicinity.

'Saar,' he said, one day, 'I have news from Morichjhāpi. There's to be a big feast there; Kusum said you should come.'

I was astonished. 'A feast? What kind of feast?'

'They've invited many people from Kolkata – writers, intellectuals, journalists. They want to tell them about the island and all they have achieved.'

This explained everything: once again I was impressed by the acumen of the settlers' leadership. Clearly, they had decided their best defence was to enlist the support of public opinion and this was to be a step in that direction. Of course I had to go. Horen said we would leave in the morning and I told him I would be ready.

When I got back home, Nilima took one look at me and said, 'What's the matter? Why've you got that look on your face?'

Why was it I'd never spoken to Nilima about Morichjhāpi before? Perhaps, in my heart, I knew she would not share my enthusiasm; perhaps I knew she would see my excitement about their project as a betrayal of her own efforts in Lusibari. In any event, these fears were soon confirmed. I described as best I could, the drama of the settlers' arrival; I told her about the quest that had brought them, from their banishment in central India, to the edge of the tide country; I explained their plans, their programme for creating a new future for themselves, of their determination to create a new land in which to live.

To my surprise, I found she already knew about the settlers and their

189

arrival: she had heard about it in Kolkata, from bureaucrats and politicians. The government, she said, saw these people as squatters and land-grabbers; there was going to be trouble; they would not be allowed to remain.

'Nirmal,' she said, 'I don't want you going there. It's not that I have anything against the settlers; I just don't want you to be in harm's way.'

I realized at that moment, with a great sense of sadness, that from now on, my relationship with Morichjhāpi would have to be conducted in secret. I had intended to tell her about the feast of the next day but now said nothing. Knowing Nilima as I did, I was sure she would find a way to prevent me from going.

Yet, I would not have lied had she not pressed me. She saw me packing my jhola and asked if I were planning to go somewhere.

'Yes, I have to leave tomorrow morning.' I made up a story about going to visit a school in Mollakhali. I knew she didn't believe me, for she looked at me closely and said, 'And who are you going with?'

'Horen,' I said.

'Oh?' she said. 'Horen?' And the inflection of her voice as she said this was enough to make me fear for the safety of my secret.

Thus was sowed the seed of our mistrust.

But to the feast I went – and it proved to be one of the strangest days of my existence. It was as if, on the eve of my retirement, I had been presented with a glimpse of the life I might have led if I had stayed in Kolkata. The guests who had been brought in from the city were exactly the people I would have known: journalists, photographers, well-known authors; there was the novelist Sunil Gangopadhyaya and the journalist Jyotirmoy Datta. Some of them I even recognized for I had known them back in the university. One of them – we used to call him Khokon in those days – had once been a friend as well as a comrade. I observed him from a distance, marvelling at how well he looked, at the bright effulgence of his face and the raven-black hue of his hair. Would this have been me, had I stayed on, living the literary life?

I became aware, as never before, of all my unacknowledged regrets.

I hung back, following at a distance, as the settlers' leaders led the guests on a tour of the island. There was much to show – even in the short while I had been away, there had been many additions, many improvements. Saltpans had been created, tubewells had been planted, water had been dammed for the rearing of fish, a bakery had started up, boat-builders had set up workshops, a pottery had been founded as well as an ironsmith's shop; there were people making boats while others were fashioning nets and crablines; little marketplaces, where all kinds of goods were being sold, had sprung up. All this in the space of a few months! It was an astonishing spectacle – as though an entire civilization had sprouted suddenly in the mud.

After all this came the feast, done in the old style and artfully arranged, with banana leaves set out on the earth and the guests seated in the shade of murmuring trees. Among those who were serving I spotted Kusum, who showed me the massive dekchis in which the food had been cooked. There were gigantic prawns, both golda and badga, and a fantastic variety of fish: tangra, ilish, parshey, puti, bhetki, rui, chitol.

I was amazed; knowing that many of the settlers went hungry, I couldn't understand how this show of plenty had been arranged.

'Where did all this come from?' I said to Kusum.

'Everyone contributed what they could,' she said. 'But there was not much to buy – only the rice. The rest came from the rivers. Since yesterday, we've all been out with nets and lines, even the children.' She pointed proudly to the parshey: 'Fokir caught six of those this morning.'

My admiration was boundless. What better way to win the hearts of these city-people than by feeding them freshly caught fish? How well these settlers understood their guests!

Kusum urged me to sit down and start eating. But I could not bring myself to sit with the guests: I was not of their number. 'No, Kusum,' I said. 'It's better you feed those who can spread the word. This is precious food – it would be wasted on me.' I hung back, in the shade of the trees and from time to time Fokir or Kusum would bring me a few morsels wrapped in a banana leaf.

It was soon evident that the occasion had served its purpose: the guests were undeniably impressed. Speeches were made, extolling the achievements of the settlers. It was universally agreed that the significance of Morichjhāpi extended far beyond the island itself. Was it possible, even, that in Morichjhāpi had been planted the seeds of what might become if not a Dalit nation, then at least a safe haven, a place of true freedom for the country's most oppressed?

When the day was almost at an end, I went up to Khokon, the writer I had once known, and stood in his line of sight, without speaking. He glanced at me without recognition and went on with his conversation. In a while, I tapped his elbow: 'Eijé; here, Khokon?'

He was annoyed at being so familiarly addressed by a stranger. 'And who, moshai, might you be?' he said.

When I told him who I was, his mouth fell open and his tongue began to flop around inside it like a netted fish. 'You?' he said at last. 'You?'

I said, 'Yes. It's me.'

'You haven't been heard from in so long, everybody thought—'

'That I was dead? As you see, I'm not.'

On the brink of saying, 'It would have been better so,' he cut himself short. 'But what have you been doing all these years? Where have you been?'

I felt then as if I had been called upon to justify the entirety of my existence, to account for the years I had spent in Lusibari.

But what I had to say in answer was very modest: 'I've been doing schoolmasteri, in a place not far from here.'

'And your writing?'

I shrugged. What was there to say? 'It's a good thing I stopped,' I said. 'My work would have been put to shame by yours.'

Writers! How they love flattery. He put his arm around my shoulder, and led me off, indulgently lowering his voice, as an elder brother might with a younger. 'So, Nirmal, tell me, how did you get mixed up with these settlers?'

'I know a couple of them,' I said. 'Now that I'm almost retired, I'm thinking of doing some teaching here.'

'Here?' he said dubiously. 'But the problem is, they may not be allowed to stay.'

'They're here already,' I said. 'How could they be evicted now? There would be bloodshed.'

He laughed. 'My friend, have you forgotten what we used to say in the old days?'

'What?'

'You can't make an omelette without breaking eggs.'

He laughed, in the cynical way of those who, having never believed in the ideals they once professed, imagine that no one else had done so either. I was tempted to tell him what I thought of him, but it struck me, with great force that I had no business to be self-righteous about these matters. Nilima – she had achieved a great deal. What had I done? What *was the work of my life? I tried to find an answer but none would come to mind.*

It is afternoon now and Horen and Kusum have gone to see if they can find some fish. Fokir is sitting here with a crabline, what is called a 'don' in the tide country, and as I watch him play with it, my heart spills over. There is so much to say, so much in my head, so much that will remain unsaid: oh those wasted years, that wasted time. I think of Rilke, going for years without writing a word and then, producing in a matter of weeks, in a castle besieged by the sea, The Duino Elegies. *Even silence is preparation. As the minutes pass, it seems to me I can see every object in the tide country with a blinding brightness and clarity. I want to say to Fokir, 'Do you know that every* don *has one thousand morsels of bait tied at gaps of three arms' lengths each? That each line is thus equal to the length of three thousand arms?'*

How better can we praise the world but by doing what the Poet would have us do: by speaking of potters and ropemakers, by telling of

> *'some simple thing shaped for generation after generation*
> *until it lives in our hands and in our eyes, and it's ours.'*

Catching up

After her shower, Piya sank into the chair by her window and found she could not get up again. After days of squatting and sitting cross-legged it was strange to have a support behind your back and to be able to swing your legs freely, without worrying about tipping over. She could still feel the rocking motion of the boat in her limbs and the sighing of the wind, blowing through the mangroves, was still in her ears.

The feeling of being back on the boat suddenly brought back the terror she had felt that morning. It had happened so recently that the sensations seemed still to be present, unprocessed, in her mind – they had not yet been absorbed as memory. She saw once again the wrenching, twisting motion of the reptile's head as its jaws closed over the spot where her wrist had been: it was as if it had been so certain of its aim, so sure of seizing her arm, that it had already launched into the movement that would drag her out of the boat and into the water. She imagined the tug that would have pulled her below the surface and the momentary release before the jaws closed again, around her midsection, pulling her into those swift, eerily glowing depths where the sunlight had no orientation and there was neither up nor down. She remembered her panic in falling from the launch and it made her think of the numbing horror that would accompany the awareness that you were imprisoned in a grasp from which there was no escape. The overlapping of these images created a montage of such vividness that her hands began to tremble: and now, with Fokir absent, the experience seemed even more frightening than it had been at the time.

She forced herself to sit up and look out of the window. The moon was not up yet and it was dark outside. She could not see much except the outlines of a few coconut palms, and beyond that a striated emptiness that suggested a closely shorn field. Then she caught the sound of a conversation, in Bengali, drifting in from the front of the house: a woman's voice was counterpointed against Kanai's deep baritone.

She made herself get up and go downstairs. Kanai was standing by the door, with a lantern in his hands, talking to a woman in a red sari. The woman was facing away from her, but at Piya's approach she looked over her shoulder so that one side of her face was suddenly brightened by the glow of Kanai's lantern. Piya saw that she was about her own age, with a full figure, a wide mouth and large, luminous eyes. Between her eyebrows was a large red *bindi* and a streak of vermilion *shindur* ran like a wound through the parting in her shiny black hair.

'Ah, there you are, Piya!' cried Kanai, in English, and from the overly spirited sound of his voice Piya guessed they had been talking about her. The woman's eyes were steady and clear as they looked her over, and Piya had the distinct impression that she had, somehow, been recognized and was being assessed. Then, with an abruptness no less unsettling than the frankness of her scrutiny, the woman looked away. Handing Kanai a stainless-steel container, she headed down the steps and vanished into the night-shrouded compound.

'Who was that?' said Piya to Kanai.

'Didn't I tell you?' said Kanai. 'That was Moyna, Fokir's wife.'

'Oh?'

Moyna was so unlike the wife she had envisaged for Fokir, that it took Piya a moment to absorb this. Presently she added, 'I should have guessed.'

'Guessed what?'

'That she was his wife. Her son has her eyes.'

'Does he?'

'Yes,' said Piya. 'And what was she doing here?'

'She was delivering this tiffin carrier.' Kanai held up a set of stainless-steel containers joined by a brace. 'Our dinner's inside. Moyna's brought it for us from the hospital's kitchen.'

195

Piya's attention drifted away from Kanai to the woman who was Fokir's wife. She felt a twinge of envy at the thought of her going back to Fokir and Tutul, while she returned to the absence upstairs. This embarrassed her and to cover up she smiled at Kanai and said briskly, 'She isn't at all like I expected.'

'No?'

'No.' Now again Piya found herself fumbling for the right words. 'I mean, she's very attractive, isn't she?'

'You think so?'

Piya knew she should drop the matter – but instead, she went on, as if she were picking at a scab. 'Yes,' she said. 'I think she's quite beautiful in a way.'

'You're right,' said Kanai smoothly, recovering himself. 'She's very striking. But she's more than that: in her own way, she's an unusual and remarkable woman.'

'Really? How?'

'Just think of the life she's led,' said Kanai. 'She's struggled to educate herself, against heavy odds. Now she's well on her way to becoming a nurse. She knows what she wants – for herself and her family – and nothing is going to keep her from pursuing it. She's ambitious, she's tough and she's going to go a long way.'

There was an edge to his voice that implied a comparison of some kind and Piya could not help wondering how she, Piya, would fare by these lights – she who'd never had much ambition and had never had to battle her circumstances in order to get her education? In Kanai's eyes, she knew, she must appear hopelessly soft and spoilt, a kind of stereotype. And she could not blame him for seeing her in this way – any more than she could blame herself for seeing him as an example of a certain kind of Indian male, overbearing, vain, self-centred – yet, for all that, not unlikeable.

Piya switched to a more neutral subject. 'And are Moyna and Fokir from around here?' she said conversationally. 'From Lusibari?'

'No,' said Kanai. 'Both she and Fokir are from another island, quite a long way off. It's called Satjelia.'

'Then how come they live here?'

'Partly because she's training to be a nurse and partly because she's trying to give her son an education. That's why she was so upset that Fokir had taken him away on this fishing trip of his.'

'Does she know I was on the boat with them these last couple of days?'

'Yes,' said Kanai. 'She knows all about it – about the guard taking the money, about your fall and about Fokir diving in after you. She knows about the crocodile – the little boy told her everything.'

Piya noticed that the mention of the boy: did this mean Fokir hadn't said much about the trip? Or that he had given her a different account? She wondered if Kanai knew the answer to either of these questions, but she could not bring herself to ask. Instead, she said, 'Moyna must be curious about what I'm doing here.'

'She certainly is,' said Kanai. 'She asked me about it and I explained you're a scientist. She was very impressed.'

'Why?'

'As you can imagine,' said Kanai, 'she has a great respect for education.'

'Did you tell her we're going to visit them tomorrow?'

'Yes,' said Kanai. 'They'll be expecting us.'

They were back upstairs now, in the Guest House, and Kanai had placed the *tiffin* carrier on the dining table. 'I hope you're hungry,' he said, taking the containers apart. 'She always brings too much food so there should be plenty for both of us. Let's see what we have here – there's rice, daal, fish curry, chorchori, begun bhaja. What would you like to start with?'

She gave the containers a look of dubious appraisal. 'I hope you won't be offended,' she said, 'but I don't think I want any of that. I have to be very careful about what I eat.'

'What about some rice, then?' said Kanai. 'You could have some of that, couldn't you?'

She nodded. 'Yes. I guess I could – if it's just plain white rice.'

'There you are,' he said, ladling a few spoonfuls of rice on her plate. Rolling up his sleeves, he gave her a spoon and then dug into the rice on his own plate with his hands.

During dinner, Kanai talked at length about Lusibari. He told

197

Piya about Daniel Hamilton, the settling of the island and of the circumstances that had led to Nirmal and Nilima's arrival. He seemed so knowledgeable that Piya remarked at last, 'It sounds like you've spent a lot of time here? But you haven't, have you?'

He was quick to confirm this. 'Oh, no. I only came once as a boy. To be honest, I'm surprised by how vividly I still remember the place – especially considering it was a kind of punishment.'

'Why are you surprised?'

He shrugged. 'I'm not the kind of person who dwells on the past,' he said. 'I like to look ahead.'

'But we're in the present now, aren't we?' she said with a smile. 'Even here, in Lusibari?'

'Oh, no,' he said emphatically. 'For me Lusibari will always be a part of the past.'

Piya had finished her rice, so she rose from the table and started clearing away the plates. This seemed to fluster Kanai.

'Sit down,' he said. 'You can leave those for Moyna.'

'I can do them just as well as she can,' said Piya.

Kanai shrugged. 'All right, then.'

As she was rinsing her plate, Piya said, 'Here you are, putting me up, feeding me and everything. And I feel like I know nothing about you – beyond your name that is.'

'Is that so?' Kanai gave a startled laugh. 'I wonder how that could have happened? I'm not known for being unusually reticent.'

'It's true, though,' she said. 'I don't even know where you live.'

'That's easily remedied,' he said. 'I live in New Delhi. I'm forty-two and I'm single most of the time.'

'Oh?' Piya was quick to turn the conversation in a less personal direction. 'And you're a translator, right? That's one thing you did tell me.'

'That's right,' said Kanai. 'I'm an interpreter and translator by profession – although right now I'm more of a businessman than anything else. I started a company some years ago when I discovered a shortage of language professionals in New Delhi. Now I provide translators for all kinds of organizations: businesses, embassies, the media, aid organizations – in short, anyone who can pay.'

'And is there much of a demand?'

'Oh, yes,' He nodded vigorously. 'New Delhi's become one of the world's leading conference cities and media centres; there's always something happening. I can barely keep up. The business just seems to keep growing and growing. Recently we started a speech-training operation, to do accent modification for people who work in call centres. It's become the fastest-growing part of the business.'

The idea that the currency of language could be used to build a business came as a surprise to Piya. 'So I guess you know many languages yourself, right?'

'Six,' he said immediately, with a grin. 'Hindi, Urdu and Bengali are my mainstays nowadays. And then there's English, of course. But I have two others I fall back on from time to time: French and Arabic.'

She was intrigued by the odd combination: 'French and Arabic! How did you come by those?'

'Scholarships,' he said with a smile. 'I always had a head for languages and, as a student, I used to frequent the Alliance Française in Calcutta. One thing led to another and I won a *bourse*. While I was in Paris an opportunity turned up to learn Arabic in Tunisia. I seized it and have never looked back.'

Raising a hand, Piya pinched the silver stud in her right ear, in a gesture that was childlike in its unselfconsciousness yet adult in its grace. 'Did you know then that translation would be your profession?'

'Oh no,' he said. 'Not at all. When I was your age I was like any other Calcutta college student – my mind was full of poetry. At the start of my career, I wanted to translate Jibanananda into Arabic and Adonis into Bangla.'

'And what happened?'

He breathed a theatrical sigh. 'To put it briefly,' he said, 'I quickly discovered that while both Bengali and Arabic possess riches beyond accounting, in neither is it possible to earn a living by translating literature alone. Rich Arabs have no interest in Bengali poetry and as for rich Bengalis, it doesn't matter what they want – there aren't enough of them to make a difference anyway. So at a certain point I reconciled myself to my fate and turned my hand to commerce. And I have to say I was lucky to get into it when I did: there's a lot going on in India right now and it's exciting to be a part of it.'

Piya recalled the stories her father had told her about the country he had left: it was a place where there were only two makes of car and where middle-class life was ruled by a hankering for all things foreign. She could tell that the world Kanai inhabited was as distant from the India of her father's memories as it was from Lusibari and the tide country.

'Do you ever feel you might want to translate literature again?' she said.

'Sometimes,' he replied. 'But not often. On the whole, I have to admit I like running an office; I like knowing I'm giving people work, paying salaries, employing students with otherwise useless degrees. And, let's face it, I like the money and the comfort. New Delhi is a good place for a single man with some money. I get to meet lots of interesting women.'

This took Piya by surprise and for a moment she was not sure of how to respond. She was standing at the basin, stacking the dishes she had just washed. She put away the last plate and yawned, raising a hand to cover her mouth.

'Sorry.'

He was immediately solicitous. 'You must be tired – after everything you've been through?'

'I'm exhausted. I think I've got to go to bed.'

'Already?' He forced a smile, although it was clear he was disappointed. 'Of course. You've had a long day. Did I tell you that the electricity would be switched off in an hour or so? Be sure to keep a candle with you.'

'I'll be asleep long before that.'

'Good, I hope you get a good night's rest. And if you need anything, just come up and knock: I'll be up on the roof, in my uncle's study.'

Storms

I would have gone back to Morichjhãpi the very next week but was prevented by all the usual procedures and ceremonies that accompany a schoolmaster's retirement. At the end, however, it was all over and I was officially reckoned a man who had reached the completion of his working life.

A few days later Horen knocked on my study door. 'Saar!'

'I've just come from the market at Kumirmari,' he said. 'I met Kusum there and she insisted I bring her here.'

'Here!' I said with a start. 'To Lusibari? But why?'

'To meet with Mashima. The Morichjhãpi people want to ask Mashima for help.'

I understood at once: this too was a part of the settlers' efforts to enlist support. Yet I could have told them that in this instance it was unlikely to bear fruit.

'Horen, you should have stopped Kusum from coming,' I said. 'It'll serve no purpose for her to meet with Nilima.'

'I did tell her, Saar. But she insisted.'

'So where is she now?'

'She's downstairs, Saar, waiting to see Mashima. But look who I've brought upstairs.' He stepped aside and I saw now that Fokir had been lurking behind him all this while. 'I've got to go to the market, Saar, so I'll just leave him here with you.' With that he went bounding down the stairs, leaving me alone with the five-year-old.

As a schoolteacher I was accustomed to dealing with children in the plural. Never having had a child of my own, I was unused to coping with them in the singular. Now, subjected to the scrutiny of a lone pair of wide-open, five-year-old eyes, I forgot everything I had planned to say.

201

In a near panic I led the boy across the roof and pointed to the Bidya's mohona.

'Look, comrade,' I said. 'Look. Follow your eyes and tell me. What do you see?'

I suppose, he was asking himself what I wanted. After looking this way and that he said at last, 'I see the bãdh, Saar.'

'The bãdh? Yes, of course, the bãdh.'

This was not the answer I had expected but I fell upon it with inexpressible relief. For the bãdh is not just the guarantor of human life on our island; it is also our abacus and archive, our library of stories. So long as I had the bãdh in sight I knew I would not lack for something to say.

'Go on, comrade; look again; look carefully. Let's see if you can pick out the spots where the embankment has been repaired. For each such repair I'll give you a story.'

Fokir lifted a hand to point. 'What happened there, Saar?'

'Ah, there. That breach happened twenty years ago, and it was neither storm nor flood that caused it. It was made by a man who wanted to settle a score with the family who lived next door to his. In the depths of the night he made a hole in the dyke, thinking to drown his neighbour's fields. It never entered his mind to think that he was doing just as much harm to himself as to his enemy. That's why neither family lives here any more – for ten years afterwards nothing grew on their fields.'

'And there, Saar? What happened there?'

'That one began simply enough, with an exceptionally high tide, a 'kotal gon' that came spilling over the top. The contract for the repairs was given to a man who was the brother-in-law of the head of the Panchayat. He swore he would fix it so that never again would a drop of water leak through. But they found later that the contractor had put in only half the materials he had been paid for. The profits had been shared by many different brothers-in-law.'

'And over there, Saar?'

Even storytellers know that discretion is sometimes a wiser course than valour. 'As for that one, comrade, I had better not tell you too much. Do you see the people who live there, in those dwellings that run beside the embankment? It happened once that the people of that 'para' had voted for the wrong party. So when the other party came to power they decided to settle scores. Their way of doing it was to make a hole in the bãdh.

202

Of such things, my friend, are politicians made, but let's not dwell on this too much – it may not be good for our health. Look there, instead; follow my finger.'

I pointed him in a direction where a kilometre length of the embankment had been beaten down, in the 1930s, by a storm.

'Imagine, Fokir,' I said. 'Imagine the lives of your ancestors. They were new to this island, freshly arrived in the tide country. After years of struggle they had managed to create the foundations of the bādh; they had even managed to grow a few handfuls of rice and vegetables. After years of living on stilt-raised platforms, they had finally been able to descend to earth and make a few shacks and shanties on level ground. All this by virtue of the bādh. And imagine that fateful night, when the storm struck, at exactly the time that a kotal gon was setting in; imagine how they cowered in their roofless huts and watched the waters, rising, rising, gnawing at the mud and the sand they had laid down to hold the river off. Imagine what went through their heads as they watched this devouring tide eating its way through the earthworks, stalking them wherever they were. There was not one among them, I will guarantee you, my young friend, who would not rather have stood before a tiger than have looked into the maws of that tide.'

'And were there other storms, Saar?'

'Yes, many. Look there.' I pointed to an indentation in the island's shore, a place that looked as if some giant had bitten off a part of Lusibari's coast. 'Look: that was done by the storm of 1970. It was a bhangon, a breaking: the river tore off a four-acre piece of land and carried it away. In an instant it was gone – its huts, fields, trees were all devoured.'

'Was that the worst storm of all, Saar?'

'Oh no. No, comrade, no. The worst storm of all, they say, was long before my time. Long before the settlers first came to this island.'

'When, Saar?'

'It was in 1737. The Emperor Aurangzeb had died some thirty years before and the country was in turmoil. Calcutta was a new place then – the English had seized their opportunity and made it the main port of the east.'

'Go on, Saar.'

'It happened in October – that's always when the worst of them strike, October and November. Before the storm had even made landfall the tide

203

country was hit by a huge wave, a wall of water twelve metres in height. Can you imagine how high that is, my friend? It would have drowned everything on your island and on ours too. Even we on this roof would have been under water.'

'No!'

'Yes, comrade, yes. There were people in Calcutta, Englishmen, who took measurements and recorded all the details. The waters rose so high that they killed thousands of animals and carried them upriver and inland. The corpses of tigers and rhinoceroses were found kilometres from the river, in rice-fields and in village ponds. There were fields covered with the feathers of dead birds. And as this monstrous wave was travelling through the tide country, racing towards Kolkata, something else happened – something unimaginable.'

'What, Saar, what?'

'The city was hit by an earthquake.'

'No!'

'Yes, my friend. Yes. That's one of the reasons why this storm became so famous. There are people, scientists, who believe there is a mysterious connection between earthquakes and storms. But this was the first known instance of these two catastrophes happening together.'

'So what happened, Saar?'

'In Kolkata tens of thousands of dwellings fell instantly to the ground – Englishmen's palaces as well as houses and huts. The steeple of the English church toppled over and came crashing down. They say there was not a building in the city left with four walls intact. Bridges were blown away, wharves were carried off by the surging waters, godowns were emptied of their rice, and even the gunpowder in the armouries was scattered by the wind. On the river were many ships at anchor, large and small, from many nations. Among them there were two English ships, of five hundred tons each. The wind picked them up and carried them over the tops of trees and houses; it threw them down half a kilometre from the river. People saw huge barges fluttering in the air like paper kites. They say that over twenty thousand vessels were lost that day, including boats, barges, dinghies and the like. And even among those that remained, many strange things happened.'

'What, Saar? What?'

'A French ship was driven on shore with some of its cargo intact. The day after the storm, the remaining members of the crew went out into *the fields to try to salvage what they could from the wreckage. A crewman was sent down into one of the holds to see what had been spared. After he had been gone a while, his mates shouted to ask him what was taking him so long. There was no answer so they sent another man. He too fell quickly silent, as did the man who followed him. Now a panic set in and no one else would agree to go until a fire had been lit to see what was going on. When the flame was kindled they saw that the hold was filled with water, and swimming in this tank was an enormous croco- dile – it had killed those three men.'*

'And this, my friend and comrade, is a true story, recorded in documents stored in the British Museum, the very place where Marx wrote Das Kapital.'

'But, Saar, it couldn't happen again, Saar, could it?'

I could see Fokir was trying to gauge the appetite of our rivers and I would have liked to put his young mind at rest. But I knew also that it would have been wrong to deceive him. 'My friend, not only could it happen again – it will *happen again. A storm will come, the waters will rise and the bādh will succumb, in part or in whole. It is only a matter of time.'*

'How do you know, Saar?' he said quietly.

'Look at it, my friend: look at the bādh. See how frail it is, how fragile. Look at the waters that flow past it and how limitless they are, how patient, how quietly they bide their time. Just to look at it is to know why the waters must prevail, later if not sooner. But if you're not convinced by the evidence of your eyes, then perhaps you will have to use your ears.'

'My ears?'

'Yes. Come with me.'

I led him down the stairs and across the fields. People must have stared to see us, me in my flapping white dhoti with my umbrella unfurled against the sun, and Fokir, in his ragged shorts, racing along at my heels. I went right up to the embankment and put my left ear against the clay. 'Now put your head on the bādh and listen carefully. Tell me what you hear and let's see if you can guess what it is.'

'I hear a scratching sound, Saar,' he said in a while. 'It's very soft.'

'But what is making this sound?'

He listened a while longer and then his face lit up with a smile. 'Are they crabs, Saar?'

'Yes, Fokir. Not everyone can hear them but you did. Even as we stand here, untold multitudes of crabs are burrowing into our bādh. Now ask yourself: how long can this frail fence last against these monstrous appetites – the crabs and the tides, the winds and the storms? And if it falls, who shall we turn to then, comrade?'

'Who, Saar?'

'Who indeed, Fokir? Neither angels nor men will hear us, and, as for the animals, they won't hear us either.'

'Why not, Saar?'

'Because of what the Poet says, Fokir. Because the animals

> "already know by instinct
> we're not comfortably at home
> in our translated world".'

Negotiations

Like every other trainee nurse, Moyna lived in the Lusibari hospital's staff quarters. This was a long barracks-like building situated close to the island's embankment. It was on the periphery of the Trust's compound, about a five-minute walk from the Guest House.

The space allotted to Moyna was on the far side of the building and consisted of one large room and a small courtyard. Moyna was waiting on her threshold when Kanai and Piya arrived. Joining her hands, she greeted them with a smiling 'nomoshkar' and ushered them into the courtyard, where a few folding chairs had been put out to await their arrival.

Piya looked around as she was seating herself. 'Where's Tutul?'
'In school,' said Kanai, after relaying the question to Moyna.
'And Fokir?'
'There.'

Turning her head, Piya saw that Fokir was squatting in the dwelling's doorway, half-hidden by a grimy blue curtain. He did not look up and offered no greeting nor any sign of recognition: his eyes were lowered to the ground and he seemed to be drawing patterns with a twig. He was wearing, as usual, a T-shirt and a lungi, but somehow in the setting of his own home, his clothes looked frayed and seedy in a way Piya had not thought them to be before. There was a fugitive sullenness about his posture that suggested he would rather be anywhere but where he was: she had the impression it was only under great pressure (from Moyna or his neighbours?) that he had consented to be present at this occasion.

It stung Piya to see him looking like this, beaten and afraid. What was he afraid of, this man who hadn't hesitated to dive into the river, after her? She would have liked to go up to him, to look into his eyes and greet him in a straightforward, ordinary way. But she thought better of it, for she could tell from his stance that, with Moyna and Kanai present, this would only add to his discomfiture.

Kanai too was watching Fokir. 'I thought only parrots could sit like that,' he said to Piya in a whispered aside.

It was then that Piya noticed that Fokir was not squatting on the floor as she had thought. There was a raised lintel at the bottom of the doorframe and it was on this that he had seated himself, squatting on his haunches and using his toes to grip the wood, like a bird perching on the bar of a cage.

Since Fokir clearly wanted to have no part of the conversation, Piya decided it might be best to address his wife. 'Will you translate for me, please?' she said to Kanai.

Through Kanai, Piya conveyed her gratitude to Moyna and told her that in return for all Fokir had done for her, she wanted to give a gift to the family.

Piya had already prepared a wad of banknotes. She was taking them out of her money-belt when she noticed that Kanai was leaning back to make room for her to reach over to the chair beside his. Moyna in the meanwhile, was sitting forward with an expectant smile. It was evident that they had both assumed she would hand the money not to Fokir, but to Moyna. This was exactly what Piya herself had intended a moment ago, but now, with the money in her hands, her sense of justice rebelled: it was Fokir who had risked his life in pulling her out of the water and it was only fair the money should go to him. After everything he had done, she, Piya, could not treat him as if he didn't exist. Whether he chose to give the money to his wife or his family was his business – it was not for her to make that decision for him.

Piya rose from her chair, but was quickly pre-empted by Moyna who stopped before her with an extended palm. Thus forestalled, there was nothing Piya could do: she handed the money to Moyna with as much grace as she could muster.

'Moyna says she's very happy to accept your gift on behalf of her husband.'

Fokir, she noticed, had sat through this without making a move: it was as if he had grown accustomed to being treated as though he didn't exist.

Piya was going back to her chair when she heard Fokir say something that provoked a sharp response from Moyna.

'What did he say?' Piya whispered to Kanai.

'He told her it didn't bode well to take money for something like this.'

'And what was her answer?'

'She told him they had no choice: there was no food in the house and no money either. Nothing except a few crabs.'

Piya turned to look directly at Kanai. 'Look,' she said, 'I don't want to interfere in whatever's going on between them, but I also don't want this to be just between Moyna and me. Isn't there any way we could pull Fokir into the conversation? It's him I really need to talk to.'

'I'll see what I can do,' said Kanai. Rising from his chair, Kanai went up to Fokir and said, in a loud, hearty voice, attempting friendliness, '*Hā-ré* Fokir; do you know me? I'm Mashima's nephew, Kanai Dutt.' Fokir made no answer, so Kanai added, 'Has anyone told you that I used to know your mother?'

At this Fokir tipped his head back. Now, looking him full in the face for the first time, Kanai was startled by the closeness of his resemblance to Kusum: he could see her likeness in the set of his jaw, in his deep-set, opaque eyes, even in his hair and the way he held himself. But Fokir, it seemed, had no interest in pursuing the conversation. After briefly locking eyes with Kanai, he looked away without answering his question. Kanai glared at him for a moment, then shuffled his feet and went back to his chair.

'What was that about?' said Piya.

'I was just trying to break the ice,' said Kanai. 'I told him I knew his mother.'

'His mother? You know her?'

'I did,' said Kanai. 'She's dead now. I met her when I came here as a boy.'

'Did you tell him that?'

'I tried to,' said Kanai with a smile. 'But he gave me pretty short shrift.'

Piya nodded. She hadn't understood what had passed between the two men, but there was no mistaking the condescension in Kanai's voice as he was speaking to Fokir: it was the kind of tone in which someone might address a dimwitted waiter, at once jocular and hectoring. It didn't surprise her that Fokir had responded with what was clearly his instinctive mode of defence: silence.

'Let's leave him where he is,' Piya said. 'Maybe we should just get started?'

'I'm ready.'

'Please tell him this.'

With Kanai translating, Piya explained to Fokir that she was doing research on the species of dolphin that frequented the Garjontola 'pool'. After these last two days, she said, it had become clear to her, as it evidently was to him, that the dolphins left the pool to forage when the water was running high during the day. Now she wanted to trace their routes and map the patterns of their movement. The best way to do this, she had decided, was for her to return to Garjontola with him, Fokir. They would take a bigger boat, a motorboat if possible; they would anchor near the dolphins' pool and Fokir would help her survey the dolphins' daily migrations. The expedition would last a few days – maybe four or five, depending on what they found. She would pay all expenses of course – the rent for the boat, the provisions and all that – and she would also pay Fokir a salary plus a per diem. On top of that, if all went well there'd be a bonus at the end; all told, he would stand to make about three hundred US dollars.

Kanai had been translating continuously as Piya was speaking, and when he finished, Moyna gave a loud gasp and covered her face with her hands.

'Was the money not enough?' Piya asked Kanai anxiously.

'Not enough?' Kanai said. 'Can't you see Moyna's overjoyed? This is a windfall for them. I'm sure they really need the money.'

'And what does Fokir say? Will he be able to arrange for a launch?'

Kanai paused to listen. 'He says, yes, he'll do it; he'll start making the arrangements right away. But there are no motor-boats here. You'll have to use a *bhotbhoti*.'

'What's that?'

'That's what diesel boats are called in these parts,' said Kanai. 'They're named for the hammering sound of their engines.'

'I don't care what kind of boat it is,' said Piya. 'The thing is: can he arrange for one?'

'Yes,' said Kanai, 'he'll arrange for one to be here tomorrow. You can look it over.'

'Does he know the owner?'

'Yes. It belongs to someone who's like a father to him.'

Piya recalled her last experience of hiring a launch and the trouble she had had with the forest guard and his relative. She said, 'Do you think this man will be reliable?'

'Yes,' said Kanai with a nod. 'I know the man, actually. His name is Horen Naskor. He used to work for my uncle too. I can vouch for him.'

'OK, then.'

Glancing at Fokir, Piya saw there was a grin on his face now and for a moment it was as though he had become, once again, the man she had known on the boat, not the sullen, resentful creature he evidently was on land. She could not tell whether it was the prospect of being back on the water that had lifted his spirits or the possibility of escaping from whatever it was that so weighed him down in his home: it was enough that she had been able to offer him something that mattered, whatever it was.

'Listen, Piya,' Kanai nudged her with his elbow. 'Moyna has a question for you.'

'Yes?'

'She wants to know why a highly educated scientist like you needs the help of her husband – someone who doesn't even know how to read and write.'

Piya frowned, puzzling over this. Could Moyna really be as dismissive of her husband as her question seemed to imply? Or was she trying to suggest that Piya should hire someone else? But there was no one else that she wanted to work with – especially if the alternatives were men like the forest guard.

'Could you please tell Moyna,' Piya said to Kanai, 'that her husband knows the river well. His knowledge can be of help to a scientist like myself.'

When this was explained Moyna responded with a retort sharp enough to draw a laugh from Kanai.

'Why are you laughing?' said Piya.

'She's clever, this girl,' said Kanai.

'Why? What did she say?'

'She made a funny little play on the word *gyan*, which means knowledge, and *gaan*, which means song. She said that her life would be a lot easier if her husband had a little more gyan and a little less gaan.'

Habits

———

Nilima was none too pleased by Kusum's visit. That evening, she said to me, 'Do you know that Kusum came to see me today? She was trying to get me involved with that business in Morichjhãpi. They want the Trust to help them set up some medical facilities there.'

'So what did you say?'

'I told them there's nothing we could do,' Nilima said, in her flattest, most unyielding voice.

'Why can't you help them?' I protested. 'They're human beings; they need medical attention as much as people do anywhere else.'

'Nirmal, it's impossible,' she said. 'Those people are squatters; that land doesn't belong to them; it's government property. How can they just seize it? If they're allowed to remain, people will think every island in the tide country can be seized. What will become of the forest, the environment?'

To this I answered that Lusibari was forest too once – this too once belonged to the government. Yet Sir Daniel Hamilton was allowed to take it over in order to create his experiment. And all these years, Nilima had often said that she admired what he did. What was the difference, then? Were the dreams of these settlers less valuable than those of a man like Sir Daniel just because he was a rich shaheb and they impoverished refugees?'

'But Nirmal,' she said, 'what Sir Daniel did happened a long time ago. Just imagine what would become of this whole area if everybody started doing the same thing today. The whole forest would disappear.'

'Look, Nilima,' I said, 'that island, Morichjhãpi, wasn't really forest, even before the settlers came. Parts of it were already being used by

213

the government, for plantations and so on. What's been said about the danger to the environment is just a sham, in order to evict these people, who have nowhere else to go.'

'Be that as it may,' said Nilima, 'I simply cannot allow the Trust to get involved in this. There's too much at stake for us. You're not involved in the day-to-day business of running the hospital, so you have no idea of how hard we've had to work to stay on the right side of the government. If the politicians turn against us, we're finished. I can't take that chance.'

It was all clear to me now. 'So, Nilima,' I said, 'what you're saying is that your position has nothing to do with the rights and wrongs of the case. You're not going to help these people, because you want to stay on the right side of the government?'

Nilima made her hands into fists and put them on her waist. 'Nirmal, you have no idea of what it takes to do anything practical,' she said. 'You live in a dream world – a haze of poetry and fuzzy ideas about revolution. To build something is not the same as dreaming of it: building is always a matter of well-chosen compromises.'

I rarely argued with Nilima when she used this tone of voice. But this time, I too wouldn't let go: 'I don't see that this compromise is well chosen.'

This made Nilima even angrier. 'Nirmal,' she said, 'I want you to remember something. It was for your sake that we first came to Lusibari, because your political involvements got you into trouble and endangered your health. There was nothing for me here, no family, friends or a job. But over the years I've built something – something real, something useful, something that has helped many people in small ways. All these years, you've sat back and judged me. But now it's there in front of you, in front of your eyes – this hospital. And if you ask me what I will do to protect it, let me tell you, I will fight for it like a mother fights to protect her children. The hospital's future, its welfare – they mean everything to me, and I will not endanger them. I've asked very little of you all this time, but I'm asking you now: stay away from Morichjhãpi. I know the government will not allow the settlers to stay and I know also that they will be vengeful towards everyone who gets mixed up in this business. If you get involved with those settlers you will be endangering my life's work. Just keep that in mind. That's all I ask.'

214

There was nothing more to say. No one knew better than I the sacrifices she had made for me. I recognized that my idea of teaching the children of Morichjhãpi was just an old man's hallucination, nothing more than a way of postponing an inevitable superannuation. I tried to purge it from my head.

The new year, 1979, came in, and soon afterwards Nilima left to go off on one of her periodic fund-raising tours for the hospital. A rich Marwari family in Kolkata had agreed to donate a generator; a cousin of hers had become a minister in the state government and she wanted to see him. There was even to be a trip to New Delhi to meet with a senior official in Prime Minister Morarji Desai's government. All of this had to be tended to.

On the morning of Nilima's departure, I went to the jetty to see her off, and just before leaving she said, 'Nirmal – remember what I said to you about Morichjhãpi. Remember.'

The boat sailed away and I went up to my study: with my school-master's duties at an end, time hung heavy on my hands. I opened my notebooks for the first time in many years, thinking that perhaps I would write something. I had long thought of compiling a book about the tide country, a volume that would include all I knew, all the facts I had gathered over these years.

For several days I sat at my desk, gazing at the mohona of the Rainangal in the distance. I remembered how when I first came to Lusibari, the sky would be darkened by birds at sunset. Many years had passed since I'd seen such flights of birds. When I first noticed their absence, I thought they would soon come back but they had not. I remembered a time when at low tide, the mudbanks would turn scarlet with millions of swarming crabs. That colour began to fade long ago and now it is never seen any more. Where had they gone, I wondered, those millions of swarming crabs, those birds?

Age teaches you to recognize the signs of death. You do not see them suddenly; you become aware of them very slowly over a period of many, many years. Now it was as if I could see those signs everywhere, not just in myself, but in this place that I had lived in for almost thirty years. The birds were vanishing, the fish were dwindling and from day to day the land was being reclaimed by the sea. What would it take, to submerge the tide country? Not much – a minuscule change in the level of the sea would be enough.

215

As I contemplated this prospect, it seemed to me that this might not be such a terrible outcome: these islands had seen so much suffering, so much hardship and poverty, so many catastrophes, so many failed dreams that perhaps humankind would not be ill served by its loss?

Then I thought of Morichjhãpi: what I saw as a vale of tears was for others truly more precious than gold. I remembered the story Kusum had told me, of her exile in Bihar and how she had dreamed of returning to this place, of seeing once more these rich fields of mud, these trembling tides; I thought of all the others who had come with her to Morichjhãpi and of all they had braved to find their way here. In what way could I ever do justice to this place? What could I write of it that would equal the power of their longing and their dreams? What indeed would be the form of the lines? Even this I could not resolve: would they flow, as the rivers did, or would they follow rhythms, as did the tides?

I put my books aside and went to stand on the roof, to gaze across the waters. The sight was almost unbearable to me at that moment; I felt myself torn between my wife and the woman who had become the muse I'd never had; between the quiet persistence of everyday change and the heady excitement of revolution – between prose and poetry.

Most haunting of all, was I overreaching myself even in conceiving of these confusions? What had I ever done to earn the right to address such questions?

I had reached that point where, as the Poet says, we tell ourselves:

> 'Maybe what's left for us
> is some tree on a hillside
> we can look at day after day,
> and the perverse affection of a habit
> that liked us so much it never let go.'

A Sunset

Towards the end of the day, when the sun was dipping towards the Bidya's mohona, Piya decided to take advantage of Kanai's invitation: she went up to the roof of the Guest House and knocked on the door of the study.

'*Ké?*' He blinked as he opened the door and she had the impression that she had woken him from a trance.

'Did I disturb you?'

'No. Not really.'

'I thought I'd take in the sunset.'

'Good idea – I'm glad you came up.' He put away the cardboard-covered book he was holding and went to join her by the parapet. In the distance the sky and the mohona were aflame with the colours of the setting sun.

'It's magnificent, isn't it?' said Kanai.

'It is.'

Kanai proceeded to point out Lusibari's sights: the village maidan, the Hamilton House, the school, the hospital and so on. By the end of the recital they had done a turn around the roof and were facing in the direction of the path they had followed that morning, looking towards the staff quarters of the Lusibari Hospital. Piya knew they were both thinking about the morning's meeting.

'I'm glad it went well today,' she said.

'Did you think it went well?'

'Yes, I did,' she said. 'At least Fokir agreed to go on this expedition. In the beginning I didn't think he would.'

'I didn't know what to think, frankly,' Kanai said. 'He's such a peculiar sulky fellow. One doesn't know what to expect.'

217

'Believe me,' said Piya, 'he's very different when he's out on the water.'

'But are you sure you'll be all right with him?' said Kanai. 'For several days?'

'Yes, I'm sure.' She was aware of a certain awkwardness in discussing Fokir with him, especially because she could tell that he was still smarting from the silent snub of the morning. Quietly, she said, 'Tell me about Fokir's mother. What was she like?'

Kanai stopped to consider this. 'Fokir looks a lot like her,' he said. 'But it's hard to see any other resemblance. Kusum was spirited, tough, and full of fun and laughter. Not like him at all.'

'And what happened to her?'

'It's a long story,' said Kanai, 'and I don't know all of it. All I can tell you is that she was killed in some kind of confrontation with the police.'

Piya caught her breath. 'How did that happen?'

'She'd joined a group of refugees who'd occupied an island nearby. The land belonged to the government, so there was a stand-off and many people died. That was in 1979 – Fokir must have been five or six. But Horen Naskor took him in after his mother's death: he's been a father to him ever since.'

'So Fokir wasn't born here?'

'No,' said Kanai. 'He was born in Bihar – his parents were living there at the time. His mother came back here when his father died. Fokir was only five at the time.'

Piya remembered the family she had imagined for Fokir: the parents she had given him and the many siblings. She was shamed by her lack of insight. 'Well, that's one thing we have in common, then,' she said. 'Fokir and me.'

'What?'

'Growing up without a mother.'

'Did you lose your mother when you were little?' said Kanai.

'I wasn't as little as he was,' said Piya. 'My mother died of cancer when I was twelve. But actually I felt I'd lost her long before.'

'Why?'

'Because she'd kind of cut herself off from us – my dad and

218

me. She was a depressive, you see – and her condition got worse over the years.'

'It must have been very hard for you,' said Kanai.

'Not as hard as it was for her,' said Piya. 'She was like an orchid in a way, frail and beautiful and dependent on the love and labour of many, many people. She was the kind of person who should never have strayed too far from home. In Seattle she had no one – no friends, no servants, no job, no life. My father, on the other hand, was the perfect immigrant – driven, hard-working, successful. He was busy getting on with his career, and I was absorbed in the usual kid stuff. I guess my mother kind of fell through the cracks. At some point she just gave up.'

Kanai put his hand on hers and gave it a squeeze. 'I'm sorry.'

There was a catch in his voice that surprised Piya: she had judged him to be too self-absorbed to pay much attention to other people. Yet his sympathy now seemed genuine.

'I don't get it,' she said with a smile. 'You say you're sorry for me, but you don't seem to have much sympathy for Fokir. Even though you knew his mother. How come?'

His face hardened and he gave a snort of ironic laughter. 'So far as Fokir is concerned I'm afraid my sympathies are mainly with his wife.'

'What do you mean?'

'Didn't you feel for her this morning?' said Kanai. 'Just imagine how hard it must be to live with someone like Fokir while also trying to provide for a family and keep a roof over your head. If you consider her circumstances – her caste, her upbringing – it's very remarkable that she's had the forethought to figure out how to get by in today's world. And it isn't just that she wants to get by – she wants to do well; she wants to make a success of her life.'

Piya nodded. 'I get it.' She understood now that for Kanai there was a certain reassurance in meeting a woman like Moyna, in such a place as Lusibari: it was as if her very existence were a validation of the choices he had made in his own life. It was important for him to believe that his values were, at bottom, egalitarian, liberal, meritocratic. It reassured him to be able to think, 'What I want for myself is no different from what every-body wants, no matter how rich or poor; everyone who has any drive, any energy wants to get on in the world – Moyna is the proof.' Piya understood too that this was a looking-glass in which a man like Fokir could never be anything other than a figure glimpsed through a rear-view mirror, a rapidly diminishing pres-ence, a ghost from the perpetual past that was Lusibari. But she guessed also that despite its newness and energy, the country Kanai inhabited was full of these ghosts, these unseen presences whose murmurings could never quite be silenced no matter how loud you spoke.

Piya said, 'You really like Moyna, don't you?'

'I admire her,' said Kanai. 'That's how I would put it.'

'I know you do,' Piya said. 'But has it occurred to you that she might look a little different from Fokir's angle?'

'What do you mean?'

'Just ask yourself this,' said Piya. 'How would *you* like to be married to her?'

Kanai laughed and when he spoke again his voice had an edge of flippancy that made Piya grate her teeth. 'I'd say Moyna is the kind of woman who would be good for a brief but exciting dalliance,' he said. 'A fling, as we used to say. But as for anything more lasting – no. I'd say someone like you would be much more to my taste.'

Piya raised her hand to her earstud and fingered it delicately, as if for reassurance. With a wary smile she said: 'Are you flirt-ing with me, Kanai?'

'Can't you tell?' he said, grinning.

'I'm out of practice,' she said.

'Well we have to do something about that, don't we?'

He was interrupted by a shout from below. 'Kanai-babu.'

Looking over the parapet, they saw that Fokir was standing on the path below. On catching sight of Piya he dropped his head and shuffled his feet. Then, after addressing a few words to Kanai, he turned abruptly on his heel and walked away, in the direction of the embankment.

'What did he say?' said Piya.

'He wanted me to tell you that Horen Naskor will be here

tomorrow with the bhotbhoti,' said Kanai. 'You can look it over and if it's OK you can leave day after tomorrow.'

'Good!' cried Piya. 'I'd better go and organize my stuff.'

She noticed that the interruption had annoyed him as much as it had pleased her. He was frowning as he said, 'And I suppose I'd better get back to my uncle's notebook.'

Transformation

And if it were not for Horen, perhaps I would have been content to live out my days in the embrace of all the habits that liked me so much they would never let go. But he sought me out one day, and said, 'Saar, it's mid-January, almost time for the Bon Bibi puja. Kusum and Fokir want to go to Garjontola and I'm going to take them there. She asked if you wanted to come.'

'Garjontola?' I said. 'Where is that?'

'It's an island,' he said. 'Deep in the jungle. Kusum's father built a shrine to Bon Bibi there. That's why she wants to go.'

This offered a dilemma of a new kind. In the past, I had always taken care to hold myself apart from matters of religious devotion. It was not just that I thought of these beliefs as false consciousness: it was also because I had seen, at first hand, the horrors that religion had visited upon us at the time of Partition. As headmaster I had felt it my duty not to identify myself with any set of religious beliefs, Hindu, Muslim or anything else. This was why, strange as it may seem, I had never seen a Bon Bibi puja or indeed, taken any interest in this deity. But I was no longer a headmaster and the considerations that had once kept me from taking an interest in such matters were no longer applicable.

But what about Nilima's injunctions? What about her plea that I stay away from Morichjhãpi? I persuaded myself that this trip would not count as going to Morichjhãpi, since we would, after all, be heading to another island. 'All right, Horen,' I said. 'But remember – not a word to Mashima.'

'No, Saar, of course. No.'

The next morning Horen came at dawn and we set off.

A couple of months had passed since I was last at Morichjhãpi, and

222

when we got there, it was clear at a glance that much had changed in the meanwhile: the euphoria of the time before had given way to fear and slow, nagging doubts. A wooden watchtower had been erected for instance, and there were groups of settlers patrolling the island's shore. When our boat pulled in, we were immediately surrounded by several men. 'Who are you?' they asked. 'What's your business here?'

We were a little shaken when we got to Kusum's thatch-roofed dwelling. It was clear that she too was under strain. She explained that in recent weeks the government had been stepping up the pressure on the settlers: policemen and officials had visited and offered inducements for them to leave. When these proved ineffective, they had made threats. Although the settlers were unmoved in their resolve, a kind of nervousness had set in: no one knew what was going to happen next.

The morning was quite advanced now, so we made haste to be on our way. Kusum and Fokir had made small clay images of Bon Bibi and her brother Shah Jongoli. These we loaded on Horen's boat, and then pulled away from the island.

Once we were out on the river, the tide lifted everyone's spirits. There were many other boats on the waters, all out on similar errands. Some of them had twenty or thirty people on board. Along with massive, well-painted images of Bon Bibi and Shah Jongoli, they also had singers and drummers.

On our boat were just the four of us: Horen, Fokir, Kusum and me.

'Why didn't you bring your children?' I asked Horen. 'What about your family?'

'They went with my father-in-law and my wife's family,' said Horen sheepishly. 'Their boat is bigger.'

We came to a mohona, and as we were crossing it, I noticed that Horen and Kusum had begun to make genuflections of the kind that are usually occasioned by the sight of a deity or a temple – they raised their finger-tips to their foreheads and then touched their chests. Fokir, watching attentively, was attempting to do the same.

'What's happening?' I asked, in surprise. 'What do you see? There's no temple nearby: this is just open water.'

Kusum laughed and at first wouldn't tell me. Then, after some pleading and cajolery, she divulged that just at that moment, in the very middle of that mohona, we had crossed the line Bon Bibi had drawn to divide the tide country. In other words we had crossed the border that separates the realm of human beings from the domain of Dokkhin Rai and his demons. I realized, with a sense of shock, that this chimerical line was, to her and to Horen, as real as a barbed-wire fence might be to me.

And now, indeed, everything began to look new, unexpected, full of surprises. I had a book in my hands to while away the time and it occurred to me that in a way a landscape too is not unlike a book – a compilation of pages that overlap without any two ever being the same. People open the book according to their taste and training, their memories and desires: for a geologist the compilation opens at one page, for a boatman at another and still another for a ship's pilot, a painter and so on. On occasion these pages are ruled with lines that are invisible to some people, while being for others, as real, as charged and as volatile as high-voltage cables.

To me, a townsman, the tide country's jungle was an emptiness, a place where time stood still: I saw now that this was an illusion, that exactly the opposite was true. What was happening here, I realized, was that the wheel of time was spinning too fast to be seen. In other places it took decades, even centuries for a river to change course; it took an epoch for an island to appear. But here, in the tide country, transformation is the rule of life: rivers stray from week to week, and islands are made and unmade in days. In other places forests take centuries, even millennia, to regenerate; but mangroves can recolonize a denuded island in ten to fifteen years. Could it be that the very rhythms of the earth were quickened here so that they unfolded at an accelerated pace?

I remembered the story of 'The Royal James and Mary', an English ship making its passage through the shoals of the tide country in the year 1694. Night stole unawares upon the many-masted ship and it capsized after striking a sandbank. What would be the fate of such a shipwreck in the benign waters of the Caribbean or the Mediterranean? I imagined the thick crust of underwater life that would cling to the vessel and preserve it for centuries; I imagined the divers and explorers who would seek their fortunes in the wreck. But here? The tide country digested the great galleon within a few years. Its remains vanished without trace.

Nor was this the only such. Thinking back, I remembered that the channels of the tide country were crowded with the graves of old ships. Wasn't it true that in the great storm of 1737 more than two dozen ships

224

had foundered in these waters? And didn't it happen that in the year 1885 the British India Steam Navigation Company lost two proud steamers here, the 'Arcot' and the 'Mahratta'? And wasn't the 'City of Canterbury' added to that list in 1897? But today on those sites nothing is to be seen; nothing escapes the maw of the tides; everything is ground to fine silt, becomes something else.

It was as if the whole tide country was speaking in the voice of the Poet: 'life is lived in transformation'.

It is afternoon now in Morichjhâpi and Kusum and Horen have just returned from a meeting of the settlers of this ward. The rumours have been confirmed. The gangsters who have massed on the far shore will be brought in to drive the settlers out. But the attack, they say, will likely start tomorrow, not today. I still have a few hours left.

A Pilgrimage

When dinner arrived, Piya had the feeling that someone had spoken to Moyna about her eating preferences. Today, apart from the usual fare of rice and fish curry, she had also brought some plain mashed potatoes and two bananas: touched, Piya put her hands together in a *namaste* to thank Moyna.

Later, when Moyna had gone, she asked Kanai whether it was he who'd spoken to her and he shook his head: 'No. It wasn't me.'

'Must have been Fokir, then.' Piya served herself an eager helping of mashed potatoes. 'All I'm missing now is some Ovaltine.'

'Ovaltine?' Kanai looked up from his food in surprise. 'You like Ovaltine?' He began to laugh when she nodded. 'Do they even have Ovaltine in America?'

'It was a habit my parents brought over,' Piya said. 'They used to buy their stocks in Indian shops. I like it now because it's easy to carry and convenient when you're out on the water.'

'So you live on Ovaltine while you're tracking these dolphins of yours?'

'Sometimes.'

Kanai shook his head ruefully as he filled a plate with rice, daal and chhechki. 'You go through a lot for these creatures, don't you?'

'That's not how I think of it.'

'So are they fetching, these beasts of yours?' said Kanai. 'Do they hold one's interest?'

'They're interesting to me,' said Piya. 'And I can give you at least one good reason why they should be of interest to you.'

'I'm listening,' said Kanai. 'I'm willing to be persuaded. Why?'

'Because some of the earliest specimens were found in Calcutta,' Piya said. 'How's that for a reason?'

'In Calcutta?' Kanai said incredulously. 'You're telling me there were dolphins in Calcutta?'

'Oh yes,' said Piya. 'Not just dolphins. Whales too.'

'Whales?' Kanai laughed. 'Now I know you're pulling my leg.'

'Not at all,' said Piya. 'Calcutta was once a big place for cetacean zoology.'

'I don't believe you,' Kanai said flatly. 'I think I'd know if that were the case.'

'But it's true,' Piya said. 'And let me tell you – last week when I was coming through Kolkata? I actually went on a kind of cetacean pilgrimage.'

Kanai burst into laughter. 'A cetacean pilgrimage?'

'Yes,' said Piya. 'My cousins laughed too – but that was exactly what it was – a pilgrimage.'

'And who are these cousins of yours?' said Kanai.

'My mashima's daughters,' Piya said. 'They're younger than me; one's in high school and one's in college – both really bright, smart kids. They had a car and driver and they said they'd take me wherever I wanted to go in Calcutta. I guess they figured that I'd want to buy some souvenirs or something. When I told them where I wanted to go, they were like, "*The Botanical Gardens! What are you going to do there?*"'

'I can see the point of that question,' Kanai said. 'What do the Botanical Gardens have to do with dolphins?'

'Everything,' said Piya. 'You see in the nineteenth century the garden was run by some very good naturalists. One of them was William Roxburgh, the man who identified the Gangetic dolphin.'

It was in Calcutta's Botanical Gardens, Piya explained, that Roxburgh had written his famous article of 1801, announcing the discovery of the first-known river dolphin. He had called it *Delphinus gangeticus* ('*Soosoo* is the name it is known by amongst the Bengalese around Calcutta') but the name had been changed later, when it was discovered that Pliny the Elder had already named the Indian river dolphin, as far back as the first century CE – he had called it *Platanista*. In the zoological inventory the

Gangetic dolphin had come to be listed as *Platanista gangetica* Roxburgh 1801. Years later, John Anderson, one of Roxburgh's successors at Calcutta's Botanical Gardens, actually adopted an infant Gangetic dolphin. He had kept it in his bathtub and it had lived for several weeks.

'But you know what?' Piya said. 'Although he had a dolphin in his bathtub, Anderson never found out that platanista is blind – or that it prefers to swim on its side.'

'Is that what it does?'

'Yes.'

'So did you find the bathtub?' said Kanai, reaching across the table for the rice.

Piya laughed. 'No. But I wasn't too disappointed. It was good just to be there.'

'So what was the next station in your pilgrimage?' Kanai said.

'This one will surprise you even more,' said Piya. 'Salt Lake.'

Kanai's eyebrows shot up. 'You mean the suburb?'

'It wasn't always a suburb, you know,' Piya said, peeling another banana. 'In 1852, it was just a wetland, with a few scattered ponds.'

In July that year, Piya said, an unusually high tide caused a sudden surge in the rivers of the delta. The wave travelled deep into the hinterland, flooding the swamps and wetlands that surrounded Calcutta. When the tide turned and the waters began to recede, a rumour swept the streets of the city: a school of giant sea-creatures had been stranded in one of the salt lakes on the city's western outskirts. The then superintendent of Calcutta's Botanical Gardens was one Edward Blyth, an English naturalist. The news worried him. The year before, on the Malabar coast, a stranded whale, a full twenty-seven metres in length, had been dismembered by the local people: they had set upon it with knives, axes and spears and hacked it apart. A nearby English clergy-man was shown the meat, both dried and fresh, and was told that it was 'first chop beef'. What if these creatures were cut up and consumed before they had been subjected to a proper exam-ination? The thought of this sent Blyth hurrying across town to the salt lake.

'It wasn't that he cared about their being killed,' Piya said. 'He just wanted to do it himself.'

The marshes were steaming under a blazing sun and the water had fallen back to its accustomed levels. He arrived to find some twenty animals floundering in a shallow pond. Their heads were rounded and their bodies black, with white undersides. The adult males were over four metres in length. The water was too low to keep them fully submerged and their short, sharply raked dorsal fins were exposed to the sun. They were in great distress and their moans could be clearly heard. Mr Blyth was inclined to identify the animals as short-finned pilot whales, *Globicephalus deductor*. This was a common Atlantic species named and identified some six years before by the great British anatomist J. E. Gray.

'Of *Gray's Anatomy*?' Kanai said.

'That's the one.'

A large crowd had gathered but somewhat to Mr Blyth's surprise they had not set upon the whales. On the contrary, many of them had laboured through the night to rescue the creatures, towing them through a channel into the river. Apparently these villagers had no taste for whale meat and no knowledge of the oil that could be extracted from the animals' carcasses. Mr Blyth learned that many whales had been saved and that the twenty remaining ones were the last of a school of several dozen. With the rescues proceeding apace, there was clearly no time to be lost. Mr Blyth chose two of the best specimens and ordered his men to secure them to the bank with poles and stout ropes: his intention was to return the next day with the implements necessary for a proper dissection.

'But when he came back the next morning,' said Piya, 'they were all gone.' The chosen animals had been cut loose by the bystanders. But Mr Blyth was not easily thwarted and managed to get hold of two of the last remaining whales. These he quickly reduced to perfect skeletons. After a prolonged examination of the bones, he decided that the animals were an unknown species. He called it the Indian pilot whale, *Globicephalus indicus*.

'I have a theory,' Piya said with a smile, 'that if Blyth hadn't gone out to Salt Lake that day, he'd have become the man who identified the Irrawaddy dolphin.'

229

Kanai was licking a grain of rice off his forefinger. 'Why?'

'Because six years later he made a terrible mistake when he found the first specimen of Orcaella.'

'And where did he find it?'

'In a Calcutta fish-market,' Piya said with a laugh. 'Someone told him about it and he went running over. He gave it a once-over and decided it was a juvenile pilot whale like the animals he'd seen out near the salt lake. He couldn't get those creatures out of his head.'

'So he wasn't the one who identified your beloved dolphin?' Kanai said.

'No,' said Piya. 'Old Blyth missed his chance.'

A quarter of a century later, another carcass of a small, round-headed cetacean was found at Vizagapatnam, six hundred and fifty kilometres down the coast from Calcutta. This time the skeleton found its way to the British Museum where it occasioned much curiosity. The anatomists of London saw what Blyth had failed to see: this was no juvenile pilot whale! It was a new species, a relative of none other than the killer whale, *Orcinus orca*. But where the killer whale grew to lengths of over ten metres its cousin rarely exceeded two and a half; while the killer whale liked the icy waters of the subpolar oceans, its cousin preferred the warmth of the tropics and appeared to thrive both in fresh water and in salt. Compared to the mighty orca this creature was so mellow as to need a diminutive: it became Orcaella – *Orcaella brevirostris* to be exact.

A puzzled frown appeared on Kanai's forehead. 'So this killer-ella of yours was first netted in Calcutta and then in Vizagapatnam?'

'Yes.'

'Then why is it known as the "Irrawaddy dolphin"?'

'That's another story,' said Piya.

The name was the doing of John Anderson, she said, the very one who'd tried to rear a Gangetic dolphin in his bathtub. In the 1870s Anderson accompanied two zoological expeditions that travelled through Burma to southern China. While sailing up the Irrawaddy, Anderson found no Orcaella in the lower part of the river. In the upper reaches, on the other hand, they were present in great numbers. There appeared also to be a few small anatomical differences between the animals that lived in fresh water and those that lived in salt water. From this Anderson drew the conclusion that there were two species of Orcaella: to *Orcaella brevirostris* he awarded a cousin, *Orcaella fluminalis*. This, he decided, was the Irrawaddy dolphin, the true inhabitant of Asia's rivers,

'The name stuck,' Piya said, 'but his conclusions didn't.' The great Gray of London examined several skeletons and handed down a definitive judgement: Orcaella was one species, not two. It was true that there were coastal populations and riverine populations and it was true also that the two did not mix. But anatomically there was no difference. In the Linnaean bestiary the animal's name became *Orcaella brevirostris* Gray 1886.

'And you know what the real irony was?' Piya said. 'Poor old Blyth was wrong on all counts. Not only did he blow his chances of identifying Orcaella; he also misidentified the stranded whales of Calcutta's Salt Lake: they were just short-finned pilot whales. Gray showed there was no such thing as *Globicephalus indicus*.'

Kanai nodded. 'That's how it was in those days,' he said. 'London was to Calcutta as orca to Orcaella.'

Piya laughed as she carried her plate to the sink. 'Are you convinced now? About Calcutta being a centre of cetacean zoology?'

Piya raised her hand to her earlobe in the gesture that Kanai had noticed before. That movement made her seem at once as graceful as a dancer and as vulnerable as a child and it made Kanai's heart stop. He could not bear to think that she would be leaving the next day.

Leaving his plate on the table he went to the bathroom to wash his hands. A minute later, he came hurrying out and went to stand at Piya's elbow, beside the sink.

'I have an idea for you, Piya,' he said.

'Yes?' she said cautiously, alarmed by the shine in his eye.

'Do you know what your expedition lacks?'

'What?' She turned away from him, pursing her lips.

'A translator!' Kanai said. 'Neither Horen nor Fokir speaks English. How are you going to communicate with them?'

'I managed OK over the last few days.'

231

'But you didn't have a whole crew to deal with.'

She acknowledged the truth of this with a nod: she could see that there would be advantages to having him along. But her instincts told her to be careful: that his presence might lead to trouble. Playing for time, she said, 'But don't you have stuff to do here?'

'Not really,' said Kanai. 'I'm getting to the end of my uncle's notebook – and it doesn't necessarily have to be read right here. I could take it with me. Frankly, I'm getting a little tired of this Guest House – I wouldn't mind a little break.'

His eagerness was obvious and she was aware of a twinge of guilt: there was no denying that he had been very hospitable; she would feel more at ease about staying in the Guest House if she knew his generosity was not going to go unreciprocated.

'Well, then, sure,' she said, after a moment's hesitation. 'You're welcome to come along.'

He made a fist and punched it into his open palm. 'Thank you!' But this display of enthusiasm seemed to cause him some embarrassment, for a moment later he added, affecting nonchalance, 'I've always wanted to be on an expedition. It's been an ambition of mine ever since I learnt that my great-great-uncle was the translator on Younghusband's expedition to Tibet.'

Destiny

⁓

Putting away my book, I said to Kusum: 'What is this place we're going to? Why is it called Garjontola?'

'Because of the garjon tree, which grows in great abundance there.'

'Oh?' I had not made this connection: I'd thought that the name of the place came from the other meaning of the word garjon, to 'roar'. 'So it's not because of a tiger's cry?'

They laughed. 'Maybe that too.'

'So why is it Garjontola we're going to? Why there and nowhere else?'

'It's because of my father, Saar,' Kusum said.

'Your father?'

'Yes. Once, many years ago, his life was saved on this island.'

'How? What happened?'

'All right, Saar, since you asked, I'll tell you the story; I know you'll probably laugh: you won't believe me.

'It happened long, long ago, before I was born: fishing alone, my father was caught in a storm. The wind raged like a fiend and tore apart his boat; his hands fell on a log and somehow he stayed afloat. Swept by the current, he came to Garjontola; climbing a tree, he tied himself with his gamchha. Attached to the trunk, he held on against the gale, till suddenly the wind stopped and a silence fell. The waves were quieted, the tree stood straight again, but there was no moon and not a thing could be seen.

'Now, in the dark of the night, he heard a garjon; soon he caught the smell of the unnameable one. Terror seized his heart and he lost all consciousness; he'd have fallen if the gamchha hadn't held him in place. He dreamed, in his oblivion, of Bon Bibi: "Fool!" she said. "Don't be

233

afraid; believe in me. This place you've come to, I value it as my own; if you're good at heart, here you'll never be alone.

"'When day breaks, you'll see it is time for low tide; cross the island and go to the northern side. Keep your eyes on the water; be patient and you'll see: you're not on your own; you're not far from me. You'll see my messengers, my ears and my eyes; they'll keep you company till the waters rise. Then will you know that deliverance is at hand; a boat will pass by and take you back to your land.'"

Who could fail to be charmed by such a story, so well told? 'I suppose you will tell me', I said, smiling, 'that this was exactly how it happened?'

'Why yes, Saar, it did. And afterwards my father came back and built a shrine to Bon Bibi on the island. Through the rest of his life, every year we came here on this day, when it was time to do a puja for Bon Bibi.'

I laughed: 'And the messengers? I suppose you will say that they were real too?'

'Why, yes, Saar,' she said. 'They were. And even you will see them soon.'

'Even I?' I laughed louder still. 'An unbelieving secularist? I too am to be granted this privilege?'

'Yes, Saar,' she persisted in the face of my scepticism. 'Anyone can see Bon Bibi's messengers if they know where to look.'

I took a little nap, in the shade of my umbrella, and then woke to the sound of Kusum's voice telling me we had arrived.

I'd been looking forward to the moment when I would be able to confound her credulousness. I sat quickly upright. It was low tide and we were becalmed in a stretch of still water: the shore was still some distance away. There was nothing to be seen, no messengers nor any other divine manifestation. I could not help preening myself a little as I savoured my triumph. 'So where are they, Kusum?' I said. 'These messengers of yours?'

'Wait, Saar. You'll see them.'

Suddenly there was a sound, like that of a man blowing his nose. I turned around in astonishment, just in time to see a little patch of black skin disappearing into the water.

'What was that?' I cried. 'Where did it come from? Where did it go?'

'Look,' said little Fokir, pointing in the other direction, 'over there.'

I turned to see another of these creatures, rolling through the water.

This time I also caught a glimpse of a small, triangular fin. Although I had never before seen this animal, I knew it had to be a dolphin: yet, it was clearly not the susuk I was accustomed to seeing in our waters, for those had no fins on their backs.

'What is it?' I said. 'Is it some kind of susuk?'

It was Kusum's turn to smile. 'I have my own name for them,' she said. 'I call them Bon Bibi's messengers.' The triumph was hers now; I could not deny it to her.

All through the time our boat was at that spot, the creatures kept breaking the water around us. What kept them there? What made them linger? I could not imagine. Then there came a moment when one of them broke the surface with its head and looked right at me. Now I saw why Kusum found it so easy to believe that these animals were something other than they are. For where she had seen a sign of Bon Bibi, I saw instead, the gaze of the Poet. It was as if he were saying to me:

> 'some mute animal
> raising its calm eyes and seeing through us,
> and through us. This is destiny . . .'

The *Megha*

In the morning Piya and Kanai hired a cycle-van to take them across the island to look at the bhotbhoti Fokir had arranged. On the way, as they were rattling down the brick-paved path that led to the village, Piya said, 'Tell me about the owner of this boat. Did you say you knew him?'

'I met him when I came here as a boy,' said Kanai. 'His name is Horen Naskor. I can't really claim to know him, but he was close to my uncle.'

'And what's his relation to Fokir?'

'Oh he's like an adopted parent,' said Kanai. 'Fokir lived with him after his mother died.'

Horen was waiting at the foot of the embankment, with Fokir at his side. Kanai recognized him at once: he was squat and wide-bodied, just as he remembered, but his chest seemed even broader now than before because of the substantial paunch that had burgeoned beneath it. With age the folds of Horen's face had deepened so that his eyes seemed almost to have disappeared. Yet it was clear that the years had also added stature to his presence, for his demeanour was now that of a patriarch, a man who commanded the respect of all who knew him. His clothes too were those of a man of some means: his striped lungi was starched and carefully ironed and his white shirt was spotlessly clean. On his wrist was a heavy watch with a metal strap, and sunglasses could be seen protruding from his shirt pocket.

'Do you remember me, Horen-da?' said Kanai, joining his hands in greeting. 'I'm Saar's nephew.'

'Of course,' said Horen matter-of-factly. 'You came here as a punishment in 1970. It was the year of the great Agunmukha cyclone – but you left before that, I think.'

'Yes,' said Kanai. 'And how are your children? You had three then, I remember.'

'They have grown children of their own now,' said Horen. 'Look, here's one of them.' Horen beckoned to a lanky teenager who was dressed in jeans and a smart blue T-shirt. 'His name is Nogen and he's just out of school. He's going to be on our crew.'

'Good.' Kanai turned to introduce Piya. 'And this is the scientist who wants to hire the bhotbhoti: Shrimati Piyali Roy.'

Horen bobbed his head in greeting to Piya. 'Come,' he said, pulling up his lungi. 'My bhotbhoti's waiting.'

Following him up the embankment, Piya and Kanai saw that he was pointing to a vessel anchored off the sandspit that served as Lusibari's jetty. Painted in white lettering on its bow, was the legend 'M.V. *Megha*'.

At first sight there was little to recommend the vessel: it sat awkwardly in the water and its hull had the bruised and dented look of a tin toy. But Horen was proud of his bhotbhoti and spoke of its merits at some length. The *Megha* had carried a great number of passengers, he said to Kanai, and none had ever had cause for complaint. He proceeded to recount many tales about the picnickers he had taken to Pakhiraloy and the bridegrooms and *borjatris* he had ferried to weddings. These stories were not hard to believe, for despite its general decrepitude the boat was clearly intended to cater to large, if huddled, numbers. The lower deck was a cavernous space criss-crossed with wooden benches and curtained with sheets of yellow tarpaulin; the galley and the engine room were located at opposite ends of this space. On top of this was a small upper deck, with a wheelhouse and two tiny cabins. Over the stern hung a tin-walled toilet. This was the head, and, being little more than a hole in the floor, it was reasonably clean.

'She's not much to look at,' Kanai admitted. 'But she might be just right for us. You and I could each have a cabin on the upper deck, and that would keep us away from the noise and fumes.'

'And what about Fokir?' said Piya.

'He'd be on the lower deck,' said Kanai. 'Along with Horen and the helper he's bringing with him, his fifteen-year-old grandson I believe.'

'Is that going to be the whole crew?' said Piya. 'Just the two of them?'

'Yes,' said Kanai. 'We're not going to be crowded for space.'

Piya gave the *Megha* a doubtful look. 'It isn't the research ship of my dreams,' she said. 'But I could live with it. Except for one thing.'

'What's that?'

'I don't get how this old tub is going to follow the dolphins. I can't see it going into all those shallow creeks.'

Kanai relayed Piya's question to Horen and then translated the answer for her benefit: Fokir's boat would be accompanying them on the journey; the *Megha* would tow it all the way and, on reaching their destination, the bhotbhoti would stay at anchor, while Piya and Fokir tracked the dolphins in the boat.

'Really?' This was exactly what Piya had been hoping to hear. 'I guess Fokir was ahead of me on this one.'

'What do you think?' said Kanai. 'Will it work?'

'Yes,' said Piya. 'It's a great idea. It'll be much easier to follow the dolphins in his boat.'

With Kanai translating, the bhotbhoti's terms were quickly agreed. Although Piya would not allow Kanai to contribute to the rental, she agreed to split the costs of the journey's provisions. They handed over a sum of money for Horen to buy rice, daal, oil, tea, bottled water, a couple of chickens and, specifically for Piya, a plentiful supply of powdered milk.

'It's so exciting,' said Piya, as they headed back to the Guest House. 'I can't wait to leave. I'd better get all my washing done this morning.'

'And I'd better go and tell my aunt I'm going to be away for a couple of days,' said Kanai. 'I don't know how she's going to take it.'

Nilima's door was open and Kanai entered to find her sitting at her desk, sipping a cup of tea. Her smile of greeting turned quickly into a curious frown. 'What's the matter-*ré* Kanai? Is something wrong?'

'No, there's nothing wrong,' said Kanai awkwardly. 'I just wanted to tell you, Mashima, that I'm going to be away for a few days.'

'You're going away?' she said in surprise. 'But you've only just come.'

'I know,' said Kanai. 'I hope you won't mind. But Piya's hired a bhotbhoti to track her dolphins. She needs someone to translate.'

'Oh I see!' said Nilima, in English, drawing out the words. 'So you're going with her, then?'

Knowing how precious Nirmal's memory was to her, Kanai said gently, 'And I thought I would take the notebook along with me. If it's all right with you?'

'You'll be careful with it, won't you?'

'Yes, of course.'

'How much have you read?'

'I'm well into it,' said Kanai. 'I'll be done by the time I get back.'

'All right, then. I won't ask you any more about it now,' Nilima said. 'But tell me this, Kanai. Where exactly are you going?'

Kanai scratched his head. The fact was, he didn't know and had not thought to ask. But a habitual unwillingness to acknowledge ignorance led him to pick the name of a river at random: 'I think we'll be going down the Tarobāki River – into the forest.'

'So you're heading into the jungle?' said Nilima, looking him over speculatively.

'I suppose so,' Kanai said, uncertainly.

Nilima rose from her desk and came to stand in front of him. 'Kanai, I hope you've thought this over properly.'

'Yes, of course I have,' said Kanai, feeling suddenly like a schoolboy.

'No I don't think you have, Kanai,' said Nilima, with her hands on her hips. 'And I don't blame you. I know that for outsiders it's very hard to conceive of the dangers.'

'The tigers you mean?' Kanai said. A smile lifted the corners of his lips. 'Why would a tiger pick me when it could have a tasty young morsel like Piya?'

'Kanai,' scolded Nilima, 'this is not a joke. I know that in this day and age, in the twenty-first century, it's difficult for you to imagine yourself being attacked by a tiger. The trouble is that over here it's not in the least bit out of the ordinary. It happens several times each week.'

'As often as that?' said Kanai.

'Yes. More,' said Nilima. 'Look, I'll show you something.' Nilima took hold of Kanai's elbow and led him across the room to one of the many stacks of shelves that lined the walls. 'Look,' she said, pointing to a sheaf of files, 'I've been keeping unofficial records for years, based on word-of-mouth reports. My belief is that over a hundred people are killed by tigers here each year. And, mind you, I'm just talking about the Indian part of the Sundarbans. If you include the Bangladesh side, the figure is probably twice that. If you put the figures together, it means that a human being is killed by a tiger every other day in the Sundarbans – at the very least.'

Kanai raised his eyebrows. 'I knew there were killings,' he said. 'But I never thought there were as many as that.'

'That's the trouble,' said Nilima. 'Nobody knows exactly how many killings there are. None of the figures is reliable. But of this I'm sure: there are many more deaths than the authorities admit.'

Kanai scratched his head. 'This must be a recent trend,' he said. 'Perhaps it has something to do with overpopulation? Or encroachment on the habitat, or something like that?'

'Don't you believe it,' Nilima said scornfully. 'These attacks have been going on for centuries – they were happening even when the population here was a fraction of what it is today. Look.' Standing on tiptoe, she pulled a file off a shelf and carried it to her desk. 'Look over here – do you see that number?'

Kanai looked down at the page and saw that the tip of her finger was pointing to a numeral: 4,218.

'Look at that figure, Kanai,' Nilima said. 'That's the number of people who were killed by tigers in lower Bengal in a six-year period – between the years 1860 and 1866. The figures were compiled by J. Fayrer – he was the English naturalist who coined the phrase "Royal Bengal Tiger". Think of it, Kanai – over four thousand human beings killed. That's almost two people every day, for six years! What would the number add up to over a century?'

'Tens of thousands.' Kanai frowned as he looked down at the page. 'It's hard to believe.'

'Unfortunately,' said Nilima, 'it's all too true.'

'And why do you think it happens this way?' Kanai said. 'What's behind this?'

Nilima sat at her desk and sighed. 'I've heard so many theories, Kanai; I just wish I knew which to believe.'

The one thing everyone agreed on, Nilima said, was that the tide country's tigers were different from those elsewhere. In other habitats, tigers only attacked human beings in abnormal circumstances: if they happened to be crippled or were otherwise unable to hunt down any other kind of prey. But this was not true of the tide country's tigers; even young and healthy animals were known to attack human beings. Some said that this propensity came from the peculiar conditions of the tidal ecology, in which large parts of the forest were subjected to daily submersions. The theory went that this raised the animals' threshold of aggression by washing away their scent markings and confusing their territorial instincts. This was about as convincing a theory as Nilima had ever heard, but the trouble was that even if it were true, there was nothing that could be done about it.

But every few years there was some new theory and some yet more ingenious solution. In the 1980s a German naturalist had suggested that the tigers' preference for human flesh was somehow connected with the shortage of fresh water in the Sundarbans. This idea had been received with great enthusiasm by the Forest Department, and several pools had been excavated to provide the tigers with fresh water.

'Just imagine that!' said Nilima. 'They were providing water for tigers! In a place where nobody thinks twice about human beings going thirsty!'

The digging was in vain, however. The pools had made no difference. The attacks continued as before.

'Then there was the electric-shock idea,' said Nilima, with laughter shining in her eyes.

Someone had decided that tigers could be conditioned with the methods Pavlov had used on his dogs. Clay models of human beings had been rigged up with wires and connected to car batteries. These contraptions were distributed all over the islands. For a while they seemed to be working and there was much jubilation. 'But then the attacks started again; the tigers just ignored the clay models and carried on as before.'

Another time, a forester came up with another equally ingenious idea: what if people wore masks on the backs of their heads? Tigers always attacked human beings from behind, the reasoning went, so they would shy away if they found themselves looking at a pair of painted eyes. This idea too was taken up with great enthusiasm. Many masks were made and distributed; word was put out that a wonderful new experiment was being tried in the Sundarbans. There was something so picturesque about the idea that it caught the public imagination: television cameras descended, film-makers made films.

The tigers, alas, refused to co-operate: 'Evidently they had no difficulty in discriminating between masks and faces.'

'So are you saying the tigers are actually able to think these things through?' said Kanai.

'I don't know, Kanai,' Nilima said. 'I've lived here for over fifty years and I've never seen a tiger. Nor do I want to. I've come to believe what people say in these parts: that if you see a tiger the chances are you won't live to tell the tale. That's why I'm telling you, Kanai, you can't go into the jungle on a whim. Before you go you should ask yourself whether you really need to.'

'But I'm not planning to go into the jungle at all,' Kanai replied. 'I'm going to be on the bhotbhoti, well removed from any harm.'

'And you think a bhotbhoti is going to keep you from harm?'

'We'll be out on the water, well away from shore. What can happen there?'

'Kanai, let me tell you something. Nine years ago, a tiger killed a young girl, right here in Lusibari. They found later that it had swum all the way across the Bidya's mohona and back again. Do you know how far that is?'

'No.'

'Six kilometres, each way. And that's not unusual: they've been known to swim as much as thirteen kilometres at a stretch. So don't for a moment imagine that the water will give you any safety. Boats and bhotbhotis are attacked all the time – even out in midstream. It happens several times each year.'

'Really?'

'Yes.' Nilima nodded. 'And if you don't believe me, just take a close look at any of the Forest Department's boats. You'll see they're like floating fortresses. Their windows have steel bars as thick as my wrist. And that's despite the fact that forest guards carry arms. Tell me: does your bhotbhoti have bars on its windows?'

Kanai scratched his head. 'I don't remember.'

'There you are,' Nilima said. 'You didn't even notice. I don't think you understand what you're getting into. Leave aside the animals – those boats and bhotbhotis are more dangerous than anything in the jungle. Every month we hear of one or two going down. '

'There's no reason for you to worry,' said Kanai. 'I won't take any risks.'

'But Kanai, don't you see? To our way of thinking, you *are* the risk. The others are going because they need to – but not you. You're going on a whim, a *kheyal*. You don't have any pressing reason to go.'

'That's not true; I do have a reason—' Kanai had spoken without thinking and cut himself off abruptly, in mid-sentence.

'Kanai?' said Nilima. 'Is there something you aren't telling me?'

'Oh it's just—' He could not think of what to say next and hung his head.

She looked at him shrewdly: 'It's that girl, isn't it? Piya?'

Kanai looked away, in silence, and she said suddenly, with a bitterness he had never heard in her voice before, 'You're all the same, you men. Who can blame the tigers when predators like you pass for human beings?'

She took hold of Kanai's elbow and led him to the door. 'Be careful, Kanai – just be careful.'

Memory

After we had spent a half-hour with the dolphins, Horen began to row towards the shore of Garjontola. As we were drawing closer, Horen looked to me with a mischievous smile. 'Saar,' he said, 'now the time to go ashore is at hand. Tell me, Saar, bhoi ta ter paisen? Do you feel the fear?'

'The fear?' I said. 'What do you mean, Horen? Why should I be afraid? Aren't you with me?'

'Because it's the fear that protects you, Saar; it's what keeps you alive. Without it the danger doubles.'

'So are you afraid, then, Horen?'

'Yes, Saar,' he said. 'Look at me. Don't you see the fear on my face?'

And now that I looked more closely, it was true that I could see something out of the ordinary on his face – an alertness, a gravity, a sharpening of the eyes. The tension was of a kind that communicated itself readily: it didn't take long before I could say to Horen, truthfully, that I was just as afraid as he was.

'Yes, Horen. I feel it.'

'That's good, Saar; that's good.'

When the boat was some twenty metres from the shore, Horen stopped rowing and put away his oars. Shutting his eyes, he began to mumble and make gestures with his hands.

'What is he doing?' I said to Kusum.

'Don't you know, Saar?' she said. 'He is a "bauley". He knows the mantras that shut the mouths of the big cats. He knows how to keep them from attacking us.'

Perhaps in another circumstance I would have laughed. But it was true that I was afraid now: I did not need to feign my fear. I knew Horen

244

could no more shut the mouth of a tiger than he could conjure up a storm – but I was still reassured by his meaningless mumbles, by his lack of bravado. His manner was not that of a magician weaving a spell: he was more like a mechanic, giving a spanner an extra turn, in order to leave nothing undone. This reassured me.

'Now listen to me, Saar,' said Horen. 'Since you haven't done this before, I must tell you a rule.'

'What rule, Horen?'

'The rule, Saar, is that when we go ashore, you can leave nothing of yourself behind. You cannot spit or urinate; you cannot sit down to relieve yourself; you cannot leave behind your morning's meal. If you do, then harm will come to all of us.'

Although no one laughed, I was conscious of a mild sense of affront. 'Why, Horen,' I said, 'I have done my business already. Unless my fear reaches such a pitch as to overwhelm me, I will have no need to leave anything of myself behind.'

'That's good, Saar. I just thought I'd tell you.'

Then he started to row again and when the shore had come closer, he leapt over the side to push the boat. To my astonishment, Fokir followed him almost instantly. Even though the water came up to his neck, the boy quickly put his shoulder to the boat and began to push.

No one else was surprised by the child's adeptness. His mother turned to me and I saw she was choking with pride: 'See, Saar: the river is in his veins.'

What would I not have given at that moment to be able to say that this was true also of myself, that the river flowed in my veins too, laden with all its guilty burdens? But I had never felt so much an outsider as I did at that moment. Yet, I was glad at least, that my years in the tide country had taught me how to use my feet in the mud: when it came time to step off the boat, I was able to follow them ashore without difficulty.

We headed into the badabon, with Horen in the lead, clearing a path for us with his dâ. Kusum was behind him, with the clay image balanced on her shoulder. I was in the rear, and not for a moment did the thought leave my mind that if a tiger were to fall upon me then, in those dense thickets of mangrove, it would find me all but immobile, a caged feast.

But nothing untoward happened. We came to a clearing and Kusum led the way to the shrine, which was nothing more than a raised platform

245

with bamboo sides and a thatched covering. Here we placed the images of Bon Bibi and her brother Shah Jongoli, and then Kusum lit a few sticks of fragrant dhoop and Fokir fetched some leaves and flowers and laid them at their feet.

So far there was nothing unusual about the proceedings, except its setting – otherwise it was very much like the small household pujas I remembered my mother performing in my childhood. But then suddenly Horen began to recite a mantra, and to my great surprise I heard him say:

> *Bismillah boliya mukhey dhorinu kalam / poida korilo jini tamam alam* baro meherban tini bandar upore / taar chhani keba achhe duniyar upore**

> *(In Allah's name, I begin to pronounce the Word / Of the whole universe, He is the Begetter the Lord* To all His disciples, He is full of mercy / Above the created world, who is there but He*)*

I was amazed. I'd thought I was going to a Hindu puja: imagine my astonishment on hearing these Arabic invocations! Yet the rhythm of the recitation was undoubtedly that of a puja: how often, as a child, had I heard those endless chants, rolling on and on, in temples as well as in our home?

I listened enthralled as Horen continued his recitation: the language was not easy to follow – it was a strange variety of Bangla, deeply inter-penetrated by Arabic and Persian. The narrative, however, was famil-iar to me: it was the story of how Dukhey was left on the shore of an island to be devoured by the tiger-demon Dokkhin Rai, and of his rescue by Bon Bibi and Shah Jongoli.

At the end, after the others had said their prayers, we picked up our things and made our way back across the clearing towards the boat. When we were back on the boat, heading towards Morichjhãpi, I said, 'Horen, where did you learn that long recitation?'

He looked startled. 'Why, Saar,' he said. 'I've known it as long as I remember. I heard my father reciting it, and I learnt from him.'

'So is this legend passed on from mouth to mouth, and remembered only in memory?'

'Why no, Saar,' he said. 'There's a book in which it was printed. I even have a copy.' He reached down into that part of his boat where he stored his things, and pulled out a tattered old pamphlet. 'Here,' he said, 'have a look.'

I opened the first page and saw it bore the title 'Bon Bibir Karamoti orthat Bon Bibi Johuranama' (The Miracles of Bon Bibi or the Narrative of Her Glory). When I tried to open the book, I had another surprise: the pages opened to the right, as in Arabic, not to the left as in Bangla. Yet the prosody was that of much of Bangla folklore: the legend was recounted in the verse form called dwipodi poyar – with rhymed couplets in which each line is of roughly twelve syllables, each with a break, or caesura, towards the middle.

The booklet was written by a Muslim author, whose name was given simply as Abdur-Rahim. By the usual canons the work was not of great literary merit. Although the lines rhymed, in a kind of doggerel fashion, they did not present the appearance of verse; they followed continuously on each other, being broken only by slashes and asterisks. In other words they looked like prose and read like verse, a strange hybrid, I thought at first, and then it occurred to me that no, this was something remarkable and wonderful – prose that had mounted the ladder of metre in order to ascend above the prosaic.

'When was this book written?' I asked Horen. 'Do you know?'

'Oh it's old,' said Horen. 'Very, very old.'

Very, very old? But on the first page was a couplet that read, 'There are those who travel with an atlas in hand / while others use carriages to wander the land'.

It struck me that this legend had perhaps taken shape in the late nineteenth or early twentieth century, just as new waves of settlers were moving into the tide country. And was it possible that this accounted for the way it was formed, from elements of legend and scripture, from the near and the far, Bangla and Arabic?

How could it be otherwise? For this I have seen confirmed many times, that the mudbanks of the tide country are shaped not only by rivers of silt, but also by rivers of language: Bengali, English, Arabic, Hindi, Arakanese and who knows what else? Flowing into each other they create a proliferation of small worlds that hang suspended in the flow. And so it dawned on me: the tide country's faith is something like one of its great mohonas, a meeting not just of many rivers, but a circular roundabout people can use to pass in many directions – from country to country and even between faiths and religions.

247

I was so taken with this idea that I began to copy some passages of the pamphlet into the back of a notebook I was carrying in my jhola, this very one, as it happens. The print was tiny and I had to squint hard at the page to decipher it. Absent-mindedly, I handed the booklet to Fokir, as I might have to one of my pupils. I said, 'Read it out aloud, so I can copy it down.'

He began to speak the words out aloud while I wrote them down. Suddenly a thought struck me and I said to Kusum, 'But you told me Fokir can neither write nor read.'

'That's right, Saar,' she said. 'He can't.'

'Then?'

She smiled and patted him on the head. 'It's all in his head; I've told it to him so often that these words have become a part of him.'

It is evening now and Kusum has given me a candle so I can go on writing. Horen is impatient to leave: he has been entrusted with the task of taking Fokir to safety. Only Kusum and I will remain. We can hear the patrol boats, which have encircled the island. Horen will use the cover of darkness to slip past.

Horen wants to go now: I say to him – just a few more hours. There's a whole night ahead. Kusum joins her voice to mine, she leads him outside: 'Come, let's go down to your boat. Let's leave Saar alone.'

Intermediaries

By the time Piya had organized her notes, washed her clothes and cleaned her equipment, the day was over and night had fallen. She decided to turn in without waiting for dinner. There was no telling how long it would be before she found a proper bed again. She might as well make the most of this one and get a good night's sleep. She decided not to interrupt Kanai, who was upstairs, in the study. She mixed a tumbler of Ovaltine for herself and took it downstairs, into the open.

The moon was up, and in the silvery light Piya spotted Nilima standing outside her door. She appeared to be deep in thought, but her head turned as Piya approached.

Piya sketched a wave with her free hand: 'Hello.'

Nilima answered with a smile and a few words of Bengali. This drew a rueful response from Piya. 'I'm sorry,' she said, shaking her head. 'I'm afraid I don't understand.'

'Of course,' said Nilima. 'I'm the one who should apologize. I always forget. It's your appearance that gets me mixed up – I keep having to remind myself not to speak to you in Bangla.'

Piya smiled. 'My mother used to say that a day would come when I'd regret not knowing the language. And I guess she was right.'

'But tell me, my dear,' Nilima said. 'Just as a matter of interest: why is it your parents never taught you any Bangla?'

'My mother tried a little,' said Piya. 'But I was not an eager student. And as for my father, I think he had some doubts.'

'Doubts? About teaching you his language?'

'Yes,' said Piya. 'It's a complicated story. You see, my father's parents were Bengalis who'd settled in Burma – they came to India as refugees, during the Second World War. Having moved around a lot, my father has all these theories about immigrants and refugees. He believes that Indians – Bengalis in particular – don't travel well, because their eyes are always turned backwards, towards home. When we moved to America, he decided he wasn't going to make that mistake: he was going to try to fit in.'

'So he always spoke English to you?'

'Yes,' said Piya, 'and you have to understand that it was a real sacrifice for him because he doesn't speak English very well, even to this day. He's an engineer and he tends to sound a bit like a construction manual.'

'So what did he speak with your mother?'

'They spoke Bengali to each other,' said Piya with a laugh. 'But that was when they were speaking, of course. When they weren't, I was their sole means of communication. And I always made them translate their messages into English – or else I wouldn't carry them.'

Nilima made no response and her silence led Piya to wonder whether she had taken offence at something she had said. But just then, Nilima reached for the hem of her sari and brought it up to her face. Piya saw that her eyes had filled with tears.

'I'm sorry,' Piya said quickly. 'Did I say something wrong?'

'No, my dear,' said Nilima. 'You said nothing wrong. I was just thinking of you as a little girl, carrying your parents' words from one to the other. It's a terrible thing, my dear, when a husband and wife can't speak to each other. But your parents were lucky: at least they had you to run between them. Imagine if they had no one—'

She let the sentence die unfinished and fell silent again. Piya knew she had unwittingly touched on some private grief and she waited quietly while Nilima composed herself.

'Only once was there ever a child in our home,' Nilima said presently. 'That was when Kanai came to stay with us, as a boy. To my husband it meant more than I could ever have imagined. More than anything else he longed to have someone to whom he could pass on his words. For years afterwards he would say to me, "I wish Kanai would come again." I'd remind him that

250

Kanai wasn't a boy any more: he was a grown man. But that didn't stop my husband. He wrote to Kanai many times, asking him to come.'

'And Kanai never came?'

'No,' said Nilima. She sighed, 'Kanai was on the way to success and that takes its own toll. He didn't have time for anyone but himself – not his parents, and certainly not us.'

'Has he always been like that?' Piya said. 'So driven?'

'Some would say selfish,' said Nilima. 'Kanai's problem is that he's always been too clever for his own good. Things have come very easily to him so he doesn't know what the world is like for most people.'

Piya could see that this judgement was both shrewd and accurate but she knew it was not her place to concur. 'I haven't known him long enough to have an opinion,' she said politely.

'No, I don't suppose you have,' said Nilima. 'Just a word of warning, my dear. Fond as I am of my nephew, I feel I should tell you that he's one of those men who likes to think of himself as being irresistible to the other sex. Unfortunately, the world doesn't lack for women who're foolish enough to confirm such a man's opinion of himself, and Kanai seems always to be looking for them. I don't know how you describe that kind of man nowadays, my dear – but in my time we used to call them "fast".' She paused, raising her eyebrows. 'Do you get my meaning?'

'I sure do.'

Nilima gave her a nod and blew her nose into the hem of her sari. 'Anyway, I mustn't be rattling on like this. You have a long day ahead tomorrow, don't you?'

'Yes,' said Piya. 'We're starting early. I'm really looking forward to it.'

Nilima put an arm around her shoulders and gave her a hug. 'Do be careful, my dear. It's dangerous in the forest – and not just because of the animals.'

Besieged

A few days after my trip to Garjontola, Nilima returned from her travels, full of news of the world outside. Almost in passing, she said, 'And as for Morichjhāpi, there are soon going to be developments.'

My ears pricked up. 'What developments?'

'The government is going to take measures. Very strong measures.'

I said nothing, but began to wonder if there was any way I could get word to Kusum, to warn the settlers. As it turned out, no warning was possible. The very next day the government announced that all movement in and out of Morichjhāpi was banned under the provisions of the Forest Preservation Act. What was more, Section 144, the law used to quell civil disturbances, was imposed on the whole area: this meant it was a criminal offence for five people or more to gather in one place.

As the day wore on, waves of rumours came sweeping down our rivers; it was said that dozens of police boats had encircled the island, tear gas and rubber bullets had been used, the settlers had been forcibly prevented from bringing rice or water to Morichjhāpi, boats had been sunk, people had been killed. The rumours grew more and more disturbing as the day passed: it was as if war had broken out in the quiet recesses of the tide country.

For Nilima's sake I tried to keep up appearances, I tried to present as normal a front as I could. But I could not sleep that night and by the time morning came around, I knew I would make my way to Morichjhāpi in whatever way I could, even at the expense of a confrontation with Nilima. But fortunately that contingency did not arise – not yet, anyway. Early in the morning a group of schoolmasters came to see me; they had heard the same rumours I had, and they too had become concerned. So much so, that they had hired a bhotbhoti to take them to Morichjhāpi *to see if any intercession was possible. They asked if I wanted to join them and I was only too glad to say yes.*

We left at about ten in the morning and were in view of our destination within a couple of hours. I should say here that Morichjhãpi is a large island, one of the biggest in the tide country: its coastline is probably almost twenty kilometres in length. When we were within sight of the island, but still a good two or three kilometres away, we saw clouds of smoke rising above the island.

Not long afterwards we spotted official motorboats patrolling the rivers. The owner of our bhotbhoti now became quite concerned and we had to plead with him to take us a little closer to the island. He agreed to do so, but only on the condition that we stay close to the near shore, as far as possible from the island. And so we proceeded, hugging this shore, while all our eyes were turned in the other direction, towards Morichjhãpi.

Presently we drew close to a village. A great number of people had gathered on the shore and they were busily loading a boat – not a bhotbhoti or a sailboat, but a plain country nouko of the kind Horen owned. Even from a distance we could see that the boat was being stocked with a cargo of provisions – sacks of grain and jerrycans of drinking water. Then a number of people climbed into the boat, mainly men, but also a few women and children; some, no doubt, were day labourers who'd gone to work on some other island and been unable to return home. As for the others, perhaps they were people who had been separated from their families and were trying to get back to their homes in Morichjhãpi. Whatever their reasons for going, clearly they were pressing enough to make them take the risk of cramming themselves into that frail craft. By the time the boat was pushed into the water there must have been a good two dozen people sitting huddled inside. The boat wobbled as it drifted out into the currents; it was so heavily loaded that it seemed incredible that it would actually stay afloat. Watching from a distance, we speculated excitedly: these settlers were evidently hoping to slip through the police cordon with some provisions, to bring relief to their fellow islanders. What would the police do? Everyone offered a different theory.

Then, as if to put an end to our speculations, a police speedboat came roaring down the Bagna River. Moving at great speed, it drew level with the settlers' rowboat and began to circle around it. There was a loudspeaker on the police boat, and even though we were a good distance away, snatches of the policemen's orders reached us across the waters: they were telling the settlers to turn back, to return to the shore they had come from. What was said in answer, we could not hear, but we could tell from the gestures and gesticulations of the people on the boat that they were pleading with the policemen to let them proceed.

This had the effect of enraging the policemen who now began to scream into their loudspeaker. Suddenly, like a thunderclap, came the noise of a gunshot, fired into the air.

Surely the settlers would turn back now? In our hearts we prayed they would. But what happened instead was something unforeseen: the people in the boat joined together their voices and began to shout, in unison, 'Amra kara? Bastuhara. Who are we? We are the dispossessed.'

How strange it was to hear this plaintive cry wafting across the water. It seemed at that moment, not to be a shout of defiance, but rather a question being addressed to the very heavens, not just for themselves, but on behalf of a bewildered humankind. Who, indeed, are we? Where do we belong? And as I listened to the sound of those syllables, it was as if I were hearing the deepest uncertainties of my heart being spoken to the rivers and the tides. Who was I? Where did I belong? In Kolkata or in the tide country? In India or across the border? In prose or in poetry?

Then we heard the settlers shouting a refrain, answering the questions they had themselves posed: 'Morichjhãpi chharbona. We'll not leave Morichjhãpi, do what you may.'

Standing on the deck of the bhotbhoti, I was struck by the beauty of this. Where else could you belong, except in the place you refused to leave.

I joined my feeble voice to theirs: 'Morichjhãpi chharbona!'

It had not struck me to ask how the policemen, in their motorboat, would interpret these cries. The motorboat, which had been idling for a few minutes, suddenly started up its engine. Its bow came around and it began to move away from the settlers. For a few minutes it seemed the policemen might even have decided to look the other way and let the boat pass.

That their intention was utterly otherwise became clear when the motorboat wheeled around in the water. Suddenly, picking up speed it came shooting towards the wobbling nouko with its boatload of passengers and provisions. It hit the boat square in the middle: in front of our eyes the timbers flew apart. Suddenly the water was full of struggling men, women and children.

It occurred to me that Kusum and Fokir might be on that boat. My heart stopped.

On our bhotbhoti, we shouted to the pilot to move closer so that we could be of help. He was hesitant, afraid of the police, but we persuaded him that the police would not harm a group of schoolmasters, he had nothing to fear.

We edged closer, moving slowly so as not to hit anyone in the water. Leaning over the side, we extended our hands to those in the water. We pulled in one, two, a dozen people. The water fortunately was not deep, and many were able to wade ashore.

I asked one of the men we had pulled in, 'Do you know Kusum Mandol? Was she on the boat?'

He knew her; he shook his head. She was still on the island, he told me and I was giddy with relief. Little did I know how things were shaping up there.

Soon the policemen came speeding up to us. 'Who are you people?' they demanded to know. 'What are you doing here?'

They paid no heed to answers; they told us that with Section 144 having been declared, we could be arrested for unlawful assembly.

We were just schoolmasters, most of the men had families, children. We quailed; we went to the shore to drop off the people we had pulled from the water and then we turned back.

My pen is out of ink and I must switch to my pencil stub. Every footstep I hear is a reminder that Kusum and Horen will soon be back, and that Horen will want to leave at once. But I cannot stop. There's too much to tell.

Words

Ensconced in Nirmal's study, Kanai forgot about dinner. He was still reading when the compound's generator shut down and the lights went off. He knew there was a kerosene lamp somewhere in the study and he was fumbling for it in the dark, when he heard a footfall in the doorway.

'Kanai-babu?'

It was Moyna, holding a candle. 'Do you need a match?' she said. 'I came to get the tiffin carrier and saw you still hadn't eaten.'

'I was on my way down,' said Kanai. 'I was just looking for the hurricane lamp.'

'There it is.'

Moyna went over to the lamp, candle in hand, and snapped back the glass cover. She was trying to light the wick when her hands slipped, sending both the lamp and candle crashing to the floor. The glass shattered and the study was suddenly filled with the acrid smell of kerosene.

The candle had rolled into a corner and although the flame was out, Kanai saw that the wick was still glowing. 'Quick.' Falling to his knees, he lunged for the candle. 'Pinch out the wick or it'll set fire to the kerosene. The whole place will burn down.'

He took the candle out of Moyna's hands and squeezed the glowing wick between finger and thumb. 'It's all right – it's out now. We just have to sweep up the glass.'

'I'll do it, Kanai-babu,' she said.

'It'll be quicker if we both do it.' Kneeling beside her, Kanai began to brush his hands gingerly over the floor.

'Why did you let your dinner get cold, Kanai-babu?' Moyna said. 'Why didn't you eat?'

'I was just busy getting ready for tomorrow,' Kanai said. 'You know we're leaving early in the morning? I'm going too.'

'Yes,' said Moyna, 'I heard. And I'm glad you're going, Kanai-babu.'

'Why?' said Kanai. 'Are you tired of bringing me my meals?'

'No,' she said. 'It's not that.'

'Then?'

'I'm just glad that you'll be there, Kanai-babu; that they won't be alone.'

'Who?'

'The two of them.' Her voice was suddenly serious.

'You mean Fokir and Piya?'

'Who else, Kanai-babu? I was really relieved when I heard you were going to be with them. To tell you the truth, I was hoping you would talk to him a little.'

'To Fokir? Talk about what?'

'About her – the American,' Moyna said. 'Maybe you could explain to him that she's just here for a few days – that she's going to be gone soon.'

'But he knows that, doesn't he?'

He could hear her sari rustling in the darkness as she pulled it tight around herself. 'It would be good for him to hear it from you, Kanai-babu. Who knows what he's begun to expect – especially when she's giving him so much money? Maybe you could speak with her too – just to explain she would do him harm if she made him forget himself.'

'But why me, Moyna?' Kanai said in surprise. 'What can *I* say?'

'Kanai-babu, there's no one else who knows how to speak to both of them – to her and to him. It's you who stands between them: whatever they say to each other will go through your ears and your lips. But for you neither of them will know what is in the mind of the other. Their words will be in your hands and you can make them mean what you will.'

'I don't understand, Moyna,' Kanai said, frowning. 'What are you saying? What exactly are you afraid of?'

'She's a woman, Kanai-babu.' Moyna's voice sank to a whisper. 'And he's a man.'

Kanai glared at her in the dark. 'I'm a man too, Moyna,' he said. 'If she had to choose between me and Fokir, whom do you think it would be?'

Moyna's reply was non-committal and slow in coming: 'How am I to know what she has in her heart, Kanai-babu?'

Her hesitation provoked Kanai. 'And you, Moyna? Who would you choose, if you could?'

Moyna said quietly, 'What are you asking, Kanai-babu? Fokir is my husband.'

'But you're such a bright, capable girl, Moyna,' said Kanai insistently. 'Why don't you forget about Fokir? Can't you see that as long as you're with him you'll never be able to achieve anything?'

'He's my son's father, Kanai-babu,' Moyna said. 'I can't turn my back on him. If I do, what will become of him?'

Kanai laughed. 'Moyna, it's true he's your husband – but then why can't you talk to him yourself? Why do you want me to do it for you?'

'It's *because* he's my husband that I can't talk to him, Kanai-babu,' Moyna said quietly. 'Only a stranger can put such things into words.'

'Why should it be easier for a stranger than for you?'

'Because words are just air, Kanai-babu,' Moyna said. 'When the wind blows on the water, you see ripples and waves, but the real river lies beneath, unseen and unheard. You can't blow on the water's surface from below, Kanai-babu. Only someone who's outside can do that, someone like you.'

Kanai laughed again. 'Words may be air, Moyna – but you have a nice way with them.'

He stood up and went to the desk. 'Tell me, Moyna, don't you ever wonder what it would be like to be with a different kind of man? Aren't you ever curious?'

He had said it in a light mocking way and this time he succeeded in provoking her.

She rose angrily to her feet. 'Kanai-babu, you're just making a fool of me, aren't you? You want me to say yes and then you'll

258

laugh in my face. You'll tell everybody what I said. I may be a village girl, Kanai-babu, but I'm not so foolish as to answer a question like that. I can see that you play this game with every woman who crosses your path.'

This struck home and he flinched. 'Don't be angry, Moyna,' he said. 'I didn't mean any harm.'

He heard her sari rustling as she rose to her feet and pulled the door open. Then, in the darkness, he heard her say, 'Kanai-babu, I hope it goes well for you with the American. It'll be better for all of us that way.'

Crimes

The siege went on for many days and we were powerless to affect the outcome. All we heard were rumours: that despite careful rationing, food had run out and the settlers had been reduced to eating grass. The police had destroyed the tubewells and there was no potable water left; the settlers were drinking from puddles and ponds and an epidemic of cholera had broken out.

'One of the settlers managed to get through the police cordon by swimming across the Gāral River – an amazing feat in its own right. But not content with that, the young man had somehow made his way to Kolkata where he talked at length to the newspapers. A furore broke out, citizens' groups filed petitions, questions were asked in the legislature and finally the High Court ruled that barricading the settlers was illegal; the siege would have to be lifted.

The settlers, it seemed, had won a notable victory. The day after the news reached us, I saw Horen waiting near the bādh. Neither he nor I needed to say anything: I packed my jhola and went down to his boat. We set off.

There was a lightness in our hearts now; we thought we would find the people of Morichjhāpi celebrating, in a spirit of vindication. But such was not the case: on getting there we saw that the siege had taken a terrible toll. And even though it had been lifted now, the police were not gone; they continued to patrol the island, urging the settlers to abandon their homes.

It was terrible to see Kusum: her bones protruded from her skin, like the ribs of a drum, and she was too weak to rise from her mat. Fokir, young as he was, appeared to have weathered the siege in better health and it was he who was looking after his mother.

Summing up the situation, I assumed that Kusum had starved herself in order to feed Fokir. But the truth was not quite so simple. For much of the time, Kusum had kept Fokir indoors, fearing to let him out because of the swarming police. But from time to time he had managed to go outside and catch a few crabs and fish. These, at Kusum's insistence, he had mainly eaten himself, while she had subsisted on a kind of wild green known as jadu-palong. Palatable enough at first, these leaves had proved deadly in the end, for they had caused severe dysentery. The latter, on top of the lack of proper nutrition, had proved most debilitating.

Fortunately, we had taken the precaution of buying some essential provisions on the way – rice, daal, oil – and we now occupied ourselves in storing these in Kusum's dwelling. But Kusum would have none of it. She roused herself from her mat, and hefted some of the bags on her shoulders. Fokir and Horen were made to pick up the others.

'Wait,' I said. 'What are you doing? Where are you taking those? They're meant for you.'

'I can't keep them, Saar; we're rationing everything. I have to take them to the leader of my ward.'

Although I could see the point of this, I persuaded her that she did not need to part with every last handful of rice and daal: to put aside a little for herself would not be immoral, given she was a mother with a child to provide for.

As we were measuring out the cupfuls she would keep for herself, she began to cry. The sight of her tears came as a shock to both Horen and myself. Kusum had never till now shown any flagging in courage and confidence; to see her break down was unbearably painful. Fokir went to stand behind her, putting an arm around her neck, while Horen sat beside her and patted her shoulder. I alone was frozen, unable to respond except in words.

'What is it, Kusum?' I said. 'What are you thinking of?'

'Saar,' she said, wiping her face, 'the worst part was not the hunger or the thirst. It was to sit here, helpless, and listen to the policemen making their announcements, hearing them say that our lives, our existence, was worth less than dirt or dust. "This island has to be saved for its trees, it has to be saved for its animals, it is a part of a reserve forest, it belongs to a project to save tigers, which is paid for by people from all around the world." Every day, sitting here, with hunger gnawing at our bellies, we would listen to these words, over and over again. Who are these

261

people, I wondered, who love animals so much that they are willing to kill us for them? Do they know what is being done in their names? Where do they live, these people, do they have children, do they have mothers, fathers? As I thought of these things it seemed to me that this whole world has become a place of animals, and our fault, our crime, was that we were just human beings, trying to live as human beings always have, from the water and the soil. No human being could think this a crime unless they have forgotten that this is how humans have always lived – by fishing, by clearing land and by planting the soil.'

Her words, and the sight of her wasted face, affected me so much – useless schoolmaster that I am – that my head reeled and I had lie down on a mat.

Leaving Lusibari

~~~~~~~~~

Lusibari was shrouded in the usual dawn mist when Kanai walked down the path to the hospital. Early as it was, there was already a cycle-van waiting at the gate. Kanai led it back to the Guest House and, with the driver's help, he and Piya quickly loaded their baggage on to the van – Kanai's suitcase, Piya's two backpacks and a bundle of blankets and pillows they had borrowed from the Guest House.

They set off at a brisk pace and were soon at the outskirts of Lusibari village. They had almost reached the embankment, when the driver spun around in his seat and pointed ahead. 'Look: something's happening over there, on the bãdh.'

Kanai and Piya were facing backwards. Craning his neck, Kanai saw that a number of people had congregated on the crest of the embankment. They were absorbed in watching some sort of spectacle or contest taking place on the other side of the earth-works: many were cheering and calling out encouragement. Leaving their baggage on the van, Kanai and Piya went up to take a look.

The water was at a low ebb and the *Megha* was moored at the far end of the mudspit, alongside Fokir's boat. The boat was the focus of the crowd's attention: Fokir and Tutul were standing on it, along with Horen and his teenage grandson. They were tugging at a fishing line that was sizzling as it sliced through the water, turning in tight, zigzag patterns.

The catch, Kanai learnt, was a *shankor-machh*, a sting-ray. Now, as Piya and Kanai stood watching, a flat grey form broke from the water and went planing through the air. Fokir and the others hung on as if they were trying to hold down a giant kite. The men had gamchhas wrapped around their hands and with all of them exerting their weight, they slowly began to prevail against the thrashing ray: the struggle ended with Fokir leaning over the side of the boat to plunge the tip of his machete-like *daa* into its head.

When the catch had been laid out on the shore, Kanai and Piya joined the crowd clustering around it. The ray was a good metre and a half from wing-tip to wing-tip and its tail was about half as long again. Within minutes a fish-seller had made a bid and Fokir had accepted. But before the catch could be carted off, Fokir raised his daa and with a single stroke, cut through the tail. This he gave to Tutul, handing it over with some ceremony, as though it were a victor's spoils.

'What's Tutul going to do with that?' said Piya.

'He'll make a toy out of it, I suppose,' said Kanai. 'In the old days landlords and zamindars used those tails as whips, to punish unruly subjects: they sting like hell. But they make good toys too. I remember I had one as a boy.'

Just then, as Tutul was admiring his trophy, Moyna appeared suddenly before him, having pushed her way through the crowd. Taken by surprise, Tutul darted out of her reach and slipped behind his father. For fear of hurting the boy, Fokir raised his dripping daa above his head, with both hands, to keep the blade out of his way. Now Tutul began to dance around his father, eluding his mother's grasp and drawing shouts of laughter from the crowd.

Moyna was dressed for duty, in her nurse's uniform, a blue-bordered white sari. But by the time she finally caught hold of Tutul, her starched sari was spattered with mud and her lips were trembling in humiliation. She turned on Fokir, who dropped his eyes and raised a knuckle to brush away a trickle of blood that had dripped from the daa on to his face.

'Didn't I tell you to take him straight to school?' she said to Fokir, in a voice taut with fury. 'And instead, you brought him here?'

To the sound of a collective gasp from the crowd, Moyna wrung the sting-ray's tail out of her son's hand. Curling her arm, she flung the trophy into the river, where it was carried away by the current. The boy's face crumpled as his mother led him away. He stumbled after her with his eyes shut, as though he were trying to blind himself to his surroundings.

Moyna checked her step as she was passing Kanai, and their eyes met for a brief instant before she went running down the embankment. When she had left, Kanai turned around to find that Fokir's eyes were resting on him too, summing him up – it was as if he had noticed the wordless exchange between him and his wife and was trying to guess its meaning.

Kanai was suddenly very uncomfortable. Spinning around on his heels, he said to Piya, 'Come on. Let's start unloading our luggage.'

The *Megha* pulled away from Lusibari with its engine alternately sputtering and hammering; in its wake came Fokir's boat, following fitfully, as its tow-rope slackened and tightened. To prevent accidental collisions, Fokir was travelling in his boat rather than in the bhotbhoti: he had seated himself in the bow and was holding an oar in his hands, so as to fend off the larger vessel in case it came too close to his own.

Kanai was on the upper deck where two deep, wood-framed chairs had been placed near the wheelhouse, in the shade of a canvas awning. Although Nirmal's notebook was lying open on his lap, Kanai's eyes were on Piya: he was watching her make her preparations for the work of the day.

Piya had positioned herself to meet the wind and the sun head-on, at the point where the deck tapered into a jutting prow. After garlanding herself with her binoculars, she proceeded to strap on her equipment-belt, with its flapping clipboard and its two dangling instruments – the GPS tracker and the depth-sounder. Only then did she take her stance and reach for her glasses, with her feet wide apart, swaying slightly on her legs. Although her eyes were unwavering in their focus on the water, Kanai could tell she was alert to everything happening around her, on the boat and on shore.

As the sun mounted in the sky, the glare off the water increased

265

in intensity until it had all but erased the seam that separated the water from the sky. Despite his sunglasses, Kanai found it hard to keep his eyes on the river – yet Piya seemed to be troubled neither by the light nor by the gusting wind: with her knees flexed to absorb the shaking of the bhotbhoti, she seemed scarcely to notice its rolling as she pivoted from side to side. Her one concession to the conditions was a sunhat, which she had opened out and placed on her head. From his position in the shade, Kanai could see her only in outline and it struck him that her silhouette was not unlike that of a cowboy, with her belt-load of equipment and wide-brimmed hat.

Around mid-morning there was a flurry of excitement when Fokir's voice was heard, shouting from the boat. Signalling to Horen to cut the bhotbhoti's engine, Piya went running to the back of the deck. Kanai was quick to follow but by the time he had made his way aft the action was over.

'What happened?'

Piya was busy scribbling on a data sheet and didn't look up. 'Fokir spotted a Gangetic dolphin,' she said. 'It was about two hundred metres astern on the starboard side. But don't bother to look for it; you won't see it again. It's sounded.'

Kanai was conscious of a twinge of disappointment. 'Have you seen any other dolphins today?'

'No,' she said cheerfully. 'That was the only one. And frankly I'm not surprised, considering the noise we're making.'

'Do you think the bhotbhoti is scaring them off?'

'Possibly,' said Piya. 'Or it could be that they're just staying submerged until the sound fades. Like this one for instance – it waited till we were past before it surfaced.'

'Do you think there are fewer dolphins than there used to be?'

'Oh yes,' said Piya. 'It's known for sure that these waters once held large populations of marine mammals.'

'What's happened to them then?'

'There seems to have been some sort of drastic change in the habitat,' said Piya. 'Some kind of dramatic deterioration.'

'Really?' said Kanai. 'That was what my uncle felt too.'

'He was right,' said Piya grimly. 'When marine mammals begin to disappear from an established habitat it means something's gone very, very wrong.'

'What could it be, do you think?'

'Where shall I begin?' said Piya with a dry laugh. 'Let's not go down that route or we'll end up in tears.'

Later, when Piya took a break to drink some water, he said, 'Is that all you do, then? Watch the water like that?'

She seated herself beside him and tipped back her bottle. 'Yes,' she said. 'There's a method to it, of course, but basically that's all I do – I watch the water. Whether I see anything or not, it's all grist to the mill: all of it's data.'

He grimaced, miming incomprehension. 'Each to their own,' he said. 'For myself, I have to say I wouldn't last a day doing what you do. I'd be bored out of my mind.'

Draining her bottle, she laughed again. 'I can understand that,' she said. 'But that's how it is in nature you know: for a long time nothing happens, and then there's a burst of explosive activity and it's over in seconds. Very few people can adapt themselves to that kind of rhythm – one in a million, I'd say. That's why it was so amazing to come across someone like Fokir.'

'Amazing? Why?'

'You saw how he spotted that dolphin back there, didn't you?' said Piya. 'It's like he's always watching the water – even without being aware of it. I've worked with many experienced fishermen before but I've never met anyone with such an incredible instinct: it's as if he can see right into the river's heart.'

Kanai took a moment to chew this over. 'So do you think you're going to go on working with him?'

'I certainly hope he'll work with me again,' Piya said, 'I think we could achieve a lot, working as a team.'

'It sounds as though you've got some kind of long-term plan?'

She nodded. 'Yes, I do actually. I'm thinking of a project that could keep me here for many years.'

'Right here? In this area?'

'Yes.'

'Really?' Kanai had assumed Piya's stay in India would be a brief one and he was surprised to learn she was already contemplating an extended stay – and not in a city either, but, of all places, in the tide country, with all its discomforts and utter lack of amenities.

'Are you sure you'd be able to live in a place like this?' said Kanai.

'Sure.' She seemed puzzled he should think to ask this. 'Why not?'

'And if you stayed, you'd be working with Fokir?'

She nodded. 'I'd like to – but I guess it depends on him.'

'Is there anyone else you could work with?'

'It wouldn't be the same, Kanai,' Piya said. 'Fokir's abilities as an observer are really extraordinary. I wish I could tell you what it was like to be with him these last few days – it was one, of the most exciting experiences of my life.'

A sudden stab of envy provoked Kanai to make a mocking aside. 'And all that while, you couldn't understand a word he was saying, could you?'

'No,' she said, with a nod of acknowledgement. 'But you know what? There was so much in common between us it didn't matter.'

'Listen,' said Kanai, in a flat, harsh voice. 'You shouldn't deceive yourself, Piya: there wasn't anything in common between you then and there isn't now. Nothing. He's a fisherman and you're a scientist. What you see as fauna he sees as food. He's never sat in a chair, for heaven's sake. Can you imagine what he'd do if he was taken on to a plane?' Kanai burst out laughing at the thought of Fokir walking down the aisle of a jet, in his lungi and vest. 'Piya, there's nothing in common between you at all. You're from different worlds, different planets. If you were about to be struck by a bolt of lightning, he'd have no way of letting you know.'

Here, as if on cue, Fokir suddenly made himself heard again, shouting over the hammering of the bhotbhoti's engine, '*Kumir!*'

'What was that?' Piya broke off and went running to the rear of the deck and Kanai followed close on her heels.

Fokir was standing braced against his boat's hood, pointing downriver. 'Kumir!'

'What did he see?' said Piya, raising her binoculars.

'A crocodile.'

Kanai felt compelled to underline the moral of this interruption. 'You see, Piya,' he said, 'if I hadn't been here to tell you, you'd have had no idea what he'd seen.'

Piya dropped her binoculars and turned to go back to her position in the bow. 'You've certainly made your point, Kanai,' she said frostily. 'Thank you.'

'Wait,' Kanai called out after her. 'Piya—' But she was gone and he had to swallow the apology that had come too late to his lips.

Minutes later, she was back in position, with her binoculars fixed to her eyes, watching the water with a closeness of attention that reminded Kanai of a textual scholar poring over a yet-undeciphered manuscript: it was as though she were puzzling over a codex that had been authored by the earth itself. He had almost forgotten what it meant to look at something so ardently – an immaterial thing, not a commodity nor a convenience nor an object of erotic interest. He remembered that he too had once concentrated his mind in this way; he too had peered into the unknown as if through an eyeglass – but the vistas he had been looking at lay deep within the interior of other languages. Those horizons had filled him with the desire to learn of the ways in which other realities were conjugated. And he remembered too the obstacles, the frustration, the sense that he would never be able to bend his mouth around those words, produce those sounds, put sentences together in the required way, a way that seemed to call for a recasting of the usual order of things. It was pure desire that had quickened his mind then and he could feel the thrill of it even now – except that now that desire was incarnated in the woman who was standing before him, in the bow, a language made flesh.

An Interruption

Kanai had been looking for an opportunity to speak to Horen about Nirmal's notebook, and he thought he had found it when the *Megha* entered a stretch of open water. He stepped up to the wheelhouse and held up the notebook. 'Do you recognize this?' he said to Horen.

Horen's eyes flickered away from the water for just an instant. 'Yes,' he said in a quiet, matter-of-fact voice. 'Saar gave it to me, to keep for you.'

Kanai was deflated by the brevity of his response; considering how often he figured in Nirmal's notes, he had expected that the sight of it would trigger, if not a flow of sentiment, certainly a few fond reminiscences.

'He mentions you several times,' Kanai said, hoping this would catch his interest. But Horen merely shrugged without taking his eyes off the water.

Kanai saw that he would have to work hard to get anything at all out of Horen. Was this reticence habitual or was he just suspicious of outsiders? It was hard to tell.

'What happened to it?' Kanai persisted. 'Where was it all these years?'

Horen cleared his throat. 'It got lost,' he said.

'How?'

'I'll tell you, since you've asked,' Horen said. 'After Saar gave it to me, I took it home and wrapped it in plastic and glued it together so that the damp wouldn't get into it. Then I put it in the sun, for the glue to dry. But one of the children (maybe Fokir?) must have found it and thought it was a plaything. They hid it in the thatch and forgot, as children do. I looked everywhere for it, but it had disappeared. Then I forgot all about it.'

'So how did it turn up again?'

'I'm getting to that,' Horen said, in his slow, deliberate voice. 'Last year I had my old home torn down, so that I could put up a new house, made of brick and cement. That was when it was found. When they brought it to me I didn't know what to do. I didn't want to send it by post because I was sure the address wouldn't be good any more. I didn't want to take it to Mashima either – it's been years since she's spoken to me. But I remembered that Moyna goes often to the Guest House, so I gave it to her. "Put it in Saar's old study," I said. "They'll find it when it's time." That's all that happened.'

He closed his mouth firmly as if to say that he had no more to say on this subject.

The *Megha* had been on the water for some three hours when Piya heard the engine skip a beat. She was still 'on effort', on the upper deck, but there had been no sightings since that one Gangetic dolphin earlier in the day, and this had only sharpened her eagerness to get to the Orcaella's pool: a breakdown now, when they were so close, would be a real setback. Without interrupting her vigil, she tuned her ears to the engine, listening keenly. To her relief, the machine quickly resumed its noisy rhythm.

The respite was short: fifteen minutes later there was another hiccup, followed by a hollow sputtering and a few tired coughs and then, all too suddenly, total silence. The engine died, leaving the *Megha* stranded in the middle of a mohona.

Piya guessed that the delay would be a long one and she was too disappointed even to ask questions. Knowing that the news would come to her soon enough, she stayed in position, scanning the wind-whipped water.

Presently, just as she had expected, Kanai came to stand beside her. 'Bad news, Piya.'

'We're not going to make it today?'

'Probably not.'

Raising a hand, Kanai pointed across the mohona. There was a small village on the far shore, he explained, and Horen was confident that the *Megha* could make it there, by coasting on the currents. He had relatives in the village and he knew of someone there who'd be able to fix the engine. If all went well, they might be in a position to leave for Garjontola the next morning.

Piya pulled a face. 'I guess we don't have many options at this point, do we?'

'No,' said Kanai. 'We really don't.'

Horen, already in the wheelhouse, soon brought the bow around, to point in the direction of the distant village. In a while it became clear that the bhotbhoti had begun to drift across the mohona. Although the tide had turned and the currents were in their favour, their progress was painfully slow. By the time their destination came into view the day was all but over.

The village they were heading for was not situated directly on the mohona's banks: it stood in a more sheltered location, on the banks of a channel a couple of kilometres wide. With the tide at a low ebb, the riverbank now towered high above the water and nothing of the village was visible from the deck; all that could be seen was the crest of the embankment, where knots of people had gathered, as if to await the *Megha*'s arrival. As the bhotbhoti edged closer, a few men were seen wading into the mud, waving their arms in welcome. In response, Horen leaned over the rails and shouted to them through cupped hands. A short while later a boat came cannoning down the mudbank, and pulled up alongside. There were two men inside, one of whom was introduced as Horen's relative, a fisherman who lived in the nearby village; the other was his friend, a part-time mechanic. There was an extended round of introductions and greetings and then Horen disappeared below deck with the visitors. Soon the bhotbhoti's timbers began to ring to the sound of the mechanic's tools. The sun went down to the accompaniment of much banging and hammering.

A little later, the twilight was pierced by an anguished animal sound: a frantic, pain-filled lowing that brought both Kanai and Piya racing out of their cabins, flashlights in hand.

The same thought had come to both of them. 'An attack, you think?' said Piya.

'Can't tell.'

Kanai leaned over the rail to shout a question to Horen, below deck. The hammering fell silent for a second and then a burst of loud laughter came echoing up.

'What's the deal?' said Piya.

'I asked if there had been an attack,' said Kanai, with a smile. 'And they said it was just a water-buffalo giving birth.'

'How do they know?' said Piya.

'They know because the buffalo belongs to Horen's relative,' said Kanai. 'He lives right by the embankment – over there.'

Piya laughed. 'I guess we were being a little too jumpy.' Knitting her fingers together, she did a long stretch and followed this with a yawn. 'I think I'll go to bed early today.'

'Again?' said Kanai sharply. Then as if to conceal his disappointment, he said, 'No dinner?'

'I'll have a nutrition bar,' said Piya. 'That'll keep me going till tomorrow. What about you: are you going to stay up late?'

'Yes,' said Kanai. 'I'm going to eat dinner, as most mortals do. Then I'm going to stay up and finish reading my uncle's notebook.'

'Are you close to the end now?'

'Yes,' said Kanai. 'Close enough.'

Alive

~~~

I was still unwell when we returned to Lusibari, and Nilima put the blame for this purely on Horen: 'It's your fault,' she said. 'You're the one who's been taking him to Morichjhãpi. Now look at the state he's in.'

And it was true I was not well – my head was filled with dreams, visions, fears. Long days went by when I could not get out of my bed: all I did was lie awake and read Rilke in English and Bangla.

To me she spoke more gently, 'Didn't I tell you not to go? Didn't I tell you it would come to this? If you want to do something useful, why don't you help with the Trust, with the hospital? There's so much to be done; why won't you do it right here, in Lusibari? Why must you go to Morichjhãpi'

'You won't understand, Nilima.'

'Why, Nirmal?' she said. 'Tell me, because I've heard rumours. Everybody is speaking of it. Does it have something to do with Kusum?'

'How can you say that, Nilima? Have I ever given you cause for suspicion before?'

Now Nilima too began to cry. 'Nirmal – that's not what people say. There are ugly rumours afloat.'

'Nilima, it's beneath you to believe in these rumours.'

'Then bring Kusum here; tell her to work for the Trust. And you can do the same.'

How could I explain to her that there was nothing I could do for the Trust that many others could not do better? I would be no more than a hand pushing a pen, a machine, a mechanical toy. But as for Morichjhãpi, Rilke himself had shown me what I could do. Hidden in a verse I had found a message written for my eyes only, filled with hidden meaning.

It remained only for the time to come when I would receive a sign and then I would know what I had to do.

For the Poet himself had told me:

> *'**This** is the time for what can be said. **Here***
> *is its country. Speak and testify . . .'*

Days, weeks went by and there came again a time when I felt well enough to leave my bed to go up to my study. I spent my mornings and afternoons there: long swathes of empty time, spent gazing at the mohona as it filled and emptied, filled and emptied, day after day, as untiring as the earth itself.

One afternoon I headed down a little earlier than usual after my afternoon's rest. I was halfway down the stairs when I heard Nilima's voice, speaking to someone in the Guest House. I knew who it was, for I had spoken to him briefly the night before. He was a doctor, a visiting psychiatrist from Kolkata. Now Nilima was telling him she was very afraid – for me. She had heard of something that was sure to upset me; she wanted to know how best I could be shielded from learning of it.

'And what news is this?' the doctor said.

'It won't mean anything to you, daktarbabu,' Nilima said. 'It has to do with an island called Morichjhāpi, which has been occupied by refugees from Bangladesh. They simply will not leave and now I believe the government in Kolkata is going to take very strong action to evict them.'

'Oh these refugees!' said the doctor. 'Such a nuisance. But of what concern is this to your husband? Does he know anyone on that island? What are they to him and he to them?'

I heard Nilima hesitate and clear her throat. 'Doctor, you don't understand,' she said. 'Ever since his retirement, my husband, having little else to do, has chosen to involve himself in the fate of these settlers, in Morichjhāpi. He does not believe that a government such as the one we have now would act against them. He is an old leftist, you see, and unlike many such, he truly believed in those ideals; many of the men who are now in power were his friends and comrades. My husband is not a practical man; his experience of the world is very limited. He does not understand that when a party comes to power, it must govern; it is subject to certain compulsions. I am afraid that if he learns of what is going to happen he will not be able to cope with the disillusionment – it will be more than he can bear.'

'It's best not to let him know,' the doctor said. 'There's no telling what he might do.'

'Tell me, doctor,' Nilima said, 'do you think it would be best to sedate him for a few days?'

'Yes,' said the doctor. 'I think that might be wise.'

I did not need to listen any more. I went to my study and threw a few things into my jhola. Then I crept silently downstairs and went hurrying to the village. Fortunately, there was a ferry waiting and it took me straight to Satjelia, where I went to look for Horen.

'We have to go, Horen,' I said to him. 'I've heard there's going to be an attack on Morichjhãpi.'

He knew more than I did; he had heard rumours that busloads of outsiders were assembling in the villages around the island; they were people such as had never before been seen in the tide country, hardened men from the cities, criminals, gangsters. Morichjhãpi was now completely encircled by police boats; it was all but impossible to get in or out.

'Horen,' I said, 'we have to try to bring Kusum and Fokir to safety. No one knows those waters better than you do. Is there any way you can get us there?'

He thought about this for a minute. 'There's no moon tonight,' he said. 'It might be possible. We can try.'

We set off as night was approaching and took along a fair quantity of food and fresh water. Soon it was dark and I could see nothing but somehow Horen seemed to be able to keep our boat moving. We went slowly, keeping close to the banks, and kept our voices very low.

'Where are we now, Horen?' I said.

He knew our position exactly. 'We've left the Gãral and we're slipping into the Jhilla. We're not far, now; soon you'll see the police boats.' And within a few minutes, we saw them, roaring by, sweeping the river with their searchlights: first one, then another, then another. For a while we hid, staying close to the riverbank, and Horen gauged the intervals between the passage of the patrol boats. Then we cast off again, and sure enough, by starting and stopping between the patrols, we were able to slip through the cordon.

276

'We're there,' said Horen, as the boat thrust its nose into the mud. 'This is Morichjhãpi.' Between the two of us, we dragged the boat deep into the mangroves, where it couldn't be seen from the water. The police had already sunk all the settlers' boats, Horen told me. We took care to hide ours well and then, picking up the food and water we had brought, made our way quietly along the shore until we came to Kusum's dwelling.

We were amazed to find her still in good spirits. We spent the rest of the night trying to persuade her to leave, but she paid no heed.

'Where will I go?' she said simply. 'There's no other place I want to be.'

We told her about the rumours, the men gathering in the surrounding villages, preparing for the impending assault. Horen had seen them; they had come in busloads. 'What will they do?' she said. 'There are still more than ten thousand of us here. It's just a question of keeping faith.'

'But what about Fokir?' I said. 'Suppose something happens? What will become of him?'

'Yes.' Horen added his voice to mine. 'If you won't leave, let me take him away for a few days. After things settle down, I'll bring him back.'

It was clear she had already thought about this. 'All right,' she said. 'That's how we'll do it, then: take Fokir back with you. Keep him with you in Satjelia for a few days. When this wind passes, bring him back.'

By this time day had broken and it was too late to leave. 'We'll have to wait till tonight,' Horen said. 'So that we can slip past the police boats in the dark.'

It was time now for me to spring my surprise. 'Horen,' I said. 'I am staying . . .'

They were amazed and disbelieving: they kept asking me why I wished to remain but I evaded their questions. There was so much I could have told them: about the medicines that awaited me in Lusibari, about Nilima's conversation with the doctor, about the emptiness of the days I had spent in my study. But none of that seemed of the least importance. The truth was that my reason for staying was very simple. I took out this notebook and I said, 'I have to stay because there's something I must write.'

I am out of time. The candle is spluttering; my pencil is worn to a stub. I can hear their footsteps approaching, they seem, strangely, to *be laughing as they come. Horen will want to leave immediately, I know, for daybreak is not far now. I hadn't thought I'd be able to fill this whole notebook, but that is what I have done. It serves no purpose for me to keep it here: I will hand it to Horen in the hope it finds its way to you, Kanai. I feel certain you will have a greater claim to the world's ear than I ever had. Maybe you will know what to do with it. I have always trusted the young. Your generation will, I know, be richer in ideals, less cynical, less selfish than mine.*

They have come in now and I see their faces in the candlelight. In their smiles, I see the Poet's lines:

> *'Look, I'm alive. On what? Neither childhood nor*
> *the future grows less . . . More being than I'll ever*
> *need springs up in my heart.'*

Kanai found that his hands were shaking as he put down the notebook. The lamp had filled the cabin with kerosene fumes; he felt he was stifling. Picking a blanket off the bunk, he wrapped it around his shoulders and stepped out into the gangway. The sharp smell of a *biri* came to his nose and he looked to his left, towards the bow.

Horen was seated there, in one of the two armchairs. He was smoking, with his feet up on the gunwale. He looked around as Kanai closed the door of his cabin.

'Still up?'

'Yes,' said Kanai. 'I just finished reading my uncle's notebook.'

Horen acknowledged this with an indifferent grunt.

Kanai seated himself in the adjoining chair. 'It ends with you taking Fokir away in your boat.'

Horen angled his gaze downwards, into the water, as if he were looking into the past. 'We should have left a little earlier,' he said matter-of-factly. 'We would have had the currents behind us.'

'And what happened in Morichjhāpi after that? Do you know?'

Horen sucked on the end of his *biri*. 'I know no more than anyone else knows. It was all just rumour.'

'And what were the rumours?'

A wisp of smoke curled out of Horen's nose. 'What we heard,' he said, 'was that the assault began the next day; the gangsters who'd been assembling around the island were carried over in boats and dinghies and bhotbhotis. They burnt the settlers' huts, they sank their boats, they laid waste to their fields.' He grunted, in his laconic way. 'Whatever you can imagine them doing, they did.'

'And Kusum and my uncle? What happened to them?'

'No one knows for sure, but what I've heard is that a group of women were taken away by force, Kusum among them. People say they were used and then thrown into the rivers, so that they would be washed away by the tides. Dozens of settlers were killed that day. The sea claimed them all.'

'And my uncle?'

'He was put on a bus with the other refugees. They were to be sent back to the place they had come from – in Madhya Pradesh, or wherever it was. But at some point they must have let him off because he found his way back to Canning.'

Here Horen broke off and proceeded to search his pockets with much fumbling and many muttered curses. By the time he'd found and lit another biri it had become clear to Kanai that he was trying to create a diversion so as to lead the conversation away from Nirmal and Kusum. Kanai was not surprised when he said, in a comfortably affable tone: 'What time do you want to leave tomorrow morning?'

Kanai decided he would not let him change the subject. 'Tell me something, Horen-da,' he said, 'about my uncle. You were the one who took him to Morichjhãpi. Why do you think he got so involved with that place?'

'Same as anyone else,' Horen said with a shrug.

'But after all, Kusum and Fokir were your relatives,' Kanai said. 'So it's understandable that you were concerned about them. But what about Saar? Why did it mean so much to him?'

Horen pulled on his biri. 'Your uncle was a very unusual man,' he said at last. 'People say he was mad. As we say, you can't explain what a madman will do any more than you can account for what a goat will eat.'

'But tell me this, Horen-da,' Kanai persisted. 'Do you think it possible he was in love with Kusum?'

Horen rose to his feet and snorted in such a way as to indicate that he had been goaded beyond toleration. 'Kanai-babu,' he said in a sharp, irritated voice, 'I'm an unlettered man. You're talking about things city people think about. I don't have time for such things.'

He flicked his biri away and they heard it hiss as it hit the water. 'You'd better go to sleep now,' Horen said. 'We'll make an early start tomorrow.'

A Post Office on Sunday

Piya had gone to bed too early and around midnight found herself wide awake, sitting up in her bunk. She spent a few minutes trying to drift off again and then gave up. Wrapping a blanket around her shoulders, she stepped out on deck. The light of the waxing moon was so bright that she stood still for a moment, blinking. Then she saw, to her surprise, that Kanai was outside too. He was reading by the light of a small kerosene lantern. Piya went forward and slipped into the other chair. 'You're up late,' she said. 'Is that your uncle's notebook you're reading?'

'Yes. I finished it, actually. I was just looking over it again.'

'Can I have a look?'

'Certainly.'

Kanai closed the book and held it out to her. She took the notebook gingerly and allowed it to fall open.

'The writing's very small,' she said.

'Yes,' said Kanai. 'It's not easy to read.'

'And is it all in Bengali?'

'Yes.'

She closed the book carefully and handed it back to Kanai. 'So what's it about?'

Kanai scratched his head as he wondered how best to describe the notebook. 'It's about all kinds of things: places, people—'

'Anyone you know?'

'Yes. Actually, Fokir's mother figures in it a lot. Fokir too – though Nirmal only knew him when he was very small.'

Piya's eyes widened in surprise. 'Fokir and his mother? How come they're in it?'

'I told you, didn't I, that Kusum, Fokir's mother, was involved in an effort to resettle one of these islands?'

'Yes, you did.'

Kanai smiled. 'I think without knowing it, he may have been half in love with Kusum.'

'Does he say so, in the book?'

'No,' said Kanai. 'But then he wouldn't.'

'Why not?'

'Being what he was,' Kanai said, 'a man of his time and place, with his convictions – he'd have thought it frivolous.'

Piya ran her fingers through her short, curly hair. 'I don't get it,' she said. 'What were his convictions, then?'

Kanai leaned back in his chair as he thought this over. 'He was a radical at one time,' he said. 'In fact, if you were to ask my aunt Nilima, she would tell you that the reason he got mixed up with the settlers in Morichjhãpi was because he couldn't let go of the idea of revolution.'

'I take it you don't agree with her?'

'No,' said Kanai. 'I think she's wrong. As I see it, Nirmal was possessed more by words than by politics. There are people who live through poetry and he was one of them. For Nilima, a person like that is very hard to understand – but that's the kind of man Nirmal was. He loved the work of Rainer Maria Rilke, a great German poet, whose work has been translated into Bangla by some of our own best-known poets. Rilke said, "life is lived in transformation", and I think Nirmal soaked this idea into himself in the way cloth absorbs ink. To him, what Kusum stood for was the embodiment of Rilke's idea of transformation.'

'Marxism and poetry?' Piya said drily, raising her eyebrows. 'It seems like an odd combination.'

'It was,' Kanai agreed. 'But those contradictions were typical of his generation. Nirmal was perhaps the least materialistic person I've ever known. But it was very important for him to believe that he was a historical materialist.'

'And what exactly does that mean?'

'For him it meant that everything which existed was inter-connected: the trees, the sky, the weather, people, poetry, science, nature. He hunted down facts in the way a magpie collects shiny things. Yet when he strung them all together, somehow they did become stories – of a kind.'

Piya rested her chin on her fist. 'Can you give me an example?'

Kanai thought about this for a minute. 'I remember one of his stories – it has always stuck in my mind.'

'What's it about?'

'Do you remember Canning, the town where we got off the train?'

'Sure I remember Canning,' Piya said. 'That's where I got my permit. It's not what I'd call a memorable place.'

'Exactly,' said Kanai. 'The first time I went there was in 1970, when Nirmal and Nilima brought me to Lusibari. I was disgusted by the place – I thought it was a horrible, muddy little town. I happened to say something to that effect and Nirmal was outraged. He shouted at me, "A place is what you make of it." And then he told a story so unlikely I thought he'd made it up. But after I went back home, I actually took the trouble to look into it and discovered it was true.'

'What was the story?' Piya said. 'Do you remember? I'd love to hear it.'

'All right,' said Kanai. 'I'll try to tell it to you as he would have. But don't forget: I'll be translating in my head – he would have told it in Bangla.'

'Sure. Go on.'

Kanai held up a finger and pointed it to the heavens. 'All right then, comrades, listen: I'll tell you about the Matla River and a storm-struck *matal* and the *matlami* of a Lord who was called Canning. *Shono, kaan pete shono.* Put out your ears so you can listen properly.'

Like so many other places in the tide country, Canning was named by an *Ingrej*. And in this case it was no ordinary Englishman who gave it his name – not only was he a Lord, he was a *laat*, nothing less than a Viceroy, Lord Canning. This laat and his *ledi* were as generous in sprinkling their names around the country as a later generation of politicians were to be in scattering their ashes: you came across them in the most unexpected places – a road here, a gaol there, an occasional asylum. No matter that Ledi Canning was tall, thin and peppery – a Calcutta sweet-maker took it into his head to name a new confection after her. The sweet was black, round and sugary – in other words, it was everything its namesake was not, which was lucky for the sweet-maker because it meant his creation quickly became a success. People gobbled up the new sweets at such a rate that they could not take the time to say 'Lady Canning'. The name was soon shortened to *ledigeni*.

Now surely there must exist a law of speech which says that if 'Lady Canning' is to become ledigeni, then 'Port Canning' should become *Potugeni* or possibly *Podgeni*? But look: the port's name has survived undamaged and nobody ever calls it by anything but the Lord's name, 'Canning'.

But why? Why would a laat leave the comfort of his throne in order to plant his name in the mud of the Matla?

Well, remember Mohammad bin Tughlaq, the mad Sultan who moved his capital from Delhi to a village in the middle of nowhere? It was a bee from the same hive that stung the British. They got it in their heads that they needed a new port, a new capital for Bengal – Kolkata's Hooghly River was silting up and its docks, they said, would soon be choked with mud. *Jothariti*, teams of planners and surveyors, went out and wandered the land, striding about in wigs and breeches, mapping and measuring. And at last on the banks of the Matla they came on a place that caught their fancy, a little fishing village that overlooked a river so broad and wide that it looked like a highway to the sea.

Now it's no secret that the word 'matla' means 'mad' in Bangla – and everyone who knows the river knows also that this name has not been lightly earned. But those Ingrej town-planners were busy men, who had little time for words and names. They went back to the laat and told him about the wonderful location they had found: they described the wide, mighty river, the flat plain and deep channel that led straight to the sea; they showed him their plans and maps and listed all the amenities they would

284

build – hotels, promenades, parks, palaces, banks, streets. Oh, it was to be a grand place, this new capital on the banks of the mad Matla – it would lack for nothing.

The contracts were given out and the work began: thousands of *mistris* and *mahajans* and overseers moved to the shores of the Matla and began to dig. They drank the Matla's water and worked in the way that matals and madmen work: nothing could stop them, not even the uprising of 1857. If you were here then, on the banks of the Matla, you would never have known that in northern India chapatis were passing from village to village; that Mangal Pandey had turned his gun on his officers; that women and children were being massacred and rebels were being tied to the mouths of cannon. Here, on the banks of the smiling river, the work continued: an embankment arose, foundations were dug, a strand was laid out, a railway line built.

And all the while the Matla lay still and waited.

But not even a river can hide all its secrets and it so happened that at that time, in Kolkata, there lived a man of a mentality not unlike the Matla's. This was a lowly shipping inspector, an Ingrej shaheb by the name of Henry Piddington. Before coming to India, Piddington-shaheb had lived in the Caribbean, and somewhere in those islands he had fallen in love – not with a woman nor even with a dog, as is often the case with lonely Englishmen living in faraway places. No, Mr Piddington fell in love with storms. Out there, of course, they call them hurricanes and Piddington-shaheb's love for them knew no limits. He loved them not in the way you might love the mountains or the stars: for him they were like books or music and he felt for them the same affection a devotee might feel for his favourite authors or instrumentalists. He read them, listened to them, studied them and tried to understand them. He loved them so much that he invented a new word to describe them: 'cyclone'.

Now, our Kolkata may not be as romantic a place as the West Indies, but for the cultivation of Piddington-shaheb's love affair it was just as good. The Bay of Bengal, let it be said, is second to none in the violence of its storms, not to the Caribbean, nor to the South China Sea. Wasn't it our *tufaan*, after all, that gave birth to the word 'typhoon'?

285

When Mr Piddington learnt of the Viceroy's new port he understood at once the madness the river had in mind. Standing on its banks, he spoke his mind. 'Maybe you could trick those surveyors,' he said, 'but you can't make a fool of me; I've seen through your little game and I'm going to make sure that they know too.'

And the Matla laughed its mental laugh and said, 'Go on; do it. Do it now; tell them. It's you they'll call Matla – a man who thinks he can look into the hearts of rivers and storms.'

Sitting in his rooms in Kolkata, Piddington-shaheb drafted dozens of letters; he wrote to the planners and surveyors and warned of the dangers; he told them it was crazy to build a town so deep in the tide country; the mangroves were Bengal's defence against the Bay, he said – they served as a barrier against nature's fury, absorbing the initial onslaught of cyclonic winds, waves and tidal surges. If not for the tide country, the plains would have been drowned long before: it was the mangroves that kept the hinterland alive. Kolkata's long, winding sea-lane was thus its natural defence against the turbulent energies of the Bay; the new port, on the other hand, was dangerously exposed. Given an unfortunate conjunction of winds and tides, even a minor storm would suffice to wash it away; all it would take was a wave stirred up by a cyclone. Driven to desperation, Mr Piddington even wrote to the Viceroy: begging him to rethink the matter, he made a prediction – if the port was built at this location, he said, it would not last more than fifteen years. There would come a day when a great mass of salt water would rise up, in the midst of a cyclone, and drown the whole settlement; on this he would stake his reputation, as a man and as a scientist.

Of course, no one paid any attention; neither the planners nor the laat shaheb had the time to listen. Mr Piddington, after all, was nothing but a lowly shipping inspector and he stood very low in the Ingrej scale of caste. People began to whisper that he was, well, he was a man so mental that who could blame him if there was a little *gondogol* in his mind; wasn't he the one who'd once been heard to say that storms were 'wonderful meteors'?

So the work went on and the port was built. Its streets and

strand were laid out, its hotels and houses were painted and made ready, and everything went exactly as planned. One day, with much noise and drum-beating the Viceroy planted his feet on the Matla's flanks and gave the port its new name, Port Canning.

Piddington-shaheb was not invited to the ceremony. On the streets of Kolkata, people laughed and sniggered now when they saw him pass by: oh there goes that old matal Piddington. Wasn't he the one who kept bothering the laat shaheb about his new port? Hadn't he made a prediction of some kind, staking his reputation?

Wait, said Piddington, wait – I said fifteen years.

The Matla took pity on this matal. Fifteen years was a long time and Mr Piddington had already suffered enough. It let him wait one year and then one more and yet another until five long years had gone by. And then one day, in the year 1867, it rose as if to a challenge and hurled itself upon Canning. In a matter of hours, the town was all but gone; only the bleached skeleton remained.

The destruction came about exactly as Mr Piddington had said it would: it was caused not by some great tufaan but by a relatively minor storm. Nor was it the storm's winds that wrecked the city: it was a wave, a surge. In 1871, four years after the Matla's uprising, the port was formally abandoned. The port that was to be one of the reigning queens of the eastern oceans, a rival to Bombay, Singapore and Hong Kong, became instead the Matla's vassal – Canning.

'But as always, with Nirmal,' said Kanai, 'the last word was reserved for Rilke.'

He put his hand on his heart and recited aloud:

> *'But, oh, how strange the streets of the City of Pain . . .*
> *Oh, how an angel could stamp out their market of comforts,*
> *with the church nearby, bought ready-made, clean,*
> *shut, and disappointed as a post office on Sunday.*

'So now you know,' said Kanai, as Piya began to laugh. 'That is what Canning has been ever since that day in 1867 when the Matla stamped out the laat's handiwork: a Sunday post office.'

A Killing

The *Megha*'s cabins were each outfitted with a raised platform that could be used as a bunk. By piling blankets, pillows and sheets on this ledge, Kanai was able to make himself a bed that was reasonably comfortable, although far from luxurious. He was fast asleep when he was woken by the sound of voices, both near and distant. Reaching for his torch, he shone the beam on his watch and discovered it was 3 a.m. The voices of Horen and his grandson were now clearly audible, on the upper deck, joined in excited speculation.

Kanai had gone to sleep in a lungi and vest, and now, as he pushed his blankets aside was surprised to find a distinct chill in the air. He decided to wrap a blanket around his shoulders before stepping out of his cabin: Horen and his grandson were close by, leaning on the rails and watching the shore.

'What's happened?' said Kanai.

'It's not clear,' came the answer, 'but something seems to be going on in the village.'

The flood tide had set in some hours before, and with the boat anchored at midstream there was now close to a kilometre of water between them and the shore. The night was advanced enough for cottony clouds of mist to have arisen from the water's surface: although much thinner than the dense fog of dawn, it had still obscured the outlines of the shore. Through this shimmering screen, glowing points of orange flame could be seen moving quickly, here and there, as if to suggest that people were running along the shore with burning torches. The villagers' voices could be heard clearly in the distance, despite the mist's muffling effect. Even Horen and his grandson were at a loss to think of a reason why so many people would bestir themselves so energetically at this time of night.

Kanai felt a touch on his elbow and turned to see Piya standing beside him, rubbing her knuckles in her eyes. 'What's up?'

'We're all wondering.'

'Let's ask Fokir.'

Kanai went to the bhotbhoti's stern, with Piya following close behind, and shone his flashlight into the boat below. Fokir was awake, sitting huddled in the centre of his boat, with a blanket draped around his shoulders. He held up an arm to shield his face and Kanai switched off the beam before leaning over to speak to him.

'Does he know what's going on?' Piya inquired.

'No. But he's going to take his boat across, to find out. He says we can go with him if we like.'

'Sure.'

They climbed in, and Horen came to join them, leaving his grandson in charge of the bhotbhoti.

It took some fifteen minutes to cross over, and as they were approaching the shore it became clear that the commotion had a distinct focus: it seemed a crowd was congregating around exactly that part of the village where Horen's relatives lived. As the shore neared, the voices and shouts rose in volume, until they had fused into a pulsing, angry sound.

The noise inspired a peculiar dread in Kanai, and he said, on an impulse, 'Piya, I don't know if we should go any farther.'

'Why not?'

'Do you know what those voices remind me of?' said Kanai.

'A crowd?'

'A mob is what I would call it – an angry mob.'

'A mob?' said Piya. 'In a small village?'

'I know it's the last thing you'd expect,' said Kanai. 'But if I were just to listen to my ears, I'd say it was a riot and I've been in riots where people were killed. I have a feeling we're heading into something like that.'

Shading her eyes, Piya scanned the shimmering mist. 'Let's just take a look.'

Although the tide had peaked some hours before, the water was still high and Fokir had no trouble pushing his boat's prow beyond the river's muddy edge. Ahead lay a slope of damp earth, shaded with mangroves and carpeted with roots and seedlings. Fokir had steered the boat close to the point where the crowd had gathered, and beyond the shadow of the embankment the mist was lit with the orange glow of the massed torches.

Kanai and Piya were picking their way through the mangroves when Horen waved them to a stop. He took the flashlight out of Kanai's hand and shone it downwards at his feet. Going over to join him, Kanai and Piya saw that the beam had settled on a mark in the ground. The earth here was neither dry nor wet but pliable, like clay, and it had preserved an impression of a stencil-like clarity. Neither Kanai nor Piya had any doubt of what it was: the prints were as clearly marked as those of a kitten, daubed on a kitchen floor – only many times larger. The shape was so clearly defined that they could see the very texture of the circular pads and the marks made by the retracted claws. Then Horen shone the beam ahead, and they saw a trail of similar depressions, leading up towards the embankment from the shore. From the trajectory of the marks, it was easy to plot the animal's path: it had crossed over from the forested bank on the far shore of the river and had touched land at almost exactly the same point as their boat.

Piya said, 'It must have passed within sight of the *Megha*.'

'I suppose so – but since we were all asleep, it was in no danger of being spotted.'

When they neared the crest of the embankment Horen pointed to a large mark in the dust and gestured to indicate that this was the place from which the animal had surveyed the village and picked out its prey. Then he made a sign to show that it was from here that it had probably sprung to attack. The old man was beside himself with anxiety now and he went running ahead, with Fokir in close pursuit. Piya and Kanai were a few paces to their rear – and on reaching the top of the embankment their progress was brought to an abrupt halt by the spectacle that lay ahead. By the light of the torches they saw that the village was made up of clusters of mud huts, so arranged as to run parallel

291

to the embankment. Directly in front of them, a few hundred metres away, was a small mud-walled structure with a thatched roof. More than a hundred people had gathered around this little hut: most of them were men and many were armed with sharpened bamboo poles: these they were plunging into the hut, over and again. Their faces were contorted in such a way that they seemed to be in the grip both of extreme fear and uncontrollable rage. Many of the women and children in the crowd were shrieking, *Maar! Maar!* Kill! Kill!

Kanai spotted Horen on the edges of the crowd and he and Piya went to join him. 'Is this where your relatives live?' said Kanai.

'Yes,' said Horen, 'this is their place.'

'What's happened? What's going on?'

'Remember the buffalo giving birth?' Horen said. 'That's what started it. The big cat heard the sound across the water. That's what brought it here.'

The hut ahead was a livestock pen, said Horen. It belonged to his relatives who lived in a larger dwelling nearby. A scant half-hour before, the family had been awakened by a crashing sound, followed by frenzied cries from their livestock. They had looked out of a window and hadn't been able to see anything because of the darkness and the mist. But their ears told them all they needed to know: a large and powerful animal had jumped on top of the livestock pen and was trying to claw a hole in the straw roof. A moment later there was a crashing sound to indicate that the predator had succeeded in breaking into the pen.

There were six grown men in the house and they knew they had been presented with an opportunity unlikely ever to be repeated. This tiger was not new to their village; it had killed two people there and had long been preying on its livestock. Now, for the few minutes it was in the pen, it was vulnerable, because to make its escape it would have to leap vertically through the hole in the roof: even for a tiger, this would not be a simple feat, not with a calf in its jaws.

The family had quickly gathered together a number of fishing nets. Then they had made their way outside and flung the nets over the thatch, piling them on, one on top of the other, and tying them down with heavy nylon crablines. When the tiger tried to make its jump, it got entangled in the lines and fell back into the pen. It was struggling to free itself, when one of the boys thrust a sharpened bamboo pole through a window and blinded it.

Kanai had been translating continuously as Horen was speaking, but at this point Piya stopped him. In a shaking voice, she said, 'Do you mean to tell me the tiger's still in there?'

'Yes,' said Kanai. 'That's what he says: it's trapped inside and blinded.'

Piya shook her head as if to wake herself from a nightmare: the scene was so incomprehensible and yet so vivid that it was only now she understood that it was the incapacitated animal that was being attacked with the sharpened staves. She was still absorbing this when the tiger gave voice, for the first time. Instantly, the people around the pen dropped their staves and scattered, shielding their faces as if from the force of a detonation; the sound was so powerful that Piya could feel it through the soles of her bare feet, as it echoed through the ground. For a moment nobody moved, and then, as it became clear the tiger was still trapped and helpless, the men snatched up their staves and attacked with redoubled fury.

Piya clutched Kanai's arm and shouted into his ear, 'We have to do something, Kanai. We can't let this happen.'

'I wish there was something we could do, Piya,' Kanai said. 'But I don't think there is.'

'But we can try, Kanai,' she pleaded. 'Can't we?'

Then Horen whispered something and Kanai took hold of Piya's arm and tried to turn her away. 'Listen, Piya, we should go back now.'

'Go back? Go back where?'

'Back to the *Megha*,' said Kanai.

'Why?' said Piya. 'What's going to happen?'

'Piya,' said Kanai, tugging at her hand. 'Whatever it is, it's better you don't stay here to see this.'

Piya looked into his face, illuminated by the torches. 'What aren't you telling me?' she said. 'What are they going to do?'

Kanai spat into the dust. 'Piya, you have to understand – that animal's been preying on this village for years. It's killed two people and any number of cows and goats—'

'This is an animal, Kanai,' Piya said. 'You can't take revenge on an animal.'

All around them now people were howling, their faces lit by the dancing flames: *Maar! Maar!* Kanai caught hold of her elbow and tried to lead her away. 'It's too late now, Piya. We should both go.'

'Go?' said Piya. 'I'm not going anywhere. I'm going to put a stop to this.'

'Piya,' said Kanai. 'You're dealing with a mob here. They could turn on us too, you know. We're outsiders.'

'So you're just going to stand by and let it happen?'

'There's nothing we can do, Piya,' Kanai was shouting now. 'Be reasonable. Let's go.'

'You can go if you like,' she said, shaking off his hand. 'But I'm not going to run off like a coward. If you're not going to do anything about this, then I will. And Fokir will – I know he will. Where is he?'

Kanai lifted a finger to point. 'There. Look.'

Rising on tiptoe Piya saw that Fokir was in the front ranks of the crowd, helping a man sharpen a bamboo pole. Elbowing Kanai aside, she plunged into the throng and fought her way through to Fokir. There was a sudden surge of people around them and she was pushed up against the man who was standing next to Fokir. Now, at close quarters, she saw in the dancing light of the flame, that the man's spear-point was stained with blood and that there were bits of black-and-gold fur stuck between the splinters. Suddenly it was as if she could see the animal cowering inside the pen, recoiling from the bamboo spears, licking the wounds that had been gouged into its flesh. Reaching for the spear, she snatched it from the man's hands and placed her foot on it, breaking it in two.

For a moment the man was too surprised to respond. Then he began to shout at the top of his voice, shaking his fist in Piya's face. In a minute, he was joined by some half-dozen others – young men, with shawls wrapped around their heads, shouting words she could not understand. She felt a hand closing on her elbow and looked around to find Fokir standing behind her. At the sight of him, her heart lifted and she was assailed both by hope and a sense of relief: she was certain he would know what to do, that he would find a way to put a stop to what was going on. But instead of coming to her aid he put his arm around her, pinning her to his chest and carried her away, retreating through the crowd as she kicked his knees and clawed at his hands. Then she saw a knot of flame arcing over the crowd and falling on the thatch: almost at once, branches of flame sprouted from the roof of the pen. There was another roar and this was matched a moment later by the voices of the crowd, screaming, in a kind of maddened bloodlust, *Maar! Maar!* The flames leapt up and people began to stoke them with sticks and straw.

Piya began to scream as she tried to throw off Fokir's grip. 'Let me go! Let me go!'

But instead of unloosing her, he turned her around, pinned her to his body and half-dragged and half-carried her to the embankment. In the light of the leaping flames she saw that Kanai and Horen were already standing there. They gathered around her and led her down the embankment towards the boat.

Stumbling down the bank, she managed to control herself to the point where she was able to say, in an icy voice, 'Foki! Let me go. Kanai, tell him to let me go.'

Fokir loosened his grip, but gingerly, and as she stepped away from him, he made a motion as if to prevent her from running back towards the village.

She could hear the flames crackling in the distance and she smelled the reek of burning fur and flesh. Then Fokir said something to her directly, in her ear, and she turned to Kanai: 'What was that? What did he say?'

'Fokir says, you shouldn't be so upset.'

'How can I not be upset? That's the most horrifying thing I've ever seen – a tiger set on fire.'

'He says, when a tiger comes into a human settlement, it's because it wants to die.'

She turned on Fokir, covering her ears with both hands. 'Stop it. I don't want to hear any more of this. Let's just go.'

Interrogations

Daylight was breaking when they stepped back on the *Megha*, and Horen lost no time in drawing the anchor and starting the engine. It was best to get away quickly, he said; there was bound to be trouble once the news of the killing reached the Forest Department. In the past, similar incidents had led to riots, shootings and large-scale arrests.

As the bhotbhoti was making its turn, Kanai headed towards his cabin, to change, while Piya went, as if by habit, to her usual place at the head of the upper deck. Kanai assumed she would be back 'on effort' in a matter of minutes. But when he came out again she was sitting slumped on the deck, leaning listlessly against a rail and he knew from her posture that she had been crying.

He went to sit beside her. 'Look, Piya,' he said, 'don't torment yourself with this. There's nothing we could have done.'

'We could have tried.'

'It would have made no difference.'

'I guess.' She wiped her eyes, with the back of her hand. 'Anyway, Kanai,' she said, 'I feel I owe you an apology.'

'For what you said back there?' Kanai smiled. 'That's all right – you had every right to be upset.'

She shook her head. 'No – it's not just that.'

'Then?'

'Do you remember what you were telling me yesterday?' she said. 'Fact is, you were right and I was wrong.'

'I'm not sure what you're talking about.'

'You know,' said Piya. 'What you said about there being nothing in common between—?'

'You and Fokir?'

'Yes,' said Piya. 'You were right. I was just being stupid. I guess it took something like this for me to get it straight.'

Kanai choked back the first triumphant comment that came to his mind, and said instead, in as neutral a voice as he could muster, 'And how did this revelation come to be granted to you?'

'By what just happened,' said Piya. 'I couldn't believe Fokir's response.'

'But what did you expect, Piya?' Kanai said. 'Did you think he was some kind of grass-roots ecologist? He's not. He's a fisherman – he kills animals for a living.'

'I understand that,' said Piya. 'I'm not blaming him; I know this is what he grew up with. It's just, I thought somehow he'd be different.'

Kanai placed a sympathetic hand on her knee. 'Let's not dwell on this,' he said. 'After all, you have a lot of work to do.'

She raised her head and forced a smile.

The *Megha* had been under way for about an hour when a grey motorboat roared past it. Piya was in the bow with her binoculars and Kanai was sitting in the shade. They moved to the gunwale to watch as the boat sped downriver and they saw it was filled with khaki-uniformed forest guards. It seemed to be heading in the direction of the village they had left.

Horen came to join them and made a remark that made Kanai laugh. 'According to Horen,' Kanai explained to Piya, 'if you're caught between a pirate and a forester, you should always give yourself up to the pirate. You'll be safer.'

Piya nodded wryly, recalling her own experience with the forest guard. 'What do you think they're going to do to that village?' she said.

Kanai shrugged. 'There'll be arrests, fines, beatings. Who knows what else?'

Another hour went by and then, while crossing a mohona, they spotted a small flotilla of grey motorboats. These too were heading in the same direction as the motorboat they had passed earlier.

'Wow!' said Piya. 'Looks like they mean business.'

'I'm sure they do.'

Suddenly one of the motorboats parted company with the others and swung around. As it picked up speed it became clear that it had set its course to intercept the *Megha*. On catching sight of it Horen thrust his head out of the wheelhouse and spoke urgently to Kanai.

'Piya, you've got to go into your cabin,' said Kanai. 'Horen says there'll be trouble if they find you on the boat. It's something to do with your being a foreigner and not having the right kind of permit.'

'OK.' Piya carried her backpack to her cabin and pulled the door shut. She lay down on her bunk and listened to the sound of the motorboat's engine as it grew gradually louder. When it was cut off, she knew the boat had pulled up alongside. She heard people conversing in Bengali, politely at first and then with increasing acrimony: Kanai's voice was counterpointed against a number of others.

A good hour passed. Arguments went back and forth and voices rose and fell. Piya was glad she had a bottle of water with her, for the cabin grew steadily hotter as the day advanced.

At length the voices died down and the motorboat pulled away. A knock sounded on Piya's door just as the *Megha*'s engine was coming alive again. She was relieved to find Kanai standing outside.

'What was all *that* about?' she said.

Kanai made a face. 'Apparently, they'd heard a foreigner was at the village yesterday, when the tiger was killed. They're very exercised about it.'

'Why?'

'They said it's a security risk for a foreigner to be wandering about so close to the border, without a guard. But my feeling is that they just don't want the news to get out.'

'About the killing?'

'Yes,' Kanai nodded. 'It makes them look bad. Anyway, it seems they know you're at large in these parts and it's clear they're on the lookout. They kept asking if we'd seen you.'

'What did you say?'

Kanai smiled. 'Horen and I adopted a policy of unyielding denial. It seemed to be working until they spotted Fokir. One of the guards recognized him and said you were last seen on his boat.'

'Oh my God!' said Piya. 'Was it a kind of weasel-looking guy?'

'Yes,' said Kanai. 'That's the one. I don't know what he told the others but they were all set to drag Fokir off to jail. Fortunately, I was able to persuade them to change their minds.'

'And how did you do that?'

Kanai's voice became very dry. 'Shall we say I mentioned the names of a few friends and parted with a few notes?'

She guessed his ironic tone was intended to downplay the seriousness of the situation and she was suddenly grateful for his calm, urbane presence. What would have happened if he hadn't been there? She knew that in all likelihood she would have ended up on one of those official motorboats.

She put a hand on Kanai's arm. 'Thank you. I appreciate it. I really do. And I'm sure Fokir does too.'

Kanai acknowledged this by dipping his head ironically. 'Always glad to oblige.' In a graver tone of voice, he added, 'However, I do have to say, Piya, you really should think seriously of turning back. If they found you there could be trouble. You could end up in jail and there's not much I or anyone else could do. The proximity of the border changes everything.'

Piya looked into the distance as she considered this. She thought of Blyth and Roxburgh and the naturalists who had crossed these waters a hundred years before and found them teeming with cetaceans. She thought of all the years in between when, for one reason or another, no one had paid any heed to these creatures and so no one had known of their decimation. It had fallen on her to be the first to carry back a report of the current situation and she knew she could not turn back from the responsibility.

'I can't return right now, Kanai,' she said. 'It's hard to explain to you how important my work is. If I leave, who knows how long it'll be before another cetologist can come here? I've got to stay as long as I possibly can.'

Kanai frowned. 'And what if they take you off to jail?'

Piya shrugged. 'How long could they keep me, anyway? And when they let me out, the material will still be in my head.'

At midday, with the sun blazing overhead, Piya took a break and came to sit beside Kanai in the shade of the awning. There was a troubled look in her eyes that prompted Kanai to say, 'Are you still thinking about the forest guards?'

This seemed to startle her. 'Oh no. Not that.'

'Then?'

She tipped her head back to drink from her water bottle. 'The village,' she said, wiping her mouth. 'Last night: I still can't get it out of my head – I keep seeing it, again and again – the people, the flames. It was like something from some other time – before recorded history. I feel like I'll never be able to get my mind around the—'

Kanai prompted her as she faltered. 'The horror?'

'The horror. Yes. I wonder if I'll ever be able to forget it?'

'Probably not.'

'But for Fokir and Horen and the others – it was just a part of everyday life, wasn't it?'

'I imagine they've learned to take it in their stride, Piya. They've had to.'

'That's what haunts me,' said Piya. 'In a way that makes them a part of the horror too, doesn't it?'

Kanai snapped shut the notebook: 'To be fair to Fokir and Horen, I don't think it's quite that simple, Piya. I mean, aren't we a part of the horror as well? You and me and people like us?'

Piya ran a hand through her short, culy hair. 'I don't see how.'

'That tiger had killed two people, Piya,' Kanai said. 'And that was just in one village. It happens every week that people are killed by tigers. How about the horror of that? If there were killings on that scale anywhere else on earth it would be called a genocide, and yet here it goes almost unremarked: these killings are never reported, never written about in the papers. And the reason is just that these people are too poor to matter. We all know it, but we choose not to see it. Isn't that a horror too –

that we can feel the suffering of an animal, but not of human beings?'

'But Kanai,' Piya retorted, 'everywhere in the world dozens of people are killed every day – on roads, in cars, in traffic. Why is this any worse?'

'Because, we're complicit in this, Piya; that's why.'

Piya dissociated herself with a shake of the head 'I don't see how I'm complicit.'

'Because it was people like you,' said Kanai, 'who made a push to protect the wildlife here, without regard for the human costs. And I'm complicit because people like me – Indians of my class, that is – have chosen to hide these costs, basically in order to curry favour with their Western patrons. It's not hard to ignore the people who're dying – after all they are the poorest of the poor. But just ask yourself whether this would be allowed to happen anywhere else? There are more tigers living in America, in captivity, than there are in all of India – what do you think would happen if they started killing human beings?'

'But Kanai,' said Piya, 'there's a big difference between preserving a species in captivity and keeping it in its habitat.'

'And what is that difference exactly?'

'The difference, Kanai,' Piya said slowly and emphatically, 'is that it was what was *intended* – not by you or me, but by nature, by the earth, by the planet that keeps us all alive. Just suppose we crossed that imaginary line that prevents us from deciding that no other species matters except ourselves. What'll be left then? Aren't we alone enough in the universe? And do you think it'll stop at that? Once we decide we can kill off other species, it'll be people next – exactly the kind of people you're thinking of, people who're poor and unnoticed.'

'That's all very well for you to say, Piya – but it's not you who's paying the price in lost lives.'

Piya challenged him. 'Do you think I wouldn't pay the price if I thought it necessary?'

'You mean you'd be willing to die?' Kanai scoffed. 'Come on, Piya.'

'I'm telling you the truth, Kanai,' Piya said quietly. 'If I thought giving up my life might make the rivers safe again for the

Irrawaddy dolphin, the answer is, yes, I would. But the trouble is that my life, your life, a thousand lives would make no difference.'

'It's easy to say these things—'

'Easy?' There was a parched weariness in Piya's voice now. 'Kanai, tell me, do you see anything easy about what I do? Look at me: I have no home, no money and no prospects. My friends are thousands of kilometres away and I get to see them maybe once a year, if I'm lucky. And that's the least of it. On top of that is the knowledge that what I'm doing is more or less futile.'

She looked up and he saw that there were tears in her eyes. 'There's nothing easy about this, Kanai,' she said. 'You have to take that back.'

He swallowed the quick retort that had come to his lips. Instead, he reached for her hand and placed it between his own. 'I'm sorry,' he said. 'I shouldn't have said that. I take it back.'

She snatched her hand away and rose to her feet. 'I'd better get back to work.'

He called out as she was going back to her place, 'You're a brave woman. Do you know that?'

She shrugged this off, in embarrassment. 'I'm just doing my job.'

Mr Sloane

It was late afternoon when Garjontola came into view and the water was at its lowest ebb. Piya was on watch as the *Megha* approached the 'pool' and her heart leapt when she saw that the dolphins had congregated there, punctually following the flow of the tides. For the sake of their safety, she signalled to Horen to drop anchor while the *Megha* was still a kilometre or so away.

Kanai had come to the bow to stand beside her and she said, 'Would you like to look at the dolphins close up?'

'Absolutely,' he said. 'I'm anxious to meet the beast to which you've pledged your troth.'

'Come along, then. We'll go in Fokir's boat.'

They went aft, to the *Megha*'s stern, and found Fokir waiting with his oars in hand. Piya stepped over and went to her usual place, in the bow, while Kanai seated himself in the boat's mid-section.

A few strokes of Fokir's oars brought them to the pool and soon two dolphins approached the boat and began to circle around it. Piya recognized them as the cow-and-calf pair she had identified earlier and she was delighted to see them again. She had the impression – as she often did with Orcaella – that they had recognized her too, for they surfaced repeatedly around the boat, and on one occasion, the adult even made eye contact.

Kanai in the meanwhile, was watching the dolphins with a puzzled frown. 'Are you sure these are the right animals?' he said at last, in a tone of disbelief.

'Of course I'm sure.'

'But look at them,' he said in a tone of plaintive complaint. 'All they do is bob up and down while making little grunting sounds.'

'They do a lot more than that, Kanai,' Piya said. 'But mostly they do it underwater.'

'I thought you were going to lead me to my Moby Dick,' said Kanai. 'But these are just little floating pigs.'

Piya laughed. 'Kanai – you're talking about a cousin of the killer whale.'

'Pigs have impressive relatives too, you know,' Kanai said.

'Kanai, Orcaella don't look remotely like pigs.'

'No – they do have that thing on their back.'

'It's called a fin.'

'And I'm sure they don't taste as good as pigs.'

'Kanai,' said Piya. 'Stop it.'

Kanai laughed. 'I just can't believe we've come all this way to look at these ridiculous porcine little things. If you're going to risk jail for an animal, couldn't you have picked something with a little more sex appeal? Or any appeal for that matter?'

'Orcaella have a lot of appeal, Kanai,' Piya said. 'You just have to have the patience to discover it.'

Despite his jocular tone, Kanai's perplexity was genuine. In his imagination, dolphins were the sleek steel-grey creatures he had seen in films and aquariums. The appeal of those animals he could readily understand, but he could see nothing interesting in the phlegmatic, beady-eyed creatures circling the boat. He knitted his brows. 'Did you always know you were going to be tracking these animals around the world?'

'No. It was an accident,' said Piya. 'I knew nothing about the species when I met my first Orcaella. It happened about three years ago.'

She had been interning with a team doing a marine-mammal survey in the South China Sea. At the end of the survey, the ship stopped at Port Sihanouk, in Cambodia. A few members of the team went up to Phnom Penh to visit friends who were working with an international wildlife conservation agency. That was how they learnt that a river dolphin had been found stranded near a small village in central Cambodia.

'I thought I'd go and take a look.'

The village, it turned out, was an hour's journey from Phnom Penh and a long way inland from the Mekong River: Piya was driven there on a hired motorcycle. The terrain was a patchwork of huts, rice-fields, irrigation ditches and shallow reservoirs. It was in one of these reservoirs, a body of water no bigger than a swimming pool, that the dolphin had been confined. The animal had swum inland with the floodwaters of the rainy season, and had failed to depart with the rest of its pod; in the mean-while, the irrigation ditches had run dry, shutting off its escape routes.

This was Piya's first glimpse of *Orcaella brevirostris*: it was about a metre and a half in length, with a steel-grey body and a short dorsal fin. It lacked the usual bill-like dolphin snout, and its rounded head and large eyes gave it an oddly ruminative, bovine appearance. She named it Mr Sloane after a high-school teacher to whom it bore a distinct resemblance.

Mr Sloane, the dolphin, was clearly in trouble: the water was drying up fast and there were no fish left in the reservoir. Piya went with her motorcycle-driver to the next kampong and brought back some fish from the market: she spent the rest of the day sitting beside the reservoir, feeding the dolphin. Next day, she went back again with a cooler filled with fish. Although there were many farmers and children present, Mr Sloane ignored the others and went straight over to Piya's side of the reservoir.

'I swear to you it recognized me.'

Back in Phnom Penh there was much concern in the small wildlife community. The Orcaella population of the Mekong was known to be declining rapidly and was expected soon to fall below sustainable levels. The Mekong Orcaella had shared Cambodia's misfortunes: in the 1970s they had suffered the ravages of indiscriminate American carpet bombing. Later they too had been massacred by Khmer Rouge cadres who had hit upon the idea of using dolphin oil to supplement their dwin-dling supplies of petroleum. The once abundant population of Orcaella in the Tonle Sap, Cambodia's great freshwater lake, had been reduced almost to extinction. These dolphins were hunted with rifles and explosives and their carcasses were hung up in the sun so that their fat would drip into buckets. This oil was then used to run boats and motorcycles.

'Do you mean to tell me,' Kanai said, 'that they were melted down and used as diesel fuel?'

'Yes, in effect.'

In recent years the threat to Orcaella had grown even more serious. There was a plan afoot to blow up the rapids of the upper Mekong in order to make the river navigable as far as China: this would mean the certain destruction of the dolphin's preferred habitats. Thus the stranding of Mr Sloane was not just an individual misfortune; it was a catastrophe for an entire population.

Piya was given the job of caring for the stranded dolphin while arrangements were made for transporting the animal back to the river. Every day for six days, Piya travelled up to the reservoir bearing fresh cooler-loads of fish. On the morning of the seventh she arrived to find that Mr Sloane had disappeared. She was told that the animal had died during the night, but she could find no evidence to support this. There was no explanation of how the remains had been removed from the pool. What she did find were the tread marks of a heavy vehicle of some kind, probably a truck; they went all the way up to the water's edge. What had happened was all too obvious – Mr Sloane had fallen victim to the flourishing clandestine trade in wildlife. New aquariums were opening throughout eastern Asia and the demand for river dolphins was growing. Mr Sloane was a valuable commodity – Irrawaddy dolphins had been known to fetch as much as one hundred thousand US dollars on the market.

'One hundred thousand dollars?' said Kanai in disbelief. 'For these?'

'Yes.'

Piya was not inclined to be sentimental about animals. But the idea that Mr Sloane would soon be sold off to an aquarium, as a curiosity, made her stomach churn. For days afterwards she was haunted by a dream in which Mr Sloane was driven into a corner of his tank by a line of hunters armed with fishnets.

Trying to put the incident behind her, she decided to go back to the States to register for a PhD at the Scripps Institute in La Jolla. But then an unforeseen opportunity came her way: a wildlife conservation group in Phnom Penh offered her a contract to do a survey of Mekong Orcaella. The offer was perfect in every way: the money was enough to last a couple of years, and the material would count towards her PhD. She took the job and moved upriver to the sleepy town of Kratie. In the three years since she had become one of a tiny handful of Orcaella specialists. She had worked everywhere Irrawaddy dolphins were to be found: Burma, northern Australia, the Philippines, coastal Thailand – everywhere, in fact, except the place where they first entered the record-book of zoological reckoning, India.

It was only when she reached the end of her story that Piya realized, with a guilty start, that she had not said a single word to Fokir since she stepped on the boat.

'Listen, Kanai,' she said, 'there's something I've been kind of puzzled about. Fokir seems to know this place so well – this island, Garjontola. He seems to know all about the dolphins and where they go. I wish I knew what first brought him here, how he learnt about these things? Could you ask him?'

'Of course.' Kanai turned away to explain the question and then, as Fokir began to speak, he swivelled around to face Piya. 'This is what he says.

'"I cannot remember a time when I didn't know about this place; back when I was very little, long before I had even seen these islands and these rivers, I had heard about Garjontola from my mother. She would sing to me and tell me tales about this island. This was a place, my mother said, where no one who was good at heart would ever have cause for fear.

'"As for the big *shush*, the dolphins who live in these waters, I knew about them too, even before I came here. These animals were also in my mother's stories: they were Bon Bibi's messengers, she used to say, and they brought her news of the rivers and khals. They came here during the bhata, my mother said, so they could tell Bon Bibi about everything they had seen. During the jowar they scattered to the ends of the forest and became her eyes and her ears. This secret her own father had told her, and he had told her also that if you could learn to follow the shush, then you would always be able to find fish.

'"I had heard these stories long before I came to the tide country, and ever since I was little I had always wanted to come and see this place. When we came to live in Morichjhãpi I would say to my mother, 'When will we go? When will we go to Garjontola?' There was never time – there was too much to do. The first time she brought me was just a few weeks before her death. Maybe this was why, after her death, whenever I thought of her I thought also of Garjontola. I came here time and again and it happened that the shush became like my friends. I followed them where they went.

'"That day, when you came in that launch, with the forest guard, and stopped my boat: this was where I was coming, with my son. The night before, my mother had come to me in a dream and she had said, 'I want to see your son; why do you never bring him to Garjontola? It will soon be time for you and me to be reunited – after that who knows when I will see him again? Bring him to me as soon as you can.'

'"I could not tell my wife this, because I knew she would be upset and she would not believe me. So the next day, instead of taking Tutul to school, I took him to my boat and we set off to come here: on the way we stopped to catch some fish and that was when you came upon us in your launch."'

'And what came of it?' Piya said. 'Do you think she saw him, your mother?'

'"Yes: the last night we were here, in my boat, I dreamed of my mother again. She was smiling and happy and she said, 'I'm glad I've seen your son. Now take him home and come back, so that you and I can be together again.'"'

Up to this point Piya had been listening as if she were under a spell: Kanai seemed almost to have vanished, creating the illusion that she was speaking directly with Fokir. But now suddenly, the spell broke and she stirred as if she had been jolted awake from her sleep.

'What does he mean by that, Kanai?' she said. 'Ask him: what does he mean?'

'He says it was just a dream.'

Kanai turned away from her to say a few words to Fokir, and suddenly, to Piya's surprise Fokir began to sing, or rather, chant, in a quick rhythm.

'What's he saying?' Piya said to Kanai. 'Can you translate?'

'I'm sorry, Piya,' Kanai said. 'But this is beyond my power: he's chanting a part of the Bon Bibi legend and the metre is too complicated. I can't do it.'

Kratie

The tide turned with the waning of the day and as the level of the water crept up, the dolphins began to drift away from the pool. When the last animal had left, Fokir turned the boat towards the *Megha* and began to row.

On board, in the meantime, Horen and his grandson had strung up a couple of tarpaulin sheets to create an enclosed bathing area in the bhotbhoti's stern. After a long day under the sun, the prospect of cleaning up was all too welcome and Piya lost no time fetching her towel and toiletries. She found two buckets in the enclosure, of which only one was full. The other had a rope attached to its handle to draw water from the river. Piya threw it overboard and emptied it over herself, revelling in the bracing chill. The other bucket was filled with fresh water and she dipped into it sparingly with an enamel mug, to wash off the soap. When she was done, it was still half full.

On the way back to her cabin, she passed Kanai. He was waiting in the gangway with a towel slung over his shoulder.

'I've left plenty of fresh water for you.'

'I'll make good use of it.'

In the distance, she heard someone else splashing and knew it was probably Fokir, bathing in the stern of his own boat.

Later, after she had changed into fresh clothes, she went out on deck. The tide was now nearing full flood and the currents were drawing patterns on the river's surface as they whirled around the anchored vessel. Some of the distant islands had shrunk into narrow spars of land, and where there had been forest before, there were now only branches visible, bending like reeds to the sway of the tide.

Piya was pulling a chair up to the rails when Kanai appeared beside her, with a cup of steaming tea in each hand. 'Horen asked me to bring these up,' he said, handing one to Piya.

He pulled up a chair too and for a while they were both absorbed in watching the slow submersion of the landscape. Piya braced herself, expecting a joke or a satirical remark, but somewhat to her surprise, he seemed content to sit quietly. There was something companionable about the silence and in the end it was she who spoke first.

'I could watch it forever,' she said. 'This play of tides.'

'That's interesting,' he said. 'I once knew a woman who used to say that – about the sea.'

'A girlfriend?' said Piya.

'Yes.'

'Have you had many?'

He nodded, and then, as if to change the subject, said, 'And what about you? Do cetologists have private lives?'

'Now that you ask,' said Piya, 'I have to say that there aren't many who do – especially not among us women. Relationships aren't easy, you know, given the kinds of lives we lead.'

'Why not?'

'We travel so much,' Piya said. 'We never stay long in one place. It doesn't make things easy.'

Kanai raised his eyebrows: 'But you don't mean to say, do you, that you've never had a relationship – not even a college romance?'

'Oh, I've had my share of those,' Piya allowed. 'But none of them ever led anywhere.'

'Never?'

'Well, once,' Piya said. 'There was this one time when I thought it was leading somewhere.'

'And?'

Piya laughed. 'It ended in disaster. What could you expect? It was in Kratie.'

'Kratie?' he said. 'Where's that?'

'In eastern Cambodia,' she said, 'a couple of hundred kilometres from Phnom Penh. I used to live there once.'

Kratie stood on a bluff above the Mekong, and a few kilo-metres north of the town was a riverbed pool that served as a dry-season home for a pod of some six Orcaella. This was where Piya had begun her research. As the town was both convenient and pleasant, she had rented the top floor of a wooden house with the intention of making it her base for the next two or three years. One of the advantages of Kratie was that it housed an office of the Fisheries Department, a branch of government with which she had to have many dealings.

One of the local representatives of the department was a young official who was reasonably proficient in English. His name was Rath and he was from Phnom Penh. Without friends or family in Kratie, he was often at a loose end, especially in the evenings. Kratie was very small, no larger than a couple of city blocks, and inevitably Piya found her path crossing Rath's quite frequently. It turned out that he often ate in the same waterfront café where she usually went for her evening meal of noodles and Ovaltine. They took to sitting at the same table and their everyday small talk evolved slowly into real conversations.

One day, in passing, Rath revealed he had spent a part of his childhood in a death camp of the Pol Pot era: his parents had been transported there after the Khmer Rouge took Phnom Penh. Although Rath had offered this as a throwaway scrap of information, his revelation had made such an impression on Piya that she had responded by telling him about her own childhood. In the weeks that followed she found herself talking to him as she never had to any man she had known before: she had told him about her parents and their marriage, about her mother's depression and her last days in hospital.

How much did Rath understand of what she was saying? The truth was, she had no idea. Was it a delusion to think he too had made some kind of revelation about himself when all he had done was to talk about an experience more common than not among his contemporaries? She was never to know.

A day came when she found she was thinking of Rath all the time, even when her attention was meant to be focused on the dolphins and their pool. Although she realized she was falling in love, she was not alarmed. This was mainly because of the

312

kind of man Rath was – like her, he was shy and a little solitary by nature. She took comfort in his hesitancies, taking them as proof that he was as inexperienced with women as she was with men. But she was still very cautious and it was not until some four months had passed that their intimacy progressed beyond the sharing of meals and memories. It was the light-headedness of the aftermath that caused her to dispense with her habitual caution: this was it, she decided, she was going to become one of those rare exceptions among female field biologists – one who'd had the good fortune to fall in love with the right man in the right place.

At the end of the dry season, she was scheduled to go to Hong Kong for six weeks – partly to attend a conference and partly to earn some money by working in a survey team. When she left, everything seemed settled. Rath came to Pochentong airport to see her off and for the first couple of weeks they exchanged emails every day. Then the messages began to tail off until she could not get a response out of him. She didn't call his office because she was trying to save money – and anyway, she assumed, what could happen in a couple of weeks?

On stepping off the boat, at Kratie, she knew immediately something was wrong: she could almost hear the whispers running up and down the street as she walked back to her flat. It was her landlady who told her, conveying the news with a ghoulish glee: Rath had married and taken a transfer to Phnom Penh.

At first, trying to think the whole thing through, she had decided that he had been forced into a marriage of convenience by his family – this was a predicament she could have understood and it would have sweetened the pill a little. The rejection would have seemed a little less direct, a little less brutal. But even that consolation was denied her, for she soon found out that he had married a woman from his office, an accountant. Apparently he had started seeing her after she had left to go to Hong Kong: it had taken him just six weeks to decide.

Despite everything, she might still have found it in her to forgive Rath: she could see, that in her absence, it might have occurred to him to ask himself what it would mean, in the long run, to be married to a foreigner, a habitual peripatetic at that? Could he really be blamed for deciding that he could not deal with it?

She found some solace in this until she met Rath's replacement. He was a married man in his thirties, and he too spoke some English. Within a short while of meeting her, he shepherded her down to the same waterfront café that she and Rath had once frequented. With the sun setting across the Mekong, he had gazed into her eyes and begun to ask sympathetic questions about her mother. It was then that she realized that Rath had told him everything: that the most intimate details of her life were common knowledge among the men of the town; that this awful oily man was actually trying to use those confidences in some sort of clumsy attempt at seduction.

That was it. The next week she packed her things and moved a hundred kilometres upriver, to Stung Treng. In the end it was not the pain of what she had lived through with Rath that drove her out, but the sheer humiliation of having had her life laid bare before the whole town.

'But that wasn't even the worst part,' Piya said.

'What was the worst part, then?'

'That came when I went back to the States. I met up with some friends. All women, all doing research in field biology. They just laughed when they heard my story. They'd all been through something similar. It was as if what I'd been through wasn't even my own story – just a script we were all doomed to live out. That's just how it is, they said: this is what your life's going to be like. You're always going to find yourself in some small town where there's never anyone to talk to but this one guy who knows some English. And everything you tell him will be all over the town before you've said it. So just keep your mouth shut and get used to being on your own.'

Piya shrugged. 'So that's what I've been trying to do ever since.'

'What?'

'Get used to the idea of being on my own.'

Kanai fell silent as he thought about the story she had just told. It seemed to him that he had not till this moment been able to see her for the person she was. Her containment and her usual economy with words had prevented him from acknowledging, even to himself, her true extraordinariness: she was not just his equal in mind and imagination; her spirit and heart were far larger than his own.

Kanai had been leaning back, with his feet up on the gunwale. Now, allowing his chair to right itself, he sat forward and looked into her face. 'It doesn't have to be like that you know, Piya. You don't have to be on your own.'

'You have a better idea?'

'I do.'

Before he could say any more, they heard Horen's voice, echoing up from the lower deck, summoning them to dinner.

Signs

Piya went to bed early again. Not having slept much the night before, Kanai tried to do the same. But despite his best efforts, sleep proved elusive for him that night: there was a strong wind blowing outside and, as if in response to the bhotbhoti's rocking, a recurrent childhood nightmare came back to visit him – a dream in which he was taking the same examination over and over again. The difference now was in the faces of the examiners, which were not those of his teachers but of Kusum and Piya, Nilima and Moyna, Horen and Nirmal. In the small hours he sat up suddenly, in a sweat of anxiety: he could not remember what language he had been dreaming in, but the word *pariksha*, 'examination', was ringing in his head and he was trying to explain why he had translated the word in the archaic sense of 'trial by ordeal'. It was not till the small hours that these dreams yielded to a deep, heavy sleep which kept him in his bunk until the dawn fog had lifted and the tide was about to reverse itself.

Kanai stepped out of his cabin to find that the wind had died down, leaving the river's becalmed surface as still as a sheet of polished metal. Having reached full flood, the tide was now at that point of perfect balance when the water appears motionless. From the deck the island of Garjontola looked like a jewelled inlay on the rim of a gigantic silver shield. The spectacle was at once elemental and intimate, immense in its scale, and yet in this moment of tranquillity, oddly gentle.

He heard a footstep on the deck and turned to see Piya coming towards him. She was armed with a clipboard and data sheets and her voice was all business: 'Kanai, can I ask you a favour? For this morning?'

'Certainly. Tell me: what can I do for you?'

'I need you to do some spotting for me,' Piya replied.

The timing of the tides had created a small problem for her, Piya said. Her original plan had been to follow the dolphins when they left the pool at high tide. But right now the flood seemed to be setting in early in the morning and late in the evening: this meant the animals would be migrating in the dark. Tracking them would be hard enough in the day; without good light it would be impossible. What she had decided to do instead was to make a log of the routes they followed when they came back to the pool. Her plan was to post watches at the two approaches to the pool, one upstream and one downstream. She herself would take the upstream watch on the *Megha*: the river was wide there and it would be impossible to cover it without binoculars. Fokir could take the other watch, in his boat: if Kanai could join him, that would be so much the better – to have two pairs of eyes on the boat, would compensate for the lack of binoculars.

'It just means you'll have to spend a few hours in the boat with Fokir,' said Piya. 'But that's not a problem, is it?'

Kanai was affronted to think she had the impression that he was somehow in competition with Fokir. 'No,' he said quickly. 'Not at all. I'll be glad to have a chance to talk to him.'

'Good. That's settled, then. We'll get started after you've had something to eat. I'll knock on your door in an hour.'

By the time Piya came to get him, he had breakfasted and was ready to go. In preparation for a day under the sun, he had changed into light-coloured trousers, a white shirt and sandals. He had also decided to take along a cap and sunglasses. These preparations met with Piya's approval. 'Better bring these as well,' she said, handing him two bottles of water. 'It's going to get very hot out there.'

They went together to the *Megha*'s stern and found Fokir ready to leave, with his oars placed crosswise across the gunwales. After

Kanai had crossed over to the boat, Piya showed Fokir exactly where he was to position his boat. The spot was about two kilometres downstream of the *Megha*, at a point where the island of Garjontola curved outwards, jutting into the river so that the channel narrowed.

'The river's only a kilometre wide over there,' said Piya. 'I figure that if you anchor at midstream, you'll have all the approaches covered, between the two of you.'

Then she turned to point upstream, where the river's mouth opened into a vast mohona. 'I'll be over there,' said Piya. 'As you can see, it's very wide but being on the *Megha* I'll have some elevation. With my binoculars I'll be able to keep it covered. We'll be about four kilometres apart. I'll be able to see you, but you probably won't be able to see me.'

She waved as Fokir cast off the boat's moorings. Cupping her hands around her mouth, she shouted, 'If it gets to be too much for you, Kanai, just tell Fokir to bring you back.'

'I'll be fine,' said Kanai, waving back. 'Don't worry about me.'

The boat had not gone very far when puffs of black smoke began to spurt from the *Megha*'s funnel. Slowly the bhotbhoti began to move and for several minutes Fokir and Kanai were shaken by the turbulence of its bow-wave. Only when it had disappeared from view was the water calm again.

Now, with the landscape emptied of other human beings, it was as if the distance between Kanai and Fokir had been reduced a hundredfold – yet if the boat had been two kilometres in length, they could not have been further apart. Kanai was positioned in the bow, while Fokir was in the stern, behind the hood. Separated by the thatch, neither of them could see the other and for their first couple of hours on the water very little was said. Kanai made a couple of attempts to break the silence and was answered on each occasion with nothing more than a perfunctory grunt.

Around noon, when the level of the water had begun to ebb, Fokir jumped to his feet in great excitement and pointed down-river: '*Oi-jé* – Over there.'

Shading his eyes, Kanai spotted a sharply raked dorsal fin arcing through the water.

'You'll see better if you hold on to the hood and stand up.'

'All right.' Kanai made his way to the boat's midsection, pulled himself to his feet, and steadied his balance by leaning on the hood.

'Another one. Over there.'

Guided by Fokir's finger, Kanai spotted another fin slicing through the water. This was followed in quick succession by two more dolphins – all of them spotted by Fokir.

This flurry of activity seemed to have created a small opening in the barrier of Fokir's silence, so Kanai made another attempt to draw him into conversation. 'Tell me something, Fokir,' he said, glancing down the length of the hood. 'Do you remember Saar at all?'

Fokir shot him a glance and looked away again. 'No,' he said. 'There was a time when he used to visit us, but I was very small then. After my mother died I hardly ever saw him. I hardly remember him at all.'

'And your mother? Do you remember her?'

'How could I forget her? Her face is everywhere.'

He said this in such a plain, matter-of-fact way that Kanai was puzzled: 'What are you saying, Fokir? Where do you see her face?'

He smiled and began to point in every direction, to the ends of the compass as well as to his head and feet: 'Here, here, here, here. Everywhere.'

The phrasing of this was simple to the point of being child-like and it seemed to Kanai that he had finally understood why Moyna felt so deeply tied to her husband, despite everything. There was something about him that was utterly unformed, and it was this very quality that drew her to him: she craved it in the same way that a potter's hands might crave the resistance of unshaped clay.

'So tell me, then, Fokir; do you ever feel like visiting a city?'

It was only after he had spoken that he realized that he had inadvertently addressed Fokir as *tui*, as though he were indeed a child. But Fokir seemed not to notice. 'This is enough for me,' he said. 'What'll I do in a city?' He picked up his oars as if to mark the end of the conversation. 'Now it's time to go back to the bhotbhoti.'

The boat began to rock as Fokir dipped his oars and Kanai retreated quickly to his place in the bow. After sitting down, he looked up to see that Fokir had changed his place: he had moved to the boat's mid-section, seating himself so that he would be rowing with his face turned towards Kanai.

In the steaming midday heat a haze was rising from the river, giving the impression of mirages dancing on the water. The heat and haze induced a kind of torpor in Kanai and as if in a dream he had a vision of Fokir, travelling to Seattle with Piya. He saw the two of them walking into the plane, she in her jeans and he in his lungi and scuffed T-shirt; he saw Fokir squirming in a seat that was not like any he had ever seen before: he pictured him looking up and down the aisle with his mouth agape. And then he thought of him in some icy Western city, wandering the streets in search of work, lost and unable to ask for directions.

He shook his head to rid himself of this discomfiting vision.

It seemed to Kanai that the boat was passing much closer to the island of Garjontola than it had on the way out. But with the water at its lowest level, it was hard to know whether this was due to a deliberate change of course or to an optical illusion caused by the usual shrinkage of the river's surface at ebb-tide. As they were passing the island Fokir raised a flattened palm to his eyes and peered at the sloping sandbank to their left. Suddenly he stiffened, rising slightly in his seat. As if by instinct, his right hand gathered in the hem of his unfurled lungi, tucking it between his legs, transforming the ankle-length garment into a loincloth. With his hand on the gunwale, he rose to a half-crouch, setting the boat gently asway, his torso inclining forward in the stance of a runner taking his mark. He raised a hand to point: 'Look over there.'

'What's the matter?' said Kanai. 'What do you see?'

Fokir raised a hand to point: 'Look.'

Kanai narrowed his eyes as he followed his finger. He could see nothing of interest, so he said, 'What should I look for?'

'Signs, marks – like we saw yesterday. A whole trail of them, running from the trees to the water and back.'

Kanai looked again and caught sight of a few depressions in the ground. But the bank at this point was colonized mainly by stands of 'garjon' – a species of mangrove that breathed through spearlike 'ventilators' connected by subterranean root systems. The surface of the bank was pierced by so many of these upthrust organs that it was impossible to distinguish between one mark and another. The depressions that had caught Fokir's eye looked nothing like the sharply defined marks of the night before. They seemed to Kanai to be too shapeless to signify anything in particular; they could just as well have been crabs' burrows, or runnels formed by the retreating water.

'See how they form a track?' Fokir said. 'They go right to the edge of the water. That means they were made after the tide had ebbed – probably just as we were heading this way. The animal must have spotted us and come down to take a closer look.'

The thought of this, a tiger coming down to the edge of the water in order to watch their progress across the mohona, was just far-fetched enough to make Kanai smile.

'Why would it want to look at us?' said Kanai.

'Maybe because it smelled you,' said Fokir. 'It likes to keep an eye on strangers.'

There was something about Fokir's expression that convinced Kanai he was playing a game with him, perhaps unconsciously, and the thought of this amused him. He understood all too well how the dynamics of their situation might induce Fokir to exaggerate the menace of their surroundings. He himself had often stood in Fokir's place, serving as some hapless traveller's window on an unfamiliar world. He remembered how, in those circumstances, he too had often been tempted to heighten the inscrutability of the surroundings through subtly slanted glosses. To do this required no particularly malicious intent; it was just a way of underscoring the insider's indispensability; every new peril was proof of his importance; each new threat evidence of his worth. These temptations were all too readily available to every guide and translator – not to succumb was to make yourself dispensable; to give in was to destroy the value of your word, and thus your work. It was precisely because of his awareness of this dilemma that he knew too that there were times when a translator's bluff had to be called.

Kanai pointed to the shore and made a gesture of dismissal.

'Those are just burrows,' he said smiling. 'I saw crabs digging into them. What makes you think they have anything to do with the big cat?'

Fokir turned to flash him a bright, white smile. 'Do you want to know how I know?'

'Yes. Tell me.'

Leaning over, Fokir took hold of Kanai's hand and placed it on the back of his neck. The unexpected intimacy of this contact sent a shock through Kanai's arm and he snatched his hand back – but not before he had felt the goosebumps bristling on the moist surface of Fokir's skin.

Fokir smiled at him again. 'That's how I know,' he said. 'It's the fear that tells me.' Rising to a crouch, Fokir directed a look of inquiry at Kanai. 'And what about you?' he said. 'Can you feel the fear?'

These words triggered a response in Kanai that was just as reflexive as the goosebumps on Fokir's neck. The surroundings – the mangrove forest, the water, the boat – were suddenly blotted from his consciousness; he forgot where he was. It was as though his mind had decided to revert to the functions for which it had been trained and equipped by years of practice. At that moment nothing existed for him but language, the pure structure of sound that had formed Fokir's question. He gave this inquiry the fullest attention of which his mind was capable and knew the answer almost at once: it was in the negative; the truth was that he did not feel the fear that had raised bumps on Fokir's skin. It was not that he was a man of unusual courage – far from it. But he knew also that fear was not – contrary to what was often said – an instinct. It was something learnt, something that accumulated in the mind, through knowledge, experience and upbringing; nothing was harder to share than another person's fear, and at that moment he certainly did not share Fokir's.

'Since you asked me,' Kanai said, 'I'll tell you the truth. The answer is no; I'm not afraid, at least not in the way you are.'

Like a ring spreading across a pool, a ripple of awakened interest passed over Fokir's face. 'Then tell me,' he said, leaning closer, 'if you're not afraid, there's nothing to prevent you from taking a closer look. Is there?'

His gaze was steady and unblinking and Kanai would /
himself to drop his eyes: Fokir had just doubled the s/
it was up to him now to decide whether he would b_
or call his bluff.

'All right,' Kanai said, not without some reluctance. 'Let's go.'

Fokir nodded and turned the boat using a single oar. When
the bow was pointing to the shore he started to row. Kanai glanced
across the water: the river was as calm as a floor of polished
stone and the currents etched on its surface appeared almost
stationary, like the veins in a slab of marble.

'Fokir, tell me something,' said Kanai.

'What?'

'If you're afraid, then why do you want to go there – to that
island?'

'My mother told me,' Fokir said, 'that this was a place where
you had to learn not to be afraid. And if you did, then you might
find the answer to your troubles.'

'Is that why you come here?'

'Who's to say?' He shrugged, smiling, and then he said, 'Now,
can I ask you something, Kanai-babu?'

He was smiling broadly, leading Kanai to expect he would
make some kind of joke. 'What?'

'Are you a clean man, Kanai-babu?'

Kanai sat up startled. 'What do you mean?'

Fokir shrugged: 'You know – are you good at heart?'

'I think so,' Kanai said. 'My intentions are good anyway – as
for the rest, who knows?'

'But don't you ever want to know for sure?'

'How can anyone ever know for sure?'

'My mother used to say that here in Garjontola, Bon Bibi
would show you whatever you wanted to know.'

'How?'

Fokir shrugged again. 'That's just what she used to say.'

As they drew close to the island a flock of birds took wing,
breaking away from the upper level of the canopy and swirling
around in a cloud before settling down again. The birds were
parrots, of a colour almost indistinguishable from the emerald
tint of the mangroves; for a moment, when they rose in the air

ogether, it was as though a green mane had risen from the tree-tops, like a wig lifted by a gust of wind.

The boat picked up speed as it approached the bank and Fokir's final stroke rammed the prow deep into the mud. Tucking his lungi between his legs, he dropped over the side of the boat and went running over the bank to examine the marks.

'I was right,' cried Fokir triumphantly, dropping to his knees. 'These marks are so fresh they must have been made within the hour.'

To Kanai the depressions looked just as shapeless as they had before. 'I don't see anything,' he said.

'How could you?' Fokir looked up at the boat and smiled. 'You're too far away. You'll have to get off the boat. Come over here and look. You'll see how they go all the way up.' He pointed up the slope to the barrier of mangrove looming above.

'All right, I'm coming.' Kanai was turning to jump when Fokir stopped him: 'No. Wait. First, roll up your pants and then take your slippers off. Or else you'll lose them in the mud; it's better to be barefoot.'

Kanai kicked off his sandals and rolled his trousers up to his knees. Then, swinging his feet over the gunwale, he dropped over the side and sank into the mud. His body lurched forward and he reached quickly for the boat, steadying himself against the gunwale: to fall in the mud now would be a humiliation too painful to contemplate. He pulled his right foot carefully out of the mud and planted it a little way ahead. In this way, by repeating these childlike steps, he was able to get across to Fokir's side without mishap.

'Look,' said Fokir, gesturing at the ground. 'Here are the claws and there's the pad.' He turned to point up the slope: 'And see: that's the way it went, past those trees. It might be watching you even now.'

There was a mocking note in his voice that stung Kanai. He stood up straight and said, 'What are you trying to do, Fokir? Are you trying to frighten me?'

'Frighten you?' said Fokir smiling. 'But why would you be frightened? Didn't I tell you what my mother said? No one who is good at heart has anything to fear in this place.'

Then, turning on his heel, Fokir went back to the boat, across the mudbank, and reached under the hood. When he straightened up again, Kanai saw that he had drawn out his daa.

As Fokir advanced towards him, blade in hand, Kanai recoiled reflexively. 'What's that for?' he said, raising his eyes from the instrument's glistening edge.

'Don't be afraid,' said Fokir. 'It's for the jungle. Don't you want to go and see if we can find the maker of these marks?'

Even in that moment of distraction, Kanai noticed – so tenacious were the habits of his profession – that Fokir was using a different form of address with him now. From the respectful *apni* that he had been using before, he had now switched to the same familiar tui Kanai had used in addressing him: it was as though in stepping on the island, the authority of their positions had been suddenly reversed.

Kanai looked at the tangled barrier of mangrove ahead and knew that it would be madness to walk into that with Fokir: his daa could slip, anything could happen. It was not worth the risk.

'No,' said Kanai. 'I'm not going to play this game with you any more, Fokir. I want you to take me back to the bhotbhoti.'

'But why?' said Fokir with a laugh. 'What are you afraid of? Didn't I tell you? A man like yourself should have nothing to fear in this place.'

Stepping into the mud, Kanai shouted over his shoulder: 'Stop talking nonsense: you may be a child, but I'm not—'

Then suddenly it was as though the earth had come alive and was reaching for his ankle. Looking down, he discovered that a ropelike tendril had wrapped itself around his ankles. He felt his balance going and when he tried to slide a foot forward, to correct it, his legs seemed to move in the wrong direction. Before he could do anything to break the fall, the wetness of the mud slapped him full in the face.

At first he was completely immobile: it was as though his body were being fitted for a mould in a tub of plaster. Trying to look up, he discovered that he could not see: the mud had turned his sunglasses into a blindfold. Scraping his head against his arm, he shook the glasses off and allowed them to sink out of sight. When Fokir's hand descended on his shoulder he brushed it off and

325

tried to push himself to his feet on his own. But the consistency of the mud was such as to create a suction effect and he could not break free.

He saw that Fokir was smiling at him. 'I told you to be careful.'

Suddenly the blood rushed to Kanai's head and obscenities began to pour from his mouth: *'Shala, banchod, shuorer bachcha.'*

His anger came welling up with an atavistic explosiveness, rising from sources whose very existence he would have denied: the master's suspicion of the menial; the pride of caste; the townsman's mistrust of the rustic; the city's antagonism to the village. He had thought that he had cleansed himself of these sediments of the past, but the violence with which they came spewing out of him now suggested that they had only been compacted into an explosive and highly volatile reserve.

There had been occasions in the past – too many of them – when Kanai had seen his clients losing their temper in like fashion: where rage had made them cross the boundaries of selfhood, transporting them to a state where they were literally 'beside themselves'. The phrase was apt: their emotions were so intense as almost to spill outside the physical boundaries of their skin. And almost always, no matter what the proximate cause, he was the target of their rage: the interpreter, the messenger, the amanuensis. He was the life-preserver that held them afloat in a tide of incomprehension; the meaninglessness that surrounded them became, as it were, his fault, because he was its only named feature. He had survived these outbursts by telling himself that these episodes were merely a professional hazard – 'nothing personal' – it was just that his job sometimes made him a proxy for the inscrutability of life itself. Yet, despite his knowledge of the phenomenon, he was powerless to stop the torrent of obscenities that were pouring out of his mouth now. When Fokir offered a hand to help him up, he slapped it aside: *'Ja, shuorer bachcha, beriye ja!* Get away from me, you son of a pig!'

'All right, then,' said Fokir. 'I'll do as you say.'

Raising his head, Kanai caught a glimpse of Fokir's eyes and suddenly the words withered on his lips. In Kanai's professional life there had been a few instances in which the act of interpretation had given him the momentary sensation of being transported out of his body and into another. In each instance it was as if the instrument of language had metamorphosed – instead of being a barrier, a curtain that divided, it had become a transparent film, a prism that allowed him to look through another set of eyes, to filter the world through a mind other than his own. These experiences had always come about unpredictably, without warning or apparent cause, and no thread of similarity linked these occasions except that in each of them he had been working as an interpreter. But he was not working now and yet it was exactly this feeling that came upon him as he looked at Fokir: it was as though his own vision were being refracted through those opaque, unreadable eyes, and he were seeing not himself, Kanai, but a great host of people – a double for the outside world, someone standing in for the men who had destroyed Fokir's village, burnt his home and killed his mother; he had become a token for a vision of human beings in which a man such as Fokir counted for nothing, a man whose value was less than that of an animal. In seeing himself in this way it seemed perfectly comprehensible to Kanai why Fokir should want him to be dead – but he understood also that this was not how it would be. Fokir had brought him here not because he wanted him to die, but because he wanted him to be judged.

Kanai lifted a hand to wipe the mud from his eyes and when he looked up again, he found that Fokir had stepped out of his field of vision. Something prompted Kanai to look back, over his shoulder. Squirming in the mud, he turned just in time to see the boat slipping away. He could not see Fokir's face, only his back; he was in the stern, rowing vigorously.

'Wait,' said Kanai. 'Don't leave me here.' It was too late: the boat had already vanished around a bend.

Kanai was watching the boat's bow wave, fanning across the river when he saw a ripple cutting slantwise across the water. He looked again carefully, and now it seemed certain that there was something there, beneath the water's surface: obscured by the darkness of the silt, it was making for the shore, coming towards him.

Kanai's head filled suddenly with visions of the ways in which the tide country dealt out death. The tiger, people said, killed you instantly, with a swipe of its forepaw, breaking the joint between your shoulder and neck. You felt no pain when it happened; you were dead already of the shock induced by the tiger's roar, just before the moment of impact. There was undeniably a quality of mercy to this, to the human mind, at least: wasn't this why people who lived in close proximity with tigers so often regarded them as being something more than just an animal? Because this was the only animal that forgave you for being so little at ease in your translated world?

Or was it because they knew of the horror of a reptilian death? It's the crocodile, he remembered, that most loves the water's edge: crocodiles can move faster on mud than a man can run on grass; the clay doesn't impede them; because of their sleek underbodies and their webbed feet they can use its slipperiness to their advantage. A crocodile, it's said, will keep you alive until you drown; it won't kill you on land; it'll drag you into the water while you're still breathing. Nobody finds the remains of people who're killed by crocodiles.

Every other thought vanished from his mind; rising to a crouch, he began to push himself backwards, higher up the bank, unmindful of the rooted spear-points that were raking his skin. As he retreated up the bank the mud thinned and the mangrove's shoots grew taller and more numerous. He could no longer see the ripple in the water, but it did not matter: all he wanted was to get as far from the water as possible.

Rising gingerly to his feet, he took a step and almost immediately there was an excruciating pain in the arch of his foot: it was as though he had stepped on the point of a nail, or on a shard of broken glass. In wrenching out his foot, he caught a glimpse of a mangrove's ventilator, sunk deep in the mud: he had jabbed his foot directly into its spearlike point. Then he saw that the spores were everywhere around him, scattered like booby traps; the roots that connected them ran just below the surface like camouflaged tripwires.

The barrier of mangrove, which had looked so tangled and forbidding from the boat, now seemed a refuge, a safe haven.

Picking his way through the minefield of ventilators, he went crashing into the vegetation.

The mangroves' branches were pliable and sinuous; they bent without breaking and snapped back like whips. When they closed around him, it was as if he had passed into the embrace of hundreds of scaly limbs. They grew so thick he could not see beyond a metre; the river disappeared from view and if it were not for the incline of the slope he would have been unable to judge whether he was heading away from the water or not. Then, all at once, the barrier ended and he broke through to a grassy clearing dotted with a few trees and palms. He sank to his knees; his clothes were in shreds and his body was covered in cuts and scratches. Flies were settling on his skin and clouds of mosquitoes were hovering above.

He could not bring himself to look around the clearing. This was where it would be, if it were here, on the island – but what was he thinking of? He could not recall the word, not even the euphemisms Fokir had used: it was as if his mind, in its panic, had emptied itself of language. The sounds and signs that had served, in combination, as the sluices between his mind and his senses, had collapsed: his mind was swamped by a flood of pure sensation. The words he had been searching for, the euphemisms that were the source of his panic, had been replaced by the thing itself, except that without words it could not be apprehended or understood. It was an artefact of pure intuition, so real that the thing itself could not have dreamed of existing so intensely.

He opened his eyes and there it was, directly ahead, less than a hundred metres away. It was sitting on its haunches, with its head up, watching him with its tawny, flickering eyes. The upper parts of its coat were of a colour that shone like gold in the sunlight, but its belly was dark and caked with mud. It was immense, of a size greater than he could have imagined, and the only parts of its body that were moving were its eyes and the tip of its tail.

At first, his terror was such that he could not move a muscle. Then, collecting his breath, he pushed himself to his knees and began to move slowly away, edging backwards into the thickets of mangrove, keeping his eyes fixed on the animal all the while, watching the tip of its twitching tail. Only when the branches of mangrove had closed around him did he rise to his feet. Turning around he began to push his way through the enclosing greenery, oblivious now to the thorns and splinters that were tearing at his limbs. When at last he broke through to the mudbank, he fell forward on his knees and covered his eyes with his forearm as he tried to prepare himself for the moment of impact, for the blow that would snap the bones of his neck.

'Kanai!' The shouted sound of his name made him open his eyes just long enough to see Piya, Fokir and Horen running towards him, across the bank. Now once again, he fell forward on the mud and his mind went dark.

When next he opened his eyes, he was on his back, in the boat, and a face was taking shape above him, materializing slowly against the blinding brightness of the afternoon sun. Slowly he came to understand that it was Piya, that she had her hands under his shoulders and was trying to prop him up.

'Kanai? Are you OK?'

'Where were you?' he said. 'I was alone so long on that island.'

'Kanai, you were there just ten minutes,' she said. 'Apparently it was you who sent Fokir away. He came hurrying back to get us and we came as quickly as we could.'

'I saw it, Piya. I saw the tiger.' He saw Horen and Fokir crowding around him too, so he added in Bangla, 'It was there, the cat – I saw it.'

Horen shook his head. 'There was nothing there,' he said. 'We looked, Fokir and I. We looked and saw nothing. And if it had been there, you wouldn't be here now.'

'It was there, I tell you.' Kanai's body was shaking so much that he could hardly get the words out of his mouth. Piya took hold of his wrist in an effort to calm him.

'Kanai,' she said gently, 'it's all right. You're safe now. We're with you.'

He tried to answer but his teeth were chattering and his breath kept getting caught in his throat.

'Don't try to talk,' Piya said. 'I've got a sedative in my first-aid bag. I'll give it to you when we get to the *Megha*. What you need is a good rest. You'll feel much better afterwards.'

Lights

Daylight was fading when Piya put away her data sheets and stepped out of her cabin. As she passed Kanai's cabin, on her way to the bow, she paused to listen at his door: he had slept through the afternoon, after taking the pill she had given him, but she sensed he was awake now for she could hear him moving about inside. She raised her hand to knock, thought better of it and went on her way, across the deck and to the bow.

With the setting of the sun the island of Garjontola, all but engulfed by the rising tide, had turned into a faint smudge of land, outlined against the darkening sky. In the dying light the island seemed to be drifting peacefully to sleep. But suddenly, just as Piya was stepping up to the bow, the dark blur was lit up by tiny points of phosphorescence. The illumination lasted only an instant and then the island went dark again. But a moment later the lights twinkled once more, in perfect synchrony: there were thousands, possibly millions of glowing pinpricks of light, just bright enough to be seen across the water. As her eyes grew used to the rhythm of the flashing, she was able to make out the sinuous shapes of roots and branches, all outlined by the minuscule gleams.

Piya turned on her heel and ran to knock on Kanai's door: 'Are you up? You've got to see this. Come on out.'

When the door opened, she stepped back in surprise, as if the man before her was not the one she had expected to see. Kanai's face and body were scrubbed clean and he was dressed in a *lungi* and vest he had borrowed from Horen. His hair lay plastered on his head and there was a look on his face so different from his usual expression of buoyant confidence that she was hard put to recognize him.

'Kanai, what's up? Are you OK?'

'Yes. Just a little tired. But I'm fine.'

'Then come and look at this.' She led him to the bow and pointed to Garjontola.

'What is it?'

'Wait.'

Suddenly the lights flashed on and Kanai gasped. 'My God,' he said. 'What are those?'

'They're just glow-worms, flashing their lights in rhythm,' said Piya. 'I've read about it: they say it happens mainly around mangroves.'

'I've never seen anything like it.'

'Nor have I,' she said.

They watched intently as the lights flashed on and off, growing brighter as the sky darkened. She heard Kanai clearing his throat and sensed he was bracing himself to say something, but it was a while yet before he spoke and he took her by surprise when he did. 'Listen, Piya,' he said suddenly. 'I wanted to tell you – I'm going back tomorrow.'

'Back where?'

'To Lusibari – then New Delhi.'

'Oh?' She feigned surprise, although she realized now that she had known all along what he was going to say. 'So soon?'

'Yes,' he said. 'It's time for me to get back to my office. It'll be nine days tomorrow and I told everyone I'd be home in ten. If I leave early in the morning I'll be able to make it back to New Delhi by the day after. The people in my office will begin to worry if I'm not there.'

She knew from his voice, that he was holding something back. 'And is that the only reason you're going? Because of your office?'

'No,' he said tersely. 'It's also that I don't really have much reason to stay here, now that I've finished with my uncle's notebook. It's not as if I'm of much use to you – I think you'll be able to manage perfectly well without a translator.'

'You certainly don't have to stay on my account,' she agreed.

'But, if you don't mind my asking, does your decision have anything to do with what happened today – on the island?'

His answer, when it came, seemed to be pronounced with some reluctance. 'This is not my element, Piya,' he said. 'What happened today certainly showed me that.'

'But what exactly *did* happen, Kanai?' she said. 'How did you end up on that island?'

'Fokir suggested we go and take a look at it,' Kanai said, 'and I couldn't think of any reason not to go. That's about all there is to it.'

Despite his evident unwillingness to speak of the incident, Piya pressed him a little further. 'Was it Fokir's fault, then? Did he leave you behind deliberately?'

'No,' said Kanai firmly. 'I happened to fall in the mud and lost my temper. He actually wanted to help – I was the one who shouted at him and told him to go away. He's not to blame.' He pursed his lips as if to tell her that the subject was closed so far as he was concerned.

'You seem to have made up your mind,' Piya said. 'So I won't try to stop you. But when exactly are you planning to leave?'

'At daybreak tomorrow,' Kanai said. 'I'll arrange it with Horen. If we make an early enough start, I'm sure he can get me to Lusibari and be back here by nightfall. I imagine you were planning to spend the day on the water anyway, in Fokir's boat?'

'Yes, I was,' said Piya.

'Well, then, it won't matter if the *Megha* is away during the day, will it? You won't miss it.'

Piya thought with regret of the hours they had spent together, 'No, I won't,' she said. 'I will miss our talks, though. It's been good to have you along. I've enjoyed your company.'

'And I've enjoyed yours, Piya.' He paused briefly as if he were trying to collect himself. 'Actually, I was hoping—'

'Yes?'

'I was hoping you'd come too, Piya. To New Delhi, I mean.'

'To New Delhi?' Piya was taken so much by surprise that a hiccup of laughter bubbled up into her throat.

'Does that seem funny to you?' Kanai said.

'I'm sorry,' she said quickly. 'It was just so unexpected. New Delhi is a long way and I have so much to do right here.'

'I know that,' he said. 'I didn't mean immediately. I meant after you'd finished your survey. I was hoping maybe you could come then.'

Piya was unsettled by the tone of Kanai's voice. She remembered her first meeting with him on the train and recalled the certainty of his stance and the imperiousness of his gestures. It was hard to square those memories with the halting, diffident manner of the man who stood before her now. She turned away to look in the direction of Garjontola, where the moon was climbing slowly above the horizon.

'What exactly do you have in mind, Kanai?' she said. 'Why do you think I should go to New Delhi?'

Kanai pinched the bridge of his nose as if he were hoping the gesture would help him find the words he wanted. 'I won't lie to you, Piya – I don't know what I have in mind. It's just that I want to see you again. And I want you to see me – on my own ground, in the place where I live.'

She tried to think of his life in New Delhi and she imagined a house filled with employees – a cook, a driver, people to fetch and carry. It seemed as remote from her own life as something she might see on film or television. It was impossible for her to take it seriously – and she knew that no purpose would be served by pretending otherwise.

She reached over to touch his arm. 'Listen, Kanai,' she said. 'I hear what you're saying. And believe me I appreciate it; I appreciate everything you've done and I wish you the best. I'm sure one day you'll meet the woman who's right for you. But I don't think I'm the one.'

He nodded resignedly to indicate that this was more or less what he had expected to hear. 'There's so much I want to tell you, Piya,' he said, 'and maybe it would be easier to put it into words if I didn't want to so much. It's like Moyna says.'

Piya was jolted by the sound of that name. 'What does she say?'

'That words are like the winds that blow ripples on the water's surface. The river itself flows beneath, unseen and unheard.'

'What did she mean?'

'She was talking about how she feels about Fokir,' Kanai said.

'And?'

'He means everything to her, you know, although you wouldn't think it. She's terrified he's going to leave her.'

'And why would he do that?'

Kanai's voice fell. 'Because of you, maybe?'

'Kanai, that's absurd,' Piya protested. 'There's no reason why she or anyone else should think that.'

'None at all?'

Piya could feel her annoyance growing and she tried to calm her voice. 'Kanai – what are you getting at?'

'I'll tell you what Moyna thinks,' he said softly. 'She believes you're in love with Fokir.'

'And what about you?' Piya shot back. 'Do you believe that too?'

'Well are you?'

There was an edge to his voice now and she chafed against its rasp. 'Are you asking on her behalf, Kanai? Or are you asking for yourself?'

'Does it matter?'

'I don't know, Kanai. I don't know what to tell you – any more than I know what to tell her. I don't know the answers to any of these questions you're asking.' Raising her hands, Piya clamped them on her ears as if to shut out the sound of his voice. 'Look, I'm sorry – I just can't talk about this any more.'

The moon had risen over Garjontola now and in its waxing light the island's glowing sparks had faded and become almost invisible. Piya stared at the dimming lights, trying to remember how magical they had seemed just a few minutes before. 'It was beautiful while it lasted, wasn't it?'

When Kanai answered, his voice sounded just as constricted as her own. 'My uncle would have said that it was like a tide country mirage.'

A Search

At dawn, when Piya stepped out of her cabin, the *Megha* was so thickly shrouded in fog that she could see neither its stern nor its bow. On her way to the foredeck she all but fell over Kanai who was sitting in a chair with a pad on his knees and a lantern by his side.

'Up already?'

'Yes.' He gave her a tired smile. 'Actually, I've been up for hours.'

'How come?'

'I've been working on something,' he said.

'So early?' She could not conceal her surprise. 'It must be important to get you out of bed at that hour of night.'

'It is important,' he said. 'In fact, it's for you – a present. I wanted to have it done before we each went our own way.'

'A present for me?' she said. 'Can you tell me what it is?'

He gave her a deprecatory smile and made a face. 'You'll see when it's finished.'

'So it's not done yet?'

'No,' he said. 'But it will be by the time we're ready to be off.'

'OK – I'll be back.' She went to her cabin to change and by the time she had brushed her teeth and had a quick breakfast of bananas and Ovaltine, Horen was already in the wheelhouse and Fokir was in his boat, preparing to cast off its moorings. She handed Fokir the backpack in which she had placed her equipment, a couple of bottles of water and a few nutrition bars. Then she went to the foredeck and found Kanai still seated in his chair.

'So is it done yet?' she said.

'Yes.' Rising to his feet he handed her a large manila envelope. 'Here it is.'

She took it from him and turned it over in her hands. 'You still won't tell me what it is?'

'I'd like it to be a surprise.' He looked down at the deck and shuffled his feet. 'And if you should want to let me know what you think of it – you'll find my address on the back of the envelope. I hope you'll write.'

'Of course I'll write, Kanai,' she said. 'We're friends, aren't we?'

'I hope so.'

She would have given him a peck on the cheek if she hadn't known that Horen's eyes were boring into her back. 'Take care,' she said.

'And you too, Piya – take care and good luck.'

The fog hung so heavy on the water that it seemed to slow the currents with its weight. When Fokir dipped in his oars, the boat slipped easily forward with the fog frothing around its bow, like whipped milk. A few strokes of the oars was all it took to carry the boat out of sight of the *Megha*: the vessel vanished into the mist within minutes.

As the boat headed downriver, Piya glanced at the envelope Kanai had given her – she could tell from its size that there were several sheets of paper inside. She decided against opening the letter straight away; instead, reaching into her backpack she tucked the envelope away and pulled out her positioning monitor. After taking a reading on the boat's position, she allowed herself to succumb to the dreamy quiet of the fog.

Over the last couple of days her body had become attuned to the shuddering and the noise of the diesel-powered bhotbhoti: the boat's silence was a comforting contrast. Now, as she looked around herself, examining the texture of the boat's wood and the ashen colour of its thatch, it seemed to Piya that she was seeing these things properly for the first time. She ran her fingers over the plywood strips that covered the boat's deck and tried to decipher the smudged lettering stamped on some of them; she looked at the speckled grey sheet of plastic that had once been a US mailbag and remembered how much it had surprised her when she first recognized it for what it was. It was strange that these ordinary things had seemed almost magical at that moment, when she was lying on this deck, trying to recover from the experience of almost drowning. Looking at these discarded odds and ends in the light of another day, she saw it was not the boat but her own eyes that had provided them with that element of enchantment. Now they looked as plain and as reassuringly familiar as anything she had ever thought of as belonging in a home.

Piya shook her head to clear it of daydreams. Rising to a crouch, she signalled to Fokir to pass her another pair of oars. She had no definite idea of where he was taking her but she guessed he was going to explore one of the routes the dolphins took when they went to forage. The flood tide had peaked an hour or so before and the Garjontola 'pool' was still empty of dolphins. Fokir seemed to know where to find them.

The currents were in their favour and, with two pairs of oars between them, they made short work of the rowing. It was not long before Fokir motioned to Piya to let her know they had reached their destination. For a couple of minutes he allowed the boat to drift and then, leaning over the side, he threw out his anchor and paid out the line.

The fog had thinned now and Piya saw that the boat was so positioned as to command a view of the entrance to a broad creek. Fokir pointed several times to the creek's mouth, as if to assure her that the dolphins would soon be coming towards them from that direction. Piya took another reading of the GPS before raising her binoculars to her eyes. She found they had come some eight kilometres since they had parted from the *Megha* at Garjontola.

At the start Fokir watched the creek in a casual, almost negligent way – he seemed to have no doubt in his mind that the dolphins would soon come at them from this direction. But when two hours had passed without a sighting, he seemed less certain of his ground, and his attitude began to change, confidence yielding slowly to a bemused doubt.

They stayed on watch, in the same place, for another couple of hours but again, despite the near-perfect conditions of visibility, there was no sign of the dolphins. In the meanwhile, the tide had ebbed and the day had grown steadily hotter with the sun's ascent. Piya's shirt was damp with sweat. Thinking back, Piya could not remember any other time since her arrival, when the temperatures had been so high so early in the day.

Shortly after midday, with the tide running low, Fokir pulled in the anchor, as a signal that they were about to move on. At first Piya thought he had given up the watch, and was planning to head back to Garjontola. But when she reached for her oars, Fokir shook his head. He pointed to the mouth of the creek they had been watching all morning and motioned to her to stay on alert, with her binoculars. He turned the boat into the creek and, after a couple of hundred metres, made another turn, into a still narrower channel.

It was only after they had spent an hour, winding between creeks and gullies, that Fokir stopped to take stock of the stretch of water ahead: there was still no trace of a dolphin. With an impatient click of his tongue, Fokir reached for his oars again and turned the boat in a new direction.

In a while, as the boat continued its passage, Piya took another reading of the GPS and discovered that they were still heading away from Garjontola. They had covered a distance of a little more than fifteen kilometres since the morning. Their progress, however, had been anything but direct: on the monitor, the line that traced their route looked like a strand of wool that had come unravelled from an old scarf.

The air was still and heavy and the water's surface was like glass, unscarred by the faintest touch of wind. Fokir was drenched in sweat and the look of puzzlement on his face had been replaced by an expression of concern: after seven hours of watching the water they had seen nothing of any interest. Piya gestured to Fokir, urging him to stop and rest, but he paid no attention: he seemed to be intent on penetrating ever deeper into the tidal labyrinth.

* * *

The initial part of the journey to Lusibari led through a part of the tide country that was little frequented and for the first few hours after its departure from Garjontola, they encountered no other vessels, large or small. But then its route brought the bhotbhoti in view of a major seaward channel, the Jahajphoron River, and suddenly the waterways were as inexplicably busy as they had been empty before. With the river's width lying athwart the bow, it became evident, even from a distance, that there were a great many boats out on the water. This would not have seemed untoward if it were not for the fact that the boats were all heading in the same direction – inland, and away from the sea.

Having had little rest the night before, Kanai had fallen asleep soon after the *Megha* left Garjontola. He was woken by the sound of Horen's voice, summoning his grandson from the deck below.

Sitting up in his bunk, Kanai found his clothes and sheets soaked in sweat. He had shut the door at dawn, when the air was still chilly, but now, with hours to go before noon, the cabin's bulwarks were already radiating heat. Kanai stepped out to find Horen standing at the bow, peering at the broad river ahead while Nogen tended the wheel.

'What's the matter, Horen-da?' Kanai said, as he made his way forward to the bow. 'What do you see?'

'Look over there,' Horen answered, raising a hand to point ahead.

Kanai shaded his eyes as he considered the sight. Unused though he was to these waterways, he sensed there was something odd about the traffic in front of them. But the exact nature of the problem eluded him. 'All I see is a lot of boats,' he said.

'Don't you see, they're all heading in the same direction?' Horen said gruffly. 'They seem to be going back to their villages.'

Glancing at his watch, Kanai saw that it was a little after ten in the morning. It struck him suddenly that it was early in the day for fishermen to be bringing home their catch. 'Why're they heading back at this hour?' he said. 'Isn't it the wrong time?'

'Yes,' said Horen. 'You wouldn't usually see them going that way until quite late in the evening.'

'So what could the matter be?'

'At this time of year,' Horen said, 'it's usually only one thing.'
'And what's that?'

Horen shrugged, and his eyes seemed to disappear into the enigmatic folds of his face. 'We'll find out soon enough.' He turned away and went back to the wheelhouse to take over the steering.

It took another ten minutes to cover the distance to the river ahead. Once Horen had executed the turn into the main channel of the Raimangal, he cut the engine so that the *Megha* drifted almost to a standstill. Then, with Nogen handling the wheel, Horen went to the stern and waited for a fishing boat to draw abreast. Soon, a whole cluster of boats gathered there and shouts rang back and forth as the returning fishermen exchanged questions and answers with Horen. Then the boats sailed on and Horen came hurrying back to the wheelhouse, grim faced and glowering. A muttered command sent Nogen racing down to start the engine, while Horen took hold of the wheel.

Kanai was aware of a stab of apprehension as he looked at the set cast of Horen's profile. 'So, Horen-da,' he said, 'what is it? What did you find out?'

Horen answered brusquely, 'It's exactly what I thought. What else would it be at this time of year?'

There was a storm on its way, Horen explained. A *jhor*. The weather office in New Delhi had put out warnings since the day before that it might even be a cyclone. The coastguard had been out on the Bay since dawn, turning back the fishing fleet: that was why the boats were heading home.

'But what about—?' Kanai's first thought was for Piya and Fokir, out on their boat at Garjontola.

Horen cut him short before he could complete the question. 'Don't worry. The storm won't be on us until midday tomorrow. This gives us plenty of time. We'll go back to Garjontola to wait for them to get back. Even if they don't return until late in the evening, we'll be fine. If we set off early enough tomorrow morning, we'll be back in Lusibari before the storm hits.'

The engine sprang back to life and Horen used his shoulders to hold the wheel to a tight turn. Within a few minutes, the *Megha* was heading back the way it had come, retracing the morning's journey from Garjontola.

It was one o'clock when they reached Garjontola and neither Kanai nor Horen was surprised to find no one there. Only seven hours had passed since they had waved the boat off that morning. They knew that Piya and Fokir were probably planning to come back to Garjontola much later – in time to meet the *Megha* on its return from Lusibari, which was scheduled for the end of the day.

There was one thing that puzzled Kanai: the boat was anchored well within sight of the Garjontola 'pool', yet, although it was low tide, there were no dolphins in the water. He recalled that the dolphins usually gathered there when the tide ebbed and it was clear, even to his unpractised eye, that the water was running low. He went to Horen to confirm this, and was told that this was indeed the ebb-tide, the bhata – the jowar would not set in for another two or three hours.

'But Horen-da, look,' said Kanai, pointing towards Garjontola. 'If it's the bhata, then why is the water empty?'

Horen frowned as he took this in. 'What can I tell you?' he said at last. 'The world isn't like a clock. Everything doesn't always happen on time.'

There was no arguing with this: yet, in the pit of Kanai's stomach was a gnawing sensation that told him something was wrong. 'Horen-da,' he said, 'instead of waiting here, why don't we set out to look for Fokir's boat?'

There was an amused grunt from Horen. 'To look for a boat here would be like trying to find a grain of grit in a sackful of rice.'

'It won't do any harm,' Kanai insisted. 'Not if we're back by sunset. If all's well, the boat will be here then and we'll meet up with them.'

'It'll serve no purpose,' Horen grumbled. 'There are hundreds of little khals criss-crossing these islands. Most of them are too shallow for a bhotbhoti.'

Kanai could sense his resistance lessening and said lightly, 'We're not doing anything else, after all – so why not?'

'All right, then.' Bending over the gunwale, Horen shouted to Nogen to start the engine and draw anchor.

Kanai stood leaning on the wheelhouse as the bhotbhoti pulled away from Garjontola and headed downriver. There was not a cloud in the sky and the landscape seemed tranquil in the soporific heat of the afternoon sun: it needed some stretching of the mind to imagine that bad weather could be on its way.

Casualties

The tide was turning when at last Piya caught sight of a dorsal fin: it was a kilometre or so ahead of the boat, very close to the shore. A quick read on the dolphin's position showed its location to be almost twenty kilometres south-east of Garjontola. When she put the binoculars back to her eyes she made another discovery – the dolphin she had spotted earlier was not alone; it was accompanied by several others. They seemed to be circling in the same place, much as they did in the Garjontola 'pool'.

She saw at a glance that the water was still at mid-level and a look at her watch told her that it was three in the afternoon. She was conscious now of an excitement similar to that which she had felt when Fokir first led her to the dolphins at Garjontola. If several dolphins had congregated here at low tide, surely it could only mean that this was yet another 'pool' and these dolphins were from another pod? This seemed like the best news she could have had, yet a glance at Fokir's face was enough to indicate that something was not quite right – there was a cautionary look in his eyes that put her on guard.

When the dolphins were just a couple of hundred metres ahead of the boat, she caught sight of a steel-grey form lying inert on the mudbank. Instantly she shut her eyes, knowing what it was, and yet hoping it would be something else. When she looked again it was still there and it was exactly what she had feared – the carcass of an Irrawaddy dolphin.

A closer look brought yet another shock: the animal's body was relatively small and she knew at once that it was probably the newborn calf she had watched for the last several days, swimming beside its mother. Its body appeared to have been deposited on the shore some hours before, by the falling tide. Now, with the water rising again, it seemed to be teetering on the water's edge.

Piya's intuition told her that these dolphins belonged to the same pod that usually congregated at Garjontola at low tide. The carcass explained the dolphins' departure from their usual routines: it seemed they were reluctant to return to their 'pool' while one of their number lay dead in plain view. Piya had the sense that they were waiting for the tide to set it afloat again.

Fokir had spotted the carcass too, Piya knew, for the boat's bow had turned to point towards the shore. As the boat was pulling slowly up to the bank a smell caught the back of Piya's throat. The full heat of the sun was on the dead animal and the stench was such that she had to wrap a length of cloth around her head before she could step off the boat.

Looking down on the carcass, she saw that there was a huge gash behind the animal's blowhole, where a large wedge of flesh and blubber had been torn out of the dolphin's body. The shape of the injury suggested that the dolphin had been hit by the propeller of a fast-moving motorboat. This puzzled Piya because she had seen so few such boats in these waters. It was Fokir who suggested a solution to the mystery, by sketching a peaked cap with his hands. She understood that it was probably some kind of official boat, used by uniformed personnel – maybe from the coastguard or the police or even the Forest Department. It had gone speeding down the channel, earlier in the day, and the inexperienced calf had been slow to move out of its way.

Piya took a tape measure out of her backpack and spent a while taking the measurements required by the Norris protocols. Then, pulling out a small pocket knife, she took samples of skin, blubber and a few internal organs. These were wrapped in foil and slipped into Ziploc bags. Armies of crabs and insects were now swarming all over the dead calf, eating into the exposed flesh of its wound.

Piya remembered how her heart had leapt when she first saw the newborn surfacing beside its mother and she could not bear to look at the carcass any longer. She gestured to Fokir to pick it up by the flukes while she took hold of the fins. Between them, they swung it back and forth a couple of times and then heaved it out into the river. She had expected it to bob up again, immediately, but to her surprise it sank quickly from view.

This was as much time as Piya could stand to spend in this place. She went back to the boat, threw in her equipment and helped Fokir push it away from the bank.

As the current was pulling them away, Fokir stood up and began to point, upriver and downriver, east and west. Presently, as his gestures became more explicit, she understood he was telling her that what she had seen was not an uncommon sight. He had come upon three such carcasses: one of them had washed up a short distance downriver from this very place – that was why he had thought of coming this way.

By the time they were in midriver, the dolphins appeared to be dispersing – except for one, which seemed to be lingering in the wake of the pod. Piya had the sense that this animal was circling over the sunken carcass as the currents rolled it along the riverbed. Was this the mother? There was no way of knowing for sure.

Then, all at once, the dolphins sounded and disappeared. Piya would have liked to follow them, but she knew it would be impossible. It was a little past four in the afternoon now and the tide was flooding in. The currents, which had favoured them in the morning, were now pushing powerfully against them. Even with two of them rowing, their progress was certain to be painfully slow.

After three hours of unrewarded wandering, Horen said, in a tone of gruff vindication, 'We've looked enough. We have to turn back now.'

Kanai's eyes were weary from the effort of peering into creeks and gullies. Now that the sun was dipping towards the horizon, the light would be directly in their eyes and it would be even harder to maintain an effective watch. But the anxiety gnawing at his stomach would not go away and he could not bring himself to accept there was nothing more to be done. 'Do we have to turn back already?' he said.

Horen nodded. 'We've wasted a lot of fuel. Any more and we won't be able to get back to Lusibari tomorrow. Besides, the boat is probably back at Garjontola now.'

'And what if it's not?' said Kanai sharply. 'Are we just going to abandon them?'

Horen turned to squint at him through narrowed eyes. 'Look,' he said, 'Fokir is like a son to me. You should know that if there was anything more to be done, I would do it.'

Kanai was quick to acknowledge the justice of this reproof. 'Yes,' he said with a nod. 'I know that, of course.' He felt a twinge of shame for having doubted Horen's diligence during the search. As the *Megha* changed course, he said, in a more conciliatory voice, 'Horen-da, you have experience of these things. Tell me – what'll happen here when the cyclone strikes?'

Horen looked pensively around him. 'It'll be as different as night from day.'

'You were caught in a cyclone once, weren't you?'

'Yes,' said Horen in his slow, laconic way. 'That was the year when you visited: 1970.'

It was well after the end of the monsoons, and Horen had gone out to sea in his uncle Bolai's boat. The crew consisted of just three men: Horen, his uncle and another man whom he didn't know. They were on the edge of the Bay of Bengal, a couple of kilometres from the mouth of the Raimangal River, within sight of land. There was no proper system of warning in those days and the storm had taken them completely by surprise. One minute there was sunshine and a stiff breeze; half an hour later, a gale had hit them from the south-west. The visibility had suddenly become very poor and they had lost sight of all their usual landmarks. They had had no compass on board: their eyes were the only instruments they used in navigating and, in any case, it was rare for them to venture out of sight of the coast. Nor would any instrument have been of much help, for the gale did not leave them the option of steering in a direction of their choice. The wind was so fierce that there was no resisting its thrust. It had swept them before it, in a north-easterly direction. For a couple of hours they could do nothing other than cling to the timbers of their boat. Then, all of a sudden, they had found themselves heading towards a stretch of flooded land: they could see the crowns of some trees and the roofs of a few dwellings – huts and shacks for the most part. The storm's surge had drowned most of the shoreline; the flood was so deep that they didn't know they had made landfall until their boat slammed into a tree trunk. The boat's wooden planks came apart instantly, but Horen and his uncle managed to save themselves by clinging on to the tree. The third member of their crew also took hold of a branch but it broke under his weight. He was never seen again.

Horen, then just twenty years old, had great strength in his arms. He was able to pull both himself and his uncle out of the raging water, into the tree's higher branches. The two men used their gamchhas and lungis to tie themselves to the tree. They joined hands and held on as the gale howled around them. At times, the wind was so fierce that it shook the tree as though it were a giant *jhata*, a reed broom – but somehow Horen and Bolai had managed to cling on.

When the wind abated a little, they discovered that the water had deposited a great deal of debris in the tree, including some pans and utensils that had been swept out of the surrounding dwellings. Horen salvaged a round-bellied clay *hāri*, which he then used to collect some rainwater: if it wasn't for his foresight, thirst would have driven them from the tree the next day.

In the morning the sky was bright and clear but a torrent was still raging under their feet: the floodwaters were so high as to reach most of the way up the tree trunk. Looking around them, they saw that they were not the only people to take shelter in a tree: many others had saved their lives in a similar fashion. Whole families, young and elderly alike, were sitting on branches. Presently, when greetings were shouted from one tree to another, they learnt that they had been blown nearly fifty kilometres from where they had been when the storm hit. They had been carried across the border and thrust ashore near the Agunmukha – Fire-mouthed – River, not far from the town of Galachipa.

'It's in Bangladesh now,' Horen said. 'In Khulna district, I think.'

They spent two days on the tree, without food or any additional water. When the floodwaters subsided they tried to make their way to the nearest town. They had not gone far before they turned back: it was as if they were in the vicinity of some terrible battlefield massacre. There were corpses everywhere and the land was carpeted with dead fish and livestock. They found out that three hundred thousand people had died.

'Like Hiroshima!' said Kanai, under his breath.

Horen and Bolai were fortunate soon to meet up with some fishermen who had managed to salvage their own boat. Making their way through unfrequented creeks and *khals* they had managed to slip back into India.

That was Horen's experience of a cyclone and the memory of it would last him through a second lifetime – he never wanted to have it repeated.

Horen finished his story just as Garjontola was coming into view.

A carpet of crimson light lay upon the island's watery threshold, covering the 'pool' and stretching all the way to the sun, now setting on the far side of the distant mohona. The angle of the light was such that any boat, even a very low one, would have cast a long shadow: but there were no boats or any other vessels in sight. Piya and Fokir had not returned.

A Gift

At sunset, taking a read on the boat's position, Piya saw that they were still a good twelve kilometres from Garjontola. She knew then that it would be impossible to get back to the *Megha* by the end of the day – but it wouldn't matter much, she decided; there was no reason to think that Horen would be especially worried. He would know that they had gone too far afield to make it back by nightfall.

She guessed that Fokir had come to the same conclusion, for it soon became clear that he was looking for a place to anchor the boat for the night. A likely spot showed itself just as the last glow of daylight was fading from the sky – a stretch of water where a small channel flowed, at a right angle, into a wider one. At this time, with the water at its height, even the narrower channel looked like a river of substantial size, but Piya knew that when the tide turned it would shrink into a comfortable creek. The land on every side was thickly forested and the failing light gave the mangroves the look of a solid barricade of greenery.

There was a patch of relatively calm water where the channels met and it was here that Fokir dropped anchor. Before dropping anchor, he made a gesture that took in their surroundings and told Piya the name of the place: Gerafitola.

Once the boat was at anchor, Piya noticed that the moon had risen. It was almost perfectly spherical, except for a thin shaving missing on one side. Around its edges was a halo with a faint copper tint. The moist, unmoving air seemed to have a magnifying effect, for this moon was larger and brighter than any she could ever remember seeing.

As she was taking in the sight, Fokir crawled through the boat's hood and came to sit beside her; raising a finger he traced an arc upon the darkening purple backdrop of the sky. When Piya shook her head to tell him she saw nothing there, he gestured to her to look more closely. Again his finger described an arc, circling around and over the moon. Now, as her eyes grew accustomed to the silvery light, she saw a faint spectrum of coloured light: it seemed to hang in the air for an instant and then it was gone. She glanced at Fokir to ask if he had seen it too and he gave her an affirmative nod. Then his finger traced another arc in the sky, a vast one this time, spanning the horizon, and it dawned on her suddenly that he was thinking of a rainbow of some kind. Was that what he had shown her, a rainbow made by the moon? He gave her an earnest nod and she nodded too – she had seen it after all, or at least glimpsed it, so what did it matter that she had never heard of such a phenomenon before?

Piya's eyes strayed from the moon and the shadows of the forest, and then fell to the currents playing upon the river's surface: it was as if a hand, hidden in the water's depths, were writing a message to her in the cursive script of ripples, eddies and turbulence. She remembered a snatch of something Kanai had said, about Moyna – something about the unseen flow of the water and the visible play of the wind. Did he, Fokir, understand what it meant to be the kind of person who could inspire and hold such constancy, especially when it was overlaid with so much pain and so many difficulties? What could she, Piya, offer him that would amount to even a small part of what he already had?

They sat unmoving, like animals who had been paralysed by the intensity of their awareness of each other. When their eyes met again it was as if he knew at a glance what she was thinking. He reached for her hand and held it between his, for a moment, and then, without looking in her direction again he moved off to the stern and began to kindle a fire in his portable stove.

When the meal was ready, he offered her a plate of food with some rice and spiced potatoes. She could not bring herself to decline it, for the plate seemed like an offering, a valedictory gesture. It was as if their shared glimpse of the lunar rainbow had somehow broken something that had existed between them, as if something had ended, leaving behind a pain of a kind that could not be understood because it had never had a name. Afterwards, when the stove and the utensils had been put away, Piya took one of Fokir's blankets and went to her usual place in the bow, while he retreated to the shelter of the hood.

She remembered the letter Kanai had given her and took it out of her backpack. It would be good to have the distraction – she needed to think of something else. Fokir saw her peering at the envelope in the moonlight, and he passed her a matchbox and a candle. She lit the wick and placed the candle on the boat's prow, using its own drippings to fasten it in its place. The night was so still and airless that the flame held perfectly steady and needed no sheltering.

Tearing open the envelope, she began to read.

'Dearest Piya

'What does it mean when a man wants to give a woman something that is beyond price – a gift that she, and perhaps only she, will ever truly value?

'This is not a purely rhetorical question: it is inspired by a genuine perplexity for I have never known this impulse before. For someone like me, a man whose chief concerns have always been with the here and now – and, let us admit it, with myself for the most part – this is new ground, uncharted terrain. The emotions that have generated this impulse are of a shocking novelty. Would it be true then to say that I have never been in love before? I had always prided myself on the breadth and comprehensiveness of my experience of the world: I had loved, I once liked to say, in six languages. That seems now like the boast of a time very long past: at Garjontola I learnt how little I know of myself and of the world.

'Suffice it to say then that I have never before known what it was to want to ensure someone's happiness, even if it should come at the cost of my own.

'Yesterday it dawned on me that I have it in my power to give

353

you something that no one else can. You asked me what Fokir was singing and I said I couldn't translate it: it was too difficult. And this was no more than the truth, for in those words there was a history that is not just his own but also of this place, the tide country. I said to you the other day that there are people who live their lives through poetry. My uncle was one such and, dreamer that he was, he knew how to recognize others of his kind. In his notebook he tells a story of an occasion when Fokir, at the age of five, recited from memory many of the cantos that comprise a tide country legend: the story of Bon Bibi, the forest's protectress. To be specific, he remembered a part of the story where one of its central figures, a poor boy called Dukhey, is betrayed by Dhona, a ship's captain, and is offered to the tiger-demon, Dokkhin Rai.

'My uncle was amazed by this feat, because then, as now, Fokir knew neither how to read or write. But Nirmal recognized also that for this boy those words were much more than a part of a legend: this was the story that gave this land its life. That was the song you heard on Fokir's lips yesterday: it lives in him and in some way, perhaps, it still plays a part in making him the person he is. This is my gift to you, this story that is also a song, these words that are a part of Fokir. Such flaws as there are in my rendition of it I do not regret, for perhaps they will prevent me from fading from sight as a good translator should: for once, I shall be glad if my imperfections render me visible.

'From the epic of the tide country, as told by Abdur-Rahim: *Bon Bibir Karamoti orthat Bon Bibi Johuranama* – "The Miracles of Bon Bibi or the Narrative of Her Glory."'

The Story of Dukhey's Redemption

The next day at dawn, Dhona spoke to all his men. 'Let's turn and go back to Kedokhali again.'

From his perch Dokkhin Rai watched the ships setting sail. He thought, 'Ah, he's decided to follow this trail.'

So to Kedokhali went the demon deva, gathering his followers from near and afar. His honeybees came swarming; they numbered in lakhs. He ordered them all to yield their honey and wax. The forest was filled by the buzzing of bees, as the swarms set to work, hanging their hives from trees.

Soon, on his boat, Dhona sighted Kedokhali. His heart filled with joy at the thought of all he would see. After his men had beached their ships on the shore, he said, 'Come, let us look for beehives once more.' To the forest they went, Dhona leading the way; and there they were, not just one, but an amazing array. When they turned back at last, gladness lightened Dhona's head. After much food and drink, he went off to his bed; but late at night he began once more to dream. Suddenly Dokkhin Rai appeared, his eyes agleam. 'The time', said the demon, 'is at hand for our tryst; be sure to say my name when you go to the forest. Although the bees will leave at the sound of my name, do not think that the honey is all yours to claim. And there is one more thing I must tell you about: however large your party, let there be no doubt. Let no man touch the hives that hang in the jungle – your sailors must only look and marvel. The bees will open the hives and carry the combs; they'll load them on your boats for you to take to your homes. But remember, on Dukhey we've made a bargain; he must be left behind when you board your sampan. Take care! Beware! I want no excuse or pretext – or it will be your life that's in jeopardy next.'

With these words the deva vanished into the night, while Dhona slept on, till the first crack of daylight. He spoke to his men at the first *namaaz* of the day, 'We must go to the forest, all except Dukhey.'

When the boy learnt he was to be left behind, he cried out aloud, 'Chacha, I must speak my mind.' Wiping the tears from his cheek with an unsteady hand, he said, 'I know it's all going just as you'd planned. Do you think I don't know of your deal with the deva? You're going to sail home, leaving me here forever.'

'Who told you this?' said Dhona, feigning a laugh. 'Wherever did you hear such a tale and a half?'

Leaving Dukhey to cook dinner, Dhona led the way; in the forest they were met by a dazzling display. Though they whispered and marvelled, not one of the men dared touch the hives till the deva's name was spoken. At the sound of those words the bees began to swarm, and a demon host came flying, raising a storm. Hearing their lord's name they rushed into the forest, to load Dhona's boats and to speed him on his quest.

Then said Dokkhin Rai, 'Look Dhona, watch my power; my army will load your boats within the hour.' He spoke to the demons and ghostly *ganas*, the *dainis*, the *pishaches* and all the *rakshasas*. They made the honey into a portable hoar and took it to the boats, carrying it on board. When all was ready, Dokkhin Rai said, 'My job's done. Your boats are full to the brim, every single one.'

Dhona went to the boats and with his own eyes saw: they were all loaded and could not take any more. Then said the deva, 'Here's a still better reward: empty your boats and throw the honey overboard. With a rich load of wax I'll fill your boats instead; it'll freshen your fortune and bring luck on your head. Forget the honey – your kismet is much better; take the wax instead: you'll see, it'll make you richer.'

So into the river Dhona poured his honey, and so that creek came to be known as Madhu Khali. And the place where Dhona chose to pour his cargo, there the brackish tides turned sweet and mellow.

Then it was time for a new and richer hoard. 'Now listen to what I say,' said the demon lord. 'When you sell this, you'll see I've given you a boon; you'll live like a king and it'll bring you good fortune. But don't forget to leave the boy; be warned, listen; recall how this began – Dukhey was the reason. Don't try any tricks or attempt any ruse; I'll drown you in the Ganga and all your ships you'll lose.'

With these words, he left, vanishing beyond appeal. In the meantime Dukhey sat in the boat, trying to cook a meal. But the firewood was wet and the pots would not boil – tears were the result of his unrewarded toil. Then he spoke a name, his voice muted by sorrow, and Bon Bibi heard him in distant Bhurukundo. In the blink of an eye she crossed the divide; she spoke to the child, standing close by his side. 'Why did you call me?' she said. 'What's happened to you?'

'I'm in trouble,' said he. 'I don't know what to do. Chacha told me to prepare a meal for tonight, but the kindling's all wet and the fire won't light.'

'All will be well,' she said. 'Don't worry in the least. With the help of the Lord, I will make you a feast.'

With these words of kindness, she gave him reassurance; then raising her hand she passed it over his pans. And such was her *barkot*, so strong her benediction, that the pots filled instantly with rice and with *saalan*. This was a feast that needed neither fire nor heat; she said to the boy, 'Look! They'll have plenty to eat!'

But Dukhey, still fearful, importuned her once more. 'Dhona'll set sail tomorrow, leaving me ashore. Mother of the earth, tell me: who'll save me then?'

'My child,' said Bon Bibi, 'do not fear this demon. He cannot kill you; he's not of so fine a fettle, that he'd survive a blow of my brother's metal.'

With these last words, Bon Bibi took leave of Dukhey, and soon enough Dhona returned from his foray. His first words to the boy were, 'Here, Dukhey, tell me: where's our food? Where have you put it – on which dinghy?'

'Here it is,' said Dukhey. 'It's on this boat, Chachaji. Look: I've cooked the meal and kept it ready.'

Dhona and the others went where he had pointed. And then, seating themselves, they waited to be fed. The food they were served was so fine, so ambrosial, that some began to say it was hardly credible. How could such a fine feast be a mere boy's doing? Or, for that matter, any human being's? Now, in under-tones, they began to speculate. Had Bon Bibi perhaps taken a hand in his fate? 'On his own the boy can't find his way to the *ghat*. For sure Bon Bibi has taken him to heart.'

And so sat the men, talking in the dimming light, until the day had waned and dusk had turned to night. The others slept in their boats, without care or qualm, but to fretful Dukhey, sleep was proscribed, *haraam*. He could not close his eyes for fear and worry. 'They'll be off tomorrow,' he thought, 'abandoning me. I'll be left behind, as the demon's *shikar*; Dokkhin Rai will hunt me in his tiger avatar.'

Hour after hour he sat bewailing his plight; not a single wink of sleep blessed his eyes that night. The other men slept in peace, happily replete; not till daybreak did they wake, after night's retreat. Standing amidst the ships Dhona said to his men, 'Undo the moorings: it's time to be off again.' Six boats were unloosed, at Dhona Mouley's behest. Only one stayed where it was, apart from the rest.

'Why are you waiting?' said Dhona. 'Come on; let's go.'

'There's no wood to cook with,' they said. 'We need some more.'

Dhona turned to Dukhey, when the crew had spoken. 'Go and fetch some firewood; there's not enough for these men.'

'Oh Chachaji,' said Dukhey, 'please don't give me this chore. Why not send someone else? I don't want to go ashore. There's no lack of men here: ask another to rise. Why is it me that you must always tyrannize?'

'You've sat on my boat,' said Dhona, 'and eaten your fill; yet when I make a request you defy my will? Right in my face, you fling this stinging reply: "I won't go ashore, I won't even try?" I'm hurt by these insults, this insolence and pride.'

'Chachaji,' said Dukhey, 'it's for you to decide. Of your pact with the deva, I'm not unaware. I know that he wants you to leave me right here. While the demon devours me, in a tiger's guise, you'll go home rich, carrying this fabulous prize. Back in the village, you'll go to see my mother. "What could I do?" you'll say. "He met a tiger." When you first came to our home, what a tale you spun: on the strength of that she gave you her only son. Your sacred pledge you're now going to dishonour; you'll send me away and be off within the hour. When the news reaches my home, when my mother hears, her life will be over and she'll choke on her tears.'

'You're a sly one,' said Dhona, 'an expert in deceit. Getting you to obey is a singular feat. If you know what's best for you, you'll do as I say; or I'll just kick you off – you'll have to go either way.'

'Wasn't it only for this that you brought me along? You knew I'd die while you grew rich and strong. So then why so much slander, why so much abuse? If the tiger takes me, what do you have to lose? Now salaam chacha, I touch your feet,' said Dukhey. 'Point me in the right direction, show me the way.'

Raising a finger, Dhona pointed to the forest. Dukhey stepped off, sorrow swelling in his breast. And even as he crossed the deep mud of the banks, back on the boats they were pulling in the planks.

Then, in his heart's silence, Dhona began to say, 'Listen, Dokkhin Rai: now I've given you Dukhey. For the wrongs of the past, Deva please forgive me. I wash my hands; now it's all up to Bon Bibi.'

Away they sailed, and when the boy saw that they'd left, he could move no more; he was utterly bereft. It was then from afar that the demon saw Dukhey. Dhona had kept his word, he had left him his prey. Long had he hungered for this much-awaited prize; in an instant he assumed his tiger disguise. 'How long has it been since human flesh came my way? Now bliss awaits me in the shape of this boy Dukhey.'

On the far mudbank Dukhey caught sight of the beast: 'That tiger is the demon and I'm to be his feast.'

Raising its head, the tiger reared its immense back; its jowls filled like sails as it sprang to attack. The boy's life took wing, on seeing this fearsome sight: 'Oh Ma, Bon Bibi, deliver me from this plight. Where are you O mother? Why're you keeping away? If you don't come now, it'll mean the end for Dukhey.'

With these words on his lips, Dukhey lost consciousness. But Bon Bibi, far away, had heard his cry of distress. 'I heard the child call,' she said to Shah Jongoli. 'The demon will kill him, brother. Quick, come with me. That devil's desires have outrun him of late; his appetites have grown: they're like a flood in spate. We can't let the boy vanish into that vast maw.' In the blink of an eye they crossed to the far shore.

Bon Bibi saw Dukhey lying motionless, and took him to her lap with a gentle caress. There lay his body, unmoving and dust-defiled, while the world's mother strove to rouse the inert child. Then Shah Jongoli knelt beside Dukhey's inert form, and breathed life into him with the *ism-e-aazam*.

Roused to anger, Bibi spoke to Shah Jongoli, 'It's time to cure this demon of his devilry. Brother, strike him a blow that will fill him with dread.'

Picking up his staff, Shah Jongoli ran ahead. So eager was he to carry out his command, that he struck the tiger with the flat of his hand. The demon reeled, so great was the force of the blow, and in panic fled south as fast as he could go.'

When she reached the end, Piya went to sit in the middle of the boat, and before long Fokir came to sit beside her as she knew he would. His hands were on the gunwale, so she put her palm on his wrist. 'Sing,' she said. 'Bon Bibi – Dukhey – Dokkhin Rai. Sing.'

He hesistated momentarily before yielding to her plea. Tilting back his head, began to chant and suddenly the language and the music were all around her, flowing like a river, and all of it made sense; she understood it all. Although the sound of the voice was Fokir's, the meaning was Kanai's, and in the depths of her heart she knew she would always be torn between the one and the other.

She turned over the last sheet in the sheaf of pages Kanai had given her and saw a postscript on the back. It said, 'And in case you should wonder about the value of this, here is what Rilke says:

> 'Look, we don't love like flowers
> with only one season behind us; when we love,
> a sap older than memory rises in our arms. O girl,
> it's like this: inside us we haven't loved just some one
> in the future, but a fermenting tribe; not just one
> child, but fathers, cradled inside us like ruins
> of mountains, the dry riverbed
> of former mothers, yes, and all that
> soundless landscape under its clouded
> or clear destiny – girl, all this came before you.'

Fresh Water and Salt

The heat of the night was such that Kanai had to get up and open the door of his cabin to let in some air. Returning to his bunk, he left the door ajar, and found that the gap had given him a view of a slice of the surroundings. The moon was bright enough to eke shadows from the trees on Garjontola, creating dark patches on the silvery surface of the water. A wedge of moonlight had even crept into the cabin, illuminating the heap of mud-soaked clothes Kanai had discarded the day before.

Sleep was slow in coming and what there was of it was anything but restful: time and again Kanai was shaken awake by his dreams. At four in the morning he gave up the struggle and got out of his bunk. Pulling his lungi tight around his waist, he stepped out on deck and found, to his surprise, that Horen was already seated there, on one of the two armchairs. He was watching the river with his chin resting on his fists. At Kanai's approach he raised his head and glanced over his shoulder. 'So you couldn't sleep either?' he said.

'No,' Kanai replied, taking the other chair. 'And how long have you been up?'

'About an hour.'

'Were you watching for the boat?'

Horen made a rumbling noise at the back of his throat. 'Maybe.'

'But is there enough light right now?' Kanai said. 'Could they find their way back at this time of night?'

'Look at the moon,' said Horen. 'It's so bright tonight. Fokir knows these khals better than anybody else. He could find his way back if he wanted to that is.'

Kanai could not immediately unravel the suggestion implicit in this. 'What do you mean by that, Horen-da?'

'Maybe he doesn't want to come back tonight.' Horen looked him full in the eyes and his face creased into a slow, wide smile. 'Kanai-babu,' he said, 'you've seen so many places and done so many things. Do you mean to tell me you don't understand what it is for a man to be in love?'

The question struck Kanai with the force of a blow to the chest – not just because he could not summon an immediate answer but also because it seemed so much out of character, so strangely fanciful, coming from a man like Horen.

'Do you think that's what it is?' Kanai said.

Horen laughed again. 'Kanai-babu – are you just pretending to be blind? Or is it just that you cannot believe that an unlettered man like Fokir could be in love?'

Kanai bridled at this. 'Why should you say that, Horen-da? And why should I believe any such thing?'

'Because you wouldn't be the first,' Horen said quietly. 'It was the same with your uncle, you know.'

'Nirmal? Saar?'

'Yes, Kanai-babu,' Horen said. 'That night when he and I landed on Morichjhãpi in my boat? Do you really think it was just the storm that blew us there?'

'Then?'

'Kanai-babu, as you know, Kusum and I were from the same village. She was six or seven years younger than me and when I was married off she was still a child. I was fourteen at the time and had no say in the matter – as you know, these things are often decided by the elders. But Kusum's father I knew well because I sometimes worked on his boat. I was with him on his last trip and I was standing on the bãdh, with Kusum, at the time he was killed. After that I felt I had a special obligation to Kusum and her mother, even though there was little I could do for them. I was young, barely twenty, and I had a wife and children of my own. I knew things had become very bad for them when her mother told me she had approached Dilip to find her a job. I tried to warn her; I tried to tell her about the kind of job he would find for her. She wouldn't listen to me, of course

362

– she knew so little of the world that these things were beyond her imagining. But after she left, I felt that Kusum was more than ever my responsibility: that was why I brought her to your aunt, in Lusibari. But when it became clear that even this would not be enough to protect Kusum from Dilip I helped her get away – from Lusibari, from the tide country. I thought I was protecting Kusum but she was, in her own way, much stronger than me: she did not need my protection or anyone else's. This I discovered on the day I took her to the station at Canning, so she could go to look for her mother. Once we got there, I realized I might never see her again. I told her not to go; I begged her to stay. I feared for her safety, a girl, wandering so far afield alone. I told her I would leave my wife, my children; I said I would live with her and marry her. But she wouldn't hear of it. She was determined to do what she wanted and so she did. To this day, I remember the sight of her, as I put her on the train. She was still wearing a frock and her hair had not grown out yet. She looked more like a child than a grown woman. The train vanished, but that image stayed in my heart.

'Eight years went by and then we began to hear rumours about refugees coming to lay claim to Morichjhãpi. People said Kusum was with them, that she had returned from the mainland as a widow and had brought her son with her. I found out exactly where she was living and two or three times rowed past her house in my boat, but I could not summon the courage to go in. That day when I took your uncle to Kumirmari, all I could think of was Kusum, and how close she was. And then, on the way back, the storm came up, as if it had been willed by none other than Bon Bibi.

'And from that day on, I could not stop going to Morichjhãpi. Your uncle became my excuse for going there, just as I became his. I saw that he, like me, could not stop thinking of her: she had entered his blood just as she had mine. At her name he would come alive, his step would change, words would come pouring out of him. He was a man of many words, your uncle – and I had very few. I knew he was wooing her with his stories and tales – I had nothing to give her but my presence, but in the end it was me she chose.

'The night before the killing, Kanai-babu – while your uncle was writing his last words in his notebook, Kusum said to me, "Give him some more time; come let's go outside." She led me to my boat and there she gave me proof of her love – all that a man might need. It was high tide and the boat, which I had hidden among the mangroves, was rocking gently in the water. We climbed in and I wiped the mud from her ankles with my gamchha. Then she took my feet between her hands and washed them clean. And then it was as if the barriers of our bodies had melted and we had flowed into each other as the river does with the sea. There was nothing to say and nothing to be said; there were no words to chafe upon our senses: just an intermingling like that of fresh water and salt, a rising and a falling as of the tides.'

Horizons

At daybreak, when she woke, Piya's face and hair were wet with dew – but to her surprise, the water's surface was almost completely clear of the usual early morning fog. She guessed this had something to do with the unusually warm night and was pleased to notice that a brisk breeze had started up and was stirring the river: it looked as though the weather would be somewhat more pleasant than it had been the day before.

Fokir was still asleep, so she lay motionless in her place, taking in the sounds of the early morning: the hooting of a distant bird, the rustle of the wind blowing through the mangroves and the lapping of the swift currents of high tide. As her ears grew attuned to her surroundings, she became aware of a sound that did not fit with the rest – a brief, breathy noise not unlike a sigh. It sounded like an exhalation, and yet it was not at all like the breathing of an Irrawaddy dolphin. She turned quickly over on her stomach, while reaching at the same time for her binoculars: her instincts told her it had to be a Gangetic dolphin, *Platanista gangetica*. Moments later she spotted a finless back rolling through the water some two hundred metres from the boat's bow. Yes, that was what it was; she was excited to have her intuition so quickly confirmed. And nor was it just a single animal, there were maybe three of them in the immediate vicinity of the boat.

Piya sat up excitedly. So far the paucity of her encounters with platanista had disappointed her – this sighting was an unexpected bonus. She quickly took a reading of the GPS and then reached into her backpack for some data sheets.

It was the data sheets that made her suspect something was

amiss. Logging the dolphins' appearances, she saw that they were surfacing with unusual frequency, with barely a minute or two separating their exhalations. And more than once, along with the breathing, she heard a sound not unlike a squeal.

There was something odd here, she decided; this was not the way these animals normally behaved. She put away her data sheets and raised her glasses to her eyes.

As she was puzzling over the dolphins' behaviour, her mind wandered idly back to an article she had read some years before. It was by a Swiss cetologist, Professor G. Pilleri, one of the pioneers in river-dolphin studies, a doyen of the field. So far as she could recall, the article had been written in the 1970s. Pilleri's research had taken him to the Indus River, in Pakistan, and he had paid some fishermen to catch a pair of Platanista, a male and a female. The article, she remembered, had described the process in great detail. It was no easy task to capture these dolphins, for Platanista's echo-location was so accurate that they were usually able to detect and evade a net once it had been lowered into the water. The fishermen had resorted to a strategy of luring the animals into places where nets could be dropped on the unwary animals from above.

Once his two specimens had been secured, Pilleri's next step was to transport them to his laboratory in Switzerland. The story of this journey, Piya recalled, was so complicated that it had made her laugh out loud as she was reading it. The animals had been wrapped in wet cloths and taken by motorboat to a roadhead on the Indus. Then a truck had been hired to take them to a railway station and they had travelled by train to Karachi. All through the journey their bodies had been regularly moistened with water from their native river. A Land-Rover was waiting at the Karachi railway station and it had taken them to a hotel where a swimming pool had been prepared for the two cetaceans. After the dolphins had rested for a couple of days, the Land-Rover came back to take them to Karachi airport. There they were driven on to the tarmac and loaded into a Swissair plane. With the two dolphins in its hold, the plane made a stopover in Athens before proceeding to Zurich where the temperature was well below freezing. Warmed by blankets and hot-water bottles, the animals were put into a heated ambulance and driven to an anatomical institute in Berne where a special pool awaited them – a tank in which the water was always of a temperature similar to that of the Indus.

It was in this strange habitat – this Indus in the Alps – that Pilleri had observed a curious and previously unknown aspect of Platanista's behaviour. These animals were very sensitive to atmospheric pressure: weather fronts passing over Berne would cause them to behave in markedly unusual ways.

Piya was trying to recall the exact details of their behaviour when her glasses strayed away from the river and gave her a glimpse of the horizon to the south-east. Although the rest of the sky was cloudless, at this point of the compass the horizon had acquired a peculiar, steel-grey glow.

Piya let her glasses drop and looked from the sky to the dolphins and back again. Suddenly she understood. Without thinking, she began to shout, 'Fokir, there's a storm coming! We have to get back to the *Megha*.'

Horen's finger pointed Kanai's eyes to the south-western quadrant of the sky, where a dark stain had spilled over the horizon, like antimony from an eyelid. 'It's come quicker than I thought,' Horen said, glancing at his watch. 'It's half past five now. I'd say we can wait for exactly thirty minutes more. Any longer than that and we won't be able to make it back to Lusibari.'

'But Horen-da,' Kanai said, 'just ask yourself, how can we go off to safety leaving them here, to face the cyclone on their own?'

'What else can we do?' Horen said. 'It's either that or we'll all go down with this bhotbhoti, right here. It's not just my life or yours I'm concerned about: there's my grandson to think of too. As for safety, don't think too much about that – it's not sure we're going to make it back either.'

'But couldn't you find a sheltered spot somewhere nearby?' Kanai said. 'Some place where we could wait out the storm?'

Horen's forefinger swept over the landscape. 'Kanai-babu, look around. Where do you see any shelter? Do you see all these islands around us? When the storm hits, they're going to be under several feet of water. If we stayed here, this bhotbhoti would either capsize in midstream or be driven aground. We have no chance here. We have to go.'

'And what about them?' said Kanai. 'What are their chances?'

Horen put a hand on Kanai's shoulder. 'Look. It won't be easy, but Fokir knows what to do. If anyone has a chance, he does; his grandfather is said to have survived a terrible storm on Garjontola. Beyond that, what can I say? It's not in our hands.'

Losses

It was just after five-thirty when Fokir nudged his boat out of the creek's mouth. Although the wind had stiffened, Piya took heart from the fact that the sky was clear for the most part. And in the beginning the wind and the waves were more a help than a hindrance: they were pushing the boat in the direction they wanted to go, so it was like having extra pairs of hands to help with the rowing. Piya had her back to the bow, so at the outset, when the wind was behind them, she was able to watch the waves as they advanced on the boat from the rear. At this point they were just undulations on the water's surface and there was no foam on their crests – they swept up quietly from behind the boat, raising the stern and then dropping it again before moving on.

After half an hour Piya took a reading on their position and was reassured by the results. If they managed to keep up the pace, she calculated they would be back at Garjontola in a couple of hours – probably before the storm broke.

But as the minutes crept by, the wind kept strengthening and the dark stain in the sky seemed to spread faster and faster. Their route, in any case, was a circuitous one, involving many changes of direction. Every time they turned the wind came at them from a different angle, sometimes hitting them in such a way as to make the boat list to one side. As the speed of the wind mounted, the waves grew taller and flecks of white appeared along their crests. Although there was no rain, the wind carried the churning spray right into their faces. Piya's clothes were soon wet and she had to lick her lips to keep them from developing a crust of salt.

On entering their first mohona, they ran into waves much taller than those they had already faced. When the water curled up ahead of them, they had to strain against the oars to carry the boat over the crest. They seemed to be working twice as hard to cover half the distance: it was as if a once-level track had now been stretched over a range of hills and valleys.

Piya took her next reading on their position after they had crossed the mohona – brief as it was, the operation gave her a minute to catch her breath. But there was nothing heartening about the reading itself: it confirmed her impression about the drop in their pace – it had slowed to a crawl.

Piya was reaching for her oars when something brushed against her cheek and fell into her lap. She glanced at it and saw that it was a mangrove leaf. She looked to her left, the direction from which the leaf had come. It so happened that they were in the centre of a wide-bodied river – she estimated that the wind had carried the leaf a good two kilometres, from the shore to the boat.

They made another turn and now Piya found herself rowing with her back to the wind. It was oddly disorientating to be hit by waves coming from her blind side; after they had lifted her up there would be a dizzying moment when the boat seemed to hang upon the crest of the watery ridge. Then suddenly she would find herself tobogganing backwards into the wave's trough, clutching at the gunwales to keep her balance. Water came sluicing over the bow with each wave and it felt as if a bucket were being emptied on her back.

The impact of these descents soon began to shake loose the assorted bits of plywood that covered the boat's deck. They began to quiver and rattle and the wind suddenly caught hold of one of them and tore it off the boat: it vanished in an instant. Minutes later, another slat of plywood went spinning away, and then another, exposing the boat's bilges: Piya found she could see right into the hold where Fokir stored his crabs.

Another turn brought the wind around so that it was hitting them side on, tilting the boat steeply to one side. The oar in Piya's right hand was now almost a third of a metre higher than the other: she had to lean sideways, over the gunwale to bring it into contact with the water. As the boat tilted, her backpack began to roll around under the hood. She had thought it would be dry there, but now it hardly seemed to matter. The spray was coming at them from so many different angles that everything on the boat was soaked. The boat lurched again and the pack was tossed up into the air; it would have gone over, but for the hood. Piya dropped her oars and scrambled forward, to throw herself on the backpack. All her equipment was in it – her binoculars, her dip-sounder, everything except her GPS monitor, which she had attached to a belt loop on her pants. The backpack also contained all the data she had gathered over the last nine days: she had wrapped the sheets in a plastic bag and fastened them to her clipboard.

Piya was looking for some means of securing this precious piece of luggage, when Fokir interrupted his rowing to pass her a length of rope. She took it from him gratefully and after threading it through the pack's straps, she bound it tightly to one of the bamboo hoops of the hood. Then she opened the flap just wide enough to check her equipment. The backpack was made of a heavy, waterproof material and its contents were more or less dry. As she was closing the pack her eyes fell on the pocket where she kept her cellphone: she had not activated it for use in India, so it hadn't been charged or turned on since her arrival. Now, even as the boat was heaving and listing below her, the onset of a sudden seizure of curiosity made her press the power button. Her spirits leapt at the sight of the familiar green glow of the screen, only to fall again when an icon appeared to indicate that there was no coverage where she was. She put it back in the bag and fastened the flap again before returning to her oars.

The wind seemed even stronger now and the boat's tilt was even more pronounced than before. As she was pushing at the oars, her mind strayed back to the phone. She remembered reading accounts of people making calls from under the wreckage of derailed trains; from the rubble of houses that had been demolished by earthquakes, from the burning towers of the World Trade Center.

Who would she have called? Not her friends on the West Coast

– they didn't know where she was and it would take too long to explain. Kanai maybe? She remembered that along with his address, he had also written down a couple of phone numbers on the back of his 'present' – one of them was for a cellphone. He was probably on a plane, on his way to New Delhi; or maybe he was in his office already? It would be strange to reach him: he was sure to say something that would make her laugh. She bit her lip at the thought of this: it would be good to laugh right now, with the boat groaning as if it was going to come apart at any minute.

She shut her eyes tight, as she used to when she was little. Let it be on land, she said to herself, muttering aloud, as if in prayer. Whatever happens, let it be on land. Not the water, please. Not the water.

The boat banked into another turn, and after they had rounded the corner, Fokir rose to a crouch and pointed in the direction of a distant spit of land: Garjontola.

'The *Megha*?' she said. 'Horen?' He shook his head and she raised herself to get a better look. It took just a glance to confirm what Fokir had indicated – the boat was not there. The waters that flanked the island were empty except for the white-flecked waves.

She was still trying to absorb this when the wind caught hold of the grey plastic sheet that lined the boat's hood – the remains of the US mailbag Piya had recognized when she first stepped into the boat. Suddenly, a part of the sheet broke out from under the thatch of the hood. It billowed outwards like a sail and there was a fearsome cracking sound in the timbers. It was as if the wind were a clawed animal doing all it could to tear the boat apart.

The boat's stern reared up as the sheet strained at its ties, pushing down the bow. Fokir dropped his oars and threw himself forward to cut the mailbag free. But even as he was hacking at the plastic bindings there was a loud cracking sound and suddenly the entire hood tore away from the boat and went sailing off into the sky with Piya's backpack trailing behind, like a streamer from a kite. Within minutes the whole unlikely assembly of objects – the hood, the plastic sheet, and the backpack with all its equipment, its data and Kanai's gift – were carried so far off as to become a small speck upon the inky sky.

It was almost eleven when the *Megha* steamed into the Raimangal's mohona and turned in the direction of Lusibari. The water, Kanai noticed, had become peculiarly translucent: against the steely darkness of the sky the brown water seemed to glow like neon, as though lit up from beneath.

This was the widest expanse of water they had crossed and the waves were taller than any they had encountered yet. The sound of the bhotbhoti's engine changed in rhythm with the waves, rising to a plaintive whine as it ploughed into the swells. There was so much water flying over the bow that the windows of the wheelhouse were continually awash in spray.

Through most of the journey Kanai had sat in the wheelhouse, with Horen, who had grown increasingly taciturn as the wind picked up speed. Now, as the *Megha* met the waves of the mohona, Horen turned to Kanai and said, 'We're taking in a lot of water. If it gets into the engine, we're finished. You'd better go below and see what you can do.'

Kanai nodded and rose to his feet, stooping to keep his head from bumping into the low roof. Pulling up the hem of his lungi, he tucked it in at the waist before opening the door.

'Be careful,' Horen said. 'The deck will be slippery.'

No sooner had Kanai turned the handle than the wind tore the door from his grip and slammed it back on its hinges. Kanai kicked off his sandals and left them in the wheelhouse. Then he went around to deal with the door. He had to step around and put his shoulder behind it, to push it shut against the wind. Step by step, keeping his back against the bulwark, he began to move towards the ladder that led to the deck below. The ladder was exposed to the wind and he felt the gusts clawing at him as he put his foot on the first rung – had he been wearing sandals they would have been torn from his feet. The wind was pulling at him so hard that he knew it would take only a slight slackening in his grip for the wind to tear him from the ladder and send him into the churning water below.

When he stepped off the last rung and entered the cavernous

galley, his foot sank immediately into three centimetres of water. He spotted Nogen, deep in the deck's unlit interior, standing beside the casing that housed the diesel engine, grimly baling water with a plastic bucket.

Kanai waded through the ankle-deep water. 'Is there another bucket?'

Nogen answered by pointing to a tin container afloat in a slick of oily water. Kanai took hold of its handle but when he reached for the water he was all but knocked off his feet by a sudden lurch of the bhotbhoti's hull. Righting himself, he found that to fill the bucket was far more difficult than it might seem, for the *Megha*'s pitching kept the water moving in such a way that it seemed almost to be toying with them, making them lunge ineffectually from side to side. In a while Nogen broke off to point to the shore. 'We're close to Lusibari now,' he said. 'Is that where you're going?'

'Yes. Aren't you?'

'Not us,' said Nogen. 'We have to go to the next island: it's the only sheltered place in this area. You'd better go and ask my grandfather how we're going to drop you off. It won't be easy in this wind.'

'All right.' Kanai clawed his way back up the ladder and went step by step along the slippery gangway, to the wheelhouse.

'How is it down there?' Horen said.

'It was bad when we were in the middle of the mohona,' said Kanai. 'But it's better now.'

Horen flicked a thumb at the windshield. 'Look, there's Lusibari. Do you want to get off there, or do you want to come with us?'

Kanai had thought this over already. 'I'll get off at Lusibari,' he said. 'Mashima is alone. I should be with her.'

'I'll take the bhotbhoti as close to the bank as I can,' Horen said. 'But after that you'll have to wade across.'

'What about my suitcase?'

'You'd better leave it behind. I'll bring it to you later.'

Kanai cared about only one thing in the suitcase. 'I'll leave everything but the notebook,' he said. 'I'll wrap it in plastic, so it won't get wet. I want to take it with me.'

'Here, take this.' Horen reached under the wheel and handed him a plastic bag. 'But be quick now. We're almost there.'

Kanai let himself out of the wheelhouse and stepped into the gangway. A couple of steps brought him to the cabin and he opened the door just wide enough to slip inside. In the half light, he unlocked his suitcase, took out Nirmal's notebook and wrapped it carefully in plastic. The engine went dead just as he was stepping out again.

Horen was waiting for him in the gangway. 'You don't have far to go,' he said, pointing to Lusibari's embankment, some thirty metres away. Along the base of the earthworks, where the waves of the mohona were crashing against the island, there was a fringe of foaming white surf. 'The water isn't deep,' Horen said. 'But be careful.' As an afterthought, he added, 'And if you see Moyna tell her that I'll go back to get Fokir as soon as the storm lets up.'

'I want to go too,' Kanai said. 'Be sure to stop at Lusibari.'

'I'll pick you up when the time's right.' Horen held up a hand to wave him off. 'But be sure to let Moyna know.'

'I will.'

Kanai went aft to the stern where Nogen had already pushed out the gangplank. 'Step on it backwards,' Nogen said. 'Use your hands to hold on, as if it were a ladder. Or else the wind will knock you off.'

'All right.' Kanai tucked the plastic-wrapped notebook into the waist of his lungi, in preparation for the descent. Then he turned around and stooped to take hold of the edges of the gangplank with his hands. Immediately, he knew he would have been blown into the water had he not taken heed of the boy's advice: without using his hands he would not have been able to withstand the pressure of the wind. He crawled backwards, on all fours and straightened up just as he was stepping off the plank. He held on to the plank for a moment, steadying himself as his feet sank slowly through the water and into the mud. The water was about hip deep and he could feel the currents surging around him. He moved the notebook up so that it was pressed against his chest. Then, keeping his eyes fixed on the shore, he began to wade towards the embankment, stepping carefully with his bare feet, making sure of his footing. When the water fell to the level of his knees he breathed more easily – he was almost there now and knew he would make it. He heard the bhotbhoti's engine starting up, somewhere behind him and turned to look.

And then it was as if the wind had been waiting for this one unguarded moment: it spun him around and knocked him side-wise into the water. He thrust his hands into the mud and came up spluttering. He scrambled to his feet just in time to see the notebook bobbing in the current, some ten metres away. It stayed on the surface for a couple more minutes before sinking out of sight.

Going Ashore

The tide should have been at a low ebb when the boat reached Garjontola, but because of the wind the level of the water was higher than Piya had ever seen it before. The gale was blowing so hard that it seemed to be holding the surface of the river at an incline: it was as if the water had been mounded into a sloping ramp that reached well past the island's banks. Fokir was able to take the boat over the barrier of mangrove roots, right into a thicket of tree trunks. Piya noticed that he had not steered the boat to his usual Garjontola landing place; rather, he had taken it towards the most elevated point on the island, a headland that jutted into the river.

When the bow was just short of the tree trunks, Fokir vaulted over the gunwale to pull the boat even deeper into the island. He put himself at the front end, where it was easier to manoeuvre the boat. Piya went to the rear, so she could put her whole weight behind the stern. Between the two of them they were able to push the boat into a position where it was lodged between the trunks of several trees. Then Fokir jumped in again and removed the cover from the boat's rear hold. Piya climbed in too, to look over his shoulder, and saw, somewhat to her surprise that the hold and its contents had survived the battering of the wind. Along with Fokir's stove and utensils, there were some nutrition bars and a couple of bottles of water rolling around inside. She stuffed the bars into the pocket of her jeans and handed Fokir one of the bottles of water. Although her throat was parched, she was careful to sip very sparingly from her bottle: there was no telling how long it might have to last.

Then, Fokir took out the old sari he had once given Piya to use as a pillow. Sheltering the fabric with his body, he twisted it into a rope and gestured to Piya to tie it around her waist. She could not see the point of this but did it anyway. While she was doing this, Fokir reached into the hold again and took out the coiled line that he used for catching crabs. He handed Piya the nylon roll and motioned to her to handle it carefully, because of the sharp edges of the bits of tile and bait that were attached to it. After they had stepped off the boat, he showed her how to pay out the line, while keeping the coils sheltered from the wind with her chest. He upturned the boat and ran the line through its timbers and around the trunks of the surrounding trees. Piya's job, she quickly realized, was only to see that the line stayed taut as it was paid out: any slack was instantly picked up by the wind, which threatened to turn the weights and the bait into vibrating projectiles.

In a few minutes, the line became a densely spun web, anchoring the boat to the forest. Yet, despite the care he had taken, Fokir had not been able to keep the line's attachments out of his way. By the time he was done, his face and chest were crosshatched with nicks and cuts.

Now, Fokir took hold of Piya's arm and led her deeper into the island, crouching almost double against the wind. They came to a tree that was, for a mangrove, unusually tall and thick-trunked. Fokir gestured to her to climb up and he followed at her heels as she pulled herself into the branches. When they were about three metres from the ground, he chose a sturdy branch and motioned to her to sit astride it, facing the trunk. Then he seated himself behind her, like a pillion rider on a motor-cycle, and made a sign to ask her for the rolled-up sari tied around her waist. She saw now what it was for – he was going to use it to tie them both to the tree trunk. She gave him one end of the fabric and helped him pass it around the trunk. After another turn, the sari was all paid out and Fokir tied its ends into a tight knot.

Powerful as it already was, the gale had been picking up strength all along. At a certain point its noise had reached a volume where its very quality had undergone a change. It sounded no longer like the wind but like some other element – the usual blowing, sighing and rustling had turned into a deep, ear-splitting rumble, as if the earth itself had begun to move. The air was now filled with what seemed to be a fog of flying debris – leaves, twigs, branches, dust and water. This dense concentration of flying objects further reduced the visibility in what was already a gathering darkness. The light was as dim as it might be at the approach of night, but Piya's watch told her it was just one in the afternoon. It was difficult to imagine that the wind could grow any stronger or more violent, yet Piya knew it would.

In his bare feet, with his body and clothes caked in mud, Kanai scrambled over the embankment and crouched low beneath it, to shelter himself from the wind. Drenched as he was, he suddenly became aware that the wind had grown colder as it picked up strength; he wrapped his arms around his chest and looked up, shivering, at the sky.

Although it had lost all trace of blue, the sky was not uniformly dark: the clouds above were a multiplicity of shades, ranging from an ashen grey to a leaden blue-black. There seemed to be many distinct layers of cloud, each distinguished by a minute difference of shading, each travelling on its own trajectory. It was as though the sky had become a dark-tinted mirror for the waters of the tide country, with their myriad cross-cutting currents, eddies and whirlpools, all with their slight but still discernible distinctions of colouring.

The casuarina trees that lined the embankment were now bent almost double in the wind and the fronds of the surrounding coconut palms had been twisted into flame-shaped knots. As a result, Kanai was able to look much further into the interior of the island than he might have in other circumstances. The hospital, being one of Lusibari's tallest structures was easy to spot.

Kanai started towards the hospital at a run but after a few steps was forced to slow down because the path was slippery and his bare feet kept sliding on the mud. For much of the distance he saw no one about – many of the islanders seemed to have abandoned their dwellings, while others had fortified themselves behind closed doors. But once the compound's gate came into view, Kanai saw that streams of people were heading there, in order to take shelter inside the hospital – it was easy to see why, for there was something immensely reassuring about the building's squat solidity. Mostly these people were on foot, but there were many also who were seated on cycle-vans, principally the elderly and the very young. Kanai joined the throng, and on stepping into the building's portico, he saw that a full-scale evacuation was under way. Teams of nurses and other volunteers were at work, guiding patients down corridors and helping them climb the stairs that led to the fortified cyclone shelter on the upper floor.

At the far end of the ground-floor veranda stood the diminutive figure of a small boy. Winding his way through the crowd, Kanai went up to him: 'Tutul?'

The boy didn't recognize him and made no answer, so Kanai squatted on his heels and said, 'Tutul, where's your mother?'

Tutul nodded at one of the wards, and just as Kanai was rising to go towards it Moyna came hurrying out, dressed in her white nurse's uniform. She stared at his wet lungi and mud-caked shirt: it was clear she hadn't recognized him.

'Moyna,' said Kanai. 'It's me, Kanai.'

She clapped a hand over her mouth as she took this in. 'But what happened to you, Kanai-babu?'

'Never mind that, Moyna,' he said. 'Listen. I have to tell you something—'

She cut him short. 'And where are *they* – my husband and the American?'

'That's what I was about to tell you, Moyna,' he said. 'They're at Garjontola – we had to leave them there.'

'You left them behind?' Her eyes flared in angry indignation. 'With the cyclone coming – you left them in the jungle?'

'It wasn't my decision, Moyna,' Kanai said. 'It was Horen who decided. He said there was nothing else to be done.'

'Oh?' The mention of Horen seemed to calm her a little. 'But what will they do – out there, with no shelter, nothing?'

'They'll be all right, Moyna,' Kanai said. 'Fokir will know what to do; don't worry. Others have survived storms on that island, his grandfather included.'

Moyna nodded, in resignation. 'There's nothing to be done now. All we can do is pray.'

'Horen wanted me to tell you he's going to go back for them as soon as the storm blows over. I'll be going too – he's going to come here to pick me up.'

'Tell him I want to come too,' said Moyna taking hold of Tutul's hand. 'Be sure to tell him.'

'I will,' said Kanai with a glance in the direction of the Guest House. 'And now I'd better go and see how Mashima is.'

'Take her upstairs to the Guest House,' Moyna said. 'I've closed the shutters. You'll be fine up there.'

The Wave

The minutes crept by and the objects flying through the air grew steadily larger. Where first there had been only twigs, leaves and branches there were now whirling coconut palms and spinning tree trunks. Piya knew that the gale had reached full force when she saw something that looked like a whole island hanging suspended above their heads: it was a large clump of mangroves, held together by the trees' intertwined roots. Then Fokir's hand tightened on her shoulder and she caught a glimpse of a shack spinning above them. She recognized it immediately: it was the shrine he had taken her to, in the interior of Garjontola. All at once the bamboo casing splintered and the images inside went hurtling off with the wind.

The stronger the gale blew the more closely her body became attuned to the buffers between which she was sandwiched: the tree in front and Fokir behind. The branch they were sitting on was so positioned that it was on the sheltered side of the tree, pointing away from the wind. This meant that Piya and Fokir, sitting astride the branch, were facing in the direction of the wind, taking advantage of the 'shadow' created by the tree's trunk. But for this lucky circumstance, Piya knew, they would have been pulverized by the objects the gale was hurling at them. She felt it in her bones every time a branch broke off or a flying object struck against the tree; at times the wood would creak and shudder under the force of these collisions and the roll of fabric around her waist would bite into her skin. Without the sari they would long since have been swept off the branch.

Sitting behind her, Fokir had his fingers knotted around her stomach. His face was resting on the back of her neck and she could feel his stubble on her skin. Soon her lungs adapted to the rhythm of his diaphragm as it pumped in and out of the declivity of her lower back. Everywhere their bodies met their skin was joined by a thin membrane of sweat.

Then the noise of the storm deepened and another roar made itself heard, over the rumbling din of the gale: a noise like that of a cascading waterfall. Stealing a glance through her fingers Piya glimpsed something that looked like a wall, hurtling towards them, from downriver. It was as if a city block had suddenly begun to move: the river was like pavement, lying at its feet, while its crest reared high above, dwarfing the tallest trees. It was a tidal wave, sweeping in from the sea; everything in its path disappeared as it came thundering towards them. Piya's mind went blank as disbelief yielded to recognition. Up to this point there had been no time for terror, no time to absorb the reality of the storm and to think about anything other than staying alive. But now it was as if death had announced its approach and there was nothing to do but to wait for its arrival. Her fingers went numb in fear and she would have lost her hold on the tree, if Fokir hadn't taken her hands in his own and held them fast against the trunk. Piya felt his chest expand as he gulped in a deep draught of air, and she did the same, swallowing as deep a breath as she could manage.

And then it was as if a dam had broken over their heads. The weight of the rushing water bent the tree trunk almost double. Encircled in Fokir's arms, Piya felt herself being tipped over and then upended as the branch met the ground. All the while, the water raged around them, circling furiously, pulling at their bodies as if it were trying to dismember them. The tree strained at its roots and it seemed that at any moment it would be torn from the earth and added to the storm of turbulence following the wave.

Piya knew, from the pressure in her lungs, that the water above them was at least three metres deep. The sari that had seemed like a godsend before, now became an anchor tethering them to the riverbed. Pulling her hands away from Fokir's grip she began to tear at the knot so that they would be able to break free and rise to the surface. But instead of coming to her aid, Fokir took hold of her fingers and ripped them from the knot. His whole weight was on her now, and he seemed to be fighting to keep her where she was. But she could not stop struggling – it was impossible to hold still when the air was almost gone from your lungs.

And then, even as she was struggling to slip out of Fokir's imprisoning grip, she felt the pressure of the water diminishing. The crest of the wave had moved on and the tree had begun to straighten itself. She opened her eyes and saw that there was light above, faint but discernible: it came closer and closer and suddenly, just as her lungs were about to burst, the tree snapped almost upright and their heads were above water. The crest of the wave having passed on, the trough had caught up, forcing the water to subside a little: it fell not to its earlier level, but to a point just below their feet.

Rain was arrowing down from the sky as Kanai slipped out of the hospital and began to run towards the Guest House. The drops felt more like pellets than rain: they had the bite of liquid metal and each created a small crater in the mud.

There were no lights in Nilima's window but this did not surprise Kanai. The Trust's generator had not been turned on all day and to light a lantern was probably not worth the trouble because of the draughts and the wind.

He hammered on her door: 'Mashima! Are you there?' A minute passed and he beat his fist on the door again: 'Mashima! It's me, Kanai.' He heard her fumbling with the latch and shouted. 'Be careful!'

The warning made no difference; the moment the latch came undone, the door was snatched out of her hand and slammed back against the wall. A stack of files fell off the shelf and a storm of paper went circling around the room. Nilima staggered back, shaking a wrenched wrist, and Kanai hurried to shut the door. Putting an arm around her, he led her to her bed.

'Does it hurt? How bad is it?'

'It'll be all right,' she said, putting her hands together on her lap. 'I'm so glad to see you, Kanai – I was getting very worried about you.'

'But why are you still down here?' Kanai said urgently. 'You should be upstairs, in the Guest House.'

'Why there?'

'The river's bound to flood,' said Kanai. 'And you don't want to be trapped in here when it does. If the water gets high enough it'll be in here too.' He glanced around the room, assessing its contents. 'Let's spend a few minutes putting together your most essential things. Some we'll take upstairs with us; the rest we'll pile up on your bed. It's high enough that they'll be safe.'

Nilima pulled out a couple of suitcases and, working together, they quickly filled one with files and papers. Into the other went some clothes and such food as Nilima had at hand in her small kitchen – a little rice, daal, sugar, oil and tea.

'Now wrap some towels around yourself,' Kanai said. 'It's raining so hard we'll be soaked before we can get around the house, to the stairs.'

When Nilima was ready, he put the suitcases outside and let her through the door. The colour of the sky was even darker now and the lashing rain had churned the earth into mud. Kanai pulled the door shut and locked it; then, with the suitcases in his hands and Nilima holding on to his elbow, he led her around to the stairs.

They were drenched by the time they reached the shelter of the stairwell, but the extra layers of covering had kept Nilima dry underneath. Unwinding the towels, she wrung them out before following Kanai up the stairs. Once they stepped into the Guest House, the storm seemed suddenly to recede. With the shutters securely fastened, the wind could be heard but not felt: it was strangely pleasurable to be able to listen to it from within the safety of four solid walls.

Kanai put the suitcases down and reached for one of Nilima's wrung-out towels. After drying his hair he pulled off his mud-soaked shirt and wrapped the towel around his shoulders. Nilima, in the meanwhile, had seated herself at the dining table.

'Kanai,' she said, 'where are the others? Piya? Fokir?'

'We couldn't find Piya or Fokir,' Kanai said grimly. 'We had to leave them behind. We waited as long as we possibly could, and then Horen said we had to go. We're going to return tomorrow, to look for them.'

'So they're going to be outside?' Nilima said. 'During the storm?'

Kanai nodded. 'Yes. There was nothing to be done.'

'Let's hope—' Nilima didn't finish her sentence and Kanai cut in.

'And I have some other bad news.'

'What?'

'The notebook.'

'What about it?' she said, sitting up in alarm.

Kanai went around the table and sat beside her. 'I had it with me till this morning,' he said. 'I was bringing it back here, carefully wrapped in plastic. But I slipped in the water, and it was swept out of my hands.'

Her mouth shaped itself into a horrified circle as she took this in.

'You can't imagine how I feel,' he said. 'I would have done anything to save it.'

She nodded, collecting herself. 'I know. Don't blame yourself,' she said softly. 'But tell me, Kanai, did you read it?'

'Yes.' He nodded.

She looked closely at him. 'And what was it about?'

'Many different things,' he said. 'History, poetry, geology – many things. But mainly it was about Morichjhãpi. He wrote all of it in the course of one day and the better part of a night. He must have finished writing just hours before the assault started.'

'So it doesn't describe the attack?'

'No,' said Kanai. 'By that time he'd given it to Horen, who had left Morichjhãpi earlier that day, with Fokir. It was a lucky thing: that's how it survived.'

'What I don't understand,' Nilima said, 'is how it got into his study.'

'It's a strange story,' Kanai said. 'Horen wrapped it up very carefully, in plastic, with the intention of sending it to me. But it got lost and they just found it again recently. Horen gave it to Moyna, who slipped it into the study.'

Nilima fell silent as she thought about this. 'Tell me, Kanai,' she said, 'did Nirmal say why he didn't leave the notebook to me?'

'Not in so many words,' Kanai said. 'But I suppose he felt you wouldn't be very sympathetic.'

'Sympathetic?' Rising angrily to her feet Nilima began to pace the room. 'Kanai, it's not that I wasn't sympathetic. It's just that my sympathies had a narrower focus. I am not capable of dealing with the whole world's problems. For me the challenge of making a few little things a little better in one small place is enough. That place for me is Lusibari. I've given it everything I can and yes, after all these years, it has amounted to something: it's helped people; it's made a few people's lives a little better. But that was never enough for Nirmal. For him it had to be all or nothing, and of course that's what he ended up with – nothing.'

'Except for the notebook,' Kanai corrected her. 'He did write that.'

'And that's gone too now,' said Nilima.

'No,' said Kanai. 'Not in its entirety. A lot of it is in my head, you know. I'm going to try to put it back together.'

Nilima put her hands on the back of his chair and looked into his eyes. 'And after you've put together his notebook, Kanai,' she said quietly, 'will you put my side of it together too?'

Kanai could not fathom her meaning. 'I don't understand?'

'Kanai, the dreamers have everyone to speak for them,' she said. 'But those who're patient, those who try to be strong, who try to build things – no one ever sees any poetry in that, do they?'

He was moved by the directness of her appeal. 'I do,' he said. 'I see it in you—' Suddenly, the dining table began to rattle and he was cut short. Somewhere in the distance was a rushing sound, powerful enough to make itself heard above the gale.

Kanai went to the shutters and put his eye to a chink between the slats of wood. 'It's the tidal surge,' he said to Nilima. 'It's coming down the channel.'

A wall of water was shooting towards them. On its side, where it was cut off by the embankment, a huge plume of spray was shooting up into the air. The island was filling with water, like a saucer tipped on its side, as the wave encircled the island. Kanai and Nilima watched aghast as the water rose and kept rising, up the flight of stairs that led into Nilima's flat, stopping just short of the door.

'It'll take a long time to get the water out of the soil again, won't it?' Kanai said.

'Yes, but people's lives matter more.' Nilima had inclined her head to catch a glimpse of the hospital. A row of people could be seen, on the second floor, braving the wind in order to look at the floodwater.

'Just think of all the people who've been saved by that cyclone shelter,' Nilima said. 'And it was Nirmal who made us build it. If it weren't for his peculiar interest in geology and meteorology and we would never have thought of it.'

'Really?'

'Yes,' said Nilima. 'Making us build it was probably the most important thing he did in his whole life. You can see the proof of that today. But if you'd told him that, he'd have laughed. He'd have said "It's just social service – not revolution."'

The diminution of the noise was the first indication of the eye's arrival: the sound didn't stop; it just pulled back a little, and as it retreated the wind slowed down and seemed almost to die. Piya opened her eyes and was amazed by what she saw. A full moon was shining down on them from the top of what seemed to be a twisting well, a whirling stovepipe that reached far into the heavens. The light of the moon was shining through this spinning tube, illuminating the still centre of the storm.

Stretching away from them, in every direction, as far as Piya's eye could reach, was a heaving carpet of leaves: almost nothing was visible of the water's surface; the usual ripples, eddies and currents had disappeared under this layer of green. As for the island itself, it was entirely submerged and its shape could only be deduced from the few thickets of trees whose uppermost reaches were still visible above water. These trees had a skeletal, forlorn look; few had any branches remaining and there was scarcely one that still had a leaf attached. Many had been snapped in half and reduced to shattered stumps.

A white cloud came floating down from the sky and settled on the remnants of the drowned forest. It was a flock of white birds and they were so exhausted as to be oblivious of Piya and Fokir. Piya loosened the knot in the sari and pushed back from the tree to stretch her aching limbs. One of the birds was so close she was able to pick it up in her hands: it was trembling and she could feel the fluttering of its heart. Evidently the birds had been trying to stay within the storm's eye. How far had they flown? Piya could not imagine. Releasing the bird, she rested her back against the tree.

Fokir, she noticed, was already standing, balancing on the branch and stretching his legs. She had the impression that he was looking around urgently, searching for another branch to move to. But there was nothing in sight: their tree had lost all its limbs except the one they were sitting on.

Suddenly, Fokir lowered himself to a crouch and touched her knee, making a small, barely perceptible gesture. She saw that he was pointing across the island, to another thicket of trees: following his finger, she saw a tiger pulling itself out of the water and into a tree, on the far side of the island. It seemed to have been following the storm's eye, like the birds, resting whenever it could. It became aware of their presence at exactly the same moment they spotted it; although it was several hundred metres away she could tell that it was an immense animal, so large that it seemed incredible that the tree could sustain its weight. Without blinking, the tiger watched them for several minutes; during this time it made no movement other than to twitch its tail. She could imagine that if she had been able to put a hand on its coat, she would have been able to feel the pounding of its heart.

The tiger seemed to sense the storm's return, for it glanced over its shoulder before slipping off the branch. They saw its head bobbing in the water for a few minutes and then the moonlight dimmed and the roar of the wind filled their heads again.

Piya swung her legs on the branch and turned quickly to resume her position. When she was facing the tree, they looped the sari around the trunk and Fokir tied it into a knot. They had barely had time to get back in place when the storm was upon them. Suddenly the air was full of hurtling projectiles.

But something had changed and it took Piya a few minutes to register the difference. The wind was now coming at them from the opposite direction. Where she had had the tree trunk to shelter her before, now there was only Fokir's body. Was this why he had been looking for another branch on another tree? Had he known, right from the start that his own body would have to become her shield when the eye had passed? She tried to break free from his grasp, tried to pull him around so that for once, she could be the one who was sheltering him. But his body was unyielding and she could not break free from it, especially now that it had the wind's weight behind it. Their bodies were so close, so finely merged that she could feel the impact of everything hitting him, she could sense the blows raining down on his back. She could feel the bones of his cheeks as if they had been superimposed upon her own; it was as if the storm had given them what life could not; it had fused them together and made them one.

The Day After

Even though it was moving very slowly, the *Megha* had covered two-thirds of the distance to Garjontola when a boat was spotted in the distance – the first to be seen in hours.

It was a bright, crisp day, cool but windless. Although the level of the water had been declining steadily since the passage of the storm, the mangroves were still mostly submerged. The water's surface was covered in an undulating carpet of green, while the forest – or what little could be seen of it – was completely denuded of leaves, stripped down to trunks and stalks. With the drowning of the landscape the channels' shores had disappeared, making navigation doubly difficult. As a result, since the time of its departure from Lusibari, at dawn, the *Megha*'s speed had rarely risen above a crawl.

Horen was the first to recognize the craft in the distance. With its hood gone, its appearance was so changed that neither Kanai nor Moyna had thought to associate it with Fokir's boat. But Horen had built the boat with his own hands and it had been with him for many years before he passed it on: he knew it at once. 'That's Fokir's boat,' he said. 'I'm sure of it. The storm's ripped off the hood, but the boat is the same.'

'Who's in it?' Kanai asked, but this elicited no response from Horen.

Kanai and Moyna went to stand in the *Megha*'s bow. The water seemed to congeal as the two crafts inched towards each other. In a while Kanai realized that there was only one person on the boat: it was impossible to tell who it was, man or woman, for the figure was caked from head to toe in mud. Moyna's hands, like his own, were fastened on the gunwale and he saw that her knuckles had paled, just like his own. Even though they were right next to each other, a chasm seemed to open between them as they peered into the distance, looking at the boat and trying to guess who it was carrying towards them.

'It's her,' Moyna said at last, in a whisper that rose quickly to a cry. 'I can see. He's not there.' Balling her hands into fists, she began to pound her marital bangles upon her head. One of them broke, drawing blood from her temple.

Kanai snatched at her wrists, to keep her from hurting herself. 'Moyna, wait!' he said. 'Wait and see . . .'

She froze and again they stared across the water, as if hypnotized by the approaching boat.

'He's not there! He's gone. . . .' All of a sudden, Moyna's legs folded under her and she dropped to the deck. There was an outbreak of pandemonium as Horen came running out of the wheelhouse, shouting to Nogen to cut the engine. Between the two of them, Horen and Kanai carried Moyna into one of the cabins and laid her on a bunk.

By the time Kanai stepped out on deck again, Piya had drawn alongside the *Megha*. She was standing unsteadily upright, clutching the GPS monitor that she had been using to find her way. Kanai went to the stern and held his hand out to her. Neither of them said a word, but her face crumpled as she stepped on to the *Megha*. It seemed as though she were going to fall, so Kanai opened his arms and she stumbled against him, resting her head on his chest. Kanai said softly: 'Fokir?'

Her voice was almost inaudible: 'He didn't make it . . .'

It had happened in the last hour of the storm, she said. He'd been hit by something very big and very heavy, an uprooted stump; it had hit him so hard that she too had been crushed against the trunk of the tree they were sitting on. The sari had kept them attached to the trunk even as he was dying. His mouth was close enough to her ear so that she'd been able to hear him. He'd said Moyna's name and Tutul's before the breath faded on his lips. She'd left his body on the tree, tied to the trunk with Moyna's sari, to keep it safe from animals. They would have to go back to Garjontola to cut it down.

They brought the body to Lusibari, on the *Megha*, and the cremation was held the same evening.

There had been very few casualties on the island: the early warning had allowed those who would have been most at risk to take shelter in the hospital. As a result, the news of Fokir's death spread quickly and a great number attended the cremation.

Through that time and afterwards, Piya stayed by Moyna's side, in her room, where many mourners had gathered. One of the women fetched her some water so she could clean up and another lent her a sari and helped her put it on. Mats had been put out on the floor for the mourners, and when Piya seated herself on one, Tutul appeared beside her. He put a couple of bananas on her lap and sat with her, holding her hand, patient and unmoving. She put her arm around him and held him close, so close that she could feel his heart beating against her own ribs. She remembered then the impact of the hurtling stump that had crashed into Fokir's unprotected back; she remembered the weight of his chin as it pressed into her shoulder, she remembered how close his lips had been to her ears, so close that it was from their movement, rather than from the sounds he uttered, that she had understood that he was saying the names of his wife and his son.

She recalled the promises she had made to him, in the silence of her heart, and how, in those last moments, with the wind and the rain still raging around them, she had been unable to do anything for him other than to hold a bottle of water to his lips. She remembered how she had tried to find the words to remind him of how richly he was loved – and once again, as so often before, he had seemed to understand her, even without words.

Home: An Epilogue

～～～

Nilima was sitting at her desk, a month after the cyclone, when a nurse came running over from the hospital to tell her that she'd seen 'Piya-didi' stepping off the Basonti ferry: she was now heading towards the Trust's compound.

Nilima was unable to disguise her astonishment. 'Piya? The scientist?' she said. 'Are you sure about that?'

'Yes, Mashima: it's her. No doubt about it.'

Nilima sank back in her chair as she tried to absorb this.

A fortnight had passed since she'd said goodbye to Piya and the truth was that she had not expected ever to see her again. The girl had stayed in Lusibari for a while after the cyclone and during that time, she'd become a strangely unnerving presence in the Guest House, a kind of human wraith, inward, uncommunicative, leaden-faced. On her own, Nilima would not have known how to deal with her, but fortunately Piya had formed a friendship with Moyna during that time. Nilima had encountered them several times, in and around the Guest House, sitting silently next to each other. On occasion, Nilima had even mistaken the one for the other. Having lost her own clothes, Piya had perforce taken to wearing saris – colourful reds, yellows and greens – for Moyna had given her those of her own clothes that she herself would no longer wear. What was more, Moyna had also cut off her hair, in keeping with the custom, so it was now as short as Piya's. But this was where the resemblance ended: so far as demeanour and expression were concerned the contrast between the two women could not have been greater. Moyna's grief was all-too-plainly visible in the redness of her eyes while

Piya's face was stonily expressionless, as if to suggest that she had retreated deep within herself.

'Piya's in shock,' Kanai had said to Nilima one day, shortly before his own departure. 'It's hardly surprising. Can you imagine what it was like for her to sit through the last hours of the storm, sheltered by Fokir's lifeless body? Leave aside the horror of the memory – imagine the guilt, the responsibility.'

'I understand all that, Kanai,' Nilima had said. 'But that's why I think it would be easier for her to recover if she was in some familiar place. Don't you think it's time for her to go back America now? Or else, couldn't she go to her relatives in Kolkata?'

'I suggested that to her,' Kanai had replied. 'I even offered to arrange for a ticket to the U.S. But I don't think she heard me, really. What's uppermost in her mind right now, I suspect, is the question of her obligation to Moyna and Tutul. She needs to be left alone for a bit, to think things through.'

Nilima's response had been tinged with apprehension. 'So you're just going to go off and leave her here? For me to deal with?'

'I don't think she'll be any trouble to you,' Kanai had said. 'In fact, I'm sure she won't be. She just needs some time to pull herself together. To have me here will be no help – exactly the opposite, I suspect.'

Nilima had not raised any further objections to his departure. 'Of course, Kanai, I know how busy you are . . .'

Kanai had put his arm around her shoulder and given her a hug. 'Don't worry,' he'd said. 'It'll be all right. I'll be back soon. You'll see.'

She'd received this with a non-committal shrug. 'You know you're always welcome here . . .'

Kanai had left the next day – a week after the cyclone – and some days later Piya had come down to tell Nilima that she was leaving too.

'Yes, my dear, of course. I understand.' Nilima had made an effort to keep her voice level, so as not to betray her relief. She'd been wondering, for the last couple of days, whether Piya's presence in Lusibari might lead to trouble with the authorities. Did she have a visa? Did she have the right permit? Nilima didn't know and didn't like to ask. 'You've been through a lot,' Nilima had said, warmly. 'You must give yourself time to recover.'

'I'll be back soon though,' Piya had said, and Nilima had replied, with hearty goodwill: 'Yes, my dear, of course you will.'

But Piya's valediction was not an unfamiliar one; Nilima had heard the same words often before, on the lips of many, well-meaning foreign visitors. None of them had ever been seen or heard from again – so it was not without reason that Nilima had assumed that the same would be true of Piya. But now here she was, just as she had said.

The knock sounded before Nilima had had the time to properly prepare herself. She could think of nothing to say except: 'Piya! You're back . . .'

'Yes,' said Piya, matter-of-factly. 'Did you think I wouldn't be?'

This was, of course, exactly what Nilima had thought, so she was quick to change the subject: 'So tell me then, Piya, where did you go off to?' The girl had bought herself some new clothes, she noticed: she was dressed, as before, in a white shirt and cotton pants.

'I went to Kolkata,' Piya said. 'I stayed with my aunt and spent a lot of time on the internet. You'll be glad to know there was a terrific response.'

'Response? To what?'

'I sent out some letters explaining what happened during the cyclone and how Fokir had died. Some of my friends and colleagues took up the cause and circulated a chain letter, to raise money for Moyna and Tutul. The response was even better than we'd expected. The money's not as much as I'd have liked of course, but it's something: it'll buy them a house of their own and maybe even provide a college education for Tutul.'

'Oh?' said Nilima, sitting up. 'I'm glad to hear that – very glad indeed. I'm sure Moyna will be too.'

'But that's not all,' said Piya.

'Really?' Nilima raised her eyebrows. 'What else have you been up to?'

'I wrote up a report,' said Piya, 'on my dolphin sightings in this area. It was very impressionistic, of course, since I'd lost all my data, but it sparked a lot of interest. I've had several offers of funding from conservation and environmental groups. But I didn't want to proceed without talking to you first.'

'Me?' cried Nilima. 'What do I know about such matters?'

'You know a lot about the people who live here,' Piya said. 'And for myself I know that I don't want to do the kind of work that places the burden of conservation on those who can least afford it. If I was to take on a project here, I'd want it to be under the sponsorship of the Badabon Trust, so it could be done in consultation with the fishermen who live in these parts. And the Trust would benefit too of course. We'd share the funding.'

At the mention of funding, Nilima, ever-pragmatic, began to pay closer attention. 'Well, it's certainly worth a thought,' she said, biting her lip. 'But, Piya, have you considered the practical aspect of this? For instance, where would you live?'

Piya nodded. 'I have an idea for that too,' she said. 'I want to run it by you, to see what you think.'

'Go on.'

'I thought, if you were agreeable, that maybe I'd rent the upper floor of this house from you: the Guest House, in other words. I could really set myself up there, with a data bank and a small office. I'd need an office, because there would have to be proper accounting for the funds.'

Nilima smiled indulgently. Having had long experience in administration she could tell that Piya had no idea of what she was getting into. 'But, Piya,' she said gently, 'to start something on that scale, you'd need a staff, you'd need people to help. You can't do it on your own.'

'Yes, I know,' Piya said. 'I've thought about that too. My idea was that Moyna would manage that end of things – part-time of couse, when she's not on duty at the hospital. It would give her an additional source of income and I'm sure she'd be able to handle the work. And it would be good for me too. She could maybe teach me some Bangla in exchange for some English.'

Nilima twisted her hands together, frowning, trying to antic-ipate every possible objection to Piya's plan. 'But, Piya, what about permits and visas and so on? You're a foreigner, remember. I don't know if it'll be legally possible for you to stay here for an extended period of time.'

This, too, Piya took in her stride. 'I spoke to my uncle about that,' she said. 'He told me that I'm eligible for a card that would allow me to stay on indefinitely – it's something to do with being a person of Indian origin. And as for the permits to do research, he said that if the Badabon Trust was willing to sponsor my work he'd take care of the rest. He knows of some environmental groups in New Delhi that will intervene with the government.'

'My goodness! You really have thought of everything.' Nilima gave a bark of laughter. 'I suppose you even have a name for this project of yours?' Nilima had meant this ironically, but when Piya gravely cleared her throat, she realized that the matter was no joke for the girl. 'So you do have a name? Already?'

'I was thinking,' Piya said, 'that we might name it after Fokir, since his data is going to be crucial to the project.'

'His data?' Nilima raised her eyebrows. 'But I thought you'd lost all your data in the storm?'

Piya's eyes brightened suddenly. 'Not all of it,' she said. 'I still have this.' She took her hand-held monitor out of her pocket and showed it to Nilima. 'See: this is connected to the satellites of the Global Positioning System. On the day of the storm, it was in my pocket. It was the only piece of equipment that survived.' At the touch of a button the screen flickered on. Piya tapped a key to access the memory. 'All the routes that Fokir showed me are stored here. Look.' She pointed to a sinu-ous zig-zag line that had appeared on the screen. 'That was the route we took on the day before the storm. Fokir took the boat into every little creek and gully where he'd ever seen a dolphin. That one map represents decades of work and volumes of knowl-edge. It's going to be the foundation of my own project. That's why I think it should be named after him.'

'My goodness!' said Nilima. Her eyes strayed to the fragment of sky that was visible through the nearest window. 'So you mean to say it's all preserved up there?'

'Yes. Exactly.'

Nilima fell silent as she pondered the mystery of Fokir and his boat, writing a log of their journeys and locking it away in the stars. Presently she reached for Piya's arm and gave it a squeeze. 'You're right,' she said. 'It would be good to have a memorial for Fokir, on earth as well as in the heavens. But as for the details, you'll have to give me a little time to think it through.' She sighed and rose to her feet. 'Right now, my dear, what I need most is a cup of tea. Would you like one too?'

'Yes, I would,' said Piya. 'Thank you.'

Nilima went into her kitchen and filled a kettle with water from a filter. She was pumping her kerosene stove when Piya put her head around the door.

'And what about Kanai?' said Piya. 'Have you had any news from him?'

Nilima put a match to the stove and replaced the grille. 'Yes, I have,' she said. 'I got a letter from him just the other day.'

'And how is he?' said Piya.

Nilima laughed as she placed the kettle on the stove. 'Oh my dear!' she said. 'He's been almost as busy as you.'

'Is that so? What's he been doing?'

'Let me see,' said Nilima, reaching for a teapot. 'Where shall I begin? The most important thing is that he's restructured his company so that he can take some time off. He wants to live in Kolkata for a while.'

'Really?' said Piya. 'And what's he going to do there?'

'I'm not quite sure,' Nilima said, as she spooned some long-hoarded Darjeeling tea leaves into the pot. 'He told me he was going to write the story of Nirmal's notebook – how it came into his hands, what was in it, and how it was lost. But what exactly he means by that you can ask him yourself. He'll be here in a day or two.'

'As soon as that?'

Nilima nodded. The kettle's cover had begun to rattle now, so she took it off the stove. Pouring a stream of boiling water into the teapot, she said: 'And I hope you won't mind if Kanai stays upstairs while he's here – in the Guest House?'

Piya smiled. 'No,' she said. 'Not at all. In fact it'll be good to have him home.'

Piya's choice of words surprised Nilima so much that she dropped the spoon that she was using to stir the tea leaves. 'Did

I hear you right?' she said, directing a startled glance at Piya. 'Did you say "home"?'

Piya had said the word without thinking, but now, as she reflected on it, furrows appeared on her forehead.

'You know, Nilima,' she said at last, 'for me, home is where the Orcaella are: so there's no reason why this couldn't be it.'

Nilima's eyes opened wide and she burst into laughter. 'See, Piya,' she said. 'That's the difference between us. For me home is wherever I can brew a pot of good tea.'

Author's Note

The characters of this novel are fictitious as are its two principal settings, Lusibari and Garjontola. However, the secondary locations such as Canning, Gosaba, Satjelia, Morichjhãpi and Emilybari do indeed exist and were indeed founded or settled in the manner alluded to here.

My uncle, the late Shri Chandra Ghosh, was for more than a decade the headmaster of the Rural Reconstruction Institute, the high school founded by Sir Daniel Hamilton in Gosaba. For some years before his untimely death, in 1967, he was also the Manager of the Hamilton Estate. To him, as to his son, my cousin Subroto Ghosh, I am greatly beholden for my earliest linkages of memory with the tide country.

One of the world's leading cetologists, Professor Helene Marsh of James Cook University, was generous enough to respond to an e-mailed inquiry from an absolute stranger. I can never thank her enough for putting me in touch with her student, Isabel Beasley, a specialist in the study of *Orcaella brevirostris*. By allowing me to accompany her on a survey expedition on the Mekong, Isabel Beasley introduced me to the ways of the Irrawaddy dolphin and to those of the cetologist. My gratitude to her is exceeded only by my admiration for her fortitude and dedication.

I had the privilege of being able to travel in the tide country with Annu Jalais, one of those rare scholars who combines immense personal courage with extraordinary linguistic and intellectual gifts: her research into the history and culture of the region will, I am certain, soon come to be regarded as definite. For the example of her integrity, as for her unstinting generosity in sharing her knowledge, I owe Annu Jalais an immense debt of gratitude.

On the island of Rangabelia, which was once a part of the old Hamilton Estate, I had the good fortune of making the acquaintance of Tushar Kanjilal, the retired headmaster of the local High School. In 1969, together with his wife, the late Shrimati Bina Kanjilal, he started a small voluntary organization that was later to be merged with another such, the Tagore Society of Rural Development (TSRD). Under Tushar Kanjilal's stewardship this organization launched a number of innovative projects. In an area where the public infrastructure was all but non-existent, it succeeded in creating a range of invaluable medical and social services. Today the standard of care offered by the TSRD's hospital in Rangabelia is no less remarkable than the dedication of its staff. In this context I would like to mention, in particular, Dr. Amitava Choudhury, who became for me, in the course of my visits to the tide country, an example in idealism. The TSRD's programmes now extend well beyond the state of West Bengal and they cover such diverse fields as the empowerment of women, primary health care and the improvement of agricultural practices: in their breadth and effectiveness they are themselves the best possible tribute to their founders. Those who would like to know about the TSRD may wish to visit the following websites: www.indev.nic.in/tsrd and www.geocities.com/gosaba_littlehearts.

Around the time of its occurrence the Morichjhãpi incident was widely discussed in the Calcutta press, English as well as Bengali. Today the only historical treatment available in English is an article by Ross Mallick, *Refugee Resettlement in Forest Reserves: West Bengal Policy Reversal and the Marichjhãpi Massacre* (The Journal of Asian Studies, 1999, 58:1, pp. 103–125). Nilanjana Chatterjee's excellent dissertation, Midnight's Unwanted Children: East Bengali Refugees and the Politics of Rehabilitation (Brown University) has unfortunately never been published. Annu Jalais's article, Dwelling on Marichjhampi, is also yet to be published.

I am grateful to B. Poulin for permission to quote from A. Poulin Jr.'s 1975 translation of Rainer Maria Rilke's Duino Elegies: this remains, for me, the definitive English rendition.

All references to Bengali versions of the Elegies are to the superb translations published by Buddhadeva Basu in the late nineteen-sixties. These are now available in the collected edition of Buddhadeva Basu's poetry, Kabita Sangraha (Pancham Khanda), (ed. Mukul Guha, 1994, Dey's Publishing, Kolkata).

I would like to acknowledge also the help, support and hospitality, variously, of the following: Leela and Horen Mandol, Tuhin Mandol, the Santa Maddalena Foundation, Mohanlal Mandol, Anil Kumar Mandol, Amites Mukhopadhyay, Parikshit Bar, James Simpson, Clint Seely, Edward Yazijian, Abhijit Bannerjee and Dr. Gopinath Burman. To my sister, Dr. Chaitali Basu, I owe a special word of thanks. For the care they have taken with this book, I am greatly indebted to Janet Silver, Susan Watt and Karl Blessing, as also to Agnes Krup and Barney Karpfinger of the Karpfinger Agency.

The support of my wife Debbie was of inestimable value in the writing of this book: to her, as to my children, Lila and Nayan, my debt is beyond reckoning.